You Must

Remember This

James R. Kincaid

ISBN: 978-1-61296-648-9

PUBLISHED BY BLACK ROSE WRITING

www.blackrosewriting.com

Printed in the United States of America

Suggested retail price $18.95

You Must Remember This is printed in Garamond Premier Pro

To my dear brother Bob, who lived through all this with me, showing me how much wit and generosity could accomplish and how radiant a spot East Liverpool could be.

You Must

Remember This

The past is never where you think you left it.
~Katherine Anne Porter

CHAPTER 1

"The book says, 'We may be through with the past, but the past ain't through with us.'" Why is that line stuck in my head? Funny how that happens.

. . .

"We have your program right here... I think."

"What are you talking about?"

"What made you suppose I was Question Answerer?"

Harold stared straight ahead. He couldn't bring himself to look directly at whatever it was. A woman? White, vaporous. He tried to remember if he'd ever seen a woman so formed. A woman or anything else. See right through it – her.

"So I'm dead?"

"What'd I just let you in on?"

"Nothing."

"I said explaining isn't what I do. I don't answer questions."

"Not part of your job description." Harold hoped for jocularity but achieved only a half-strangled whine.

"I'm not an employee, Harold."

"Of course not. You're in charge, do as you like. Such as with my program. You can conceal *or reveal* just as it suits you."

"That's subtle, Harold."

"No, really." Harold felt like crying.

The Whiteness continued her paper shuffling.

"It's important, what you're doing. It may look as if you're just messing with papers, like some asshole in an office. But I can tell you're no ordinary asshole."

Silence.

"I'm not supposed to be here. You won't find me in that pile. There's been a mistake. I'm not scheduled for a program." Harold noticed for the first time that the room was like a disco he had frequented when he was young, in his late thirties, actually. Harold had always looked younger than he was. That was a big disadvantage prior to, and an occasional advantage after, age twenty-five. The room, like the old disco, kept changing color. It was hard to figure out where the color stopped and the walls began, if walls were what these were.

Woman-thing said nothing, kept fiddling the papers, also of an uncertain color. If he looked closely, they disappeared. The table was interesting, odd in some way.

"Watch them shuffling along, you gotta keep them shuffling along. So take your best gal, real pal; go down to the levee, I said to the levee." Harold sang, well. Whitey offered no praise, remained stolid, self-absorbed. Harold tried pounding the table, shiny but not reflective.

"Harold," she said, "you're hard to resist."

"Thank you?"

She rose and suddenly was upon him, kissing his ear. Then she wasn't.

"Thanks for the kiss."

"Part of the job description."

"So you do have one?"

"Not a great sense of humor, Harold. The program addresses that and many other things, too. You're going to imagine yourself lucky."

"That's good. You a fortune teller?"

"Harold, even before the program leap, your intelligence base wasn't that low. I guess you're nervous."

"You don't want me asking questions."

"Bingo!"

"If I sit tight and don't pester, all will be revealed. After that, I'll go on my way."

She ignored him, then: "Your attribute jumps are extravagant. The time – well..."

"That's good, right?"

"Somebody's going to have fun."

"Me?"

"Ha!" She pulled out a chart, for all the world like an old computer printout, fold-upon-fold.

"You're some fly-by-night operation. That printout – so out of date, so very seventies."

"Is not!"

.   .   .

Then she wasn't there. He was where he thought he used to be. Not recently.

.   .   .

It turned out to be another quasi-room, not disco-lighted. It was hollow: all space, empty air, no defining boundaries. There were pictures on the not-walls, pure smut.

"They are not, King of the Philistines."

The woman at the desk – different, not vaporous – was annoyed.

"Those are," he thought, "naked children. The photos are air-brushed and lighted so that the eye automatically travels straight to indecent parts."

"*Your* eye so travels. *Your* eye, *your* perversion. Don't blame the light."

"Anyways, how did you know I thought that about the kiddie porn? You read my mind, turn brain currents into words?"

"I was told you ask questions, Harold. Crave attention? Try providing answers. Questioning can become an addiction."

"Who made you all so nasty? I don't have a questioning addiction. I want to know."

"Know what?"

"What's going on. Where I am. You'd feel the same way. It's natural."

"Forget natural. Fact is, you never had a nature, and, anyhow, you won't."

"That's good news. You don't mind criticizing, but you won't tell me how you read minds. You some sadist? Am I dead? Satan, are you?"

"Your idea of Hell is an eternity of frustrating conversations?"

"How'd you know I thought that about kiddie porn?"

"You spoke it. Out loud."

"What?"

"You've started talking to yourself. Don't think you're necessarily crazy. Babbling is not uncommon under the circumstances."

"What are those circumstances exactly? Or not exactly. I'll take approximately. I'd be happy with a lie."

"Shit, Harold, those photographs you dismiss so complacently are by celebrated artists. Sally Mann, Edward Weston, Jock Sturges. The one way over there is by Lewis Carroll."

"There are three or four over there."

"Right."

"You aren't going to explain. I can wait."

"For what?"

"For whatever ensues."

"What's going to ensue, Harold?"

"Don't you know? You should know. Don't you know?"

"Me? Nope."

"Oh God!"

"Set you up there, Harold. Couldn't resist. Sorry."

"You're not sorry."

"Gotcha, gotcha, gotcha!"

"You're vicious, but you can't scare me. Bring it on, whatever it is. I'm ready."

"Bully."

The woman, like Albino See-Through, diddled documents. But this one was orange, oddly shaped in some indistinct way. He ootched a little off his chair to look at her legs. There they were. He sidled to the edge of the unreflecting desk to observe her profile. Everything in proportion. Not sure about her breasts, as she was wearing some sort of tunic.

"Nice tunic!"

Silence.

"Don't think I'm ogling you. I'm just curious."

"You suppose oglers aren't?"

"I'm not driven by lust, just want to see your shape."

"Your interest is architectural."

"I think there's something wrong with you, but I can't put my finger on it."

"That's witty, Harold. Your wit index is increased 64%, and you were slightly above average before. Not the best trait to have."

"Your forearms are bigger than your biceps."

"Those aren't forearms. Now let's proceed."

"What do you mean, my wit index? Is this a reincarnation center? Am I dead?"

"You'd be better – in safer territory – thinking of dreams, unconscious formations, though that'd be misleading. Best not to think. It's all real enough, what you're in. Reincarnation is way off the mark."

"Thanks for explaining. Can you tell me more?"

"I thought you were willing to wait."

"Is that what I should do?"

"Let me do my work here."

She resumed paper-flipping, picked up a pen and started making marks, then began some of the worst singing he had ever heard:

You caint always get what you wah-hant

"You know that song, Harold?"

"I'd pick something more challenging, classier. Are you all golden-oldies sorts here, residents of the trailer park of the hereafter? Not part of the heavenly choir yourself, are you?"

"You in a position to criticize?"

"I have no idea what position I have."

"Fucking A!"

•   •   •

Then he was somewhere else, a kitchen. He looked around for a desk and a woman.

"I'm here behind you."

"Damn!"

There was a Formica table of the sort his parents had been proud of in 1948. Sitting at it was a thing with bright green hair, blue mascara, and black lip gloss. She had a thick beard.

"Hungry?"

"I don't know how to tell."

"What's your specialty?"

"What do you mean?"

"Blue Lasagna? Beans and Cream? Scrod Francois? Rhubarb Fiesta?"

"You want me to cook?"

"Bingo!"

"So you're hungry, and want to eat, even if I'm not and don't?"

"Bingo!"

"Tell me what you drool after. Let your imagination soar."

"Spare ribs and kraut, green beans and potatoes with ham, pot roast."

"Is this my parents' table? Those are things my mother cooked. Your choice."

"Your mother fixation made me lose my appetite. Besides, I have work to do."

"Let me guess. You'll produce some documents, pick at them aimlessly, make random marks, and confuse me. What did I ever do to you? Why do you have it in for me?"

"Me, me, me."

"I see. This isn't about me?"

"That's rich."

"What are we talking about?"

Silence.

Harold began sniffling.

"Don't do that."

The whimpers turned to loud sobbing, bawling.

She came around the table and sat on his lap.

"Here, want my beard?"

He used it to stem the flow of snot.

"There are so many indices," she purred. "We're experienced, kind of, but none of us has ever seen anything like this, what's planned for you."

"You have to be specially careful?"

"Exactly. In a routine case, you'd not have encountered – what you've encountered."

"I'd have been through with all this long ago?"

"That way of thinking – through with it – doesn't apply. Time isn't what you think it is. Time's no one-way street. What Time is – well, it's – never mind. I have trouble keeping it straight. Just hold onto this: if you start going on that way about time, you'll upset yourself. No matter how you look at it, nothing's free, not exactly. But if you flap your wings in that direction, what would come of that? Stick with what you know."

"I know not one goddam thing. Give me something solid. One thing I can hold to."

"Your wit index will be up 62%."

"64%."

"That was a test to see if you pay attention. 64% is right. See, you've got something solid. Hold onto that, Harold. It'll be your prop and stay. Amidst other woe than yours, it will remain, a friend to man, to whom it sayest, 'lean on me, when you're not strong.'"

"You sing well."

"Thanks."

"Something's planned for me, you say. Who planned it? "

"There's a question I can answer. Nobody." She was earnest, excited. "Clutch this! It's planned. That's point one. Point two is that you must never think there's some planning place you can go to find The Planner. There's no source." She put her hand on his arm and patted, then squeezed, finally causing him to scream in pain.

"That hurt, you over-developed-forearm freak."

She pounded on the table. Scary.

"Sticks and stones. I don't believe you know what a forearm is. Oh sure, you have a loose idea, but what does that count for when the chips are down?"

"Sorry. You divide up the work?"

"Like in an old-fashioned factory. Assembly line techniques, tried and true. You figured that out. See? It's not such a mystery."

"Figured what out?"

"You see?"

"What's your name? You keep calling me by my name. I feel rude not using yours. You can understand that, right?"

"I sure can! By-de-by, Harold."

. . .

Then she was gone and so was the table.

. . .

"How does high school sound?"

"Where are you?"

"I'm known as a disembodied voice, Harold."

"Then, who are you, voice?"

"Ah, now there's a question."

14

"You people don't take well to questions."

"You noticed."

"I also noticed you purchase thrills by cheap mysteries. See how observant I am?"

"You'll be more."

"When I grow up."

"Just the opposite, though that's a confusing way to regard it."

"I understand now."

"If we had a sarcasm index, I'd see about getting yours lowered."

"Am I on the island of Dr. Moreau? You going to mate me with a puma?"

"What made you think of that?"

"All my life I've yearned to do it with a puma, asshole."

"You're trying to be abusive, seize control, and it's pathetic. You're not good at abuse, never have been, won't be, I think. I expect there's some danger..."

"But you can't be sure. OK, Dr. Mengele. So you're doing experiments. Don't say anything; that's not a question."

"Since it's not, I can respond: Harold! Harold! We don't call it an experiment, but we could, if we used such terms. It's a way of changing things, seeing what will happen. Observing. We're not omniscient. Knowing everything – who'd want that, even were it possible?"

"Are you God in His many forms, a multitude of heavenly nitwits?"

Silence.

He began to worry that he had offended *Something* and might have to pay for it. But the voice, when it returned, sounded amused.

"I'll say this. I've never seen such a radical program. Not even close. No, sir."

"You work for somebody else. That somebody else, your boss, devised the plan."

"I'm not trying to be mysterious, but all that about plans and bosses: it won't point you where you want to go."

"You mentioned high school."

"Yes, some time ago. What I said was, 'How does high school sound to you?'"

15

"How can I answer that? What high school? What's at stake? Are you going to make me attend one, give me exams, make sure I never graduate? If I answer wrong, are you going to turn me into a sparrow? Look at it from my position. How'd you feel? Wouldn't you be disoriented? You see my point."

"It wasn't a question. I was just being pleasant."

"Nothing was at stake? You get me all worked up, worrying that my life, or whatever it is, rides on the answer; then you snatch the rug from under me. Nothing's at stake?"

"My remark about high school was a way of including you. Not to be rude, but we're not in a place where your opinion matters. Nothing personal. Of course it's personal, from your point of view. What could be more personal, when you think about it? From your point of view. I can see why it would impact you in that way. Do you enjoy conversations, generally?"

"Yes I suppose I do, though this one has me riddled with anxiety. Truth is, and let's face it together, you aren't much of a conversationalist. I'll bet nobody ever picked you up in a bar."

"I was trying to make you feel at home. No need to be contumelious."

"Ohhh. Big word! Mary Jane Nerd. Never got a date to the prom!"

"I don't care what your views on high schools are."

"I don't care about yours either."

"That's a mistake."

"Yeah, well. I can live with my mistakes."

"That's just the issue. Let me explain."

"No, you won't explain. I'll let you, but you won't."

"I'll say this, exceeding what you have reason to expect: you aren't being tested."

"I'm not on trial. My life doesn't hang in the balance, tipped one way or the other by my views on high school."

"Don't put words in my mouth."

Harold stopped listening and tried to figure out the surroundings. Not a kitchen. Not what you would call a place.

The voice was trailing on. At least this one didn't sing. Harold tried to read reflections from her table. It didn't reflect.

16

"So we proceed carefully. It's a sign of the extraordinary nature of your case that so much time is needed processing, checking, preparing, anticipating, detailing, forestalling."

"How about a date?"

Silence.

"I'm not being sarcastic. I'm being respectful. You pique my curiosity, arouse me. You got a club around here, lover's lane, bowling alley?"

"Very funny."

"Yes, it is. My funny index – astronomical. I'll do stand-up in Hell."

"As a matter of fact, Harold, I think I have what I need."

"Me, too."

. . .

By now, it was predictable: a different location, different figure and voice.

"Are you girls all sisters?"

"Let me be merciful – you want to skip ahead to the disclosure?"

"We all do. I do, you do. All is revealed: the butler did it; turns out I was the heir. No more interviews. So that's it. Agreed!"

"Oh, we'll still have interviews."

"Where's the mercy come in?"

"You won't remember anything, Harold. It'll happen but you'll have no memory."

"Like drugs when you have a baby. You have the pain, just no memory of it."

"I wouldn't know about that."

"Never experienced the wonders of giving birth? Never mind. Let me drink of the cup of forgetfulness and wake in the fertile land of disclosures."

"Right. I should add, Harold, that doing it this way may make things a little less clear to you in the long run. You won't be able to remember the various meetings."

"How many more are there?"

"Harold, I won't lie to you: 147."

"Skip ahead. Drug me."

"OK, but you'll miss..."

"I'll lose the enlightening. It's a tough choice, but I'll stick with forgetting. I've always enjoyed drugs. We're not supposed to, but you know how it is. Why, once..."

Even in his haze, Harold was terrified. He knew that he was babbling, complaining – just to keep from thinking. Still, as soon as he rid himself of one panic, his mind slid on to an entirely new set of horrors.

CHAPTER 2

"So, Harold, here we are."

"Where?"

"At the end, really the beginning."

"You expect me to say, 'When are you going to put me out?' and then you can amaze me, 'Hey, it's over, bud!' I'm way ahead of you. All meetings have been concluded, all 147."

"We added some, but yes, you're through with what you inaccurately call meetings."

"Why did you add some? There a problem?"

"Perfectly routine."

"If it were routine, why was 147 not accurate? Some emergencies came up?"

"Accurate smaccurate! We value tactics, not strategies. Process rather than system."

"What?"

"Take my word for it, Harold."

"It'd be easy to be frightened by you people. Am I safe here?"

"Not unsafe in the way you suppose."

"I'm going to assume my only chance at understanding is to strangle all the questions. You can proceed without fear of interruption."

"You sure you want it that way?"

"It's the path of wisdom, right?"

"What?"

"Don't you people talk that way?"

"Nobody talks that way."

Silence.

"You really have plugged the stream of questions?"

"Right."

"I couldn't be sure. After forming that resolve, you followed with two in succession, namely, 'It's the path of wisdom, right?' and 'Don't you people talk that way?'"

Silence. Harold was prepared to wait forever. He repeated to himself the famous sentence: "I am prepared to wait until hell..." Why was Adlai Stevenson remembered for the most fatuous thing he said? Here's a man with a fine mind and prose to match, and he lives only by a cliché. Why's that?

"It's an irony of history, Harold."

"Was I speaking? I would have sworn I wasn't. You can read my mind too, like your sister? Hell, I suppose you can, since you've manufactured it. Are you Victor Frankenstein? You'll proceed as if I hadn't asked the question. Am I right?"

"I'll proceed as if you hadn't asked **several** questions, after making a vow to renounce the interrogative, then *BREAKING IT*! First, your current situation. It occurred to you, according to my notes, that you were dead. You mentioned that often, as if you were in an afterworld. You'll be glad to hear, though it's not altogether good news, that these formulations will not further your ends. Such thinking doesn't live on the same planet as what you'd call 'the truth.' Where you are now is of no importance. It couldn't be explained to you in any case, or to me either, but never mind that. I can't force you to drop your present ways of thinking. Just advising."

"Oh."

"Not much of a response. Here's a way to think of it, accuracy not being important: your life has been put on pause. You could say your aging has been proceeding all along while you're here, but only biologically, not experientially. It'll continue that way. I'm not saying that's the only way to think of it. Just a way to expand the number of tools in your shed."

"Umm."

"You have been here with us in order to work through a deep makeover, to vulgarize it. The first stage is to realize that we here are like a beauty parlor or garage. You are being tuned up, in a record-breaking radical way. It wouldn't be too much to say remade. From this point of view, transformation wouldn't be too strong a word."

"Not too strong."

"I will go through the precise details shortly."

"No need whatsoever."

"The second stage in understanding, from this point of view, is to realize that what you imagine to have been your life will be re-formed, in your case drastically."

"In my case."

"Think of it this way, if you like: you will be given the chance – you don't have a choice – to go through part of your life again, but with wildly different attributes. New name even."

"High school. That's what they said before."

"High school it is. You will return to high school, starting with day number one, at age fourteen, having just turned fourteen."

"My birthday is August 31."

"Yes, and school begins in 1951 on Tuesday, September 4, the day after Labor Day. You see, you will be fourteen. On that same day the one-millionth U.S. soldier died – in Korea."

"Horseshit. Even I know there weren't a million casualties in Korea."

"Right. I wasn't being clear. The first soldier died April 19, 1775, in Lexington. The millionth dies on September 4, 1951. The millionth over all."

"I got it. So this poor bastard dies again?"

"From our point of view, that's not the way to look at it. He dies."

"Let's talk about me. I'm dropped down in 1951, where everyone about me is fourteen. I'm seventy-eight. Maybe I'll be a little out of place. Perhaps not. My present appearance is youthful. People remark on that. 'How old are you?' they inquire. 'My guess is fourteen.' But my life experience distances me some from that age."

"We'll see. We do experiments here. That's not what they are, but it's a word you can understand. And you'll be fourteen, idiot, as I plainly said. But all of this lies inside this procedure, what we're calling, so you can understand, an 'experiment.'"

"I heard that from your sister. 'Experiments' is the term best adapted for my limited human understanding. You space creatures know what you are doing, abducting us, checking us out? I bet you probed my anus."

"You'll start school as you did in 1951. Nothing changed except you. It'll be a rerun, except your personal difference will alter things in small or perhaps large ways. Now listen to this: all others will know the new you, be adjusted. For them, Harold doesn't exist, never did, only the new you. They will have memories of the new you, not of Harold. Same goes for your memories, I think. Anyhow, from your point of view, it'll be the same first day of school right there in 1951, not in the past but the present, not made up but as real as real ever gets."

"Which isn't very."

"Good boy."

"Same pencil box and all for me. It'll be fun."

"Well, there's something I need to say about that, regarding what you'll be aware of. But let's go in an orderly way."

"One step at a time."

"So, here you'll be, altered in ways I'll enumerate, on September 4, 1951, temperature 68 degrees, at 8:05 a.m. (it'll be a hot one), getting off the school bus in front of East Liverpool Central High School."

"Step one."

"Now, still inside this viewpoint, think of it as a movie but real. Everything will be, apart from you, exactly the same, with the slight alteration I mentioned before in the inhabitants, the way they will have been adjusted to the new you, as if you had been there all along, Harold being nowhere, never being."

"Apart from that little matter, it's a perfect reproduction of the real 1951."

"No, no, no, no, no, no. Jesus Christ Almighty!" The woman, nude and tiny, rose, looking about, perhaps for a weapon.

"Don't get excited. I'm cooperating. You gotta admit this sounds awful. Maybe I have it wrong. Don't get mad now. I'll stop anticipating."

"Anticipate all you like, just understand. This is the simple part. You don't understand this, how will I be able to explain double-shadow perception?"

"Please, don't hit me."

"It isn't a simulation. *It is.* What you'll be encountering is what's what. You understand? We're sticking with this story. It's a rerun as a first run. You're not doing it again; you're doing it for the first time, only you'll be different. It won't be *LIKE* 1951. It'll *BE* 1951, and the pretty kids will be pretty as they were, and the teachers and the Truman administration and the lousy food and the polluted river and the hair on your arms and the..."

"It's not a simulation."

"What put that in your head? Think of Perry Como and Milton Berle, Martin and Lewis and 'I Love Lucy.' *The Catcher in the Rye*, the execution of the Rosenbergs, and the firing of MacArthur. 'On Top of Old Smokey' and the Roller Derby. DiMaggio retires and Willie Mays is rookie of the year. Drive-in movies and 'The Thing.' Cigarettes $0.19 per pack. The college basketball scandal and minimum wage of $0.75. The biflex bra costs $1.00 and is worth it. Johnny Ray sings 'Cry.' Ike decides to run. Amateur Hours are much loved: Horace Heidt and Arthur Godfrey and Ted Mack. *The Death of a Salesman* opens. Best of all, Ralph Kiner, from down the river in Pittsburgh, is NL home-run king, forty-two big ones."

"Painters, opera, news from the world of high culture?"

"Not in your line."

"Ouch. OK. It's a rewind to the same reality, only I will be transformed, which, as things go along, could change others a bit. Probably not a lot. I didn't exactly electrify people first time through."

"But the changes in you..."

"I know, radical."

"And others the same – apart from being reprogrammed to the new you – Harold, zippo."

"But I'll be at sea."

"You'll catch on. In time. We think."

"You think? Great God! What's my name?"

"Timothy. Timothy Mills."

"OK."

"So, on to double-shadow perception. Or, should we do details first?

"Let's do double-shadow perception, while I'm fresh. Is this real-real or just kinda real?"

"You know the answer to that."

"Yeah, some answer! Choose your story, any story. OK, so double-shadow perception!"

"I never liked that term. Imprecise, pretentious, designed to confuse."

"And?"

"We had hoped it would make clear to you and to us what sort of awareness will accompany you on this fold in time, allowing you to do your thing, as they say. Will you think you've been there before? Will it be déjà vu, or will you go through it with eager naiveté, unaware that you've returned?"

"My guess is – you ready for this? – not exactly any of the above."

"And you see why. Were you convinced of repeating, you'd feel as if you were in a performance, hampered by a consciousness of things, even of outcomes, a debilitating ability to know something of the future."

"Sounds good. Knowing the future could give me a leg up – know which girls to go after and which quests are pointless, what the test questions will be, when to keep my sunny side up."

"You'd hate it."

"So I'll not be thinking that I'm back on the old track."

"It isn't a matter of awareness or unawareness."

"Jesus Christ. Go on."

"Your idea of re-running will be inconstant, never certain. It will come now and then as a clear flash of power, like a jolting pain, a dentist strumming on a nerve. For that instant, you will feel blinded with certainty, as if a hand from the future were reaching back, touching you. Read Tennyson. He gives us the best description ever of these flashes of connection."

"Those mystic moments in 'In Memoriam.' I know about that. He uses the same language you do. Hands reaching through time and touching him, providing him an electrifying assurance that he is what he is."

"And it is temporary; immediately after, those crystalline moments of certainty are 'stricken through with doubt,' he says. I wouldn't call what you'll experience 'mystic.' Even within this plot we're treating more seriously than it deserves, understanding is an illusion. That'll be helpful for you to think on."

"Oh, it will be. So, within our plot, these jolts of certainty will come, flash blindingly, and leave behind only a doubt as to what they were. OK. I don't understand, as you say, but I – I don't know why I started that sentence."

"As you see, 'double-focus performance' doesn't get things under control."

"'Double-shadow perception.'"

"What?"

"The phrase – you got it wrong."

"That troubles you. It would me. Surely somebody told you we're not omniscient or in control. That's why these are experiments, something like. If we knew all, or even a good deal, there'd be no point. It'd just be setting wind-up dolls in motion."

"You're not fumbling idiots, though, right? You know a hell of a lot."

"Almost nothing. The only thing we can claim is that we have no interest in knowing, aren't bothered by not knowing."

"So I'm in peril. You not-knowers could be setting me up for pain. You act like it's a valuable asset, this ability to avoid understanding what the hell you're doing, even when you've got some big-whoop time machine at your disposal. That's half-assed. I could get hurt here."

"That's not our purpose. I guess that's all we can say."

"But your power to fumble around inside me, play with time, as if life were nothing but a movie you can watch, edit as you like: that doesn't sound like impotence to me. And doing it for fun doesn't sound benign."

"It probably doesn't. But we're less moralistic than you."

"Your eyes are bloodshot."

"I work very hard, keep long hours, and those aren't eyes."

"That's horrible."

"Gotcha! They're eyes."

"Anyways, speaking of Tennyson, you sound like his Lucretian Gods, 'careless of mankind,' hurling lightning bolts for sport, reckless and self-indulgent, playing cruel games."

"'Like flies to wanton boys.' I don't say you're wrong. But it's fruitless speculation: purpose, meaning, what's behind it all. If we can treat time like tidal currents, party streamers, hiccups – then what's that say?"

"Hell if I know."

"Me either. I'm not a knower."

"And proud of it."

.   .   .

"Who are you?"

"My name's Dartmouth, Harold."

"Hi, Dartmouth."

"Hi there."

"Are you female?"

"If you like. No, just yanking your chain. I'm female."

"I thought the last woman was going to give me the details, but all she did was explain double-shadow perception. Actually, I wouldn't call what she did 'explaining.' She was so busy telling me she wasn't explaining, there was no room for substance. What's wrong with her?"

"She was tired, turned the job over to me. I think she was hurt. You wounded her with that comment about bloodshot eyes, Harold. Do you think that was necessary?"

"Name's Tim, and I don't need to tell you how indifferent I am to your feelings."

"OK by me. Do you want to hear the details?"

"Fire away."

"I have them written down. Here you go."

Harold took the sheet and scanned it eagerly.

Appearance---+520%

Sex Appeal---+783%

Intelligence---+42%

Bodily Coordination---+395%

Speed---+152%
Strength---+347%
Wit---+64%
Energy Level General---+163%
Energy Level Maximum---+535%
Singing Ability---+1437%
Eyesight---+10%
Hearing---+24%
Insight into Others---+85%
Endurance, Physical---+743%
Endurance, Emotional---+423%
Patience--- -4%
Confidence---+311%
Empathy--- +121%
Self-Awareness--- +99%
Size of Penis--- to be determined
General Health (illness quotient)--- uncertain

. . .

"What do those figures mean? What's the base from which things rise?"
"You."
"So I'll have 4% less patience than I have?"
"Had."
"Oh yeah, the time fold. Than I had when I was fourteen, when I was Harold."
"Any other questions?"
"Jesus, yes. When can I start asking?"
"That's one question. You have two left."
"Oh my God!"
"A joke: the genie and three wishes. You have unlimited questions."
"OK, first, a small alteration. Let me be forty rather than fourteen.

Who'd choose to be fourteen, all things considered? So, let's change that."

"You may ask questions about the set-up, one so favorable I can't imagine you whining. You cannot make alterations, nor can I. All is established."

"By whom?"

"You know better. Besides, don't pretend it's not *you* wanting to be fourteen."

"Me? It's ridiculous being fourteen. I think you girls are feeding some adolescent porn fantasy: 'If only I knew then what I know now...' You got some bumbling voyeur running things? This is all so banal."

"There a question hidden somewhere in that rant?"

"What happens when I graduate high school? This keep going on?"

"I'm sorry you asked. No, it doesn't. Not within the perspective we're now using. Probably. Of course, there are other ways of looking at it, but this is one way of viewing things, so let's stick with it. So, let's just say, no, it doesn't keep going."

"I keep doing it over and over?"

"Just once."

"Then what?"

"Well, let me answer that this way: as near as we can, we don't interfere in natural processes. I know it looks like we're interfering to beat the band, doesn't it?"

"You want an answer? Yeah, it does look like it. But get to the point. Those natural processes that you don't much meddle with, do *what* with me?"

"Well, like they say, time marches on."

"I thought that's just what it didn't do."

"I can see why you'd think that. So, no, it doesn't, not at all, if you like."

"I have an idea. Instead of graduating in four years, could I fail a few classes, extend the time? Never mind. Anyways, when I graduate and come back to time present, roll me back again to age seventy-eight, so I won't be degenerating in the meantime, losing limbs and organs, without even knowing it. OK?"

"Like I say, this is questions-only time."

"So, whatever happens in real time, will I know it in high-school time?"

"You worry too much about hypotheticals. Leave the details to us."

"Little details like my future. It's my life, isn't it? My details?"

"Que sera, sera. Besides, shut the fuck up. Leave things to us. It'll provide you with true serenity. You don't have any choice."

"You seem upset, serenity-store manager."

"I'm doing my job. Up to me, we'd change those pluses in the profile to minuses."

"You're not a very steady sort. Must be a slim labor market here in Hell."

"OK, you ready?"

"Not quite. Let me be clear: you're changing me, only me, and everyone will imagine I'm Tim, not Harold."

"Well, Harold is erased."

"OK. Timothy is there, always has been, as far as they remember – or know. In place of klutzy old Harold is Wonder Boy and nobody's any the wiser."

"Bingo!"

"But that's some transformation. Given that I look, act, swing the bat differently – better. I was going to say screw better, but I never screwed in high school. I will now. That's what you're looking for, right? You wanta watch."

"Come now."

"Here's the thing, though. You'll set me back there with the same instincts I had before, the same patterns of behavior, expectations, defenses, psychoses, fears, slim areas of confidence, compensations that I developed back in actual 1951..."

"Sorry to interrupt, but this is actual 1951, what you're gliding into. That's the game we're playing."

"We? Right, then, the 1951 I'll be a-glidin' into will be me transformed, but transformed from a base wholly maladjusted to all these radical changes. Any chance you can follow?"

"Don't be insulting. Of course."

"So, for instance, the old me is equipped to ward off insults by little gestures of withdrawal, propitiation, implicit apology. I'll still have those, I assume, but they won't accord with what I now am. I'll be like Baryshnikov apologizing for being unable to dance."

"I see what you mean."

"And you've found ways to adjust me at this deep level."

"Of course."

"I mean, all those indices you cited about better coordination, prettier, bigger dicked: they didn't seem to touch on these developed instincts."

"Well, we included confidence, self-assurance."

"Gross categories! They don't connect with adjusting the minutiae of learned behavior."

"Sure they do."

"Have you actually addressed these things?"

"Yes – no. It's the first time it's come up – very acute of you, impressive. You talk about subtleties and we adjust only gross attributes, taken from a magazine quiz, 'Do You Have a Winning Personality?' I'm impressed that you thought of this. It's a telling criticism."

"What am I to do about your crudity, your absence of sophistication – this lousy plan I have to live inside?"

"Fuck, man, do you expect us to think of everything? You'll have to be adaptive, quick to sense and devise. Remember those areas of maladaptation and work to make them – adaptationally apt. Forewarned is forearmed."

"Thanks. One last thing. I think it's the last thing. Will I be able to help my mom and dad with money? I see that strange category, 'Ability to Attract Wealth.'"

"Yes, but it isn't very specific, is it? I think it's left *in potential.*"

"So I might be able, somehow or other, to help them, make their life easier?"

"Bingo!"

"So the future – one truly last question – will be altered, in large or tiny ways, by what happens here this time in real 1951. And please don't say 'Bingo.'"

"There was a man who had a dog, and Um-Um was his Name-O."

"Will I be able to save my father's life?"

"One too many questions. So, Timothy, Harold-that-was, I take it you're ready to go."

"Bingo."

CHAPTER 3

The past is a foreign country; they do things differently there.

•   •   •

Here I am. The place, this spot, seems to be what they promised, though I've had but a minute to check: the old Ohio-Gothic school building; the old clean bus; my old best friend, Jimmy Canton, sticking close to me and me to him; the odd '50s clothes; the half-remembered teen-talk; the air. I had forgotten the air. It's wet and visible this early in the morning, not cool. The river, five hundred yards away, sends up complex odors and this poetic fog.

So I'm here, where they said, unless it's a set. I'll take here on trust.

I'm walking along outside the bus, following the crowd, trying not to look like an alien. I have on white shoes, a white tee shirt, and jeans. The shoes are white bucks, I remember, not "remember," but know. Double-shadow perception. Wonder if I have blue suede shoes at home. Maybe that style is still to come. Soon, I hope.

I notice how clean everyone looks, and notice that I notice. The boys divide: the unhappys forced to wear gabardine slacks and a collared sport shirt, and the cool kids whose parents allow them to wear what I have on. The girls are more varied, but all look starched. Sweaters and bobby sox, saddle shoes and skirts: long and heavy or long and pleated or long and swishy.

Wonder what I look like? Good, apparently. Feel energized. I'm fourteen, not seventy-eight. That kid over there, Marshall Black (I remember!), obviously a jerk, also feels zinged. But I truly am strong, handsome, smart, equipped with an appeal no girl or boy can withstand. Looking around, there are plenty I'd love to test that on. Take some starch out of them.

That's what they'd like, the lowlifes in the sky, gathered round their TV, eating corn-curls, blobby guts sticking out, skirts hiked up above their knee-high hose.

They must be at the lout level, a special glory reserved for rednecks. Imagine picking someone from '50s East Liverpool, Ohio. Why not plant an extraordinary being like me in Paris during the Revolution, as Mary Shelley, a friend of Oscar Wilde, a decadent Roman emperor, Gandhi, Chaucer, the lover of Audrey Hepburn, Audrey Hepburn herself? What heavenly harem would go to all this work just to watch high school sports and amateur diddling at the drive-in? What kind of mind would be possessed of giant power and pigmy imagination?

"What do I look like, Jimmy?"

"Huh?"

"Oh yeah. Just kidding."

I'm off to Room 603. I can't tell if anybody thinks I'm strange. Jimmy Canton doesn't. I know him and like him for things gone by: lemonade stands, handball games that ran for weeks, unreasoning loyalty. To that extent, my memory works, though it seems to be Harold's memory. Confusing, but not as confusing as finding Room 603. But I do and know a few kids there. Everyone seems self-absorbed, paying me no never-mind. Look over here!

Am I in the same boat as all these others? Hope some of them are my friends.

Poor kids. It's the first day of school. They're scared, cast up in a game whose rules are strong but invisible. The best years of their lives, they hear. All downhill after this. The girl sitting next to me, Deanna VanClausen (her seat tag tells me), is trying to look relaxed, not succeeding. I know her from back there. What do I remember?

"Hi, Deanna."

"Hi, Tim."

"You look sensational, Deanna."

She stares at me, seems unsettled, and does look sensational. Her features are regular, so much space between everything, and all smooth. Aren't there pimples in 1951? Deanna may not be representative, but it sure is nice to gaze on the skin covering her. She looks to me for help, or maybe just looks at me.

"Don't be scared, Deanna. This isn't going to be so bad."

"What?"

Good question. What do I mean? I can't live through the next four years as a half-assed and unwanted therapist.

"I have no idea what I meant, Deanna. I guess I'm a little nervous."

"Me too. Do you think she'll be nice? She looks nice."

"Mrs. Smith. Yeah, she'll turn out to be nice."

"I'm just so nervous, Tim."

Deanna is nervous, but not me. I'm terrified.

How is it I'm aware that I'm acting? Even the terror seems both strong and assumed. I am not in the moment, fourteen and participating eagerly in experiences as they arise. I am seventy-eight, remembering only roughly what the hell all this is. They have lied to me, those women, got it wrong, awfully wrong. It really is as if I'm doing this again, only badly, as self-conscious as a timid child with the lead in the fourth-grade play. They said it'd be a new world and a new me, but it isn't, nor am I. It's more like a foggy replica of events that may have occurred before, involving someone vaguely like me, someone temporary. I miss Harold, miss the old life I'd already had. I'm an intruder, dangerous to the natives, surely, in ways I can't predict.

I feel like a tiger let loose on a playground.

Still, the sea of faces, fog, acid smells, tension, eagerness, fear, unwrinkled skin, the musty oiled floors, white bucks, bobby sox, denims with the bottoms rolled, saddle shoes, baby-blue sweaters, crew cuts.

Mrs. Smith calls role, which helps make things fit – I tell myself. In addition to homeroom, she teaches General Science, which I see I am scheduled to take sixth period. General Science: a classification from the fourteenth century. Am I also down for Natural Philosophy and Alchemy? No, just Latin, Gym, Choir, English, Algebra, American History, and Mrs.

Smith redux.

Interesting to study such things at age seventy-eight, looking fourteen. I don't have the same brain I had before, but it seems the same, despite the assurances of the Faerie Queens that I'm smarter, wittier, and other stuff I forget. Wish I'd paid more attention, taken notes.

Should I flirt with Deanna, test my allure on her?

"Tim, hissssst."

"Yeah, Deanna?"

"What did she just say?"

"She said you and I should go out in the hall and neck, write down what happened, and compose a five-paragraph essay to share with the class."

Deanna turns rosy, doesn't laugh.

"I'm sorry, Deanna – just joking. No, I wasn't."

"Good," she says matter-of-factly.

How am I to understand that? Who's in control here, super me or this schoolgirl? Doesn't seem as if I have better equipment for dealing with females than the weak tools that had served me so ill first time around.

"So, I trust you have the information you need on bus passes, excused absences, the school calendar, special activities, and weekly sock hops." This from Mrs. Smith, to whom I am listening intently, even while talking to Deanna. I'm so worried I will miss something vital – be excluded from clubs, have my bus pass revoked. She's going so fast. Probably bores her, but what about us? Why don't they hand out copies of these policies? No Xeroxing, but there's the mimeograph. I'm forgetting faster than Mrs. Smith speaks. Will everyone else remember and only I flounder? Maybe I'm dim after all.

A wave of panic crawls up my back like a cold snake. Is a part of me actually fourteen? What if I can't find my locker? What then?

I look for Deanna, but she has scrammed. Avoiding me? She's pretty and museum fresh. Tight sweater and a bushy long skirt that looked as if it would fly over her head if she bent over and a great wind or a thumb assisted it. Skinny. Almost everybody is skinny.

I'm off to Latin. Room 511, one floor down, I figure. Why are the floors numbered 500 and 600? There's another building, I remember: 100, 200,

300? Where is 400? The basement? Where they teach shop. I would never have been caught dead there, snob that I was – and am.

The hallway is packed, kids rubbing against one another in an aimless shuffle. I see Jimmy Canton over by the water fountain.

"Jimmy, I have this real problem. Believe me now, OK?"

"What's buzzin, cousin?"

"Neat expression. I can't explain, but you gotta tell me what I look like."

"You asked me that before. You just bugging me?"

"What? Anyhow, please tell me."

"Like do you have snot on your lip?"

"No, what color's my hair?"

"Blonde, like always – you know, yellow, sort of white."

I run my hand across the bristles. A crew cut. That's different. I'd never been able to maintain one first time through. Here's a meaningful advance.

All I can see of my actual self is arm-skin – tanned, hairless – long fingers, unfamiliar biceps stretching my tee shirt. Jeans. Those white shoes. No glasses. Groping around, I find that my ears, once dumbo-like, are small and flat.

As we flock toward the stairs, many people smile at me.

"Hi, Tim."

"Hi," I shoot back. What a terrific voice – high, fierce, clear. Every word a song.

"Hi" I soon change to "Yo!" or "Whassup!" sometimes pointing a finger saying, "You're the one!" I also adjust phrases like the one Jimmy knew: "What's your wish, Fish?" "Great dress, Bess!" "Like your moves, Shoes!" Once started, a witty person like me can make up funny phrases without end, really funny.

What an asshole. How easily assholishness comes to me.

All seem to tolerate my greeting, find it fun, every kid. My diagnosis: they're happy to be noticed by me. Doesn't matter how. I notice; they glow.

I start adding punches and playful-as-hell shoves. Most of the company might soon be uninviting, but now is another matter. Those who are pretty are lightning-bolt pretty.

But who in hell are they? I'm "Tim," sure enough, with some residual

Harold, it seems. Jimmy Canton is Jimmy Canton. And I know the names of another dozen or so, their names and not much else.

Then it hits me. They've dropped me back in 1951 with 2016 memories. I'm Tim with Harold's seventy-eight-year-old mind. These kids don't know I'm attending a sixty-fifth class reunion, the only attendee and I'm not even me.

Like falling back into a dream. What I have is all anticipation, a kind of erotic tingle, and a memory that is both dim and useless. How screwed up is this! Maybe in a few minutes I'll lose this displaced feeling, be here, recognize people, know their names and whether we had been friends, teammates, or sexual partners. Rule out the last. How about some effortless slide-and-glide, some escape from myself? Instead, it's an animated yearbook decades later. Concentrating as hard as I can, very few of the faces slide into familiar territory as the minutes' tick by. I guess they are ticking. I have this sensation that time isn't working right.

But still, there is the immediate, the inescapable material world I'm in.

The smell of old wood: strong, moving, and complex. I mentioned that before, but it's what's in my mind, when I'm not cursing my fate or picking out kids I'd like to ravish. Oil on top of years of dirt, discarded skin flakes, and the perfumed dust janitors sprinkle on puke to worsen the smell. Then there's the bodies, bodies as open to pleasure as they ever will be. But where's the pleasure? All around me nervous giggles are trying to pass for ease. Is anyone having fun? Hey, we're fourteen! (Were we all fourteen? I remember the "held back." It'd be nice to get to know these pariahs, save them. Slip them answers, produce future big-shots from what are now fated to be steelworkers in mills fated in a decade to downsize and in another to close.)

All this as I follow the flow of kids, then cut off down the steps to second period, Latin. I remember the teacher distinctly: she exists for me with a solidity denied to my shadowy peers. Remember her so vividly I'm ready to kiss her gray, deep-in-death face as she croaks out the roll. I copy it out as fast as I can, first names being all I can manage, not very accurately:

Luanne
Lester

Sandra
Patsy
Brenda
Marshall
Oliver
Mary Lou
Jo Ann
Shirley
Rudy
Timothy (moi)
Sondra
Jacqueline
Erla
Yvonne
Gus
Deanna
Cecil
Edna
Lynnette
Norman
Ruth Ann
Doris

However inaccurate my list, one thing is clear: not a single Jason, Tiffany, Courtney, Brendan, Brandon, Ashley, Trent, Jessica, Kristy, Kimberly, Jordan, Brett, Justin.

The class is a group of strangers, all wearing masks, serious and attentive. Before long, surely, I'll make the associations, remember the kid, our times together. As I strain and stare, I manage to haul to the surface some nearly atrophied connections: oh yeah, *that's* Yvonne!

Might as well enjoy it, being fourteen. It's no picnic, but seventy-eight's no heaven either. Where is a mirror? No matter, I'm equipped to bed every pretty girl and boy in sight. I have permission to act just as I like. If I assume that, it'll be true. People who are certain they can have sex do so, even in the

1950s. Make a list and check it twice. Letting my mind run in that stream proves to me that I have fourteen-year-old hormones. (Values too, but, hell's fire, I'm an authentic youngster top to bottom, so I'm told.) I try to retreat from the physical, think about Latin verbs, heavy-lidded Miss Adelaine Hawke.

Miss Hawke, really and truly named Adelaine, is explaining the daily quizzes, the rigors ahead, and her plan to seat the class according to each student's performance. It'll be like the BCS football rankings: "Student #1 will sit in desk #1, until displaced; student #2 will sit in desk #2, until displaced; student #3..." She goes up to #10 before, "and so on," like a comedy act with horrible material. Crazy old bat.

"Miss Hawke has too many holes in her bowling ball," I hiss to Carol Blake, the amazingly pretty girl in front of me. Her long blonde hair doesn't seem arranged, just brushed, held in place by plain clips, and her features are so soft they seem to flow together. She makes my throat constrict.

Carol's neck turns pink, but she doesn't say anything or turn around.

"You and I could swap clothes, undress right here, and she'd never notice."

This time she does respond, in a soft whisper, maybe edgy, "Tim!"

Is she offended? I sure don't want to drive away one of the prettiest girls in this or any town. Carol is wearing bobby sox and penny loafers, a full skirt, and a version of what I remember are called peasant blouses. I'm a lot taller than she (or the person for whom my desk was designed) – must be 6'5". By leaning forward, I can look down the front of her blouse, the loose elastic clinging to nothing, and see her sparkler white bra, heartbreakingly simple.

"Sorry," I whisper – and I am.

A minute later, I'm flipping through the book and listening intently to Miss Hawke explaining, with enthusiasm and a lucid futility, what a frozen language amounts to, not dead but relatively uncorrupted, available to us, she says, "as a specimen in amber might be, a sharp image of antiquity seen through a glass dimmed only by our faulty eyesight, made defective by limited imaginations and incomplete learning." What astounding eloquence, thrown away on the coal-dust-scented air. Her appreciation of

Latin's formal properties and grammatical complexity is a matter so subtle and richly aestheticized it makes me glad I'm here, dazzled, as one might be at hearing Maria Callas sing at a cock fight. Miss Hawke loves this language in a way some might love Mozart or Raphael. "Even the irregular verbs have symmetry, if not exactly a straightforward logic." How did this mad, elegant mind get imprisoned in East Liverpool? She may as well have been lecturing the flowers. Every kid is quiet and respectful, doesn't even shuffle in these granite-hard seats, solidly attached by an insanely elaborate curving metal lattice to an iron-maiden desk.

Could a teacher stand here in 1951 for the whole period, a slow tick-tocking forty-two minutes, going "google gum gim!" and command the same well-mannered attention? What a strange world, and not one I want to condemn. There is dignity in all this obedience; polite consideration comes natural to these kids. They probably find Miss Hawke loony, but they would never hurt her feelings. Maybe. Maybe they don't know their asses from their elbows.

A hand is pawing at my calf, a calf attached to a leg so long it pokes far out into the aisle, close to Carol's desk, within easy groping reach of her hand and the note drooping from it.

"Dear Tim. Want to start with shoes or hair clips? Top or bottom? Your friend, Carol."

It brings tears to my old, old eyes. "Your friend." How can I keep from lousing this up, driving away this kid, my friend?

"Dear Carol. I'll put your clips on, if you'll wear my belt. Your friend, Tim."

Despite my resolve, it's hard not to drop the note down her blouse or reach round and grind it against her thigh. You're right, reader, it's perverted: a grown (very) man wanting to fondle a trusting girl, not yet at the age licensed for fondling. If that bothers you, go engage in something virtuous. But before you do, think of Carol – gentle Carol – and be as merciful as I am to you. I could ridicule you. Give as good as you are getting.

I settle for rubbing her shoulder, just where blouse hits skin, so as to touch both.

Carol reads the note, takes out some hair clips and passes them over her shoulder. When I see them coming, I whip off my belt and slip it round the corner. It's hard to find enough hair to clip, but I manage. Carol has no trouble getting my belt round her.

Note again: "Are your pants falling down, Tim? I hope so. How do I keep the belt up?"

And mine: "I won't know till I stand up. Should I pretend to have a cramp and leap to my feet? As for the belt, how about tying it like a rope?"

Hers: "Better not stand up. Miss Hawke might have a heart attack – if she noticed. I'd notice. Nice suggestion about the belt – very fashionable."

Mine: "It goes better with my pants than your skirt. You should really be wearing jeans. Mine would fit perfect. Want them? They're no good to me around my knees."

Hers: "OK. Then you can wear my skirt, and we'll both be decent. You want to be decent, don't you?"

I'm in over my head, but I can't stop: "I'd rather not be decent. But my pants won't look right without my underoos. You have to wear them too."

Hers: "Underoos? Describe them."

Too much. I have to draw back or explode. My God, was this going to be four years of teasing, no-holds-barred titillation, without release?

Mine: "Now you have me embarrassed. My bad."

Hers: "I'm sorry I embarrassed you, Tim. I didn't mean anything by it."

The bell rings. I lean over as she is getting up, hug her sideways. Let go quickly.

"That was fun." What a lame thing to say!

She looks at me – quizzically, angry, shocked?

"Well," I burble, "I'm off to English. We can swap underwear tomorrow."

Her face lights up, dimpled and shining. "Unless I can catch you before. When you're not looking, I'll get my fingers on your zipper."

She isn't giggling or skittering away. She's blocking my path, books in front of her non-breasts, looking straight into my eyes. Her eyes are not blue, as I had thought, but light green. They jump around. I thought such eye skittering only happened in movies, a trick actresses mastered, learned in drama school. But here it is a foot away.

I recall that my self-assurance level has tripled – must have been sub-zero before. I can think of nothing to say, though I manage not to stare at the ground, shuffle, mumble. I make it sound as if it is a ghastly moment, but it isn't. She has enough poise for both of us.

She reaches out, grabs my hand, and squeezes it, not too gently. "I'm not scary," she says, with a mix of mockery and kindness.

"Uh – no, you're not, I guess."

She laughs and leaves.

. . .

Angling over toward English class, I bump into a boy. Takes a second to be certain it is a boy. He is maybe as pretty as Carol, and in much the same way.

"Tim!" he shouts. I return a cool look and, for the hell of it, a hug, which flummoxes him. Even if the hallways commonly witness girls hugging girls (uncertain) and boys hugging girls (unlikely), sure as shit no boys hug boys. Not because it is gay, gayness and its phobias still hiding around the corner, except for faint jokes. I debate doing more but figure sufficient unto the day is the trend setting thereof.

Wonder who he is?

"Where's your locker, Tim? They're giving us an extra ten minutes to get those set up. That's nice of them. I'll need it, I figure. You know where yours is?"

I stare at him for a second, enjoying his fluster, making it worse. "I heard the announcement: an additional ten minutes between classes, which should suffice, and if we need help consult any nearby teacher or associate. But I don't want their help. You can show me,"

"So where's your locker, Tim?"

"Damned if I know. D-111. You know where that is? Pay you $25 for the info."

Who is he?

Whoever it is whispers, "For you, no charge."

"OK. So, Flash, where's D-111?" He leads me and stands by as I flip the combination, cram in supplies I seem to have with me, bang shut the tinny door, and twirl the lock.

"What's your number? Let me guess. D-132. And if I'm right you owe me one."

"You're right!"

"Good!"

"Nah, its D-163 – over there."

"I'll walk you over."

He can find nothing to say, so I shove him toward the locker and, on the way, put my hand on his shoulder, but so lightly he can ignore it if he chooses. He chooses.

D-163 doesn't have English with me, so we have to part. Knowing infatuations feed on uncertainty, I walk away, silent. He calls after me, but I don't turn around. If I have in mind taking advantage of him – do I? – I'll make him frantic for any notice. On edge, obsessed.

Am I bothered by the single-minded coarseness, the triviality of my first two hours back in 1951? Am I flunking this intricate test, devised by deputies of limited competence but backed by God and His angels? Am I beginning badly, would you think? Am I seizing a healthy idea and warping it into a diseased joke? Here I am with elevated capacities, and you'd think I'd been supplied only with date-rape drugs and a ravenous libido. Why am I not thinking of medical advances I can reveal, getting a head-start on emissions control, anticipating the Salk vaccine, the hula hoop? At least I could focus on classes, eager to see how far I can go in Latin, vie for that first seat. Do I have an exalted mind, capable of lofty or, let's say, useful thoughts? If so, why do I have nothing in it but planning the seduction of Carol and Deanna and this boy, adding more from Periods 3, 4, 5, and 6? Am I worried that I should be doing better, doing something?

Well, no, I ain't. If those higher capacities I am told I possess come to the fore and lead me to what we can all agree would be loftier ends, then I'll ascend, I suppose.

I get to English class early, sit among four admirers in a desk that has seen service since the days of quill pens, judging from the inkwell and the sad, fancy graffiti. I want to read the desk, but surrounding students start yammering.

Their talk is of football. I have, it seems, starred in a grade-school league at some point. Not last year. Where I was last year is a matter clear to them, hidden from me. I have major triumphs behind me, with no way of recalling them, though I have sharp enough memories of my Harold football experiences: pain leading to a desire to avoid the pain, in any way possible, not disregarding ways leading to humiliation, leading to secret tears, leading to deeper shame, and finally back again to pain. I couldn't before bring myself actually to do what you would call "play the game." That's not possible when you are so single-heartedly devoted to protecting yourself, creating ever-new possibilities for letting time go by without being injured in it. No artist ever made such calls on imaginative ingenuity. Of course, it was (a term I tried to keep buried) shameless, being willing, as I was, to find no cowardice, no ruse beneath me.

In the terrible old days, first time around, I often made bargains with rival-team kids opposite me: get the game over, don't get stepped on, don't cry. Most, I found, had aims similar to mine. "Let's go easy on one another," I'd hiss. Sometimes they'd pretend to ignore me or tell me to kiss their tough ass – and then act out this dual fakery: grunt, shove, and lay atop one another, safely out of range of the cleats that chewed up fingers, the forearms that shivered necks, the twisting tackles, the humiliating open field. Thespians all, fooling coaches and parents alike.

In 1951 East Liverpool, one thing is foundational: real boys play football and batten on the pain. Maybe I am now, in this new 1951, a real boy. Can it be that I will endure, enjoy football, superstar that I obviously am? The way my fans talk, I'm the best to come along here in town, in any town.

"So, when's this start, football, I mean?"

They look blank, then laugh, drawing severe glances from Miss Blaine, who is sticking a pencil down her blouse, perhaps to relieve a bosom-itch.

"Tim! Sixth period, down the hill, Patterson Field – oh, you know."

"Should I try out?"

Guffaws, allowing Miss Blaine to reach into her repertoire of reprimands and grab an especially forceful one, made even more impressive by the way its insistences defeat the demands of grammar. Miss Blaine has perfected this speech over many years, many decades for that matter. Subtle rearrangements have been introduced to meet the needs of new generations, until her come-uppance now bears little resemblance to its first appearance in 1924, when Miss Blaine was considering becoming a flapper:

"You will find, students, some particular students in particular, that what is appropriate and timely behavior for some places are not appropriate and timely for other places, and one of those places is my classroom. You will apprehend this in the coming days and weeks, and I can guarantee it. Doubt that at your peril."

• • •

The day slips by happily, though by fifth period the adulation begins to seem stale. Sure, it's intense and unqualified: kids are shy of me, and a smile can throw them on their backs, legs pedaling in the air. But where's the challenge? Like winning the love of all the puppies in the kennel. Who would find that alluring? You, maybe, but not me.

All of which is bullshit. Unthinking, mouth-breathing adulation is as good as it gets, "it" being life, even this pretend, fixed-period life.

Thinking in terms of general experience, not just sexual experience (though sexual experience tops the list), why limit my hunting grounds to classes I am in? There are (if memory serves) almost a thousand kids in the high school. Some will be pretty, maybe also interesting, like Carol and Deanna. Androgynous boy seemed uninteresting, but so what? Were he forty, tubby and hairy, you'd not pick him for a desert-island buddy. But he's fourteen now and – well, you know.

Back to serious thinking. With my bankroll of talents, why not cash in? I can exploit my athletic skills, even before the age of endorsements. But there's no pro basketball, even assuming I'm a whiz. Pro football pays peanuts; it's brutal and ill attended. They have thin leather helmets, inadequate medical attendants, and none of the powerful drugs that were later to make it worth watching. Anyhow, neither sport would want a fourteen-year-old, even if I wanted them. But baseball! I could tootle on over to Pittsburgh. Get to know Ralph Kiner, Wally Westlake, Catfish Metkovich: all those I remember so fondly from first time, as they formed the heart of my hopeful life, even while lolling in last place. Lead the Pirates to the Series, or, more realistically, a .500 season. Maybe wait a year, make it more plausible? But they're used to kids in baseball, Bob Feller having started at seventeen. But fourteen?

Singing – oh yes. No reason not to do that. First, get a better grip on what's hot. I have sharp memories from before, tapes I can play in my head. But they're surely not keyed to the autumn of 1951, may indeed come from ten or twenty years later – need to straighten that out. Might also help to listen to my own voice, see if I can anticipate Elvis, go with the Met, do a lounge act, or settle in with the glee club.

· · ·

As I was saying, during the afternoon, I move from enchantment to arousals, class after class, hallway after hallway – warmed by beams of admiration shot at me from every face.

Tom something grabs my arm in the hall after sixth period, I having grabbed Tom by the shoulder earlier. Tom is bigger and toothier than earlier boy but no less charming in his naiveté. Does he know what he's getting into, seizing me? Might as well clutch Count Dracula and herd him off toward football practice.

"You're very handsome, Tom, you know that?"

"What? God, Tim. What'd you say? Never mind. That Yellow Springs talk?"

I stare at Tom, making him more flustered, then laugh it off, prick that I am, making lots of noise in the process.

Some kids look and giggle. More just look. I hadn't noticed, standing right there in the hall, a fat floppy adult in a brown double-breasted suit shaped like a bag that had been in a trunk under the spare tire. He looks at me, then Tom, then me again, produces a theatrical sigh, and walks on. Problems he can ignore, he will. Who wouldn't, especially if you devoted your life to teaching wood shop, ushering into the world thousands of bookends, napkin holders, and tie racks? The advanced students get as far as horse-head shoetrees.

CHAPTER 4

Now, I'm scared and can't shake it. Football again, pain unbounded, no matter how good I am. Tom keeps chattering away, plainly excited. We are joined by others, farting away the time as we walk toward where I gradually remember the stadium to be. It's a good twenty-minute walk. Wonder anybody has energy left for practice.

I shut up, unable to maintain my strut. My most vivid recollections of high school are wrapped around football, and I can call up something very like the ache and exhaustion, dry mouth and pulsing shame. Runny nose, sore gut, caked and bleeding hands, rubbery legs, nausea. Unable to summon any other story, I am left with naked fear. I was pretend-sick a lot that fall but hated myself so much for faking, that it was often easier to practice, get beat upon. There was a fellow pretender back then, a boy who made it all much harder, holding up a mirror. Buck Majeski was fat, graceless, cowardly – the very guy to avoid. But I couldn't help being close to him, unable to retreat into myself, discover any self-sufficiency. So I nursed this comradeship, knowing it revealed what I hoped to conceal. This time around I realize that nobody looks, nobody gives a shit, dealing, as they are, with blinding personal torments. Buck and I are no more than minor annoyances or weak comic distractions. We threaten no one, don't count.

By now we are there, Patterson Field, tromping into the locker rooms under the stands. Then the smells hit me: old pads, old hurt, old urine, old Absorbine Jr., old fungussy socks, old men hanging about, old lamentations.

We stand around, trying to appear casual, knowing. I notice Buck, now utterly alone in his hide-the-coward game. I consider befriending him, but that would expose him, draw him into the light he avoids like a night crawler.

As I'm thinking about poor lost Buck, Coach Sadon steps out of my nightmares and into the room, walking right up to me.

"OK, Mills, you just got cleared to play varsity. Think you can handle it? I doubt it, and I don't like it. I'm pretty sure you wouldn't be a starter for me. You think you can handle it? You want to chicken out now?"

"Not me, Coach!" As he speaks, all dread of this little turd slips away, leaving behind an easy contempt. I delay the "Coach" until even he will read the disrespect in my voice.

"You'll chicken out, Mills, I know." He moves in close, wanting to stare me down. I keep my eyes straight ahead, about ten inches over the top of his head, and only slowly lower them to meet his glare. I'm getting to him good, starting to settle old scores.

"I'm ready to do whatever you want, Coach. You name it. I won't chicken out."

"I'm boss here, Mills, and don't you forget it. I'm making it my business to make sure you don't forget that. So don't forget it. Ever!"

The veins are pulsing on his brick red neck. It's too much to resist. I smile pleasantly. "I'm your man, Coach. Count on me not to forget."

He badly wants to slug me. All at once I hope he will, and I concentrate on sending brain waves his way, compelling him to strike. Maybe telepathic powers are not part of my package. Anyhow, he contents himself with ordering me, "Chickenshit Mills," to proceed to the other end of the stadium to join the varsity.

Not wanting to spoil my chances for fun, I vow now to be obedient. I am All-Time All-American, and there's no point in irritating these morons in the athletic hierarchy beyond Sadon. How much can they know, even about football, if they're here? I'd better be respectful, read fawning, and keep them hot after me.

"Mills!"

"Yes, Coach."

"C'mere. I need to talk with you. Private"

"Yes, Coach."

"OK, Mills. I won't mess around with you. You were away last fall at that fancy prep school for girls, but reports on you are good. I won't say more than that. They're good. I'm not saying I believe them. I'm not saying I don't. Those are sissies over there, but that doesn't mean they don't know their stuff. Doesn't mean they do. We'll see. I'm not saying we won't. Can't trust reports. Maybe they're true. Maybe they aren't true. I've seen both. We'll have to see. I'm not going to be impressed by reports. You see where we stand?"

"Absolutely, Coach." The short and fat (easily matching Sadon) varsity coach is staring at me, probably checking to be sure I'm impressed. It's not hard to imagine real kids locked into this world being afraid of him. It'll be heaven if I can imagine them without being one of them.

"You are? You sure? I don't need some stuck-up kid. We all work the same here. No hotshots. We all put our jock straps on one leg at a time."

This is exhilarating. I look Head Varsity Coach [his name?] in the eye and try my best to appear respectful: "I understand that, Coach. I just want to help the team, if I can."

Studying his face, I use my superior powers, but detect no sign that he can read irony, and irony's not my aim. I just want a shot at the big time. Put me in coach! I'm ready to play!

Practice starts out, and stays, tedious for some considerable time. Tedious is fine, beats misery. I'm hot and sweaty but in no discomfort, though I sense it all around me. Jumping jacks, squats, pushups – all come to me effortlessly. Where suffering had been, ease now reigns. Hopping in tires is duck soup. Wind sprints. I beat everybody by a mile, though I'm pretty sure the coaches aren't noticing; being macho in walk and talk is occupying all their attention. I'm starting to think nothing is going to happen.

But then, we're having a scrimmage. The kids from last year, the vets, display some tight-mouthed familiarity – no laughter or fun, just dogged routine. Maybe everybody, everybody everywhere in the world, finds contact sports as excruciating as I had before? Is the only goal to hide chicken-shittedness? The offense lines up, gaps being quickly filled by Coach Whomever. I'm part of the leftover group standing around.

"OK, scrubs. Defense. Kennedy linebacker left, Christian linebacker right …"

Finally, "Mills, left tackle."

Tackle! Me as tackle is like stewing the finest prime tenderloin, like forcing Shakespeare to write Hallmark cards. The trick will be to kick ass at defensive tackle without kicking ass so thoroughly these creek-bed crawdads will decide they have found just the position for me.

But once we start banging about, I find it impossible not to kick ass thoroughly. At first I shove the kid opposite into the backfield and level the tailback. I do so three times and then decide to slice between tackle and guard, get there more quickly, destroying the play before it can get started. Four times I do this. I've never had so much fun with my body. It's a little like running a race with toddlers, but what do I care? Responding to a challenge is as over-rated as is hard work. There's nothing like being on the right side of a major mismatch.

The coaches are embarrassing me with praise. They are *not*. They say nothing to me, just lay into the guy opposite. "Chickenshit weakling! Yellowbelly! You want to quit, run home to mommy? Give me four laps, you yellow out-of-shape chickenshit. Everybody yell at Crugnale, 'Chickenshit! Chickenshit! Chickenshit!'"

I refuse. To be fair, nobody else yells with any enthusiasm, and a few sneak glares at me. What have I done? Maybe these coaches don't notice that Crugnale is trying hard, that I am the best defensive lineman this side of Mean Joe Greene, though I don't intend to be at this position beyond today. Good as I am, mixing it up in the mire of blundering, chunk-chapped linemen, would still mean cleats grinding atop my fingers. Also, what I want, attention, will come in lighter bundles to even the finest lineman. Then I recall that these are the days of playing both ways! But can I double as defensive tackle and hotshot tailback?

First I have to get noticed – without humiliating anyone. Not that I care much, but it'll be easier to star if teammates don't hate me. While portly Crugnale is chugging through his laps, coach makes some changes, inserting a replacement opposite me. He looks familiar – terrified.

"Jesus, Tim, you got to do that?"

He's down in his three-point stance, his knuckles white and his arm trembling.

"Sorry. I got carried away."

Just then the play starts and, by instinct, so do I, hitting my trembling friend so hard he would have flown had I not caught him and allowed us both to settle to the ground, me on the bottom. I make no move to wiggle away or launch him off me.

The coaches, oblivious to what has happened but noticing that the play has actually been run, look over and, forgetting themselves, compliment somebody.

"OK, Bailey, that's the way to handle him. Not as tough as you thought, right, Mills? Crugnale, get back in there and start playing, for Christ's sake. We need Bailey at guard."

As luck would have it, Crugnale comes panting over just as the coaches take it in their heads to explain something to the backfield. He says nothing, looking at the ground.

"Hey, Crugnale, I don't know what's wrong with me. Let's just slow dance together and get the practice over with."

Crugnale looks up at me scowling, probably thinking I'm abusing him yet more. The adjacent guard, though, one of three black guys in the vicinity, laughs in a way so friendly I could kiss him. Luckily, I don't. But he makes me laugh and, a beat later, Crugnale, too.

"Didn't know you'd be playing varsity, Mills. You a tackle?"

"Not a tackle. Hope not."

"Yeah," says one or the other, "but varsity?"

"I show up for practice and they send me over here, Sadon did, the little turd, don't know if I'll get to play much anywhere."

"Fuck yeah you will," says Crugnale. "Everybody knows about you setting records at Yellow Springs. I didn't know they'd let you be varsity. God damn good they did."

"Thanks. I'll help if I can." Not knowing where to go with that, I look to them for help. Yellow Springs?

"Shit yes, you'll help. Shit yes. You'll be fullback or something. Maybe tackle too."

So the scrimmage wanders on, grim and joyless. I let Crugnale handle me, content with tackling ball carriers running my way. I also deflect a pass and jab the ball loose from a small kid with arms too weak to ward off a half-determined stripper. Mostly, I take it so easy I hardly seem to be playing. The coaches, of course, register nothing, neither my skill nor my kindness. What a curse to be an orchid in an abandoned garden.

But they do notice, half-notice.

"Mills, in my office."

I had looked forward to watching people undress, but I can stand missing that for now, given that these bodies belong to burleys. So I go cheerily into the partitioned-off wooden cage, maybe ten yards away from the primitive benches and the worse showers.

"So, Mills, what were you doing out there?"

"Coach?"

"I said, what were you doing out there?"

How much does he know? Nothing, surely. "Just trying my best, coach."

"Hell you were! Just what were you doing out there?"

This could go on all night. "I was just going at practice speed, coach, getting my moves down, ironing out kinks."

"Huh?"

"Test my balance, try new angles, check out some things, work on basics."

"You were dogging it. Nobody dogs it on my team, Mills. You might think because you could get headlines in that prep league, you can dog it here. But you can't, Mills. Nobody dogs it on my team, Mills. You think you can, but you can't – dog it."

The words are angry but the voice is pitched a hair above a whisper.

"Well, coach, yes I was. I thought that since we are all on the same team, there was no point in maybe hurting somebody, destroying somebody's confidence."

He looks at me differently – annoyed? baffled? I can't tell, so I plunge ahead.

"Coach, I mean no disrespect. Let's understand each other." I am speaking earnestly, but at least as softly as he. "I wasn't dogging it, just not showing off."

"Yeah."

"Hell, let's be straight. Excuse me." He looks shocked. "I'm the best athlete in the country. I know that and you suspect it. I didn't ask to be, but I am. I'm the fastest and the most coordinated and the toughest. Nobody's even close."

"Yeah."

"I can't remember if there's a state championship, is there?"

"What?"

"Sorry." I had forgotten where I was. "I mean, in the state rankings, we can be number one. But let's stop dicking around. I am not going to hurt other kids in practice, though I won't be so careful in games. You let me play at some skill position – tailback and maybe linebacker or, I don't care, tackle on defense, and we'll fucking win the state title."

He looks horrified. "Your dad know you talk this way? What's got into you, Mills?"

"I mean it, Coach. You can ride me to a terrific job if you want out of here and of course you do. Just let me go at it. I don't want special treatment. Jesus, man, I can score at will and keep the other team stalled. Just let me dog it in practice. I wouldn't shit you, and also you'll see for yourself, not being blind."

Before he can respond, I realize what I have done: "Forgive me for getting carried away, coach. I'm just eager. I'm not challenging your authority. You're the one to determine things. You're the coach and I respect that. But everything I say is true. I'm just asking for a chance to show you. You'll make up your own mind."

"You're goddam right I will."

"But you'll give me a chance?"

He stares at me, glaring his best, which was pretty good, then breaks into a big smile, his face suddenly light. And he pats my shoulder.

"Get the hell out of here, Mills. And don't forget to shower. I don't want your dad telling me I sent you home smelling worse than you usually do."

I turn away. What a piece of cake! I can control adults while I play with the kids, basking in their adulation, doing good among the worthy, assaulting the appealing.

"And Mills!"

I spin around. "Yes, Coach."

"Who do you think you are? Talk to me again like that and I'll kick your teeth down your throat. And you're off the varsity. See if you can make the freshman squad, which I doubt. Let Sadon knock some sense into you."

. . .

What I remember best about my dad is that he is dead. My mother is dead too, but that event won't occur for another forty-seven years. Dad has six years to live, is only a year or two away from the first in a series of heart attacks, very near the end of what would count as his real life, the last four years being one misery after another, day after day of pain and helpless guilt.

On the bus home, I consider ways of coping with his doom, "coping" moving quickly from acceptance to rejection, to creating a new story altogether. Armed with all this knowledge, I will cheat the fates. Why should he die? I'm going to save him.

My mother does just fine for a long time. My sister, though, Joanie. Maybe this time around I can manage to see her, not just slide past.

Maybe take Dad into my confidence. Big bucks will save his life. Place bets, gamble on sure things. 1951 is Bobby Thompson and the huge home run, in just a few weeks. A wager there will set us up. When were heart transplants done? Christian Barnard. But the patient died in a couple of weeks. How can I make a bet at age fourteen, an illegal age for an illegal bet, and where will the money come from? What good will it do? One thing at a time.

Keep quiet for now. One more night of peanut butter crackers and breakfast with cream on his cereal won't make much difference in the progress of Dad's heart disease.

If this is only a four-year fake, why make Dad well? There's no carry-over, no meaning at all. Whatever happens only happens in this fenced-in plot of make-believe, doesn't "happen" at all: dolls in a dollhouse, wind-up toys. As Tweedledum says, we're shadows in the King's dream, and "if that there King was to wake," we'd "go out – bang! – like a candle!"

According to the sky girls, real life is plodding ahead while we're playing this game. The kids around me are losing their grip, losing the farm, losing limbs and lives. They'll wake up to disaster, if they wake at all. They went into this in their seventies, so they can count on crawling out in worse shape than when they entered. Me, too.

So why even think of long-term things?

I don't know. Yes I do.

These folks in charge don't seem to know much. They promise I'll fit in as smoothly as a toe in the mud, perfectly coordinated. And here I am so very far out of 1951. Did they lie? More likely they don't understand. They fumble helplessly, despite having sphincter-tightening powers. They're morons, holding the keys to time, no idea what they unlock.

So then? Who's to say this 1951 isn't as consequential as the one I went through before, if I did, if it was before, if it was me. Maybe the back then that's going on right now counts just as much, whatever that means.

Those time-warping gals have been wrong about so much, who is to say this isn't 1951 all over again? They did insist that where I am now and what's going on is *real*. Wouldn't that make more sense than a limited revival running in an alternate reality zone? Maybe they didn't want to admit the truth. What are they but file clerks? And, if they tell the truth, that it's real true 1951 and I have a full life to live, I'm likely to be cautious, future-oriented, buying insurance in more ways than one, no fun to watch. On the other hand, telling me I have a fixed terminus, nothing but a wink, would give them what they were looking for. I'll be reckless, devoted to short-term pleasures, the glories of sports, wild drama, sex. It'd be good pay tv, uncensored and hot.

But what if they are right? If I live carefully and then, after four years, the curtain falls, I'll have wasted so much, saved up for nothing.

• • •

My candle burns at both ends;
It will not last the night;
But ah, my foes, and oh, my friends—
It gives a lovely light!

• • •

Home is adjusted to me, altered in little ways. The house itself is in better repair; maybe I've developed practical skills I didn't have first time around. But some things remain: the devotion to received opinion; the exchange of self-confirming commonplaces; the skepticism regarding art, politics, unfamiliar religions; the high regard for low comforts; the small kindnesses to neighbors and those in need; the silent sacrifices for Joanie and me; the avoidance of all domestic conflict; the pleasure in routine; the substitution of gossip for genuine malice; the respect for authority; the penny-pinching to finance small holiday squanderings; the honesty; the deep-down decency; the love. And there's the kitchen table out of the heavenly sisters' lair, anchoring everything: non-reflecting gray Formica, steel tubes holding up its unsteady form.

Having no idea how to behave, I try to adopt a "natural" attitude by responding alertly to everything around me. I listen carefully to what is said, watching body language, hearing the unspoken. But everyone except Joanie is so passive, it's hard to operate this way. Maybe they're waiting for me to take the lead.

"Well, Joanie, how was first day in eighth grade?"

"Timmy! How would I know?"

"Huh?"

"I'm in seventh."

"Of course you are."

"No, I'm not."

"I know you're not."

"No, you don't."

"So, how was it?"

She giggles.

"You're so pretty when you laugh like that."

She looks at me as if I'm mocking her.

"Yeah, sure!"

"Your eyes sparkle."

"Don't have a cow!"

"You're a good sister. Bring your friends around. That's the only way I'll ever get a date. You think any of them would date me?"

"Most of them can't date yet. If they could, they'd go wild just thinking about it. Maybe I could find somebody older."

"I'll let you know my availability (which is limitless), and you can line up some candidates – or candidate, one will do."

Mom and Dad observe all this, seem happy to see the kids getting along. Didn't we always? I can't remember fighting with Joanie – just not much noticing she was there.

We're gathered round one of the two tables in our tiny house. The dining room pretends to accommodate the other, a table so outsized it leaves little space for its six chairs. By mutual and unspoken agreement, an illusion of roominess is maintained. Nothing but this set could live there: not the smallest package, not a sweater on the floor, competed with it for the chimerical space. Surviving from the brief time when Mom and Dad had been a little flush, this piece is dark mahogany with a lustrous finish. There are pads to protect it, though Dad loves to have the wood exposed, open for board games. Almost every night. It's also used for dinners, at which time food settles on a cloth laid over the pads. I suppose this table is no more than average-sized, but it looms as large now as it had in my memory. Every night, Mom carts things in to us in bowls. Strikes me that we kids never do chores, never do anything but obey the unspoken rules. Looked at it in this way, Mom's servitude is barbed wire, wrapping us into acquiescence. That sounds ungenerous. You'll say my mother was hardworking, kind, unselfish, and loving. You'll be right. It's the table we're talking about.

I mentioned before the real table, the one for relaxing round, which is in the kitchen, where there *is* a little space. Anyhow, it isn't ten minutes until I remember what I'd ignored first time around: my parents never talk about their own lives until any stock of school doings or blurted-out confidences from Joan and me is exhausted. We gave daily reports, babbling on, parents listening, nodding, now and then wedging in a polite question. As Joan is taking her turn, I consider letting fly with some obscenities, stories of drug arrests.

Mostly I'm listening to Joan. What a kindly, funny girl. It occurs to me that I'm not sexually attracted to her. Since I'm attracted to myself, this seems surprising. If it's only a set-up world, notions like "narcissism" or "incest" have no soil in which to thrive. If everything is a game, abnormal at the core, how can there be perversion? But still, what I feel toward pretty, animated Joanie is pride and protectiveness – a whole range of dull but warming emotions.

We talk, eat, sit on the back porch, finish three games of Parcheesi, visit (Joan and I) two sets of neighbor kids, put pennies on the railroad track, play volleyball over at the school, manage our Ping-Pong contests in the Canton's basement, play kick the can, listen to the radio (tales well calculated to keep you *IN SUSPENSE*), talk some more, have snacks, get ready for bed. Each activity seems to take two hours. There's a common feeling that the world contracts as we grow older, that there is no room for what was once overflowing. Maybe that's not an illusion.

Another thing I do: I make a phone call. I hadn't forgotten that our one phone is in the sardine-can living room, where are also the radio, the record player, and the other three family members. Oh well, I want a date. I get the feeling Mom and Dad think I'm a bit young to date, not that they would say so. Maybe they understand that they derive their power from the guesswork forced on Joan and me, the demand that we read unspoken signals. We're regulated by our ability to imagine what would hurt the feelings of our permissive parents. And we obey those guidelines, strict ones, we draw up out of speculation and thin air. Not entirely unpleasant, though anticipatory guilt is a lot like guilt itself.

The phone calls. First to Carol. Have trouble dredging up her last name. Thank God for Joan, who knows Carol well: Blake.

"What do you like about her, Joan?"

"The same things you do, Timmy. Well…" Then she giggles.

"Apart from that?"

"She's smart and doesn't let on. She's the prettiest girl in town and doesn't care about it. She doesn't hang out with the rich kids. She's easy to talk to."

"That's pretty remarkable. Maybe we should get her to join our family."

"You marry her, Timmy, and she could move in with me."

"Sounds like a plan."

"Where did you learn hip phrases like 'sounds like a plan' or 'whassup'?"

"I come from the future. We all talk that way in 2016."

"Not much to look forward to."

"Other things are worse."

"You gonna call Carol or talk to me until it's too late? Nervous, right?"

"Of course not. Right, I am. But I'll do it. She scares me. Should I be scared?"

"Yes."

· · ·

Nonetheless, I call.

I won't bother you with the first minutes. I'm nervous as hell for the seven seconds it takes Carol to get to the phone. Then she takes over, though I suppose I do half the talking. Maybe it's not enchantment, but I'm relaxing so deeply words emerge without touching any memory bank. That sounds corny. I'll revise it later. I hope I have the chance.

Finally, I get to the point. "I'd love to take you on a date, Carol. That's not the same thing as you wanting to go on a date with me. I shouldn't assume you'd want to."

"Of course I do, Tim. You're hot, but I'd go out despite that. I like you."

Now I am enchanted, so occupied by a friendly army of tingling nerves I can scarcely register what she's saying and have to ask her to repeat.

"I was saying, Distracted One, that my parents think dating is the road to pregnancy, atheism, motorcycle gangs, and voting Democratic. I'd love to, but I can't."

"Can't?"

"I'm sorry, Tim. It might be different if my parents didn't hate you."

"Really?"

"They like you – insofar as they like any boy. They'd like you better if you were confined to a wheel chair, a chess champion."

"Oh."

"Listen, Ace, you do want to go out?"

"Damn right!!!" I said so loudly, Mom, Dad, and Joanie all look up.

"Don't scream – I'm not proposing. So we plot. We get together, not calling it a date. Couple of weeks. Maybe that's what you had in mind, middle of October?"

"Oh sure, Carol. I had in mind Friday or Saturday."

"Let's delay. See what we can sneak up. I always love sneaky, and of course you do. You're the sneakiest boy this side of the reform school."

"Worked at it for years."

"So get somebody else to keep you company meanwhile."

"What?"

"Gotta run. My jailers are approaching."

I relay this to Joanie, who tells me I should get a date just as Carol says, since I don't want to sit home weekend nights listening to Guy Lombardo until we get our sneaks figured out, Carol and me. I figure that's right. Carol won't mind – at least she said that.

I ask Joanie if I can help her sneak, just to return the favor, cover with Mom and Dad while she goes out drinking with other eighth-graders. She glares at me.

Since Carol won't mind, dates! Of course I have almost no notion of what constitutes a date in 1951, nothing springing to mind that isn't foggy, alarmingly close to Archie comics.

Anyhow, the pressing issue is not the nature of "the date" but finding a girl to go on one.

The name comes from the most unlikely source – Mom.

"How about Mary. You've always gotten along, since you played paper dolls."

"Mary, hi."

"Hi, Timmy."

"How'd you know?"

"Maybe because we've talked on the phone every day since we were three."

"That'd explain it."

"You OK?"

This is a tight spot. Should I tell Mary? Tell her what? What would you do, reader? What I do is make matters worse.

"Just having a senior moment."

"What?"

Oh Jesus. Don't mention Alzheimer's. Don't say you're seventy-eight. "What's wrong with *you*, Mary? Senior moment. That means I'm forgetting, as seniors do – senior citizens."

"Now it's all clear. What are senior citizens?"

"Old people."

"You inventing your own language? Pick it up at Yellow Springs?"

"I guess so. Wanta go on a date, Mary?"

"Ha ha. Your parents forcing you to clean out the garage, and you want help."

"I thought you might want to go to a movie and then to — Dairyland." Thanks to the heavenly sisters for providing me, at the last second, the name of the one hot teen spot in town.

There's silence at the other end for a good ten seconds. Finally, "Timmy?"

"Yeah?"

"Never mind. Sure, I'd love to, and – never mind."

Having no idea what's going on, I take the safe route and ignore everything but the obvious: "Terrific. Friday? Or we could do it Saturday, if you'd prefer – or both."

"Friday's fine."

CHAPTER 5

And here I am, on the freshman squad, with the little kids, trying not to hurt anyone. Coach Sadon, after a few days, doesn't really seem awful. He's watched too many Knute Rockne movies and developed his own talents under coaches similarly schooled. He has, I gather, no general intelligence whatever, but he is shrewd about football. When he forgets that his mission is to humiliate one and all, he can be interesting, telling anecdotes about his days at Youngstown U. I burn to ask questions, but questioning is brown-nosing. I listen earnestly to his instructions and follow them dutifully, careful to add only minimal variations. As a result, he can't help but like me, not realizing it, of course. When he forgets himself, he discusses strategy with me.

"We're gonna have to find ways to make up for a piss-poor line, both sides of the ball. Those kids try but they just don't have it. Burns is good at center, and Burlingame's a fine tackle, nice instincts and quick. But holy Jesus beyond that. The thing is, have the weak ones submarine. That's risky. Going at ankles can trip up linemen, give you a couple seconds, or it can leave you on the ground while the guy steps on your nuts and into our backfield."

Sadon is fond of talking about nuts. Getting hit is "taking it in the nuts"; a good block is "shoving his nuts down his throat"; an off-tackle run (our offense) is "popping their nuts."

Wish I could talk to him generally, easily, but the only way to lure him into conversation is to keep my mouth shut. To reveal my own views would be to fly straight at the heart of his religion, but he can't help warming to me.

He never smiles, or relaxes his cynical disdain – but installs me at tailback. I've carefully suppressed the full range of my abilities, running at half-speed, using few fakes, allowing myself to be tackled. I'm acting the part of the best player on the team, holding back the best-player-in-the-world. I sense also that coming on like Doc Blanchard would annoy Sadon and activate perverse instincts that would land me on the bench.

We have an end, Sammy, who can catch the ball like nobody's business. Unfortunately, he has no idea of following a route and may direct his steps right into coverage. But coverage at this level doesn't amount to squat, so it's criminally easy for me to complete passes to him. Sammy battens on it, loves running like hell and finding the ball there. We work on a buttonhook and a sideline-timing pattern. Sadon notices us staying after practice and watches a minute before telling us to get into the showers, remembering to scrub our nuts.

The result of our extra work is that Sadon starts spending practice time on passing. Nobody in 1951 passes much, and he's clear-headed enough to see that it'll be one hell of a weapon for that very reason. I'm mobile enough to get out of the way of linemen coming at me, avoid them long enough for Sammy to get clear. Shrewd Sadon also puts in keepers for me, letting the three other backs do the blocking the line finds iffy. By the first game, we're set to surprise a lot of folks – not a lot, since only parents and a couple of stragglers come to freshman games. But I intend to amaze 'em by running up a big score and unleashing powers I have veiled until now.

Against our best interests for sure, the first game figures to be tough: a bigger school, Beaver Falls, up the river some twenty-odd miles and our major road trip. I had forgotten that the only highway runs along the river, winding through little towns laid back-to-back with just a bit of woods between. These burghs are mill towns when they count for anything and shanty towns when they don't, forming a gauntlet of stop lights, sharp curves taken at a crawl, hills taken at a double-crawl, old folks crossing the street, random detours, arbitrary pull-overs, and railroad crossings. The game is at four-fifteen. We leave at two-thirty, suggesting, I figure in my innocence, a quick meal on the way. We arrive at four, take five minutes finding the locker room, get dressed rapidly, and scramble out for the kickoff.

We kick, poorly, and their return man, choosing the side of the field where I ain't, stumbles and falls. Otherwise, they'd be off to a demoralizing lead. But I'm feeling as exhilarated as Wordsworth at a waterfall: for the first time, I've gone all out, flattening three of their starters without breaking stride. True, I'm more intent on bashing blockers than finding the guy with the ball. That's dumb, but now I know what I can do.

Sadon has me at middle linebacker. He didn't explain, of course, but it's obvious: from that position, I can range about, prevent disaster. I'm not unwilling to do that, but in my present state prevention seems timid. This era is long before the time of blitzing linebackers, but I figure once won't hurt.

I'm stationed behind Burns and Burlingame, our two good linemen, set beside one another to close off up-the-gut plays. That leaves the outside weak, but Sadon knows this team and their macho need to plow straight ahead. The first play they do just that, Burns and Burlingame pinching in on the ball carrier quickly. I satisfy myself with making sure there's no forward progress, holding the pile where it is, no ramming into it and hurting my own buddies.

The gain is only a yard, but I figure these blockheads will regard that failure as a challenge and doggedly repeat the play. I tell the B boys to scoot laterally, clearing space for me. As their tailback starts his count, I move up to the line, jump at the snap, and throw the center into the backfield. He hits not long after the ball arrives, me shortly behind, screaming and grabbing at everything in sight, finally the ball, which has never landed securely in anyone's grasp, so confused have things been with my berserker marauding.

Our ball!

Final score: forty-two to nuthin, us. Seven touchdowns and no extra points. Sadon stubbornly insists on giving our kicker all seven opportunities, despite sufficient evidence after a single failure, that he's as likely to get it through the uprights as is my mama. Our kicker, one Wentzel, is a nice gangly kid with no talent I can see, certainly none for timing his kicks or getting his foot into the ball squarely. I think he somehow made his one successful conversion the first time in practice, and Sadon seems reluctant to accept that success as accidental, no matter how deeply the fact sinks its teeth in his ass.

Walking to the bus, I join Sammy and two others, both black, named Martin and William. I start chortling: "You guys think Sadon'll congratulate us, buy us dinner, beers all round?"

"No."

"You kidding?"

"Why should he?"

"Because we played a great game."

"Shit, Tim. *YOU* played a great game, all over the field, keeping the Beaver Falls bastards from running a play."

"Hogging it up, you mean."

"That's just the way you are. It's great. Nobody's complaining, Tim."

"You sure? There's no point in me playing that way if you guys hate it. I mean, why should I perform to please Sadon. I hate him and I love you guys."

"You *LOVE* us?"

"I love you, that's right.

"Jesus, Tim. You don't talk that way."

"I'm from the future, Martin. Everybody loves everybody."

Silence.

"And you know what? Everybody's black. No white people."

"Black?"

"Sorry. Negroes start calling themselves black, but then everybody starts mating with everybody else, so that we're all tan, light brown, gray."

Silence.

"Anyhow, what do you think Sadon will say?"

I need work on people skills.

Sadon seems concerned we'll get "cocky." We were lucky, got an opponent almost as chickenshit as us. We won because they started practice late. Had they been ready, they'd a cut off our privates and handed them to us. Then he does – surprise – compliment several players, including Sammy and Burlingame. Me, he doesn't mention. That's fine; he and I have this secret understanding. Oh yeah!

One thing I notice is the absence of chafing, the misery (one of the miseries) recalled from last time: the way hard pads, bulky uniforms, and cleated high-top shoes rub against delicate skin and protruding bone. I'm not even tired, could play three more games back-to-back. No chickenshit me, Coach!

· · ·

I discover a few days later that the name of Donny (?) is Donny. I must have had the name lodged in my head from last time around. Odd I don't seem to remember Donny himself. Maybe I was careful to repress same-sex attraction then. I corner Donny by his locker and ask if he wants to get together and study.

"Sure, Tim!"

"My house or yours?" I suddenly remember that study at my house is limited to public areas. The bedroom provides space for my bed, a chest, and not one thing else. Also, his house is closer to the stadium, handier after practice.

"You can come over to my house."

"Can I stop over after football practice?"

"Sure, Tim. Eat with us, have supper, before you cut out, if you want."

"Thanks, Donny, it's nice of you to ask me. Sure on all fronts – study and dinner."

I call home. Mom is worried I might miss the last bus and probably isn't thrilled about me eating elsewhere, but of course won't say so. I assure her that Donny's small body is not the result of systematic underfeeding and that the last bus is at eleven, way later than I plan to stay.

Donny is clearly proud to have me at his house but isn't a jerk about it. He's shy but also cool in ways I will never be, unashamed of his parents and their poverty. He's also unconscious in his flirting ways and, as we'll come to say, way attractive.

And whatever I like he will, within limits but wide ones, adopt as his own liking.

We go to his bedroom to study – and do just that. It's a modest place, beige walls even before beige is common. Ampler space than mine by a fair margin, and he has a rickety, uncluttered table, Donny does, serving as a desk. He sits on the bed, pointing me toward the desk chair. Instead, I plop beside him and open two books at once.

We have a good time. That's the best way to put it – easy, minutes flying. He's no dummy, but it makes me feel good to explain a few things to him (algebra). We listen to some of his records – forty-five r.p.m., a speed just arrived, I think, at least in East Liverpool.

There's a cracked and graying mirror loosely attached to his chest of drawers, and I catch myself several times admiring the two of us, shocked that the prettier and stranger is me. I've been looking at myself a lot, trying to get used to the image smiling back. But it isn't working. It's a centerfold shock at every encounter.

At one point his sister Sally comes in, knocking first. Sally looks a good deal like Donny, a couple of years younger. When she laughs, her hands flutter over her mouth in a gesture of modesty that kicks off in me a reflex of something I can't name.

"Hi, my lovey Tim."

There's a history here. Hope I can catch up with it. "When are you going to marry me, Wild Woman? We could elope and take your brother with us – or not."

This seems to be the right tone. She pretends to swoon into me. I'm slow in catching her and end up having to hitch her up, unintentionally into kind of an embrace,

Sally doesn't seem to notice, or mind, and I can say with truth, cringing reader, that I loosen my hold on her at once. What am I, a deviant? She is a child, and I am a child. Makes me think of Poe, who occupies dangerous territory to enter.

Sally keeps the game going: "Take me with you now, lovey!"

"Disguise yourself. Then we'll make a break for it, head to Wellsville."

Donny to the rescue. In a voice containing no irritation, he tells her he's irritated.

"God, ankle-biter, leave Tim alone."

67

She backs up a step, takes on a new tone.

"I wanted you to tell something to Joanie, Tim. "

"I'm your trusted courier."

"Tell Joanie that it's OK about Brian."

"It's OK about Brian. You two talk in code? Does that mean you're going to blow up the grade school?"

"Just tell her, please, will you? She'll understand."

"I will: 'It's all over with Brian!'"

She smiles and is out the door.

Donny looks after her with a smile of his own, doesn't apologize, and returns to algebra and the concept of unknowns.

All this time, I've kept my hands to myself. He's a wiggler, writhing about like a well-mannered puppy. After we get through algebra, he leans into me and I wrestle him back on the bed. He's quick and extremely athletic in his way, so it really is just wrestling. I could get away with stuff, I guess, but I don't. He assumes that I know what I am doing and that he doesn't, and he trusts me so completely I feel the burden. He'd let me talk dirty, try to return the favor, and proceed from there. But how would he feel? Do I care, or am I entertaining tiresome moralistic ideas for no better reason than to let them ring?

Just as I am resigning myself to a sterile buddiness, and as it gets to be eight-thirty, fifteen minutes after I should have left, I'm hit with a wave of warm tingling, call it sexual excitement, and proceed to more wrestling, tame groping included.

I feel terrible, but the excitement is strong doing even this. I then catch a glimpse of us, this time accidental, in the mirror across the room. Our monitor. At first I think, ridiculously but acutely, that I'm watching a porn flick. As soon as I realize it's Donny I'm looking at and this stranger, I'm hit by wave after wave of what must be shame.

"Jesus, Donny, I'm sorry."

"That's OK, Tim. This is fun."

He isn't being seductive, just kind. When I said earlier he didn't care, I was wrong. He cares a lot – about me. I will study to deserve it.

Later, on the way to the bus stop, I consider how defenseless I have rendered my friend. It isn't Donny diminished. He is taking a risk and inviting me to do so – suggesting that we are playing the same game, by the same absence of rules. Agreeing beforehand with anything I decide to do, he draws me into a league of tenderness.

Enough of that for now. I have a dad to save.

. . .

There are problems with making money on my certain knowledge of what will happen in the National League pennant race and playoffs. First, I have no money; second, I have no idea how to place a bet. All I have is a million dollars' worth of illicit knowledge.

Trying hard to remember shady characters from the first time through, I realize that there were no shady characters first time through. My parents (and I) are subject to an iron rule of virtue, my father, for instance, celebrating the voluntary income tax by deciding every doubtful point in favor of the IRS: "If you don't know, then you don't deserve it." I'd remembered that in my previous life, as adult Harold filing returns, gnawed at by a painful reluctance to claim deductions. I remembered my dad's words and respected them, though I could never, twist it how I would, make them sensible. My father makes no distinction between the government and the people, finds politicians admirable, servants of the electorate, differing from one another only as honest men will. I held onto this as adult Harold, and consequently found myself shut out of political conversations. I had no irony, no sophistication.

Casting about in my old-life memory, I recall two places I knew, without being told, I was not to go. Both were located on a downtown street veering seedily off the main avenue. One of the evil dens was The River Rest, a noisome bar, and the other Meilie's, a cigar and magazine shop, or so it appeared. A front? The prohibition of Meilie's seemed mysterious and thus promising. Meilie's, unlike the Rest (as it was known), blew forth wonderful smells out onto the street, a layered mixture of tobacco, sweat, floor cleaner, and liniment. Does this den have a back room, stocked with low-lifes, gamblers? Badly in want of such, I hope so.

I walk into Meilie's early Saturday, trying hard to look like I know what I'm doing.

"Hey, kid. That you, Tim, Tim Mills?"

"Sure is. Hi!"

"Son of a bitch. Your dad'd kill you if he knew you were here. Kill me, too."

"Yeah, I know, but I need your help."

"You got it. Let me tend to this drunk on the phone."

I busy myself looking around.

"OK, Tim, what is it?"

"Well, sir, you gotta promise me to keep this quiet, OK?"

"You gonna hold up the bank, you little shit, have to stand on a stool to reach the teller!" (I was a good foot taller than he, even spotting him his greasy hat.)

"Maybe. Could we talk in private?"

"You in some kinda trouble, kid?"

"No, nothing like that."

"Come back here." Meilie looks concerned, not at all like a genuine shady character.

We enter an honest-to-God den: two pool tables, a desk, another door, leading somewhere – to the betting apparatus, phone banks, sin!

I spring it on him right away.

"You know my dad, sir, but you don't know he has a bad heart, real bad heart. Remember, this is between you and me. Whatever you do, don't let on to Dad."

"Jesus!"

"You'll keep this between us, right?"

"Yeah, but what's his problem? How long has he...?"

I interrupt: "Here's what it is, sir. I gotta get money for treatment he can't afford." I can sense that Meilie is about to produce some cash on the spot, so I hurry on. "I need to know how to place a bet. You're going to tell me that's no way to make money. Please, old friend, if you ever trusted anybody, trust me. I know what I'm doing. There's nothing crooked. I just need to know how to do it, that's all."

He's looking pained, panicked, and negative. I need to produce something more.

"I want to keep you out of it, or I'd give you all the details. It's not that I don't trust you. Hell, I'd trust you with my life."

Tears jump into his eyes. I'm afraid he's going to hug me and sob. He does neither.

"It goes against my better judgment, kid."

I know I have him, so I try to look innocent and trusting.

"OK. The simplest thing will be for you to let me do it for you. I won't ask the details. What you betting on and how much?"

"I don't know how much yet. The Giants to tie with the Dodgers for the NL Pennant, the Giants to take the three-game playoff, winning the third game in the bottom of the ninth, the Yankees to beat the Giants in the World Series in six games."

"Huh? Oh Moses in the bulrushes!"

"True. That's the bet."

"Oh shit, Tim. I can't. I can't let you do that."

"You mean we can't bet on baseball." (I feel sure it is the 'we' that gets him.)

"Sure we can, but we can't make such a stupid bet."

"The odds would be good, right?"

"Oh, shit yeah. The odds'd stretch from here to Wheeling. About the same odds you'd get on the second coming happening next Thursday over in the Diamond, where the dentists are. It ain't the odds. There's a reason the odds'd be so good."

"OK. I know what you're saying, sir."

"So, you see what I'm saying."

"If we bet a hundred bucks on what I said, in sequence, what would we make?"

"Giants have picked up a little ground, but they're still seven games back, so maybe that's two hundred to one, twenty thousand. The Dodgers would be favored to win any playoff, maybe two to one, so forty thousand, which you could balloon by predicting the number of games for the playoffs, the length of the World Series, all those odd damned details. I'd say, all together, oh maybe two hundred thousand to two-hundred fifty."

"Not bad for a one-hundred-dollar bet. What's your commission?"

"My commission is kiss my ass."

"Set it up, sir. I'll be back in two or three days, with the one hundred, maybe more."

"Set what up, piss-your-pants? All I do is call. You don't need to know any more than that. You want me to advance you the hundred? And don't call me 'sir.'"

His caution, his aversion to a stupid bet, seems to have evaporated. A real gambling fool, my buddy Meilie. But I don't want to borrow.

"I appreciate that, really! I want to do this myself, though. You understand. It'd make me feel good to do this for my dad."

"OK, kid. Whatever you say. You think your dad's gonna like this?"

"That's a problem I'll face later. You're right, though, it's no slam dunk."

"It's no what?"

"It's really a problem. But I'll solve it."

The hundred dollars is easy to get, though it comes in multiple loans from buddies, running between fifty cents and four dollars. Deanna, who doesn't have much money, is one who advances me four dollars; Jimmy Canton, who has less, is another. Donny comes up with three dollars, as does Mary, Sally with seventy-five cents. I don't ask Carol because I am a shy bumbler; I don't ask Joanie because it's too complicated.

Meilie is delighted to see me. I worry he might have slept on it, changed his mind, decided to save me from myself. Nope. He has it all set, he says, actually has placed the bets.

"Don't worry, Tim. That's the way it works. You pay me now. If you lose, kiss the money goodbye. If you win, you get it next day. Guaranteed. Course it's not me paying you. Think I have three hundred fourteen thousand lying about? Do you?"

"Yeah, I figured you had that much in the register."

Meilie stares at me aghast and then gets it. He gets it the way some people get smacked in the nose by a rock. Liquid laughter comes out of him like a geyser.

I wipe my face surreptitiously, thank him. "You said three hundred fourteen thousand?"

"As of now. Could change a little, but – you don't want to know."

I did, but figure Meilie needs to sit privately on some details to satisfy the secretiveness so central to his pretend-criminal act.

"So, friend, your commission…"

"My commission is kiss my ass." More eruptions.

"Yeah, so you said. But Meilie, how do you make any money out of this? I don't want to be taking advantage of you."

"Don't worry, little shitass, I get paid. It's all on the up-and-up."

"Really?"

"Well, no. It's not exactly illegal."

"It's not exactly legal, either. I'm with you, sir – buddy."

And I am. But the problem of getting three hundred fourteen thousand dollars, give or take, to my dad and his deteriorating heart is no closer to being solved. Then it strikes me that history might not repeat. What if Thompson, never really more than a fair hitter and only this once a star, doesn't produce his classic homer this time around? What if the bum strikes out?

• • •

I want a dream lover,
So I don't have to dream alone

CHAPTER 6

I go to Mary's door, illuminated by a porch light too small to cover the area, leaving me peeking room: can't see Mary, only a vaguely familiar tubbo, doubtless Mama. It occurs to me that I have stood right here many times, and the house slowly regains its place in my memory. I knock and wait.

A comfy woman finally answers the door, "Lord, Timmy, why in Heaven's name would you knock? You know we never hear. You ain't knocked since you were – you never knocked. Just walk right in like you always do."

"Gee, Mrs. Barber..."

"C'mon in, sweetie. My Lord, I can't get over what a tall pine tree you've become. One of those sequoias. You were knocking because it's a date you two are going on, right? All grown-up. No more paper dolls – or nudist colony. Remember when you two were doing that, right in the front yard? [Pause for choking laughter.] You were about four. I looked out and there you were, naked as jaybirds, 'playing newy camp,' you said."

"God, Mom, maybe you could find more ways to be embarrassing? Too bad you didn't take Kodak's of us."

Mary has come up behind her mother, the bigger body hiding entirely the small one for a moment, so that I have no form to attach to the voice.

"Oh, Miss Grown Up, it wasn't that long ago. And it was cute."

"Surprised you didn't join us."

Lucky they're talking together. I'm so startled by the sudden appearance; I couldn't have done more than gurgle. Mary is vivid and unmistakable, beyond pretty. Partly it is her self-possession, but partly it's a striking combination of light complexion and dark features I find magnetizing. Who wouldn't?

"Watch your mouth, missy!" Mama chortles, doing a bad imitation of a

74

good sport.

"You know what was even cuter, Mom? Timmy and I playing doctor, examining each other. So cute. And it was just last week."

I laugh like hell, though I figure Mrs. Barber will be outraged – as much by Mary's seizing the wit handle as by any off-color joke. I'm right.

"That's enough! You aren't too old to have your mouth washed out with soap."

"Sorry, Mom," Mary says with just enough sarcasm to allow her to claim innocence, were she called on it. Mary is good at this game, real good.

Mrs. Barber, absurdly outmatched, goes through a pantomime of responding angrily, then shifting clumsily to blub-faced tolerance. Strange she isn't better at it after all these years being an asshole. She bids us kiddies have a good time and lets us escape.

To what? Mary, please tell me. Don't let me flounder.

My house is some four miles from downtown, the movies and the hangouts – from anything interesting except the river. Mary's is fifty yards from mine, so we find our way together to the action. The stores are crowded, the restaurants few but busy. The town is nearly bustling now, the only quasi-boomtime East Liverpool is ever to have. With the mills rolling, working people find themselves with a few coins in their pockets and no way of knowing how soon they will disappear. It's a strange sensation; nobody has any experience with this sliver of prosperity. The citizenry responds nervously, not by amassing goods but by going to town: an embarrassed pacing, circling a vacant center. Those who once had been happy at home find reason to roam over this lumpy town: houses covering the pretty hills, the steep shale scarfing cliffs cascading down to the river. With the locals on the move, a remarkable bus system springs up, running often and late to all parts of the spidery pattern of streets.

"Well, Timmy, I'm glad you called me, but..."

"So am I. You know I was thinking..."

"Thinking what?"

"Not a damned thing, I guess. I just didn't want you to go on with that 'but.'"

"You knew what I was going to say?"

"Yeah. Well, no, it just sounded ominous."

"Me, ominous?"

"You were going to say that we could only be friends, not to get my hopes up."

Mary looks at me quickly, then away. In that split second, I am sure I read shock. I had hurt her, that's clear.

"OK, Timmy."

"Oh Lord, Mary, what a dumb thing to say. I don't feel that way; I just figured you did. You're so pretty, and we've known each other so long."

This is a disaster. I'm actually gulping.

"It's OK, Timmy. I understand what you're saying." She's regained her equilibrium, control of the situation.

"Mary?"

"Yes? Do you have something to say, or are you still just making noises?"

She's right. I'm mumbling away, hoping something kind sounding will occur to me, something kind sounding and safe. It doesn't, so I try something worse, the truth. "Do you think we might be more than paperdoll buddies, Mary? Could we start out by thinking of this as a date?"

She smiles so openly, signaling what smiles should tell us: that we are trusted not to attack. It's her first smile tonight. She doesn't smile much, Mary, but I can see why I had spent my younger childhood almost exclusively with her as my game-playing friend.

Within fifteen minutes, I've forgotten that I'm out with Mary, simply *am* out with Mary. It occurs to me that I've been awkwardly spliced onto the fabricated past of this being, Tim, and that such a past has an uncertain tie to Harold. How is Harold connected with Mary? How did past closeness, our history, now seem, at once, both startlingly new and totally familiar?

That Mary and I have the sort of too-close friendship that precludes deeper interests, that we've gone beyond the ignorance and fantasy-building that makes for sexual attraction. Why had I suggested such a thing? We hold hands in the movie, and she snuggles close to me as we walk. Sit across from one another at Dairyland and gaze, actually we do. I wish we could turn back time, re-create our nudist game.

Failing that, I decide to tell her all, though I'm sure "decide" is not what I do.

"Mary, can I talk to you about something you won't believe?"

She smiles. Near as I can tell, she isn't ridiculing me. Maybe Mary doesn't respond that way, ever, to anyone. She leans forward and licks her lips. I come close to upsetting my lemon coke right into the fries we're sharing.

"I mean it, Mary. You'll think I'm crazy, which is possible, but I don't think so, and it's strange, what I have to tell you."

"Timmy!"

"I have this sense of the future, Mary."

"That's nice."

"Dear Mary, I'm just going to tell you. You know much more about me than I do. I mean, you *do*."

Now she does look puzzled.

"That's a bad place to start. Let me begin at the beginning. Well, before I do..."

"Go ahead, Timmy. You can tell me anything."

My hands are sweating in the way bellies do in a sauna. I hate nervous laughs of the sort that now leak out of me.

"Do we have time, I mean to talk?"

"Our parents won't say anything if we come in next month. You know that. They'll make us feel guiltier than bank-robbers if we're twenty minutes later than they think we should be, but they'll never tell us what that is. We've talked about how they do this – both sets. Your parents are milder than mine, but both are big deal trusters. So, take all the time you want."

"That's funny. I really like you, Mary."

"I know. Now tell me." She leans closer.

"I can tell the story quickly. What'll take a long time is you believing it."

"Uh-huh. So... ? And why do you keep rubbing your flat top?"

"I don't know. Where can I start? Mary, I don't know how to get you to believe..." I look over at the jukebox, resisting the impulse to read the titles, flip the flaps.

"Timmy, just tell me. Don't worry about me believing you. We've spent nearly every minute together since we've been conscious. It's not in me to think you're lying."

"I'll just spill it out."

Pause.

"Spill."

"One day in 2016 – really 2016 – I find myself, myself at that point being Harold Fordyce, you don't know him, confronting a series of shadowy celestial figures who are quizzing me, telling me they're sending me back to high school. Who they are, I don't know. My impression is that they are powerful beyond reason and equally stupid, but that's another story. Harold Fordyce, which is who I was then, is seventy-eight years old in 2016, but these powerhouse women are going to make him, me, repeat high school, four years, that's all, as a kind of experiment. I know this sounds..."

"Just keep going and stop worrying about me. Your fiddling makes it hard to follow. Just tell the story, Bluto!"

I register her point and suddenly know, as if from before, that she is inevitably right. "These agents have the power not only to do a rerun of time, the years going from 1951-1955, but to effect alterations, extensive ones. So they take me, Harold, and make me into this Timothy Mills. He's about sixteen times the person Harold was. That's not being modest. Tim has Harold's athleticism, appearance, singing ability, and other stuff all increased enormously. They took what Harold had and multiplied it. I guess I'm now this Tim person, who is a lot easier to be than old Harold, let me tell you. Harold did go to this high school, had the same family, but that was the 1951 that went before. This present 1951 is running now and is sort of simulated, I guess. Real but fake, if that makes sense."

A long pause: I consider my floundering, restock my pond, gather my resources.

"You stopped, but I can tell there's more."

"Trouble is these arrangers on high told me I would fit smoothly into this new being, not even be aware that it is new. Turns out to be baloney. I remember too much Harold stuff, and it's mostly useless, worse than that. It's partly accurate and partly not. They seem to have adjusted the world surrounding me, you included, and made you think Tim has been around for the whole fourteen years. It seems right in the flow to you. Not me. True, when people like Joanie tell me things, I recall them. Maybe I'm getting more Tim every day. But for now it sucks."

"I bet it does. Sucks? Never mind."

I pause to study her, appreciate what I have in this friend. Right now, though, what rams into my mind is not her loyalty but a beauty so penetrating it hurts. The 50s style hair, the sweater over the white shirt, the glowing pink skin. And this was Mary.

"My God, Mary, you're pretty. Sorry – back to it. I know I'm not being clear. Here's one way of understanding it. I don't know if it's right, but it's a way. This 1951 we're in seems real, but we're actually seventy-eight or so in bona fide time. That life that we're real old in keeps going. We're there in 2016, only we think we're here. We're back here just for this do-over. The motives guiding this artifice aren't clear. The Heavenly Powers have readjusted everybody's memories so that they think they really *are* in 1951 and that they've known Tim Mills from before. But there are probably other ways to think of it, as I say. Oh, God."

Pause.

"Mary, I read in one life or another this terrifying line in Borges, a writer."

"I know who he is, Tim. What line?"

"'What if all time has already transpired?' Jesus Christ!"

"I understand what you're saying."

"You believe me?"

"I know you're not lying."

"But that might mean you think I'm delusional, paranoid."

"Loony, a nut, a visitor from outer space."

"Do you?"

"Why not put this the other way round? Maybe 2016 wasn't real, you just thought it was: you're here now and *this* is real? Maybe Harold is a delusion that has crept into your mind? Like a bad dream that won't go away. Harold? Really? What a lousy name."

"Yeah, it is. Maybe what you say could be, except I remember things from the future, not just personal things. For instance, the Dodgers are going to blow a big lead in the next three weeks and end up in a tie with the Giants, who will win the playoffs with a Bobby Thompson home run that will be called 'The Shot Heard Round the World.'"

"Really? You have a vision of that? Well, it's good to know you return from the future with such useful knowledge. How about x-ray glasses for all?"

"Yeah. I do know of wars to come, shit like that. It gets really screwed up. Polio gets cured though, by Jesus. But mostly it's one fucking mess after another."

"In your other life, do we talk that way? I mean it's OK, but up to now we haven't been on 'shit' and 'fuck' terms."

"I'm sorry, Mary. I'm so excited. You seem to believe me."

"Believing you's the easy part. Just what are we believing? Could it just be right, what's happening, nothing so strange?"

"I don't know. Let me tell you one thing. It's narrow and local, what's happening, and it doesn't solve that big problem about what is and isn't real. It's 1951 in all respects except that Harold has become Tim. That's what I was told, though I have no confidence in these celestials, since they seem to have been wrong in one major particular: others are adjusted to me, no complaint there, but I'm not adjusted to me or anything else. That's fucked – sorry – goofed."

"Relax, old nudey buddy. You say it's getting easier for you to be Tim."

That seems a strange way to put it. I look at her narrowly, hoping to detect some signal from her eyes, but Mary sends back pure affection.

She continues, "It's interesting, all this about what part of us is here and what part is there, which zone is real. But, Tim, doesn't this feel real to you, right now, you and me? Doesn't it matter more that we have this, how we're living, now, immediately. We have whatever it is, no matter how brief, even if it's an instant."

"An instant?"

"Even if. I mean, what counts?"

"I agree that fitting in is a minor issue, and maybe the big one doesn't matter, the nature of reality. I'm tempted to become a minor-league philosopher, wondering which 1951 is actual. I see what you mean. What counts, as you say Mary, is more important than what is. Whatever status our lives have on some other plane, we gotta live 'em. Making it a practical issue seems to offer control, but the big issue still tickles me, galls me. What is going on?"

"You OK? God, Tim, settle down. It's what we got, one way or another – or no way at all. It's all that is – *all*. This can be a kick, a whole lot of fun – even funny."

"Funny!"

"You seem to have covered a lot of attitudes, ranging from anger to panic. How about being interested, being – I don't know, amused. You quoted grim old Borges – inaccurately, but never mind. I have a better one, from Hughes Mearns:

As I was sitting in my chair,
I knew the bottom wasn't there,
Nor legs nor back, but I just sat,
Ignoring little things like that.

"You get it, goof?"

"Little things? That's wonderful, Mary."

"Ain't it! How about doing what you have no choice but to do, enjoying it, enjoying us, enjoying me?"

So beautiful, eyes shining, lips parted. "You're right. Oh, yes you are. And it's great enjoying you. And it'll keep on being great in the future."

"Stick with *is*."

"OK. Who knows, right? I mean about what'll happen?"

"You're a sweetie, Timmy, and that's what counts. Maybe what you call the big problem is just a teaser. Why bother with it? You said this, but I don't think you have it in your head: how about if it doesn't make much difference, all that about reality? It comes down to sitting in the chair that isn't there. We always go along as if stuff which isn't important actually is, and things that probably aren't real actually are. That's the way we go along. So why don't we proceed *as if*, since it's what we have? What's it matter? It won't last long."

The last part jolts me, but I lean out over the shiny, matte-finish table to meet her, grabbing her warm hand. How can she be so dear and so self-possessed, almost distant? She's both there and not, reaching inside me and nowhere to be found. She now has both hands on my one, but she also seems to be waiting for me to grasp something, something I feel sure I'll never find.

"But..."

"But?"

We're still leaning over the French fries, ignoring grease and ketchup. We're arched like a suspension bridge made of unequal parts. What a moment to sustain. It sounds awkward, but it's not. Mary's eyes are flecked with something. Should I kiss her before muddying the clear-running stream? Probably, but I don't.

"It's not everything. I got this future knowledge. And there's a particular thing."

"OK. I'll admit that makes things different, that and having the feeling you're not real and everybody else is closer to you than you are, even though everybody else doesn't know you at all but just has adjusted memories. But still, you have to go from day to day with that. Whatever the explanation, it's what you got. Go from there. Fuck it, as you would say."

"Uh-huh." Beat. "Mary, you said 'fuck'!"

"Nyah, nyah, Mr. Methodist Church, pillar of, so did you!"

"I did."

"So, what was the particular thing?"

"It's my dad. He's going to have a heart attack soon and then several others, and he'll die in six years, about. You know the money you gave me? I got some more and put this bet down with Meilie, runs the shady store downtown, on what I told you about the Giants. And I want to use the money I win – as much as three hundred thousand – to get my dad medical help."

"To save his life."

"I don't mean that exactly. Yes, I do."

"I see."

. . .

By the time history has repeated itself, happened for the first time, or whatever, and Thompson's homerun and the anti-climactic World Series have played themselves out, I still haven't talked to Dad. Now I have three hundred eighty-five thousand, minus the twenty-five thousand I foisted on Meilie. It was the hardest thing I'd done, getting that sweet, uglier-than-is-possible guy to take any money. He kept telling me his commission was "kiss my ass," and I think he'd have stuck with that had I not told him I would honor his terms. He was shocked, said I shouldn't talk that way. That started another hour of dickering. He said he'd take a sawbuck. I finally told him I'd only consider a percentage. For all his smarts, Meilie isn't used to percentages, so, before he could figure, I managed to hoodwink him.

"I can't even think of taking that much, not even close. You tricked me, you little shit."

"Look, Meilie, it's barely more than five percent, a lousy commission. You'd go broke soon if that's all you charged. Anyhow, I don't need it. My dad don't need it. And think of this: I'll have other bets and we can both get as rich as we want."

"Yeah, sure. Well, that twenty-five grand already makes me richer than I ever dreamed of. God, little Tim, it's the most dough I've ever seen at one time, hell, by a long shot. I don't know what to say, kid. Why'd you do this for me?"

"You did it, made this happen. You took a chance, trusted me. You're my friend."

He looked at me in a way that so softened his face that half of the forty thousand wrinkles disappeared: "Well, I am that. But I was that before, you little shit. OK, OK. I can't argue with you. You're smarter than me. I'll take it. I'll take it and thank you. Now get outta here before somebody tells your dad you were hangin' around with a crook."

So I have all this money, in a bank account Meilie sets up. Only I can access it and don't need his signature. Sure as hell illegal, but if I'm not to trust Meilie and Mr. Earle at the bank, where will I be? I might as well think Mary has secrets – or Donny or Carol or Jimmy Canton. This isn't a secretive bunch. I can't figure out why that is or what it means, not at the moment.

. . .

"So, Mary, what should I do with all this money, now that it's here?"

"Two choices: talk to your dad, or go behind his back and talk with Dr. Pigeon."

"Pigeon is good. He'll never say I am sneaking around. He knows Dad and will see what I'm doing."

"Plus it'll put off talking to your dad."

"Did we decide I can use the 'F' word, honey, that we'll both use it in public and in private, in daylight speech and in prayer, at home and at school, in sickness and in health?"

"No, we didn't, but why should I care if you use it?"

"Fuck you, Mary."

"I care."

"OK, but your advice is to consult with Dr. Pigeon."

"I think you should talk to your mom. She's a lot smarter than you suppose."

"Really? Wouldn't she fall apart if she thought Dad was going to get sick and die?"

"Leave out the last part. In fact, leave out anything about coming from the future. She won't like the gambling part, but she'll like the money. Or..."

"Or what?"

"No she won't. Talking to your mom's a terrible idea. Your dad is stubborn, but he won't try to make you give back the money. Your mom thinks gambling is an incurable disease and a sin. She wouldn't care if it were three hundred million you had. What's money compared to eternal damnation?"

"You're way ahead of me, Mary. Wish there were some other way to explain this money being here. By the way, you want some? I can get all we want."

"No. That's a distraction. Keep your pecker pointed in the right direction."

"Mary!"

"If you can say 'fuck,' I can say 'pecker.' Besides, I've seen yours enough. Who could erase memories of all our backyard fun? If Mother only knew that I have exact knowledge of your year-by-year pecker development."

"Did you take pictures, make drawings?"

"I committed it to memory, every wrinkle and freckle decorating that tiny wormy thing."

"But you haven't seen it recently. It's grown to enormous size, a regular giant kielbasa."

"That's appealing. I liked it better when it was Good-N-Plenty size, which it was only last month. Of course, it's all my planted-in memory. You've talked with Joanie about your dilemma? Also, does she know all about the transformation of old Howard?"

"Harold. You're playing with my identity here. Joanie knows some. I can give her the full story. But what good does that do us?"

"She'll have ideas. She's smart, and she pays attention to your parents."

. . .

"So, Joanie, you see how I made all this money. It's the future."

"Like you. My big brother from the future. Really, you are?"

"Maybe. Anyways, springtime, regarding this particular problem?"

"Talk to Dad. You can talk to Dr. Pigeon first, see how the money might be spent, where to go for the best treatment. If he knows. He's a nice man and good to Dad, but a genius or even competent? He didn't turn down the Mayonnaise Clinic to work here. Anyways, he's not going to let you understand the problem better than he does. He'll want to do the – what's that word?"

"Diagnosis. It's the Mayo Clinic."

"Is it? Gosh, I didn't realize that, Dick Tracy! But Dr. Pigeon. There's a chance he might know a little, guide you where to ask. Use all your persuasive skills."

"And if he refuses to do it?"

"Dr. Pigeon? Well, deefie, he absolutely will refuse to treat Dad as an already-serious heart patient, since it wasn't his idea. I just said so. And you don't want him to be doing that anyhow, as he'd start prescribing things from the time of George Washington, leeches maybe. See what you can dig out of Dr. Pigeon quietly, without him knowing why you want to know, and then leave him to playing golf."

"That's smart."

"I'm smart."

She says this as if she's announcing her height.

"So," I prompt.

"The real problem is getting Dad to spend any money on himself. The best way is to tell him straight out who you are, how you know. Say if he gets help, he'll make it easier for Mom. That might work. Won't be easy. You'll have to squeeze it in fast. You know how he is."

I suggest we go over to the Cantons' basement for a few games of Ping-Pong. It turns out that Ping-Pong playing is one skill the celestial oddities have neglected. I think I was better first time around. So it's useful humiliation. Jimmy, Jimmy's Dad, Jimmy's sister, Jimmy's brother, Johnny Leon, Joanie – all beat me.

• • •

Before confronting Dad, I give myself a week, wherein I discover a new playground belonging to rich kids. There are only twelve-fourteen genuine rich kids in a freshman class of four hundred. About half of that rich contingent seems affable. The others have acquired a supercilious air that is ludicrous but effective, even on me. Having more confidence than last time, but not that much more, I don't fall completely under their humiliating spell, but I do resent it.

I resent it so much I can find it in my heart to be heartless. As things stand, their rich-kid routine is humiliating, damaging to all the working-class innocents around them. The power of the privileged is airy, insubstantial, which makes them vulnerable to blunt frontal attack. Armed with that insight, I plan to turn the tables and keep them spinning upside down.

My strategy is simple: get them by way of their bodies. I have a vision, a spiritual vision, wherein these shits will be wrapped, pecker and pudenda, in the rapture of worship – of me. Then I will expose them, at least to themselves, make them whine. More specifically, I will create a theatre of degradation and cast them in roles they will enact in order to be close to me. They'll forfeit their dignity, integrity, clothing.

This will test my powers and provide the Heavenly Pervs the theater they crave.

Picturing the details involved in such a wholly vicious campaign gives me considerable pleasure, and I spend no little time inventing plots filled with X-rated particulars.

Some of these kids are pretty as well as snooty, and all have added attractions. The girls in my target group show off expensive clothes, though the boys are tied to the required uniform, needing no more, as they possess what nobody (I) could resist: teeth, though orthodontically corrected, too big for the mouth trying to hold them, causing an upper-lip curl that is less a sneer than an invitation. With such teeth leading the way, could a tongue be far behind?

I select six – the most fetching, self-absorbed, and airily confident. First comes ingratiation, being there as part of the weather. I won't work at it, just *be* their equal. They will acknowledge me as essential, without giving it a thought. Equality is the first step to dominance. I can't argue my way into their circle, but I can use the wedge of easy assumptions to do it. Fred, Francis, Joyce, Patricia, Marilyn, Glenn, the kids with the middle names, the Juniors: all will be mine, toys to fondle and torment. My pleasure, their pain. They won't like it, but they won't know they don't. Even if they do, they'll lack the will to escape.

I spend the week assuming intimacy with them, shamelessly mocking other kids I like, using a mite of the gambling winnings to arm myself with a better haircut and funds to buy sodas at Dairyland for these spoiled pussbags. They fall for it instantly. Maybe they don't need persuading, being perfectly willing to like me.

Easy game, you'll say, beneath me, beneath anyone this side of sociopathic. Not only am I triumphing viciously, but what a Lilliputian contest it is. Has polio been wiped out? Are people of color oppressed? Are children hungry? Do women enjoy equality? Can gay and lesbian people marry? Are species disappearing, the environment deteriorating? Why am I wasting precious hours chatting it up with the upper crust of this shithole town, just to bed them?

Good questions.

During this week of intense strategic activity, not once have I touched anyone, defiled my prey. I haven't gotten close, in word or body. I know what is irresistible: attention that doesn't seem like it, edging in while keeping a distance, making them hot by being cold.

CHAPTER 7

"Dad, I don't know how to say this."

We're on the back porch, Joanie having done her part by taking Mom for a neighborly visit. (Those visits are patterned: my mother and her friend, guided by random associations of words, trade anecdotes, barge in as soon as the other pauses for breath.) Looking close at my dad, I see how gentle and undefended he looks – is. I wonder how he and my boiled-potatoes mom had sired someone as lovely as Joanie, the present me not being in the equation. Dad has very kind eyes and a strong mouth and chin. He's only forty-three, though almost as craggly as Meilie, much like Walter Matthau. Right now, he's looking at me expectantly.

"Um hum."

"I'll start from the beginning." And I do, with the weird sisters, and run fast through it all, trying to sound matter-of-fact, knowing he'll slip away as soon as he senses something personal approaching.

"This is a joke." It isn't a question.

"No, Dad. I swear it's not. I can kind of prove that I've been through all this before, but I want you to believe me without proof."

"OK, I do."

"What?"

"If you want me to believe you, I will."

I have no way of reading his face, but his voice seems to hide nothing.

"OK. I'm really not lying, Dad."

"I didn't think you were. Hey, I think I can get Steelers tickets. I have this customer, you know him, Paulo, runs the produce and hardware store in Midland you like so much. Well, he says this guy at the mill..."

You're thinking I should press my advantage, get Dad back on track, riding toward health issues and the 300 thousand. You aren't here and don't see how badly he wants to run. He's begging off not because what I'm saying seems fantastic but because it threatens intimacy. Pleased beyond measure by a one-on-one with a son he finds both strange and admirable, he also is able to stand only a small amount of this up-closeness. It would have been cruel of me to carry on. Besides, I feel just as he does.

. . .

So I return to toying with the wealthy buggers, with the goal of – I've made this clear and you don't want to hear it again. Nor do I.

I decide to hone in first on Patty. Patty is short, very. There is some premium set on this mini-stature at our school, and Patty accepts the lavish awards for her wee-ness with becoming immodesty. Ask her and she'll tell you how cute she is. Way-out perky, too. Used to getting what she wants, Patty will expect to get me, which means I can get her if I pretend, for a day or two, to be indifferent to her and hot on one of her friends. Who might that be? Another cashmere-sweatered littlun, one Joycie.

Monday and Tuesday I do what I can to provoke jealousy, once turning my back on Patty so as to flirt with Joycie, who is fiddling in the locker adjacent to Patty's. My flirting is resolute, none too graceful. Luckily, grace is not what I seek, even had I possessed a supply to draw on.

Getting to know this Joycie, even a bit, isn't the best idea I've concocted. She's easy to like, snootiness being the thinnest of veneers, maybe visible only to me, through the light I'm shining on her. I notice how ditzy she is, but she's fourteen and probably no more ditzy than most, than me. Somehow, behind the wealthy veneer, she projects a casual indifference to things I want to regard as her identity markers. Joyce seems bent on becoming friends, drawing me into her charm. Charm it is, and I should be ashamed that I am able to resist. Joyce threatens to become human, but she's no match for my plan.

First, I back her into a slight corner next to the locker stack. Then I move my way-taller body between her and any but the most determined peeker.

"I swear, Joyce my pet, you have the finest handles in school."

"Tim!"

"First-class. Want me to suggest a fine way to display them?"

Giggles and token (maybe) resistance as I pretend to lift her sweater, in the process rubbing her breasts enough to bring a flush to her pretty face. Maybe I'll redirect my aims. I wonder, even at the time, if her acquiescence, as I was determined to regard it, is simply a result of her habitual agreeableness, a uniformly pleasant way of facing the world. Having no experience with such crudity as I am throwing at her, she has no script to consult for a response.

"I'm sorry, Joyce. Please know how much I respect you" – with mock super-sincerity.

"Too bad you do." She catches on – or accepts the only unstuffy role open to her.

I keep up the banter, grinning broadly, speaking louder. I figure clownish actions are requisite to standard "kidding" and a reasonable cover.

We're tucked into the locker stack, Patty taking it all in. Not quite *all*, since I hide much, allowing Patty to know little, guess more. At last I get a response:

"Joyce, come on. We're going to be late for Science."

Later, during lunch break, I accost Patty, as she seethes in the alley next to the hot-dog and fries joint that substitutes for the cafeteria we don't have. "Patty, my true love. Let's go unlock a janitor's closet and find new uses for mops."

"Hello, Tim," she says, as frostily as she can manage, which is arctic indeed. She walks slowly away, in the process moving us down the alley and toward the back of the diner, where one finds vents, fumes, garbage, and no other people.

"OK, so you're angry because of Joyce."

"Angry? Of course not. You and Joyce are a matter of no concern to me, none at all." It is good Joan Crawford.

"Let's cut through the bullshit. Time is flying, hormones raging. I made an innocent mistake. Here's the truth: I'm so hot for you, I tried to make you jealous." I do this with an earnestness that makes me proud. I move close, grasping her hand with true, true sincerity.

"Bullshit?" she says with fake consternation, "I've never heard that word before, never. What language to use to a woman you love."

"So, you're not mad?"

"Well, what you call flirting was really feeling her up. I'm not blind." She's laughing, though, and looks pretty good. If she could forget she had on expensive clothes and deserved them, she might not be so bad.

"Feeling her up! How you talk!"

"You were!"

I edge closer. This is perfect.

"I may have accidentally brushed up against her – ah."

"Yeah, accidentally! Her what?"

Either Patty or I draw closer, so there's only a horizontal inch (and 18 vertical inches) between my manly fast-beating chest and her small-breasted heaving one. I bend.

"I didn't notice, honey." I lean down to whisper in her ear, wrapping my arm round her shoulder, drawing her to me. I also nudge her further behind the building, out of sight. "Where was it I accidentally brushed her? This time I wouldn't have to pretend – ah – my emotions."

I'm holding her close, my right hand caressing her downy neck. With my left, I'm burrowing beneath her sweater, shoving her sideways. I move my mouth to hers. Patty has her mouth agape, gulping my tongue in a maneuver that would make a hooker envious.

We're backed into this smelly alley, not thirty feet from the school, built on a steep slope, sliding down toward the river. The area here by boiler rooms is understandably unfrequented.

I notice Patty's crisp smell. As she squirms so far below me, I get it: clothes dried on the line, sun and air, the sweet sense that up close to clothes is up close to grass and trees, Romantic epiphanies purchased from Ogilvie's Department Store.

I enjoy ruffling Patty's blouse and sniffing her skin so much that I pull back from mouth sucking – with a slight pop – in order to nuzzle her hair and worm her around in my arms. She seems to enjoy all this as much as I, which makes me less aware of anything judgmental.

Enough of the cuddlies. I return to her mouth and less innocent parts, advancing in fifteen-second intervals. Finally, I worm down my hand, in a gesture of big-time suavity (Cary Grant comes to mind) and massage her bottom, being careful to roust her skirt with every molding. I'm having luxuriant fun imagining how I will soon expose those pinky globes.

"You really love me?" she gasps, using six breaths in panting out five syllables.

"We are eternally united," I say, then almost laugh, as I proceed, left hand rising of its own accord (perhaps not) to find a breast beneath her birdcage frillies. At that point, I initiate even more massaging, tweaking, and rousting.

"Oh don't, Timmy. Oh, I love you. No, no, no. Not here. Oh God. I can't stand it. No, no, no. We can't. Don't, dear. Oh, God. No, please dear. Oh Jesus. Oh please, please. I love you. No, don't. God. I can't stand it. No. Oh Timmy. Oh love me. Don't please, please. Jesus. Stop, please stop. We can't. Oh, it's too much. No, no, no, no, no, no, no, no, no, no. Ohhhhh. Stop. Oh God, I love you. Yes."

Patty keeps her voice low, as if she were convincing herself.

By this time I have her sweater over her shoulder, her bra half-down. My left hand has crept under her panties and rests happily on her ass, pinching with some energy, as I realize I can now make aggression pass as passion. I use the back of my wrist to try and shove her panties down but manage only to extend them outward into a tent, pushing against and lifting her skirt.

Using her rear as leverage, I slide her to the right, opening space for my probing fingers to glide to the front.

Patty's "Oh no, Oh God, Please don't" ing becomes measurably louder and more insistent as I do so resolutely what she is so earnestly don't-ing, though she's grinding away and working her tongue (between pleas for cessation) eagerly. Her own hands have been busy on my shoulders with conviction but with a redundancy displaying a woeful lack of imagination. Shall I whisper in her ear some suggestions about zippers, initiate some movement of her hands southward? After all, she can take an equal part: I am from a time of gender equality.

No matter. We soon explode, almost together, a triumph of alley sex, all done with graceful impunity – or so I imagine. But, damn it all, I am only just in time – if I am in time – to beat the eyes of Carol, which appear, along with her body, around the corner.

"Hi, Tim! Hi, Patty!"

Patty bursts into raucous sobs, a horse with a hairball. I'm in fair order, but Patty is a mess, red-faced and hair-tossed, dress hoisted up, caught somehow in something, and her sweater still half over the shoulder.

"Hi, Carol."

Carol pushes me aside, gathers wailing Patty in her arms. Whether it's post-orgasmic hysteria, shame, or exhilaration I have no idea. I'm not in the picture. To be fair to me – which I don't deserve – my panic is mixed with sympathy. If only Patty weren't so loud. The sobs are animalistic in their authenticity, causing pity to slide quickly into discomfort and then irritation. Not that my concern for the poor assaulted (only in a manner of speaking) girl disappears entirely. I'm not a monster, much as I must look like one to Carol, and to you.

"Patty, Patty, Patty," Carol croons, rocking her in her arms.

"Is there something I can do?" I try.

Neither pays the slightest attention. It seems ungallant to leave, so I stand there, wondering what look appropriate to the occasion I can paste on: a public-spirited passer-by, eager to help but not interfere should do. Maybe offer to get somebody a glass of water?

The focus of the drama has shifted. Now utterly miserable Patty is putting her body and her reputation in the hands of Carol, and Carol is accepting the burden. The words exchanged don't amount to much, but it's obvious that these girls, certainly not friends or even well-wishers, are now locked together. It's an alliance forged by mutual vulnerability. They aren't united against me, exactly, but against a more generalized bestial force I had been the one channeling towards them. I don't exist as a specific Tim. Any male would do as well.

. . .

I tell Joanie the whole story, hoping she'll explain to me what I've done. I give her a cold version, unvarnished. What other version is there? In for a penny, I don't spare anatomical details, realizing only afterwards that I'm overstepping all sorts of boundaries, not just those set by brother-sister decency but of age. Joanie is twelve, for God's sake. She probably doesn't know what a clitoris is and for sure doesn't need that detail. Too late now.

"So, Joanie, what has happened, really?"

"I think you know."

"I mean, what have I done?"

"You worried whether Carol will forgive you, overlook this?"

"No! Yes!"

"She probably isn't surprised." She stops.

"That sucks, Joanie. I'm not a brute. I just made a mistake." I'm shocked to hear my own angry voice.

I 'm sorry at once. Joanie looks so pretty, sitting on her mini-bed in her mini-room. I'm trying to get her to work with me, stop judging me.

"What do you want from me, Timmy?"

I start to cry. Jesus Christ Almighty.

Joanie at once comes to me, just as Carol had come to Patty. Rocking, soothing. She's not, however, telling me everything is OK, that I'm OK.

When things settle down, she's the first to speak.

"Here's what you should do, Tim. Can I say?"

"Please."

"Get Carol and Patty together and explain."

"Apologize?"

"Explain."

"Couldn't I meet the two of them separately? That'd avoid confusion, don't you think?"

"No, together."

. . .

I figure I'm bound to do what Joanie says. It isn't the first time I've felt I am playing pin-the-tail-on-something, minus any game instructions. I'm stumbling about, all by myself. The party has moved on.

Joanie has set up some meeting! I run it in my head: performing courageously, hiding nothing, being abject, fair to all parties. But even with the girls obediently using the lines I write for them, I can't make things develop agreeably. At first, I'm after a happy ending; before long, I'm searching for bearable. I can find neither. Every time I envision Carol, Patty, and me as a bunch, no decent dialogue emerges, nothing but grinding humiliation.

What does Joanie have in mind? What good, for me, can come of having them together, unavailable for the cajolery I might effectively use on them seriatim? The key thing is studiously to avoid specifying what exactly we are talking about. The whole humiliating mess must remain as "it." I can hint to Carol that it was a temporary weakness, tell Patty it was badly timed but down deep an expression of my true need for her. "True need" is as far as I'm prepared to venture. I have my limits and will not claw myself out of this particular pit by digging a deeper one, which is what I'd accomplish by getting within miles of the dread word, "love." If only I could have at them separately, but now I am stuck with both – and no script at all.

No need to do anything now. I will be cheery and **not** flirty to both girls, avoiding conversation. Carol's parental imprisonment makes it easy, as does Patty's residence in the wealthy hill area. Physical avoidance doesn't solve the problem phone calls might raise, but perhaps girls don't call boys now, even to tell them that, in their opinion, the boy in question has acted badly, is, take it all in all, a complete asshole.

•   •   •

One thing I can work on right off – football. I've made some missteps with my team-mates and can smooth over misunderstandings (correct reasonable understandings unfavorable to me) with little effort. Hone my skills on the lummoxes for the more intricate challenges posed by females. It is the kids in this school I have to win back. The adults, here and elsewhere, present no problems. As I to my peers, so they to me: unseen.

Coach Sadon has kept me on his intimate list, a list of one, intimacy consisting of occasional, impersonal monologues on the team's problems. It's my teammates who matter, but in the meantime, Sadon's grousing is better than nothing. We've played five games, two to go, are undefeated, and present to the Coach a galaxy of deficiencies.

"There's no use running sweeps when both guards are so slow they can't get in front of the fullback, who is no bolt a lighting himself. We run that sweep three, four times a game, and I don't think we've got back to the line of scrimmage once."

"We did gain pretty good yardage against New Cumberland."

If he hears me, it doesn't matter. "We got to find ways to move the ball beyond just those two plays that work."

"You mean the ones where..."

"I'm going to send on to varsity nothing but a screw-loose end with some talent and no brains, two mediocre tackles, and that Mills. Hell of a coaching job."

Me being "that Mills," I figure it would be becoming of me to protest, but I'm also not foolish enough to imagine I am a living part of the conversation.

The team has remained distant from me, certainly not grateful.

I decide to buddy up to the one guy I have avoided this time through, tarring him broadly and most unfairly with Harold's humiliation. I wait until I am pretty sure he's through dressing, just so I don't get a direct, unmistakable answer to my question, "Hey, Buck, how they hanging?"

Buck's deficiencies include nearsightedness, so he blinks several times, squinting like the chucklehead he is. He doesn't say anything, probably anticipating cruelty, vicious pranks marking the only variation in the general indifference erected before him.

"Buck, you got a minute, willing to talk to me?"

"What?"

"Can I ask you something?"

"What? Why you asking me?"

Buck doesn't have what you'd call a winning personality, understandably, but his way of fronting the world does tend to invite the very treatment he's guarding against. Maybe I can offer Buck useful tips. For now, I'm the one needing help.

"Why? Because I know you're a good guy – and smart."

"Uh huh." He isn't surprised, doesn't register, I guess. Hard to tell if anything registers.

"Why don't the guys on the team like me, Buck?"

He relaxes, guessing I'm not going to inflict pain, not right now.

"You askin' me, cause I'm King of the Not Liked."

"Buck, no! Cause you're observant."

"Sure. Anyhow, I do know why nobody likes you."

I'm a trifle disheartened that he picks up my suggestion so readily. I'm earnest in my solicitation, but I'm hoping for modification, if not contradiction. Still, I can hardly retreat now, or maybe don't want to. "And why's that?"

"You're different. That's it."

"Different?"

"You're good. Not as good as you think, but good. They hate it. That's the way it is."

"Pretty cynical, Buck."

"Pretty fucking true."

"OK. So, Buck, why put yourself in situations where you're bound to get this grief?"

"My dad."

"Want me to help you get better, at football I mean, work with you?"

"No."

For the first time this re-running, I have no way to exit a conversation, and Buck doesn't help. I reach tentatively for his shoulder, why I don't know. He flinches a little – enough. I stand there, unable to dredge up a get-away line. I can't even meet his eyes. End up muttering, smacking my head in a pantomime of God knows what. Back up a few steps, turn around, stumble to my part of the bench, pull on my ugly pea coat, scramble away.

For ten years, at least, Buck has led a lousy life, being giggled at, offended, excluded, ignored. I'm not going to change any of that with one gesture. I can make things worse for him, of course, and I just had.

To see if I can't add failure to failure, I approach the one teammate I've spent time with.

"Sammy, why is it nobody likes me?"

"What do you mean?"

"Why is it nobody likes me?"

"What do you mean?"

"Fuck, Sammy. Why does everybody hate my guts?"

"Nobody hates..."

"You know what I mean. They don't hang out with me. They don't talk to me. They don't like me. Tell me, Sammy. You're the one friend I have on the team."

"Do you like them, Tim? I mean, do you want them to like you?"

"Yeah, I do."

"Really? OK. Most guys think you don't give a shit. I guess you could help them, try to teach them."

"What?"

"Everybody knows how good you are, but you act like we're just as good. We all know that's bullcrap. Maybe you could help us."

"I didn't want to act like a big shot."

"I know. Just go ahead and act like a big shot."

"I'll be damned, Sammy. You think so? Don't know what kind of a coach I am."

"Doesn't matter."

I get the point.

But I don't seem able to carry the point into the field of play. I can't grind it deep into the very fabric of anybody's balls. I spend time before and after practice, even during it when I can, making suggestions. My teammates are pleasant. They're also attentive, try to adopt my pointers. In a very few cases, I think I do help, getting an end to think about his route and not what the cornerback is doing and telling a linebacker to wait for things to open up, letting the action come to him, instead of bulling ahead and taking himself out of the play.

Problem is that I possess little knowledge on which to draw. In my other life I had devoted maybe two thousand hours to watching football, without learning a thing. I had followed the ball, as deeply attentive to the superficial at game seven hundred as at game one. I had no idea what a nickel defense was, much less why one might employ it. The sort who say "Shit!" when plays fail and give high fives when they work: that's me.

Figuring out that I'm assisting, or trying to, some of my teammates come to me for help with positions I understand as little as I understand where I am. I tell the guards and tackles to wait for the defensive lineman to hit them rather than lunging and losing their balance. "Stay low at all times." The last part is fine, but the sitting-back seems less efficacious. "What the shit are you yellow bellies doing? Martin! Dorsey! You're having your ass shoved into our own goddam backfield quicker than the ball. Why ain't you charging? You chicken?" Nobody rats on me, but demands for my tutoring taper off.

Sadon notices me working with our left guard, Phil Restelli, trying to have him charge without ending up on the ground. His idea of aggression is to get there first and jolt the defender, which in itself beats my passive idea. Trouble is that Restelli's feet are so far behind his body that he inevitably ends up prone. I'm working on getting him to keep his feet under him as he charges. Restelli seems capable only of the diving lunge or of the standing thrust. It's beyond my powers of invention, certainly knowledge, to have him both low and balanced, and I'm on the verge of becoming abusive – that goddam clumsy Restelli! One can almost sympathize with coaches who humiliate, larrup, murder inept, thickheaded players.

"Mills, c'mere!"

I trot over, tail wagging.

"What the hell you doing with Restelli?"

"Well, coach..."

"You think I'm blind. I see what you're doing."

He pauses, uncharacteristically leaving a blank, not one I can fill.

"So?"

"Well, coach…"

"Restelli spends all his time on the ground. I noticed that, Mills. You coach here?"

I generally try to avoid Sadon's eyes, simply because he scares me to the point of wetting myself, but now I look at him and notice he's smiling. Jesus Christ!

"I just thought Restelli – well, he could use about fifty coaches."

Sadon laughs, not exactly conspiratorially.

"OK, Mills. Tell Restelli to crawl."

"Crawl?"

"It's called submarining. He's not going to get balanced, which means he's not going to learn what you're trying to show him. I've had four hundred Restellis. He's not worth a shit upright. He's better off as close to underground as you can get him."

Sadon's on a roll. I nod politely.

"Look, Pop Warner, which you ain't, once Restelli's on his knees, he can upset any lineman, and then roll on top of them or hold 'em down there in the muck. If he's on top, no referee is going to notice holding. Once they're on the ground, even Restelli can manage to keep him there. See what I mean?"

"In submarining, then, he attacks, driving at the knees or below, plows into him but sacrifices his own verticality in order to muck about on the ground, right?"

Sadon blinks. "That's what I said. You tucked your brains into your balls?"

Back to the frowns and the abuse, but we have had a moment, yes we have.

• • •

Next game, our penultimate, I ride with Sammy on the bus over to

Massillon, where we are insulted annually by being permitted to play, not their regular freshman team but an adulteration of the 'A' team with some scrubs from the 'B's.

(I still have made no progress on the other issues at hand: seducing Donny, assaulting other rich kids, getting medical aid for Dad, repairing things with Carol and Patty, helping the helpless, launching a singing career. Mostly I have avoided brambles, though not entirely. I have seen Donny every day, but am slipping into a friendship that is more affectionate than erotic, too chummy to move toward seduction in a natural way – in any way at all.)

So, here we are on the way to face what would be, at full strength, the best freshman team in the state, chugging along in a bus designed to accommodate dwarfs.

I'm awakened from an empty slumber by Sadon's blare.

"Didn't want to tell you this ahead of time because you chicken shits might have chicken shitted all over yourself."

This, a new low in Sadon rhetoric, catches our attention.

"Massillon's heard we're undefeated, so they're gonna use their A team. That means we gotta play way beyond what we done so far. Now, the best way not to get hurt is to go hard. I'm not shitting you. If you ease up to protect your worthless asses, you'll end up candidates for broken bones. I'm not lying. That ain't gonna happen as often if you're running hard and hitting the shit out of them. That's the fucking truth. Sorry."

The "sorry," is for the adjective, "fuck" and its variants being one sliver of the language this molder of youth feels he should avoid. But it's clear he *is* worried about sending these little kids, his little kids, into this battle. Massillon is not only the best but the dirtiest team in the state, year after year. The steel mill there runs a recruiting program, buying players from far and wide by giving jobs to men with huge, great-athlete kids.

I notice no apprehension, much less chicken-shitting. There's an approving murmur and a mid-grade cheer. My teammates may indeed be valiant. I'm not, but I also have it in me to figure we (I) could kick Massillon ass.

"Sammy, what do you think?"

"I think we're in for getting our balls sanded."

One of the reasons I like Sammy.

"I'm sure if you and I go all out, we can beat them. We won't stop them all that well, but we can outscore them. And get some turnovers."

Sammy looks at me. His eyes are narrowed and sharp but unreadable.

"You doubting me, inscrutable one? You and I can score any time we want."

"You mean you can. What's a turnover?"

"A fumble, interception. And hell, Sammy, you told me I was pissing people off by holding back. Not today. Now I'm going to play closer to my ability, which is apparently amazing. I haven't seen it myself. But it might upset some teammates. Well, they don't like it, fuck em."

We ride in silence for a while – it's not a short trip – until Sammy tries again, "Tim, you comfortable?"

"Comfortable, Sammy? These seats were made for first-graders; the bus has no shock absorbers; we're going thirty-five when we're not in some dunghole town, which we almost always are. I feel like I'm seventy-eight years old, and, believe me, I know what that's like."

"Oh, sure you do."

That ran that table, but Sammy wanted to say something more.

"Tim, I think we all do know how good you are. You don't show it much, but when you're not thinking, you do and it's unreal. You're fast and stronger than anything I've seen, and you can do anything. It's crazy. But it's not insulting to the rest of us to not do it all the time. It leaves some things to us, even if we don't do them too well. No offense, Tim."

I take a minute to digest that. Should have taken longer.

. . .

For the first two or three minutes of the game, I play only a little better than usual, maybe at twenty-five percent of my capacity. But the Massillon Tiger A team is smart, and after running some straight-ahead plays that I mash, they start passing to sidelines and running pitch-outs. They score fast and then shut down our first two plays. That does it.

Next play I call a sweep left off a lateral. Only I don't lateral, move to the right, and outrun or trample defenders who don't buy the fake. I gain thirty yards before being squeezed out of bounds. And from that point, I do my stuff, dominating the offense and causing enough trouble on defense so we can outscore them. As they turn to passing, I drop back and watch the passing tailback's eyes (one thing I do remember from televised football). Three interceptions and a fumble recovery, all but one by me, are enough to give us the ball more than our share and, finally, the win.

Even while doing it, I feel as if I'm taking money from second-graders. Sadon says little during the game but twice takes me out for a play. It occurs to me that he's trying to get me to recall it's a team I'm on, but I'm far beyond cautionary messages. Nothing short of cabling me to the bench would prevent my display. The Massillon kids keep coming at us hard, knowing no other way, and I batten on their frustration, finding new ways to humiliate. Sometimes, when carrying the ball, I slow down so as to make a would-be tackler miss in a blundering jungle of flails. I jabber at them, mocking them and commenting on their chickenshittedness.

I'm resolutely chipper with my teammates and feel a little annoyed that they don't carry me off in triumph. True, several slap my shoulder pads and smile. I should have known something was wrong when more than a couple say, "Thanks."

"Sammy, what'd I tell you? You and me – we scored every time, one way or another. Whoo-eeee! Who's Number One now!"

"Yeah, Tim, I didn't think you'd let a team like that beat you." With that, he turns his bare ass to me and heads to the showers, very nice showers, no more than fitting for the (till-then) number one team in the state.

• • •

"Dad, let me spill this out."

We're taking a walk, which we never do, he never does. He's wearing his usual getup: hat, dress pants, white shirt, a tie (hand-painted, a tropical sunset on a seriously lime-green background) Joanie and Harold had presented him several years back. One thing from the past does endure: my kind Dad's awful neckwear.

"I told you about how I know what things are going to happen. This is the second time around for me. Now, here's what. I knew about the Giants beating the Dodgers and about the World Series. I know other things too, I suppose, but that's what came to mind. Anyhow, I talked Meilie into placing a bet for me. Don't get mad at Meilie. I forced him to do it, and he's worried you'll be mad at him. But hold that. I know you're going to get sick in about two years, Dad, and not be able to work. I wouldn't make that up. Thing is, if we get some real medical help now, you can stay well and not have that problem, not for years and years. I know, Dad, you'd never spend money on yourself, but think of Mom. As it is, she will have to go to work full-time when you get sick, take care of Joanie and me. It'll be tough on her, without us getting help. On the other hand, using this money from the bet, you can have the best treatment. Besides, it's fake money. I'm not asking you to take it to buy a yacht. I'd love it if you would, but... I'm getting off the track. The thing is to get medical help, you see."

Dad smiles. I realize again what an odd character he is, how little I know him. I feel nothing but love for him, but without analyzing it, figuring how it came about. I haven't the slightest idea how he will react, to this or anything else.

"Fake money?"

"I mean, it's not that we're taking it from good people. It's more like Monopoly money – or we found it."

"More like we stole it, your mother would say, more like we made a pact with Satan, diving into those eternal flames."

Is he smiling?

"That's true. She would. But if we wait around to make the money honestly, the kind of money this'll take, it'll be 2016."

"You're thinking I won't live till then in the natural course of things."

"Dad, it's only minor illegal. Not like I stuck up a bank."

"I gotta have a talk with Meilie."

"Oh Jesus, please don't."

"OK."

"What?"

"OK, I won't."

"Good. Will you get the treatment?"

"Yes."

"I know it'll be expensive..."

"I won't ask about that, so long as you promise me that the money comes from bets and not from some charity or some relative or do-gooder you've charmed into doing this by promising to marry his daughter."

"OK. This isn't Dr. Pigeon we're talking about, Dad. I'll talk to him to get advice, but I doubt he'll even have that."

"He's a good friend."

"I know, it's just that heart specialists aren't crowded around East Liverpool."

He laughs. "So it's heart, huh?"

"Yeah."

CHAPTER 8

Lunch hour. Truly a full hour, giving the busses time to deliver kids for a hot meal and get them back. Maybe nothing marks so clearly what is to disappear in a decade: mothers at home, no fast food, the post-Depression equation of good parenting with eating. True, once the kids get off the bus, traipse home, race back to the stop, hustle into school with seconds to spare, the nutritious lunch has to be slurped up in a few minutes. Not being sarcastic about the quality of the food. Lots of soup. No salads, of course, or crispy vegetables. Still...

I'm avoiding the subject. C'mon, Harold! Tim! Robot! Fake!

The same thing that got me in trouble before: lunchtime, the alley. What's different is the weather, drizzle replacing sunshine, that and the altered views Carol and Patty must entertain toward me. Because of the muck outside, brown-bagging students (Carol and Patty included) are in the auditorium/study hall.

I go inside myself, stare away some nerd and take the seat next to Carol. She's wearing pretty much what she always wears. I remember her family doesn't have much money. But she would look good in a gunnysack.

"Hi, Bubbles."

"Hi there – oh yeah, Tim. Haven't heard from you in a while. I thought you and I were plotting for an elopement, or at least a date."

"I thought you wouldn't want to talk to me."

"Now, why would you think that?"

"Because I was necking with Patty behind Clutter's cafeteria."

"Nobody calls it that. It's 'Clut's.'"

"Oh."

Silence. Carol turns to her history book. Pretending to read. Not pretending.

"OK, not necking but taking advantage of her, forcing myself on her, humiliating her."

"Yes you were, Tim."

"I know."

"No you weren't, not exactly. You pushed too far, but Patty did want to neck with you. I'm not sure how you interpreted her crying, and I ain't telling you. It wasn't remorse."

"So, it's OK?"

"I didn't say that. You were cold and calculating. You lied to Patty, one way or another. Her wanting the lies doesn't excuse you. Half the girls in school will go behind Clut's with you, if you let them think you love them. Since they are drooling for you, you won't even have to say it. But you'll have to lie somehow or other, and I am surprised you would."

"I am, too."

"Don't lie to me, too. You planned it."

"I did. I won't tell you it didn't mean anything, since that makes it worse."

"I have no doubt you realize that. You feel bad about it. Right now. But you did it, and it wasn't an accident."

Silence.

"One thing I'll say for you, Tim. You didn't tell me Patty was an idiot or a rich girl who deserved what she got."

I know enough to keep my trap shut. I'm learning. Maybe.

"Start over?"

"Thanks, Carol. I don't deserve it."

"Umm."

"So. I want to talk to Patty, and you too, all together, now. She's right over there."

"You do?"

"No. It's about the last thing I want to do."

"So?"

"Joanie said I should. Clear it up. Apologize – make it clear all around."

"You sure you want it clear all around?"

"No."

"You sure you know clear when you see it?"

"I wouldn't know it if it bit me in the ass. Sorry."

"Don't be. That's funny. So, you go get her and then come fetch me."

"Yeah, that way it won't look like…"

"Just do it, Mr. Windex!"

So I do, approach Patty.

"Hi, Patty."

"Swimmy-Timmy! Wanna find a pool? Skinny-dip?"

She's determined to ignore all, to reignite. I like the ignoring part, but Patty is planning a deep relationship, built on the foundation of that clammy pawing. Christ!

"Ha ha! You're a good friend, Patty."

I might as well have called her a fat slut. Her face crumples.

"Patty, I am sorry. I forced you and was rough and – I feel terrible. Would you go with me and we'll get Carol and I can tell you both straight out and clarify."

"Carol? You don't need to, Tim. It wasn't anybody's fault. It wasn't fault at all. When we feel about each other…"

It's cold in the room, but I'm leaking sweat. "Please, Patty. It'd be a kindness to me to let me tell you both."

"But why Carol?"

"She was there, and it's important…"

"Important how, Tim? Oh, honey…"

"You'll do this for me, though, please?"

"For you, I'd do anything."

This is worse going to worst. What did Joanie have in mind, and why am I taking life lessons from a twelve-year-old? So far as I can determine, Carol seems to regard this meeting as a mistake; Patty regards it as a renewal of vows; I regard it with none of the *assurance* and *clarity* I had assumed would descend on me.

We collect ourselves in a vacant part of the hall, not an alcove. I was hoping for an alcove. We need a suitable talking place in which to – talk. It's wrong just to stop a ways down the hall. I'm about to suggest that we keep going, find that alcove. We aren't allowed in the classrooms, I know; but it struck me that I should say, "Let's find a proper talking place."

Carol says, "This'll do."

"It's perfect," Patty twirps.

"You're wondering why I asked you all here," I say, chuckling. Nobody else chuckles. Carol seems embarrassed, a state I've never observed in her and am dismayed to see now. I want her to be superior as always, above the fray, and able, in a pinch, to step in, rescue me. But she isn't any closer to taking control than I. And Patty is doing everything she can to bring on disaster by being cute.

Left to my own devices, which have gone into hiding, I launch a sentence: "You see, Joanie told me – you both know Joanie?"

They stare at me.

"That doesn't matter. I got off on the wrong foot. I think I should get right to the point."

I pause. This is a rout.

"Tim wanted to apologize, Patty. I'm only here because I accidentally came on the two of you, and he wanted to clear things up, in case you were offended – or I was, I guess."

An angel out of heaven!

"This is sweet of you, Tim. You could never offend me. You know that, Tim."

Patty is fluttering her eyelids, really and truly fluttering. The idea is to let Patty down easy, end up on Carol's good side. If that means sacrificing Patty, fine. But Patty is proving tough to sacrifice.

"Well, I was brutal, Patty, forcing you against your will. No, let me finish. I said things and did things that just weren't, you know..." What a time to run out of words.

"Nice?" Patty offers.

"Fair," Carol says.

Fair is it, but I need a word of my own – *honest* will do.

"I wasn't honest, and I hate that. You deserve it, Patty, honesty. I was carried away, and got – carried away." Surely no genuine fourteen-year-old could be more idiotic.

"I was carried away, too, Tim. That's OK. Sorry, Carol. I guess we weren't too dignified, but you understand."

"No," Carol says, politely.

"Maybe you don't," Patty returns, "but we do. Tim and I don't care what others, who aren't involved in the first place, think about it or why they're thinking at all."

"OK, Patty. You shouldn't feel called upon to clarify things for me. You're right. I wouldn't understand even if you did try to explain."

"Yes, I expect so."

"I expect so, too."

This isn't my plan. I'm letting Carol take shit, for no reason, apart from my cowardice and inability to find things to say. Let there be an end to both!

"I want to say something here."

There follows a respectful silence.

"Tim, for God's sake do." I'm so blinded by fear I'm not sure who says it.

"Here's what I came to say and I'm sorry I didn't say it right off and save all of us... I'm sorry. You know this from Carol that I'm sorry, but it's more becoming if I say it. It's not right that Carol says it. I mean, not that she was wrong to say it. Not at all. I thank her for it."

"I'm right here, Tim. You sound like you're addressing an auditorium."

"I guess I do." I'm fighting back tears. If Joanie were here, I'd punch her in the mouth.

"I shouldn't have done that, Patty, and said that, because it wasn't appropriate. It wasn't honest. It wasn't fair. I sort of took advantage. That's bad. I am sorry. It's a terrible thing to take advantage of a girl by pretending to feel things."

"Pretending?" Patty's voice, hot-sauce fierce before, now trembles.

"That wasn't the word I wanted. I was – carried away. I won't do anything like that again. You can count on that, I hope."

"What?" Again I don't know who asked. I'm staring hard at the ceiling, not clean, a large crack running about two-thirds of the way across, fly spots. Where is double-shadow perception when I so badly need it?

"I think that's clear. I'm sorry to you, Carol, but you too Patty, and don't want this to go any farther – further. You can count on that. We'd better get back. They'll be checking on us."

Checking? Its fucking lunch hour. But both allow me to exit. My guess is that Carol is guided by mercy, Patty by confusion. Wait'll I get my hands on Joanie!

. . .

Now that Dad has agreed to medical treatment, it's up to me to uncover just what that might be. I speak to the locals, whose condescending blather I will spare you. They can't get beyond asking for symptoms and won't let me raise questions about the state of research, the best locations for heart surgery. They don't know, of course, so I'm not sure what I expect.

I consider using the Internet, then recall what decade I'm in. That leaves me with the public library, housed in a gorgeous Italianate building with a cupola and not many books. But they do have stereopticons and cards. At age ten, Harold had spent many hours scanning eagerly from Niagara Falls to the 1906 World's Fair. There's also a display of pots on the second floor and, on the third, journals, a complete run of bare titties inside National Geographics. They have three women librarians, unfussy and smart, dying to help anybody wandering in with the faintest interest in anything. One of them, Miss Wade, unearths three lavishly illustrated, outdated books on the human heart, pictures of the valves and cartoon figures explaining the circulatory system. As I'm glancing at these, the fifty-seven pound woman comes fluttering up with a county medical directory, current and chock full of the mediocre med-school students now licensed to try out their mistaken certainties on a credulous population.

Waste of time here, so I scuttle to Mary. I'd ask Joanie, but I'm still annoyed with her. I haven't poured my anger onto her, since I have trouble articulating precisely my grievance. I use silent signals, suspecting all along that my annoyer isn't noticing my annoyance. She's being so friendly I have trouble obeying the demands of simple justice. Catch myself smiling back. She's bright and funny, and she likes me. Right now, there seem to be few people who do: Donny, Jimmy Canton, Mary, Deanna, not Carol (?), not anybody else.

"So, Mary?"

"Make phone calls. Ohio State. The Cleveland Clinic. The Mayo Clinic. Eventually you'll get doctors who'll talk to you."

"What'll I tell them?"

"That your dad has chest pains, shortness of breath. Tell them his father died of a heart attack. Tell them you're worried and have nowhere to turn. You have this legacy from a deceased aunt. You want to help your dad, so money's no object. The best treatment is what you are after. You're desperate and don't know where to turn, so what should I do, please sir?"

So I do it. Each call finally gets me to courteous doctors, who recommend someone else, and I start over. These voices become a chorus, zeroing in on The Cleveland Clinic, where they are beyond courteous, seem moved by my devotion, say they'll help.

They set an appointment for tests, coinciding with Christmas vacation. I tell Dad, who again seems easy with it. Then I ask Joanie to figure out what story we'll feed Mom about going to Cleveland. Joanie says she'll take care of it. I knew she would.

Feeling elated with handling this and making it through a fortnight without positively offending anyone, I think I can fairly turn my attention homeward, be good to myself. Football season has ended with another win, this one against the Grade School All-Stars, which hardly counts but gives me a chance to hang back. Sadon accuses me of "dogging it," but I can tell he doesn't give a damn. I say goodbye to him warmly: "See you, Coach. Can't wait till next year." "Umm," he replies. My teammates seem less cold, or maybe just want to get the hell out of there. Nobody's celebrating the best season ever in ELHS freshman football.

What's open to me in the way of self-gratification: a singing career, philanthropy, plagiarizing *Catch-22*, convincing President Truman I can perform vital national services, setting up a try-out with the Pirates, mentoring the young, comforting the old, getting someone to screw.

I fix on the last. Can't complicate things with Patty, Carol is now a puzzle, Mary scares me. That leaves the rich kids or Donny. The rich girls might blab to Patty, but the rich boys won't leak, and all three on my list are gooduns. These rich-boy attractions are spiced with rage and shame, just as Donny's are now muted by respect and affection.

I've spent many evenings with Donny, allowing none to pass without a bit of minor-league fondling. But, as I say, our friendship makes it tough to advance.

Donny isn't witty, but he's unselfish, thoughtful in an anticipatory way, gifted at ease, and devoted to me. Friendship for him is what love ought to be: boundless.

· · ·

On Thanksgiving weekend, I get Donny over for a sleepover. Joanie likes him, Sally too, whom she invites along. Donny and Sally are taking the bus.

"You're excited about them coming, aren't you, Timmy?"

"Excited? I wouldn't say that. Well, yeah. I can't lie to you."

"Sure you can."

"I try not to, though. You know, first time around, I was so self-absorbed. I suppose I was less a liar then, but for all the wrong reasons. I'm sorry about that."

"You're always nice to me, Timmy."

"But?"

"You aren't interested. The only reason you knew I was friends with Sally is because she keeps telling you."

"That's true."

"What?"

"You expect me to deny it? I've been surprised how smart you are and kind, but beyond that..."

"That's the way families are. We don't have to be."

"Do-over. Start here: you know, Joanie, I'm very close to Donny. Don't be shocked. But maybe Sally can tell that. It's a charged atmosphere when I'm over there. Sally seems somehow included."

"She says that about you."

"I hadn't realized feeling 'close' would involve so much."

"What do you mean about Donny, me being shocked?"

"God – " (could I say this?) – "Joanie, I mean what you think I mean. I feel about Donny the way I feel about Carol – and Mary. You want to know more?"

"Sure."

"I started spending time with him because I was attracted to him, like sexually. You know about that, right? You know what I mean, sexually attracted? You know about sex?"

Silence.

"I wanted to – I'm not too sure, honestly – do things with him. Is this gross?"

"Gross? Wanting to do 'things'? No, I wouldn't call that gross. Dumb maybe. What 'things'? Play ball? I'm just kidding."

"I can't believe you aren't shocked. I wanted to mess around, you know, have sex. That's the way it started, sex fantasies. You want to know what boys do when they have sex?"

"No."

"Sorry."

"I don't mean I find it disgusting. I think I can picture it. It's harder for me to imagine what a boy would feel like having it with a boy, but I suppose it'd be cool. I think you should do what you want, if you don't hurt Donny, I mean his feelings."

I wonder what exactly she knows, but sufficient unto the day is the uncomfortable openness thereof.

"You think I might hurt him?"

"You might."

"Yeah. Now I like Donny, I don't know about having sex with him."

"Why not?"

"In 1951, homosexuality isn't out in the open, and people are rough on gays, or people who act gay, or people others suspect of being gay."

"Gay means homosexual? OK."

"Later on it gets worse and then, finally, better. People understand more, and there's lots of men and women who are openly gay or bisexual, wanting to have sex with both genders."

"Like you, bisexual."

"Yes, yes, yes. Like me. I don't see any reason not to."

"Is it new, this bisexual? I mean, not with you but those others? It sounds nice, like you don't have to say no to anybody and everybody sparks your ignition."

"Sparks your ignition, nice. True, though – maybe not everybody, not ugly people, people over eighty or under eight. Mostly."

"That leaves a lot."

"So, as a bisexual, I have a huge pasture to roam in, and no fences.

"Back to Donny. They'll be here in a minute, our bisexual friend and his sister."

"It's not really known, bisexuality isn't. Right now, if Donny has something like sex with me or finds himself wanting to do it, he'd maybe think he's a homo or some other cruel term. Gay stuff isn't an experience most boys can deal with. It may be different for girls; I'd be the last person to know. But with Donny, it could mess up his life."

"But you wouldn't force him."

"I could fool myself. If Donny realizes that's what I want to do, he might do it, just to please me, just for that reason. How can I tell for sure?"

"Do you really really want to sex him?"

"Yes, I really want to sex him."

"He's no idiot, not a baby. Talk to him, only work it out so you say it better and don't take so long, or he'll go to sleep before you get to the rolling on each other part."

"God, Joanie!"

She giggles, then shouts, "There's the bus."

Sally is off first and into my arms. She's in on the game. Wish I were.

With no need for preliminaries, we get into the fun, enjoying things. At least the other three do. I don't know why I can't, not fully. Maybe it's because I keep thinking of Humbert Humbert: three kids and a distinguished senior, a criminal senior.

So, finally adapting Hum's mode with abandon, I introduce them to the great rubba-dubba party game, TWISTER, constructing the playing surface (old sheet and crayons) and a spinner (a safety pin, a Popsicle stick).

(You suppose that this knowledge of games-to-come could be valuable for me and boost the happiness of mankind. Think of them – Chutes and Ladders, Trivia, Cards Against Humanity. I can market them, using gambling winnings, get a direct line to Parker Brothers and ride it to fame. Can I be more trifling? My inability to set off rockets is starting to bother me. How can I justify the narrow scope of my activities these first three months? I haven't found myself warding off ideas, doubtless because I'm led around by my, to put it elegantly, member.)

The game provides what I intend and what everybody, even my ashamed self, manages to engineer: elbows in crotches, forearms on breasts, faces folded into buttocks.

We then wend our way outside on this freakishly balmy November evening to join a community game of "Release the Peddler," a version of a seventeenth-century English country sport called "Marry Your Sister." I just invented that bit of history, but you believed it, sucker. Release the Peddler is a game played under a street-light, with a chalked out rectangle (the jail), one jailer, the rest of the players (escaped cons), set on arranging jail-breaks for those nabbed by the law. We have about four square miles in which to hide and sneak. The jailer, by common consent, cannot be a "base sucker," standing by the box, but has to make forays out and thus risk having his prisoners released by jail-breakers. Often, of course, the jailer herself hides, waiting for unwary runners trying to reach the rectangle before being spotted: "One, Two, Three, I see Ronald." If that's yelled out before the kid gets to the line, he lands in jail as a prisoner, hoping for a slick marauder to release him. If the kid gets there unspotted by the jailer, everyone can scatter. Any number can play, and it's one of those games that has no ending. If everyone gets caught, the first becomes the jailer and it all starts over. But it's hard to know when everybody is caught, as people join and leave the game unofficially, crawling from their houses under cars and toward the jail or, just as likely, leaving without telling anyone.

It is a version of infinity, like so many kid's games, and it brings tears to my eyes to think of it. Being inside this game means being released from time. The game goes on and on, over the hill and into the river, up on the West Virginia side, through more states and into the Atlantic, then back around, winding and rewinding like the string on a yo-yo, a perpetual motion world run by the hopeful hearts of children.

It might look like ignorance or, more sloppily, innocence. It does look like that to adults who have lost the profundity of Release the Peddler, locked in a jail not marked in chalk, where time slogs on, there are no buddies engineering jailbreaks, and bedtime is welcomed.

It isn't that kids know better. It's not what they figure out or even understand; it's what they assume, which builds on their being. They don't know better. They are better.

Or so it seems to me, as I wobble here between fourteen and seventy-eight, hoping to find a weight that will topple me backwards.

I'm so busy befogging myself that I get spotted: "One, two, three on Tim." So I'm imprisoned, chatting it up with the jailer, one Cletus Daniels, trying to distract him by such subtle feints as "Hey, Cletus, over there, behind Canton's car, the other side!" Cletus, either a nitwit or a trusting friend, bites, but not heartily enough to wander far, open lanes for raiders, get me released. Finally, a disturbance behind the Stanley house draws Cletus away far enough to allow four daring pardners to come running and spring me from the clink. It strikes me how fast most of these kids are. I don't think I observed it first time through, nor do I remember how all the players laugh their way through the game, even those in hiding, even Cletus.

There's a great concealment place in a vacant lot nearby – though I know it won't be absent a house for more than another year. From inside the weeds there, one can remain as undetected as a field mouse and still have a view of the jailer and his vulnerable hoosegow. The trouble is that the weeds are thick, milky, prickly, itchy, clinging, and smelly. But hell, for the sake of the game, one would undergo tortures worse than these.

I find myself beside a strange body, so I reach out to identify it. Turns out the shoulder I feel is actually a butt, worse, one belonging to Joanie, sprawled next to me in the darkness.

"Timmy!" she hisses.

"Hi, Joanie."

118

"Was it the voice or the ass gave me away?"

"How you talk!"

"Oh, I can't say it but you can massage it, pervert. I think you're a felon there in the future, or is everybody doing incest then?"

"I'm sorry, honey."

"That's OK. It was nice. I know you'd have gone for anybody's ass over mine, given the choice."

"Not quite everybody. Cletus has an uninviting ass. So does that girl Marlene."

"I'd agree. It's Arlene. And you're going to give me away, you're so loud. Why don't you snake over and find Martin Paul, maybe little Dolly, someone not in the immediate family."

"I have no idea who Martin Paul and Dolly are."

"You'll recognize 'em."

"Don't tell me: by their shapely asses. They're not cousins or something, are they?"

"No, but we do have blood in the game."

"We do?"

"Mom. Don't go molesting her."

"Really? She's playing?"

"No."

Before I know it, I've crawled to a small clearing in the middle of the milkweed horrors. Getting out will be as bad as getting in, but for now, I've found an oasis. Setting about to enjoy my solitude, plot some dirty business, I consider why I'm not smoking. That habit had soothed me for a few years the first time through, and a few years are probably all I have. Drinking too, harder to arrange. Lost in musings, I fail to notice company until it bites my arm, really does.

"Jesus Christ!"

"Shhhh. You'll get us caught."

"That you, Dolly?"

"Who's Dolly? No, it's your friend, Margie."

I reach down to drag this twerp from beside me, heaving a pixie, maybe about eleven years old. I get her face close to mine to study her in the semi-darkness. She seizes the opportunity to blow up my nose, so I shove her back.

Studying Margie, some memories come flooding back, indefinite but happy.

"Margie, why are you playing a game like this in a skirt?"

She looks embarrassed.

"I'm sorry, honey, did I say something wrong?"

"I like skirts."

I stare at her until her face caves in.

"My mom and dad won't let me put on shorts. They say I wear them out."

That doesn't make sense, but I shut up.

"We can't afford them, Tim. I only have these two skirts."

My impulse is to give her money, but I restrain myself. Why? I got a better idea.

Whispering to her carefully, I offer a plan: "Look, Margie, I'm serious now. I need some help on a project and I can pay you if you'll help me."

"I'll do it, Tim, but you can't pay me."

"Sure I can. I have money. I can't explain but I do."

"You just want to help me. That's OK. I don't need more clothes, and I know you don't have any money, your dad or my dad. I wish I hadn't said anything."

"You were feeling bad because I hurt your feelings. I really do need help and you gotta believe me that I have all this dough. I wouldn't lie to you."

"You're serious."

"Yeah, but in another minute I start tickling you."

"Better not."

"Margie, will you help me? I'll figure out a way to explain it to your parents, so they won't think you stole the money from Salvation Army Santas."

"Well..."

"Think about it. Let's go free those jailed jerks. I'll talk to you more about this project."

"Don't go that way, Tim. There's briars. Follow me. I'll help. No pay."

After the game winds down some, though one could never be sure that's happening, we go back into our house, into our sardine-can rooms, boy-boy, girl-girl.

I waste no time going after Donny, as soon as we are alone. "Alone" is a technical term here, a geographical fiction, given that Sally and Joanie are in the next room, separated by half-inch wallboard. Mom and Dad are way at the other end of the house, a good forty feet.

Halfway into wrestling, Donny gets up and whips off t-shirt, socks and shoes, and then peels down his jeans without unbuttoning them, so tiny are his hips. He stands there, while I sit on the bed a foot away. I have no idea what I'm thinking, probably nothing. We stay that way for what seems like fifteen minutes, probably ten seconds.

"Tim, what do you want to do?" He's whispering.

"Do?"

Donny smiles in a way I can't decode.

It's so quiet we can hear Joanie and Sally whispering in our interstices, but Donny's question occupies me fully. He seems to know what he's about, to be way ahead of me. That doesn't seem possible, but it's indisputable.

I'm unprepared, left with nothing but the truth. Wish I knew where that was. Why does Donny raise the subject, openly? What do I want to do? I understand this much: Donny intends for me to be happy. He will unbuckle our friendship from shyness.

"Donny, you know how I feel. Right now it's all I can do to keep from attacking you."

Donny starts to say something. I know what it will be.

"Here's the thing. What I mean is that I'd like to have sex with you."

Again, he starts to speak. I put my hand over his mouth so I can consider. If I go on, there's a chance I'll ruin everything.

"It's so complicated. What people of the same gender, boys, do when they have sex probably would gross you out, make you angry or ashamed. Donny, when boys are having sex, having sex in the way of – fucking. You see?" What did I just say?

He seems amused, waiting for me to stop blabbing. Something keeps me talking. I'd say it is decency, though maybe I'm just trying to make a preemptory strike on the guilt I am sure will follow any sex.

"Donny, I don't know how to say this, so I'll just go on. Here's what worries me, and it has to do with what bisexuals do. Bisexuals are people attracted both to men and women, sexually and even falling in love and all that."

"Like you."

"Yeah."

"Like me."

"You just saying that?"

"Why would I just say that?"

"Donny, I feel as if I'm feeding on your decency, your affection, and aiming you toward misery. Bisexuality sounds nice, but... What bisexual boys do to one another is..."

"Yeah?" He's smiling.

"Like you figured, they hug and fondle and – and – fiddle. You with me?"

"Yeah. I'm all over you."

His ease is making this harder. I try to ignore it and return to the horrors: "So what boys do are these things, and they also are cocksuckers, penises in the mouth, Donny. And they have sex between the legs: you put your pecker between my legs and go back and forth. And also gay people have anal sex, up butts and climax there."

"Really?"

"It's not required, but it tends to happen when boys start playing around and get excited."

"Tim, what does gay mean?"

"That's a big-city word for homosexual – fairy. That's the real problem."

"What is?"

"Nobody here has heard of bisexual, and it wouldn't matter if they had. This isn't a cruel town, but it is a cruel time. People who seem well meaning can and will become vicious, if you do anything that's different, even if it's harmless. If you and me have sex..."

"Nobody would ever know."

"Maybe not, but you'd know. Don't say anything. I can maybe have sex with you, and with girls, and not worry. I won't be here long. But you will be. I can hardly believe how gutsy you are, but I'm afraid you're mostly anxious to be good to me. I don't think you're weak or that I can handle what you can't. Hell, I have no idea whether I can handle it. I just can't help it."

This is the wrong alley to scurry down. I beat a quick retreat to sociology and the melancholy history of intolerance. "For me, we can have sex and not *be* something as a result. We can make love all we want and not be faggots. We're just two guys who want to do it and do. But how could that be for you, being here in 1951."

"What about being in 1951? What's that?"

"Oh, just our time period, you know."

His eyes are sparkling, and he's holding my hand. I hadn't noticed him doing that; it happened so smoothly.

"You won't mess up my life, Tim."

He's leaning close, pressing insistently. With his free hand he rubs my neck, an intimate gesture that seems more kindly than erotic. Laughter is dumb, but it's what I emit. Then we kiss. I lean back on the bed, and we hold hands. He starts to roll on me and I block him.

"Not now. At least let's think about it a few days. We'll have plenty of chances. Right now, let's go to sleep."

Of course we don't. We explore, fondle. But we avoid ookie bits. Mostly. Of course some things happen I'd vowed to resist, but our boyish sex play is what some might call tame. What happens – do you want to know? Shame on you. I'll just say that, while we don't keep our hands to ourselves, we pretty much avoid invading territories from which there'd be no return. Anyhow, we do what we do and are none the worse for it.

Really, we aren't. I hope. If Donny is scarred, he doesn't show it by his demeanor next morning. He's grinning as he tickles me awake. Throwing caution to the winds, we have a silent grind, with Mom's breakfast preparations no more than twelve feet away. It isn't my prudish mother, though, but my super-ego that kicks in, loudly. But grind we do.

"Well, Tim, you think you turned me into a fairy?" He's whispering with difficulty, barely holding in his giggles.

"Yep."

"Fine by me. Fuck it." His mouth is about five millimeters from my ear.

"Donny! I never heard you say that."

"You taught me. And there's so much we didn't do."

While fully aware of his delirious happiness, I'm stricken with something like terror. I can't think of anything to say, but Donny, vigilant in sensing my feelings, slugs me and tells a really awful joke that releases the tension, releases me.

"And Tim..."

"Yeah?"

"I was kidding about you teaching me. You wouldn't. You'd like to **do** it but not **say** it."

No longer able to bottle it, he explodes in such shrieks Mom asks if we are "OK in there."

. . .

For reasons all too plain, this warm-up doesn't clear the decks in the fantasy-desire boat to which I'm lashed. I find myself by the very next day horny beyond all bearing. Deciding that I should treat this condition with respect and move into territories where ethical considerations will be less pressing, I wait only two days to act.

So, the following Tuesday, as December comes on us, I make a call to one Glenn, the only kid in town with a III to his name. The III is enough to justify assault, aimed at nothing more exalted than one-way carnal pleasure. Worse, I hope to make III crawl. I have trouble imagining exactly the details of that humiliation, but it's Lear-like in its amplitude.

I convince myself that such brutality has been purchased by my weekend selflessness. You may be thinking that my description of our profligacy does not leave an impression of moderation, but you weren't there. It's terrible to admit, and I try to blind myself to it, but I'm giving myself points for half-protecting Donny, and I'm not the sort to let points go unredeemed.

Even my phone call to Glenn is pitiless. I make it seem as if he has called me, am impatient, make him sputter. "Err, Tim, would you like to come over after school – have dinner. It'd be – we'd have a good time." I almost feel sorry for him, but that won't do. Keep humanizing these kids and I'll never get laid. At least III can hold steady as a cliché. One thing for sure, he's pretty: clean-cut, slight, a curl to his upper lip, welcoming in pervs like me. He has more self-confidence than any other thirty kids – so I tell myself – and has nerve enough to wear clothes a little different from the rest of us. He isn't in my gym class, so I haven't seen him naked. That makes me keen with anticipation. You might wonder what I expect: two peckers, orange nuts?

He melts when I notice him, loses his poise, comes close to groveling. I become cooler as he liquefies, though the prospect of what is to come has made me glassy-eyed.

．　．　．

"You just talk to Carol?"

"Nope. Why'd you say that?"

"Cause you look like you're in love."

"What?"

"Or in heat."

The phone rings. Carol.

"Oh, Carol! Hang on just a second."

"Did you know Carol was calling?"

"Yes, I did. We talk..."

"OK. Yeah, Carol. I just wanted to find out what sort of double-dealing my conniving rat of a sister is up to."

Carol doesn't laugh: "She's plotting to help me seduce you."

"I don't think that requires a conspiracy."

Silence.

"I deserve that."

"Tim, I want to talk to you about something else, your dad's condition. Joanie told me more than you did, about the Cleveland Clinic. I'm not sure if you know my mom is sick."

I don't. "Heart?"

"Yeah, real bad, Dr. Pigeon thinks. She carries nitroglycerin in her purse. I peeked. Tim, can you help?"

"Yes, I can help. I'll call the Clinic and see if I can get her in the same day as my dad, for a check. Don't you think?"

"How can I get my mom to go along?"

"Oh. I'll ask Joanie."

"What?"

"Joanie will have a good idea. Sorry, that's silly."

"No it isn't. But do you have any ideas all on your own?"

"No. I mean, not no exactly, but – I'll think about it and..."

"Ask Joanie."

"I'll call you back – ten minutes."

"No need for that much speed. I hope."

"Joanie's right here."

So I do – talk to Joanie and call back. Joanie says that I should speak to Pigeon, tell him about Dad's appointment and ask him if he'll advise Mrs. Blake to look into it, plant the seed. Then call Pigeon with the appointment time so he can relay it to Mrs. Blake, as if it came from him. Makes sense. She'll never go if she thinks the arrangement originates with Carol. I relay all this and feel useful. I even find room to worry about Carol, her mom, and especially my dad, who cannot hide the gasps when he climbs the three steps to our front porch, a porch he and I and Joanie had put in, made the footers and sloshed round with garden hoes the concrete that spilled out of the mixer like sloppy oatmeal.

. . .

My grades are all A's. Did I tell you that? I take pride in that, realizing that most of this school material is new. Algebra is easier and world history, but Latin and the rest are freshly challenging – depressing, if you're the sort who gets depressed by such things. Me, I'm tied to more weighty matters, though I have as yet done little (nothing) to locate them. My singing voice, which thrills me in the tub, has been kept under wraps. Haven't figured out what to do with it, though singing might be a place to start. My athleticism has been piddled away on freshman football and will soon soar to new trivial heights in freshman basketball. Apart from this story-in-progress, I have written nothing – though I have some poems (written by others) in my head I can unloose. Can I publish Ginsberg's "Howl" or X. J. Kennedy's "For a Child Skipping Rope"

Here lies resting, out of breath,
Out of turns
Elizabeth,
Whose quicksilver heels not quite
Cleared the whirring edge of night.
Earth whose circles round us skim,
Catching e'en the lightest limb
Shelter now Elizabeth, and for her sake,
Trip up Death.

That isn't accurate, I think, but so what? Beating great poets to the punch: there's an idea only slightly less narrow than getting "Twister" on the market. Maybe I can dribble out *Harry Potter* or write (direct, star in) "The Big Lebowski."

I can invent deconstruction, but who will care? How about Pilates, a model with only half an idea in it and lots of money. Fast food? Wal-Mart? A lot like inventing AIDS. At least I can manage to do no harm with my meddlings, except to the bodies of those locals cursed with social status.

What have I done, in any area? It is only December, a little over three months into my tour of duty, so I mustn't be impatient. Still, slight and venal as have been my aims, I haven't succeeded in advancing even them. I have bedded no one, am as spotless in body as first time around. Not exactly, but I'd expected more of myself in such a run-of-the-mill activity. All over America, even in 1951, other kids, a few, are successful in advancing their sexual aims.

And yet, I have enjoyed myself immensely in ways a little hard to explain. I love being around not just Donny but, just as much, Jimmy Canton and other old friends, not to mention new ones I hadn't known very well first time around. Even among all the people I have clumsily alienated, many seem to like me, and I like more of them. I find great pleasure in small things: gossip, brushing arms, phone calls, Release the Peddler, gym class, studying Latin, getting to know and love Joanie, watching my parents' silence, listening to the radio, eating bad food, going to movies, playing with the horse weeds down by the river, thinking of Carol, wondering about Mary, riding the bus, talking to just about anybody, hearing the Saturday afternoon opera (courtesy of Texaco), watching boys undress in the locker-room, imagining I can see girls undress in theirs, admiring my dad and (without admitting it) my mom, singing in the choir, putting pennies on the railroad track behind the house, fishing in the river for catfish, flirting, board-games, being surprised by the unaffected decency of all these kids, wearing clothes that seem like costumes, taking car rides for the sake of riding, playing pinball, drinking milkshakes, dancing at sock hops, seeing girls in their sweaters and funny pointed bras, chewing SenSen, eating Mallo Cups, hearing Hit Parade ballads. They tried to tell us we're too young.

For some people that would be enough.

CHAPTER 9

Somehow, the medical scheduling works, Dad and Mrs. Blake with appointments on the same morning. Surprisingly, Dr. Pigeon is invaluable in arranging this, using acting talents doctors acquire in order to keep patients (and their practices) motoring along. Great advantages in this two-in-one: among other things, the long, slow, up-and-back drive can be shared, endured but once. It's only one-hundred miles away, but with top speeds of thirty-five and what seem like an equal number of small towns to inch through, it takes a whole morning, crammed into a Chevrolet sedan belonging to the Blakes: four parents, Carol, me. It's taken a little squiggling to get me and Carol included, partly because Carol's younger brother and Joanie have to be left behind, and partly because nobody but my dad sees any reason for "the older kids" to be included.

I have managed to get through to both sets of Clinic specialists, Dad's and Mrs. Blake's, and, wonder of wonders, convince them that I can pay and that they will tell only me the unvarnished medical truth in both cases. Why they believe me, I don't know.

We've packed a picnic lunch so as to avoid the unthinkable, a restaurant. The highway beyond Lisbon has roadside rests about every ten miles, the one we choose being among the least attractive. It's vacant, though, which suits our shy parents. I end up at a separate (uneven, sloping, ancient) table with Carol's sick mother, a strange arrangement that occurs only because nobody feels comfortable sorting things out. So here I am with Mrs. Blake, passing mountains of food back and forth across the gulf between the pine tables, redolent of creosote. There's a creek running not too far away and some trees, pretty when in leaf. But this is December, gray and grisly. We're all huddled beneath funny long coats. Gloves would have been nice, though they would also have absorbed the potato salad and smelled things up.

"How are you feeling, Mrs. Blake?"

"I'm fine, Timmy. Thanks for asking. You seem to be a very nice boy."

("For a boy, that is," she might as well have added. What could I say to that?)

"Thank you, Mrs. Blake. I think it's Carol who is the good person."

Her eyes immediately shoot out alarm rays. "Are you and Carol close friends?"

Here's the dragon guarding my love. Maybe I should tell her I hardly know Carol, am saying she's a good person because I seem to recall somebody saying something like that.

"I guess, Mrs. Blake, the truth is I wish I were a close friend. I'm an admirer."

To my slack-jawed amazement, she smiles, then changes the subject.

"Carol tells me you have a fine singing voice."

How would she know? Did I say so, brag?

"Would you like to hear it, Mrs. Blake? I could serenade us, give us some lunch music."

I'm kidding, but she nods, "I'd like that very much."

Oh Jesus! Should I choose something super-decent, maybe a hymn? Seems too obvious, so I set right into "All Through the Night," without alerting anyone. Though I'm singing softly, the others hush to listen, and I sing simply as I can. On the second verse, Mrs. Blake joins in with a nice alto and a few of the others, my mother first, a little too loudly but on key, and Carol. Wish I could say it's angelic, but the truth is Carol can't sing a lick, has one of those tonal senses that allow her to fly close to the right note without landing. But she seems unaware of it, enjoys herself, and we continue for some time. Dad looks on with an expression hard to decipher. I think I see his lips moving, but I'm probably mistaken.

I my loving vigil keeping---All through the night.

We arrive an hour early and spend the spare time reading *Argosy*, *Redbook*, *Look*, *Collier's*, *Saturday Evening Post*, and *Tales from the Crypt* comics. Several times, I'm on the verge of suggesting a walk before remembering fresh each time that there's nowhere to walk. Mean streets, blank buildings. I have warm memories of Cleveland from the first go-round. Mr. Canton had once taken Harold there with his three boys to watch Bob Feller pitch and to stay in a motel, my first such experience. The Cantons were unfussy, resourceful people, deeply kind. I remember best the car trip – Mr. Canton knew great road games. It seems as if I can bring back every smell, motion of the breeze, joke, and I-see-something-you-don't-see games, as if none of these are memories but somehow still to come, as if time has rolled in on itself and is no longer taking things away but promising more. Watching the test pattern, bothering other guests with Hide-and-Seek in the halls, story-telling contests: maybe I glamorize the memory, but no I don't.

Harold had been to Cleveland often, had lived there for many years later on in the fifties and sixties, but who cares about that? The later-on-in-my-first-life is commonplace material. Of course it counted for a good deal to Harold, but where is he?

The medical exams take a long time, allowing us to fuss, though entertainment is everywhere in the room. Aside from the magazines, there's a jigsaw puzzle the two mammas tackle. The radio is on, first to soaps – "One Man's Family," "Stella Dallas" – then to serials – "Jack Armstrong," "The Green Hornet." I love every minute of it, the sound effects and music especially: "Jack Armstrong! Jack Armstrong! Jack Armmstroonng! The Awll Americaun Boyee!" Footsteps smacking, doors creaking, guns exploding. It strikes me how tough it'd be to write serial material, rich stories that never close off. Like Release the Peddler, with ongoing misery or endless derring-do – on and on and on.

Just when we least expect it, my dad's team emerges, followed minutes later by Mrs. Blake's. Upshot is, officially, that both have "conditions." Mrs. Blake has the more advanced problem, it's revealed to me, though Dad's heart, as I knew, is very weak, with congenital this's and that's closing and caving in and bloating and clogging and fluttering, opening at the wrong time or just about refusing to open at all.

I find this out during a pretend trip to the bathroom, while Carol herds everyone, grumbling at the extravagance, down to the cafeteria for a Coke. The docs, all six of them, wink me toward an empty examining room. One thing won't change in the next sixty-odd years: the ability of these charnel-house rooms to evoke terror. This blank chamber has a smell and a moist burning taste that makes me believe I've swallowed a quart of Clorox.

Bracing for the news, I find myself backed up defensively against a slab commonly used to examine patients or, probably, lay out corpses. On Mrs. Blake, short and grim: there's nothing to do, advanced as the disease is. Were she to slow down, lose weight, walk every evening, and other stuff she won't dream of doing, she might live for "some time." I appreciate the absence of bullshit. Nobody speaks of miracles, of how you never know about these things. They do know, and they don't hide it. I wonder if they recognize how old I am, why they accept me as a person into whose hands this tough information should be delivered. Maybe they don't give a shit, though they do seem to care very much about their job. I don't know if they honor patients, exactly, much less me, but they honor their craft and, since I ask, they let me have it straight. They can load Mrs. Blake with more medications, ones more relevant to her condition, but they'd only mask (well) and prolong (not much).

With Dad, things are both more hopeful and a lot more complex. Certain possibilities for repair – risky, complicated, experimental, bold – can extend his life span, but no guarantees. Surgery without much delay. I'm not too clear what they have in mind and know there's no point in asking. They'd tell me.

I assure them again that I have money, spare no expense. I feel like a Mafia boss, all ignorant bluster, talking to doctors about dough. They seem to mind it less than I.

· · ·

"So, Dad, that's it. The surgery could give you years, for Mom and for me and Joanie. It's risky. The docs said to emphasize that. Of course you can talk to them. It's your decision naturally and you want to get facts from them, not me."

"Like hell."

"What?"

"That's fine. I'll do it. How long will I live without it? You know."

"Six or seven years."

"In bad health." It wasn't a question.

"Real bad. You start getting attacks in a year or two, two. Soon you can't work. It's pretty terrible for you."

"Pretty terrible for May."

I can't remember my dad calling Mom by her name before.

That's it. He tells Mom what exactly I don't know, and she goes into a new mode, capable and tough. It's as if her world, now focused and purposeful, allows her a better place to be.

I talk with Joanie about it. I can tell she's worried, much more tuned in to the "risky" part than I. But she won't say so, tells me I've done good. In this, she is like Mom.

Mrs. Blake comes out of the building armed with a pile of prescriptions, some of which are preventative, some for emergencies, some for pain, some for sleep, some for feeling good, some placebos. I tell Carol everything, emphasizing the moonshine and hiding from her the hopelessness. She tears up immediately, seeing through me, seeing way too much. After all, her mother is no worse than when she went in, and now has some meds that will make things nicer, even if they don't offer much in the way of treatment.

I comfort Carol as well as I can. Carol doesn't cry, is waiting for me to leave to do that.

I tell Joanie that Carol seems to be looking on the dark side of things.

"There's only the one side, right? From what you said, there's no hope."

"She's no worse off than she was." I'm stung, thinking I'd done better than that.

"God, Timmy. Now Carol knows what that means. Mr. Blake, too. They figured these experts could give them something Dr. Pigeon couldn't. Either that or Dr. Pigeon was wrong, and it was just indigestion."

"I see what you mean. Now there's no hope for anything better. But she can still live a long time, maybe."

"If she does all those things."

"Yeah."

"If she doesn't do them, it won't make much difference."

"It might."

"No it won't."

"No it won't."

• • •

Meanwhile, I'm turning my attention to my snooty, curly-lipped Glenn, to basketball, and to figuring out Mary. Also a musical surprise. Nothing much happens between the Clinic visit and the resumption of school. Carol is in no mood for subterfuge, so we make a silent agreement to let slide our plans.

Our family has established Christmas rituals, starting with candy-making, a three-day operation resulting in something called fondant, an uninteresting confection if you asked your taste buds but wonderful to dye and mold and decorate. Then there's tree buying, a few mandatory visits to family friends, *NO CHURCH*, stocking-hanging, car trips to see the lights. My parents spend what seems to be all their savings on nice presents for Joanie and me, lots of them, none terribly expensive in themselves – no bikes, watches, or stylish clothes – but high quality puzzles, balls, books, craft kits, chocolates, and games, most of all games, the latest and finest, board games especially. Dad takes his vacation, his one-week, between Christmas and New Years, and we spend every day playing games. Morning until night, with small breaks for eating, ridiculously short walks, and a couple of radio programs. Even during radio times, we practice magic tricks, mess with something like a make-your-own-toy-soldier kit, or work a jigsaw puzzle. I remembered it from the first go-round as a lovely skein of spun-out happiness. And it is. I'm so mesmerized by the warmth of it all that I forget to feel sadness, any sense that it is all gone – or going fast.

I'm thinking my health-care activities and my fledgling plans to launch a program to rescue the held-back give me a pass for low-grade hijinks. I can't find the right word for what I want with Glenn, desire to do *to* Glenn. Rape, with some semblance of consent, might describe it, though I'm not about to let that word gain center stage.

I've been over twice after school, teasing my prey, making him happy and insecure. The second time I agree to dinner with his parents and charm them. The Missus has a face and body carrying reasonably fresh memories of being pretty. She has a stiff perm – resembles a cord of piled wood – and expensive clothes. The Mister is handsome in a cornball way, looking enough like Robert Young to make you realize how remarkable the authentic thing is. Glenn Junior (my Glenn being III) wears a suit. I'll hand it to him: he knows how to assume importance, act as if he doesn't give a pile of cat shit whether you admire him or not. He does, though.

The mother (God!) is ready to jump my bones, as we'll say in fifty years. Glenn's father is busy smiling, telling anecdotes, trying to convince me that he's the biggest of shots, and I let him, knowing he'll be impressed by anyone impressed by him. He's a blowhard, but he loves it that I'm spending time with his boy. He isn't the sort to be impressed by cute, the one strong quality Glenn can lay claim to, and probably has deep-down fears that his pretty boy isn't very manly. My own unmistakable manliness reassures him, verifies his own.

I haven't counted on Glenn's sister being there, didn't know Glenn had a sister. She has an energetic, rambunctious ease missing in the rest of the family. Her eyes gleam, narrow mysteriously at odd times, when she stares at me, trying to make me uncomfortable, I guess, which she does. She laughs mockingly, offers a running satiric commentary on the goings-on. The others seem determined to ignore her, even when her ironies become direct. So she talks more to me, points her smile as she offers her sneers. I haven't seen her at school, but she must be there, a year or three our senior. She's beautiful, maybe not in repose but certainly in motion.

She complicates things. I'm drawn to her, strongly, and hate playing my Eddie Haskell part before her cool self. It's hard work, addressing her father's country club jollities, her mother's old-dog lust, her brother's beauty, and her wit. She's the least important in my scheming, but she's controlling me. It isn't the smartest thing, given my goal, but I begin adding a caustic zing to my own comments, slight inflections I hope she'll catch. She's sitting across from me, watching me steadily and with bemusement. Her eyes move so fast and reflect too much light to be read, though I can see how they might trap me. Just as I'm about to give up efforts to understand her, my problems are solved by a socked foot snaking up my leg. It's a narrow table (luckily not glass) and she's directly opposite me. Doesn't everyone else notice? By the time I get that worry formulated, I cease to worry about it.

And I can't remember her name. Beverly? Betty? Barbara?

Which of these rich kids do I want? Who in 1951 would play footsie with a boy, parents right there at table! A dissolute, cynical rich kid, that's who. I'm aware that her mocking advances don't mean she's interested. More likely, she wants to impose herself, her power, on me, show me how indifferent she is to the coolest kid anywhere.

Still, it'd be fun matching cool with her, and maybe I'm wrong about her motives. She doesn't seem vicious, just bored. And she doesn't direct her barbs at her brother.

True, I don't want to endanger the hold I have on Glenn by chasing after his hot sister, though it's doubtful anything would diminish Glenn's bedazzlement.

I decide my best bet is to engage the old folks in after-dinner chat, ignoring both Glenn and sister. Let both yearn for me, plot to attract me. Old Glenn Jr. has never had an audience so captivated, and his wife keeps googling her eyes at me.

Ten minutes later they are as sorry to see me leave as is Glenn or, I hope, sis. I could have talked them into making art movies of their kids. They would have volunteered to man the lights, fit the G-strings, play the butler and the maid.

Glenn calls the next day with a sleepover invite. I'm cool, pretend reluctance, then agree, even give him a small dose of friendly. He deserves something for being cute, rich, susceptible, and so nicely supported by a knockout sibling. You're thinking this is all horrible. Talk about gratuitous judgments!

The sleepover goes like this. Glenn and his mom – where was sis? – pick me up on Saturday. (By the way, it's now Saturday January 5, two days before the resumption of classes.) They have a black Cadillac, very original, and make the most of its blatant presumptuousness. I get in back, right beside a scrambling Glenn, Mrs. Downing making jokes about being chauffer for her two movie stars. Glenn is dithery, consumed with fidgets about what I will think – about his parents, clothes, plans. He has a multitude of ideas, spilling them out and then withdrawing them before I can speak. Torn between wanting me happy and fear that his ideas will seem uncool, Glenn is like the donkey starving between two bales of hay.

I turn to him, ooching closer, not smiling. He laughs nervously and tries unsuccessfully to keep from looking away. I put my hand deliberately on his thigh, and pat. "Glenn, I'll enjoy anything we do, or doing nothing. It's you I want to be with. I don't care what we do."

Predictably – this is playing with pre-programmed robots – Glenn's fluster jumps five notches. He puts his own hand on my thigh, thinks of what he's done, and withdraws so hastily he hits me in the shoulder. Apologies, promises, babbles, splurts.

Mrs. Downing observes this with sappy approval. I speak a little more loudly, pouring it on with all the subtlety of a sanolet cleaner. "Look, Glenn. Just be easy and have fun. That's what I want, for you to have fun. Don't worry about entertaining me, [a beat of silence as I forgot his name] Glenn. It's you I want."

Direct, but I needn't worry; it's as likely that a musk ox will catch a double entendre.

We end up going bowling, playing touch football (with the other rich kids on a big rich lawn), making fudge, playing Bingo, trying out my newly-invented Twister (with the adult Downings, not a good idea), taking a walk around the grounds, playing hide and seek (the two of us), and wrestling. All this time, Betsy (I asked Glenn) doesn't show, nor is her absence explained. Not that I lack for the stimulation I have come for, though I have been super-careful to avoid, in all our scrambling and tumbling, any fondle. I have, however, maneuvered his hands and my body so that, as often as possible, it is he going after me in improper places. None of these advances are his, of course, but they give me a chance not to react, to normalize things, which is a good idea, though also a waste of strategic brilliance. Had I spoken my desire, Glenn would have let himself be diddled by the household pet, an oversized dog with the mange.

At eleven, Glenn's Dad suggests we go to bed, so we play-punch our way upstairs and into Glenn's chambers, one of us (not me) rattled. Glenn disappears in a closet and emerges in opulent jammies. They're vaguely Turkish, the sort of thing Oscar Wilde might have worn at his sleepovers with telegraph boys at the Savoy. I feel certain they have been procured by the elder Downings on one of their nitwit tours of Europe for purposes of conspicuous consumption.

"Those are nice, buddy."

"Yours, too," said Glenn automatically, blushing furiously when he looks again. I'm wearing size-too-small J. C. Penny briefs.

"Why did you go away to change? You didn't want me to see you naked?"

"I'm sorry."

"Did you think I might attack you, get overcome with lust?"

"God, Tim, No!"

"I might." I'm not smiling.

Glenn can think of nothing to say.

Very quietly, I move slowly toward him, whispering. (What a corny villain I am.) "Are you wearing anything under those pajamas, Glenn?"

"Errrr – no."

"Oh?" I arch my eyebrows, hold out my hand.

Not having the slightest idea what to do, Glenn takes my hand, turning even more red, cheeks now splotchy, eyes registering pain.

This is too much, but so what? "Can I see what you are wearing underneath your jammies, Glenn? Since you don't trust me?"

"God, Tim, I trust you. What do you mean?"

This is indeed too much, so I laugh and hug him in Tom-Brown-schoolboy style.

"Only shitting you. We can talk about anything, right?" I continue to hold him.

"Sure!" He moves closer, but it's relief and nothing more.

"And do anything?" I slip my hand down his back and onto his butt.

"Sure," he falters. I can now feel his dick trying to drill a hole in my leg.

"Good friends can trust each other and do anything they want, don't you think?" My hand moves to the front of his pjs, opens the drawstring, and wiggles down to find his – what anyone would expect to find.

"Nawwwuuuoooohhhh," he gasps.

Given Glenn's vulnerability, I think I show Christian restraint that night. I'm even more tediously well-mannered than with Donny. Why? Don't you know? What would you have done? More than I did. I did a little.

Rolling and rubbing, reaching under and around. Clothing shoved sideways. This is normal schoolboy fun. (I seem to have recourse to that phrase a lot. I notice it, reader, so there's no need pointing it out.) True, Glenn doesn't seem to know much, but he's willing to follow my lead. The one thing he isn't eager to do is talk about it, but that part interests me.

"Did you enjoy that, Glenn?"

"Well, geez, Tim, yeah."

"You want to do that some more next time?"

"I guess."

"OK, we won't."

"No, no, Tim, like you say, friends can do anything."

"But do you want to do that?"

"Sure."

"I mean do *YOU* want to do it, or is it just because I want to?"

"God, Tim. I want to do it."

"Do what?"

"Tim!"

"OK, don't tell me. I thought we were friends."

"We are. It's just embarrassing."

"It shouldn't be embarrassing. We should be able to talk about anything. We should be open and trust everything about the other. That's what best friends are."

Glenn has been getting apoplexy trying to get his protest in: "No, Tim, no, no. OK. I really like it when you and I play with each other – with each other's dicks."

"And? Keep telling me. Trust me."

"And rub our dicks and hug and touch our butts and cum."

"Me too."

And that was that, except for the presence of Betsy in the church party, still including me in her satiric oblongata and flirting outrageously. She sits one over from me on the hard church pew, separated by her brother, but she puts her arm over bro's back, and starts playing with my hair. She advances to tickling my ear, not stopping even when Glenn glances over. What about the faithful just behind us? Betsy obviously doesn't give a shit, but she soon withdraws her hand. Suddenly, a piece of folded paper snaps over on my lap.

I give Glenn a look to keep him from peeking, then unfold it slowly, feeling both excited and apprehensive. What in hell is this maniac going to propose? A blowjob atop the baptismal font? I'm trembling a little as I open it:

Hi Tim,

I hope you and Glenn had a good time. I know he was looking forward to your visit. I'd love to be part of your games next time you're over, if I wouldn't be an intruder. I know the last thing you want is a big sister spoiling your fun. But I like Glenn a lot.

He's a wonderful brother. Be good to him.
Your friend (I hope),

Betsy Downing

Hardly the stuff of seductivesextalk.com.

• • •

I ask Mary what she thinks of Betsy. Mary, my constant and misused buddy all these months, is as enigmatic a dear friend as ever there was. She's given me to understand clearly that she loves me and knows that I love her. What isn't clear is what she means, what we mean. Here's what I understand: Mary loves me unreservedly. No need to qualify that or to say anything about how teens don't really feel love. Horseshit. They said that love's a word, a word we only heard, and can't begin to know... They really do say that.

Mary loves me but senses my – whatever it is. Reluctance? As I think about settling in with Mary, perfect Mary, it seems both thrilling and unadventurous, like *settling for* Mary. Terrible to say such a thing. It's all one can hope for, but I resist. It takes constant effort, what with Mary being what she is, so much more than I deserve. Maybe that's it. Whatever it is, I avoid serious talk with Mary that involves the state of her feelings, my feelings, or the feelings existing between us. She understands something, and, whatever it is, she accepts. It makes her miserable, but it keeps things open. And open is what I need – keep the party going, don't settle in or settle down. No endings. We'll never run out of peddlers to release.

To punctuate my desire to have an unpredictable soap opera of a time, I've dated others: Deanna Van Clausen, Sue Patterson, Jo-Ann something. For some reason, I confine myself to proper fifties dating etiquette – maybe a twiddle past the norm, if that. But how can I recognize the norm, having at my disposal only what I can gather from this heavily-coded teen culture? I have few keys. Here's what seems: handholding and a peck on first date, French-kissing on second, more French-kissing on third and subsequent dates, and on until the end of time. Donny and Glenn, even voluptuous Patty, offer no clues. I attack; they go along, sort of. These others I've dated seem warm enough. They squirm a little, waggle their tongues against mine, press against me, run fingers through hair. I sense that this is routine, an accepted ritual of the evening, meaning about as much as tooth-brushing in the morning.

Then there are the clothes. The tops seem to me kind of slutty – tight sweaters, loose blouses. The bottoms seem designed by chastity-promotion companies – ankle-length dresses of heavy wool with no give to it. True, the skirts hike up during passion-pit sessions, but not enough, even in reckless moments, to get to the knees.

The conversation, though, is often salty. I think about how that can be, decide that the self-assured girls rely on the prudish ethos of the times and their own vastly superior sophistication to protect them from anyone equating loose talk with loose behavior, open discourse with opening thighs.

That is one theory I have, not the only one.

Another is that they are as starved for advanced activity as are the boys and are reaching toward what little they can get, releasing libidinous energies by way of burning talk. Sex in the head, D. H. Lawrence's bitter description of modern eros, had been established as the only arousing practice in town. Sex in the head being better than no sex at all – maybe. For me, it isn't so much frustrating as fun. "Fun" seems an insipid term, but I can think of no better word for one of the best things I am experiencing back here in dear old 1951 East Liverpool, Ohio, home of the Potters and many fetching people.

Added to the arousing, if limited, physical fun is some skillful flirting, practiced well by nearly all the girls and poorly by all the boys. In a single between-class walk in the hall, several eye-twinkles, many hair-flips, just as many hands on the shoulders, some breast brush-againsts, and maybe even a pat or two close to butts are routine. Whorehouses are less brazen.

Mary seems outside the flirting. Maybe because she doesn't want a circular game of arousal, deferring any punctuation at the end of the sentence. She doesn't flirt, looks at me steady and clear, doesn't brush against me. But I know, were I able to summon courage and signal to her, she'd not hesitate.

I stand close, sensing that she's reading my eyes. What's she seeing? Will she tell me? I'm as curious as she to know what is crouching in my head. When I study them in the mirror, those eyes, they give back nothing. They're consistently toned, as if painted, not unlike doll eyes.

I reach out, cup her shoulder. "Hi, Mary."

"Hi, Timmy."

You remember where we were a couple of pages back? This is the girl I am about to use to get information on Glenn's forward, sexy sister. It annoys even me to admit that.

"Mary, what do you think of Betsy Downing? You know her, right?"

"Not too well. Glenn's sister, right? Your friend."

"You being sarcastic?"

"No."

"You think I have odd friends?"

142

"I like Jimmy, and Larry Talbott, Jack Probst, Sammy, Deanna, Carol, lots of your friends. I really like Donny and his wild sister."

"Um. She wild, Sally is?"

"Not in that way. She's a lot of fun."

"You're changing the subject."

"Which is?"

"Betsy Downing – and why you don't like some of my friends."

"Such as?"

"Glenn."

"I don't dislike any of your friends, Timmy. I don't know Glenn."

"But what you do know..."

"Yeah, right. No need to say. I do know his sister. She was counselor at Y-Camp when I was littler. I admired her."

"Still do?"

"Yeah. She's the smartest person I know. She's not exactly sweet but she's kind, and she's nice to poor girls and even some of the out-of-it boys. You know Michael, for instance."

This is shocking, and I have to say something irrelevant, give myself time to absorb. "But you don't think Glenn has any of that?"

"Maybe he does. It's not my business."

"C'mon, Mary."

"OK. It just seems like Glenn isn't your type. You know what I mean."

"Well, Mary, it depends on my type for what, what I want him for."

I wish I had never said that, wish I could erase the last ten seconds. Where are the celestial time fuckers when you need them?

Mary looks shocked, clearly understanding what I mean, maybe more than I mean. I hurry into the silence.

"Mary, I... I guess it's a rotten thing to do."

"You could hurt him, Tim. Why do that? He likes you, and he may be a great person, if he's anything like his sister. He's very cute. Is that it? Sorry, that's none of my business, but I do think he doesn't have much to protect himself with."

Oh shit! So much for mindless, no-consequences diddling with Glenn. Mary is as good a guilt-loader as Mom. Actually far better, as I care a whole lot what Mary thinks.

. . .

I go back and examine something I'd written to myself in mid-September, when I was cocky, operating under the illusion that I could record noteworthy, even resounding insights, make vital contributions. I hazard a look just to see why nothing is working. What have I got so wrong? What is so wrong with me?

This is not the past at all. What look like genuine real-article people are props, designed for somebody's amusement somewhere. It's a rerun, a sadistic rerun. So what matters? Is this time you're in, this fake time, disconnected entirely from what happens after? There is, in truth, no after. When this four years is over, things will pick up from their old base, not this one. Or, say that's not so, say that what happens here has consequences. Unlikely, but even if that's true and I screw up the future – so what? I'll be over eighty then. Maybe dead. You see where this is going. Why shouldn't I be as reckless with all this as the celestial authorities are with me? Outdo them in irresponsibility.

It doesn't seem anybody has been given a second chance, not even me, since I will forfeit all this superstar material when time's up. So in no sense I can grasp is this I. Nor are these people around me THEM. We aren't people, but some kind of organic toys or simulacra. The others are here as robot extras in a drama being staged for the bored. Me too, but I know it, which puts me one up on the stooges, I guess. So why not play with them myself? Why be the straight man here? Why not disrupt? Screwing all these pseudo-kids around me, these warm-blooded fakes, would be a start. Then kill some.

Of course I never did mean that part about killing, at least I hope not. I was trying to work myself up into a sense of detachment sufficient for delight. But something has happened to that detachment and to my delight. Not that I've been enveloped in goodness, but this unreal world has proved intractable. Unreal as it might be on some plain, it is *there*, at least as much as I. And whatever it is doesn't operate as a simulation. These people: they love and try and fail. If you prick us, do we not bleed?

CHAPTER 10

Basketball has kicked off with two weeks of heavy practice. I'm again on the freshman team, but at least don't have to undergo the mortification of demotion. I accept with what I regard as a good grace my assigned place alongside beginners and set about readying myself for a packed schedule. The reason we can play so often is simple: so many of the river and farm towns around who can't come up with football teams have no problem getting three gawky kids and two squirty ones to play basketball.

I plan something different this time. Mindful of how little pleasure my football experience had provided for me and my teammates, I determine to become the finest team player ever, setting world records in assists, rebounds, and steals, while leaving the scoring to others. One stimulating uncertainty: am I any good at basketball? No one has said anything about me setting prep-school records. Maybe I suck.

The collection trying out for the Potter freshman team includes a fair number of carry-overs from football, Sammy included. Sammy is his cordial self, and the others seem to have a consciousness that resets for each occasion. I don't notice Donny in the locker room, but there he is shortly thereafter in the line of kids organized by our coach. Mr. Tarinello is, I think primarily, defensive coach for the football team, but he impresses me right away by not mentioning chicken shits or drawing attention to our testicles.

The shorts we wear are so crotch-binding as to make it tough to concentrate on Tarinello's soft-voiced explanations of his policies. He has us run weave-and-circle drills, lay-ups, then three-on-three scrimmages. He knows how to keep things moving and doesn't yell at us, even encourages the clumsy ones. "Shoot off your left foot, Billy; you're right-handed. Don't worry, you'll get it." He demonstrates, clowning and getting the klutzes to enjoy themselves. Happiness athletics? This is the land of steelworkers, lives peaking at eighteen, sad dreams blasted. Not fun. But Tarinello hears a different piper.

After not much more than an hour of playing around, he calls us together.

"Don't want you boys to get exhausted the very first practice." We all look for permission to laugh and somehow get it.

"You did well. I think there's real talent here. [Truly?] One thing, though, try not to play a lot of playground ball while we're in season. I know it seems like it'd be a good idea, but trust me, it's not. You pick up bad habits and concentrate too much on shooting. Here, I want you to learn to make easy shots for others."

Right down my cleaned-up alley.

"Any questions?"

"Yeah, Coach, when are cuts?"

"There won't be. Anybody who has come out to play, will. This is to learn basketball, that's what we're doing, discovering how much fun it can be. If you want to do that, you can, and I'll try to help. I'm not saying everybody will get the same minutes in games – we want to win, too – but I'll get everybody experience. So, no cuts."

This is fantasyland. I can't tell how my be-shorted colleagues react, but I am thrilled by this generosity, though I feel a temporary shot of annoyance zing through me at the reduction in playing time I'll suffer under this Gandhi-like approach. But that passes. Amazing – even the manifestly and incurably incompetent will be included. I want to kiss craggy old Tarinello.

· · ·

All this time – did you pick up the earlier clue about "musical surprise"? – I'm working up something in the talent-show-assembly line. Now do not confuse what I am discussing with the spring concert. That's something different, and later on. This is just an all-school assembly, where the orchestra can try out its numbers prior to the spring concert, piggy-backing on a talent competition. Sounds confusing, but accuracy is all.

I sent a letter and got the rights to songs from "Carousel," a huge Broadway hit a few years earlier. A great musical, if you overlook trifling things such as wife beating, but this is the 50s, so shut up. It cost me fifteen hundred bucks to use the songs in a venue guaranteed not-for-profit. Highway robbery. But I have the money, the talent, the ego, and the plan.

I talk Dr. Lawrence Clendenning, the orchestra conductor (and a very amiable sort), into having his ensemble learn two of the songs, "If I Loved You" and "You'll Never Walk Alone." The orchestration seems complex to me – what do I know? – but the unevenly-talented crew works hard, and the pieces sound good, they really do. I had forgotten that music instruction in the schools has yet to be subjected to the growing stinginess of our country. Even here, beginning in the fourth grade, any kid can get loaner instruments, once-a-week free instruction, and cheap private lessons. Almost everyone plays something – mostly trumpets or clarinets. Clendenning has a great feel for the schmaltzy music I picked, is willing to risk overdoing it. His slow tempos and volume building are weep engendering.

A word about taste. Look here now. I know that I have the entire world of music before me, further, that I am equipped with a voice such as has never been heard. (Who will say it if not I?) Why, then, would I go to such trouble to work up clichéd ballads? Fair question. I want to show off. Something operatic would mystify and bore. A popular ballad out of Frankie Lane, Johnny Ray (just on the scene) would be possible, but humdrum, not soul-stirring. Soul-stirring is what I'm after. The "Carousel" songs have nice murky lyrics, plenty of high notes, and sweet sentiments. They encourage forceful singing, loud singing, not to put too fine a point on it. I can sing real loud. And soul-stirringly.

I have problems with "If I Loved You," an electrifying song, with aching, lovelorn, self-pitying sobs right out there, full-throated and running slowly up the spine, like electric eels let loose in the audience. But it's a duet, promising and then withdrawing love, in balanced phrases, both parties (Julie and Billy) feeling the same thing and expressing themselves in identical terms. I can hardly sing both parts, though it's tempting:

Yet somehow I can see
Just exactly how I'd be
If I loved you.

. . .

If I loved you,
Time and again I would try to say,
All I'd want you to know.
If I loved you,
Words wouldn't come in an easy way,
Round in circles I'd go!

. . .

Longin' to tell you, but afraid and shy,
I'd let my golden chances pass me by.

. . .

Soon you'd leave me, lost in the mist of the ???? [learn the lyrics!]
Never, never to know
HOWWWWWW AIIIIEEEE LOVVVVVED YEEEEWWWWWW
If I loved you.

. . .

The bare lyrics make me shake with emotion. You too.

As I say, the evident solipsism, the invitation to satiric giggling, present in doing this duet as a solo makes me cast about for a soprano. I finally find sweet-faced, short and sturdy Judith Paderewski (like the pianist). Judith has a small mouth in the midst of a white moon, a mashed-in nose, and eyes befitting a rodent. She's so shy that it's only with difficulty she can be persuaded to speak. Even then, she whispers.

"Judith, do you know the musical 'Carousel'?"

"A little," she murmurs. People have spoken more forcefully from the depths of a coma.

"What? Don't be nervous, Judith. I'm not going to make you go off the high dive."

She laughs, doesn't up her volume. Why did Dr. Clendenning suggest her, well, mention her? "You might try that Paderewski girl, Tim. I think somebody told me she could sing."

"Listen, Judith, would you try a duet with me? I think it'd be fun. You know 'If I Loved You,' right? Will you sing it with me?"

I think she hisses an assent. Only the angels or the titmice could have heard her.

But she picks up the sheet music and I start in on the prelude, a silly talky thing: "Hey, you been putting ideas in my head? What makes me think I might love you?" She goes first on the song, after a swelling orchestral prelude I can only simulate on the piano, skilled as I am. (Surprise! I couldn't play the piano at all as Harold, but this Tim fellow is accomplished, that's the word, accomplished!).

And then she starts:

"But somehow I can see, just exactly how I'd be –
If I loved you, words wouldn't come –"

I almost stop playing, so sweet and right is her voice. No accounting for it, the assurance and the power; the quality, the timbre perfect for this song. Though there isn't much polish, it's still an unusual soprano, with depth and overtones. Judith's voice may be limited by its heavy sweetness, but the sweetness is there, and, even more mysteriously, a strong lyric expressiveness. It's genuinely moving to hear her sing of an almost-love, offering it to Billy and watching him hesitate, then turn away. As the song elevates itself, so does Judith, finally soaring.

It comes my turn, and I am super-ready, echoing back to Julie Jordan her own sentiments, minus the pleading, but with all the hope. Her soprano hides beneath my tenor, as we approach the climax, but it does not cower. There's enough mutuality here to bring down the house, to saturate and elevate anyone, certainly Judith and me, sweet and doomed Julie Jordan and charming asshole (more asshole than charming) Billy Bigelow.

As the last chord dies, Judith looks at me, bidding me come to her with those teeny eyes. How can I not? We embrace operatically. A kiss would have been vulgar. I break away, shining. So shines she. No stammer and no shyness. My God, can she sing!

As for me, it's always tough to know what sounds are working out there, so trapped is my voice inside cranial cavities and their echoes. But there's little doubt. I'm not letting go with everything, but I'm not holding much in reserve either. What I'm hearing is rapturous, perhaps a little too La Boheme-ish and not enough Broadway. That can be adjusted. I'll get advice.

For now, Judith and I stand there staring at one another, wearing grins that only those outside the spell would find silly. I'm about to suggest another go, when the curtains part and the choir director, another Dr., bursts in.

I should have explained that we're rehearsing on a closed-curtained stage. That stage, deep and wide, is elevated, set at one end of an auditorium proudly serving as basketball arena, gym class territory, theater, and assembly hall – emphasis on "hall." It's huge, seating maybe 2000 on the sides, and nearly double that when the floors are be-chaired, as for a play. It has the acoustics of a padded cell. But I'll bet Judith and I make the rafters ring.

"Good Gravy! I wondered who was doing that. I thought it was a recording, I honest to John did. I had no idea. What are you two doing? I mean, who are you? What are you doing this for? You rehearsing? You getting ready for something? Who are you? Tim, I know you, right? Of course I do. Who are *you*?"

Half this quantity of dumbass browbeating would have been sufficient to yank Judith and me out of our bewitchment.

"Dr. Randolph, this is Judith Paderewski, the finest lyric soprano anywhere."

It takes a host of pledges for future engagements to disengage ourselves from Randolph, but he finally leaves and we run through it again. I thought we might have lost the oomph, but within a few bars we reach the same territory that had claimed us before, now even more at home, more willing to extend and explore.

We then move to the arrangement I've done of "You'll Never Walk Alone," putting the two voices in harmony. It hadn't sounded bad on the piano, but even Judith and I can't mask what a lousy job it was. So, we decide to dive into the difficult: doubling the phrasing in many places, adding bridges, creating two new sections. Judith is perhaps not a composition genius, but she's much closer to that than I, and she has terrific instincts about how to let one phrase grow into another. As for me, I can translate notes on a page to sounds in my head and the other way round. As her work takes shape, so does a duet of more complexity and subtlety than the song deserves. But it'll take it – and we'll deliver it.

I rough it out quickly on the piano and finally get to the point where we can try a full run-through. Minor adjustment, major adjustment, tinker, tinker rejected, my idea dropped, her idea adopted. Then we sing the whole thing at full volume.

When you walk through a storm –

We rip right through and beyond the conventional sentiments and made it into another love song.

At the end, we again embrace. Strangely, when we break apart, we laugh. It is passion, pure and simple, but it is – how shall I put this without sounding pretentious? – the passion of high art, engendered by the God Dionysus, dangerous and transcendent. Maybe more like pure high-flown adolescent excitement, born in the mind and played along the pulses.

Neither of us notices that we have been slaving into the night. In January the night comes early, but we've been warbling in the dark for a good two hours, and it's now eight o'clock, long past time for us to be home, even had we a way to get there. But there are auditorium phones, nickels to use them, and compliant parents. Judith's quiet folks give me a ride, while I try to keep alive a conversation. I feel I know mysterious grottoes hidden deep in this girl's remarkable sensibility, but I do not know her at all in the way one usually does. Inside music, though, we couple perfectly, and we're ready to spring on the student body a compulsory rapture.

．．．

You don't have to be the one to tell me that there is some ego floating all this hard work, but give me this: the act of singing sobby songs at least doesn't involve disrobing some youth who doesn't really want disrobed. That's a start, a sop to a battered conscience.

I decide to extend myself into out-and-out good deeds. I figure any dip into decency will be, as they say, a drag, but as soon as I get to planning, I discover that righteousness really is its own reward. The more I give my mind to this scheme, the more I become bubbly-boiled by it, thrilled by every mundane detail. I start with the Dean of Boys, a fifties swell fella I remember from his many kindnesses to Harold. I want him now in his capacity as a member of Rotary, a service club on the lookout for ways to make clear that it is serving.

"Tim! How's basketball?" Dean Nelson is a handsome man, no taller than Sally. He shakes my hand, a gracious gesture for an adult at my school, most of whom regard the students as defective infants.

"Basketball's fine, Dean, really fun." That's pathetic, and even a man immured to student reticence looks disappointed, so, always more than equipped to please, I proceed: "Coach Tarinello is remarkable, letting everyone play, encouraging those of us who aren't as good, taking it as his job to teach. What a difference from football."

"Is that right?" Nelson's smile doesn't diminish, but his enthusiasm is now auto-piloted.

"We're also good, if I do say so, the team, I mean. Donny's the key, I expect you know." (He stands in some sort of blood relationship to Donny, resembling him not a little.)

"Not what he tells me. You are the best athlete this school's ever seen. So, what can I do for you, bub?"

"I want to start a large-scale program to tackle the problem of good kids who have been held back in school somewhere along the line and now are in high school and feeling lost, often just waiting until they are old enough to quit."

He doesn't say anything, nodding to let me know I should go on.

"I think schools take these kids for granted, let them put in the time, and that's why our senior class is about half the size of the freshman. You know, Dean, right now these dropouts can get jobs at Hall China or Crucible Steel, but we don't know if these jobs are going to be there forever. Besides, even if they are, dropping-out limits choices. Now, some may really want to quit, but I think others might do it because they have somehow internalized – ah, been convinced that they're dumb, when they really aren't, not at all."

"That's true, Tim. Go on."

"What if we started with those freshmen who are a year or more behind, have flunked at least once. Let's call them 'at-risk,' our 'at-risk' population."

"I like that."

I knew he would. The future is coming in handy by furnishing hackneyed terms, springtime fresh now.

"Say we get a group of student volunteers and supplement them with Rotary members, form a tutoring corps, like the old CCC. We could also get community members involved. We'd be the first city to take seriously the dilemma of good kids who have special needs. We could call it 'Save the Children.'" (I know, I know.)

"God damn it! Yes!"

I like it that the Dean, Ralph we all call him, doesn't apologize for his collegial language.

"But if this is big, we need to do it right. And we need to keep it going past a burst of up-front enthusiasm. We need a full-time coordinator, a fundraiser, and a consultant on learning disabilities. That'll take some dough. I think the Rotary can handle the publicity and stir up the volunteers among its own membership and in town. I can get kids from

ELHS. But we need money to pay the three people I mentioned. Rotary, right? Fundraisers? The guys I know at SPEBSQSA could do fundraisers, and you'd know a lot more who are good at that. Those SPEBSQSA guys, some of them, would be good mentors, too. I forgot to say that we'd call our team a corps, a corps of mentors, not teachers. Often, what these at-risk kids need is not just school help, but help with life: advice, kindness, hope, an encouraging squeeze."

Dean Nelson jumps up in his chair. For a second I think he's annoyed, but then he settles back, takes out a pad and pencil. For maybe three minutes he writes quietly, looking up periodically to assure me he knows I'm there.

"Moses in the Bulrushes, Tim. This is the best idea. We can do a lot of good – not every student, though, I expect. You weren't thinking..."

"Oh no. I have no idea –"

"How many. But we'll get some, and the program will have so many side benefits. I'm not just thinking of good publicity either, but, hell, we could -

"Create a real community; nobody is left out and we share not only our money but –"

"Our caring."

That isn't where I would have taken the sentence, but it's OK by me. We pause and laugh, aware of the way we are banging oars, tipping the canoe in our excitement.

We spend a half-hour divvying up phone calls and letters, Ralph taking eighty percent of them. I've previously located a learning disabilities person and an administrator, both from Carnegie Tech, just down-river in Pittsburgh. As for a fund-raiser, I'm not sure there are such things in 1952, but someone in Rotary will know. I hadn't thought there were learning disabilities experts either, but my Carnegie Tech smarty tells me there are a few in the area. The term "learning disabilities specialist" doesn't exit, of course, but the work itself does.

I'm almost out of the office.

"Will you let Donny be involved?"

It hadn't crossed my mind. Even affection cannot blind me to Donny's limitations – or what I take to be limitations, likely imposed by me, now that I think of it.

Ralph notices my hesitation, so I hurry in. "Of course. He'll be terrific."

"Do you think so?" Ralph speaks with an equal amount of pride and hesitation, a need to be told that his little whatever (nephew?) can handle something other than a basketball.

I lose no time speaking confidently of Donny's hitherto unsuspected abilities. I'm not, after a minute, faking. Till now, I've been guilty of taking Donny's timid self-evaluation at face value. I think other kids undervalue him as much as I, and for the same reasons.

Ralph listens, soaking heartfelt assurances he clearly is happy to gather in.

"Oh thanks, Tim. You know Donny dotes on you."

It's time for something more from me, even unnecessary risk-taking. "It's mutual, Dean. Of course he won't say it. He sets records in modesty. He's better at everything than he will ever say, better than he can believe. He's a wonderful person – and friend. We're very close, Ralph – Dean."

He smiles.

"Yeah, we're close."

He doesn't blink. "He's very lucky."

"I am."

CHAPTER 11

Speaking of Donny brings to mind that this do-gooding isn't, and you knew it, meant to be its own reward. Nobody is better situated to reward me than I, so I call Carol with a plan.

"Hi, Bubbles."

"Hello there, tin man."

"I have an idea about how we can date, actually date and not just sneak around, running off to vacant lots and hotel rooms together. That's getting dangerous, don't you think?"

"Thrilling, though."

"Yeah. I love you, Carol."

How did that slip out? Too much Harold, blowsy old Harold.

Carol doesn't miss a beat. "I love you too, Tim, but I don't know if we mean the same thing. How many people are you in love with?"

No time to be dishonest.

"I know. You for sure. Donny, Mary, Glenn, Glenn's sister, whatshername."

"Not very gallant of you to forget her name."

"It's Betsy, yes it is. The reason I have trouble is that before I thought her name was Beth Ann or Bunny, and that planted the uncertainty in my mind, and – you don't care."

"Right. I like Betsy; she's fine. Is that the question?"

"No."

"And the question is?"

"OK. All I know is I love you."

"Sounds like a song."

"They always tell me I'm a fool//What do they know, when you're so cool//Owls may hoot and cows may moo//All I know is I love you!"

"You're in love with the world, like old Jesus or Miss Blaine's favorite, Walt Whitman."

"It's not that I love everybody the same, or... Anyway, Carol, I have an idea of how we can date without sneaking. And here it is: I talk to your mother and get her approval, her being the tight-ass in chief hindering our perfectly innocent and idiotically normal activity, common to all the young and the healthy. Did I mention healthy?"

"You talk to her and convince her straight out that these healthy activities of youth don't lead her daughter into being shipped off for an abortion, right?"

"Not straight out. I won't say it, not straight out, you know, not in those words."

"I hope not. OK, do it."

"Yeah?"

"Yeah."

The phone went quiet. Then I realize Carol is putting dragon mama right on the phone, oh Jesus.

"Hello, Tim." Came the fluty voice one could learn to hate.

"Hello, Mrs. Blake. Are you well?" Brilliant start.

"I'm fine, Tim. What can I do for you?"

"I'm glad. I want to ask you something, Mrs. Blake, and I hope you'll hear me out." Moving right along. "I know you're reluctant to have Carol dating, and I understand that. But what we want to do is not so much dating as being together so we can talk and have simple good times – go to basketball games, things like that, the teen center and school events that everyone goes to. That's all. We like each other. You know that. We want to spend time together, just the way friends do..." Bad time to run out of gas.

"Well, Tim, I see what you mean. You understand I don't want to keep Carol from having fun. I wouldn't want her to think of me as her jailer."

"Oh, no, Mrs. Blake, and she doesn't."

"Yes, she does, Tim. Don't say what you don't know anything about. Sorry. I don't mean to be harsh. I also don't want to be smooth-talked into doing what's wrong. You're persuasive, Tim, but I don't think you're being completely honest."

"True, I am trying to persuade you, but I'm not lying. I'm putting a spin on things."

"You're what? I guess I understand."

"We're not wild kids, Mrs. Blake."

"I think kids are kids, Tim. At your age... Never mind."

"Even if you don't trust me, you can trust Carol. I'm sure you do."

"Damn it, kid. Stop trying to persuade me. If you had any sense, you'd shut up and see that I'm about to agree with you."

"Oh."

"So, OK. It's gonna happen, and you probably aren't a whole lot worse than the run of the lot. If you hurt her..."

"So, it's OK?"

"Yes it is. I'll think up rules and curfews, but you've won."

"I didn't think it was a battle."

"Sure you did. To be fair, which I haven't been, I can see that it seemed like you were freeing a girl, breaking her out of jail. You thought you could make me see that and we'd all be friends. It's naïve of you, kid, but sweet too – maybe. When you get older..."

If she only knew. But we have, as she says, won. All sick momma can do is withdraw as gracefully as she can, be fussy, but never again in charge. One can almost feel sorry for her. She's defined herself as a caring parent, thrown all she had into that noxious being, nothing left over, and now it's all dried up and blown away. She simply isn't. Bye-bye.

Heartlessly trodding on the still-warm corpse, we set off on our first date the next day, right after school. My plan is to go for a walk, cold as it is, eat at the diner, and then take in a movie before heading to the Bide-A-Wee Motel. I don't even buy a condom, not because I decide not to but because it doesn't occur to me. Mrs. Blake needn't have worried. I'm enough a child of the fifties to imagine that it'd be disrespectful to do the old turkey trot with a decent girl. Possibly Carol's thinking on the matter is more advanced than mine; otherwise, we'll be lucky to get to hand-holding. Truth: I just want to be with her and alone.

For this time it's not imagination,
Or a dream that will fade and fall apart!

It's love!

This time it's love, my foolish heart.

(Wonder if that's been written yet? I have these absolute sure-bet hit tunes squirreled away in my head. Might as well turn it to my advantage. But not now. Besides, I fixate on what should be throwaway lines. "A dream that will fade and fall apart." Why should I think of that?)

The walk idea comes as an inspiration, though I realize as we start that date walking is not fifty-ish or East Liverpool-ish. Nobody walks for pleasure, only to get from right here to over there. Maybe, for that very reason, Carol will like it, "dig it."

She tolerates it.

I'm concentrating on noticing things. It strikes me for some reason, about six minutes into the date, that I had raced through my Harold-life so self-involved that I'd been blind and deaf, hardly recording what was passing before me. Battened in cotton wool, my senses were dimmed, automatic and uninvolved, and the world was enveloped in a sack, lumpy and indistinct. This is the time to smell, hear, see. Feel, too, which particular sensory need is doubtless fed by the body next to me, cool palm pressed to mine, now and then squeezing.

This park is, in better weather (almost any weather would be), unspoiled and comfortable, a park for the people. Nothing is here to mark it as a park beyond a road circling back to picnic pavilions and a swimming pool, now closed, way down over the hill. No nature trails, tennis courts, ball-fields. Probably the trees have been thinned out and some open areas maintained. The usual East Liverpool greenery, around the river basin, is jungle-lush, but here one can navigate easily. Of course, the January cold does in the leaves, but there is still for walkers the joy of happening onto a clearing, a rolling, sometimes steeply-graded meadow, where trees block nothing, arrange themselves for picturesque pleasures. It is possible that Carol and I are the only pleasure-walkers these grounds have ever seen. Old folks don't hobble around for health, lovers use cars, and jogging, thank God, is still in the future. People might picnic, come throw a ball, or park to neck. But we are the first to walk. Or so says me.

I'm about to mention this to Carol, but it seems goofy even as I strain to think it. Maybe I'm not cut out to be observant: truly receptive people would produce more easy-flowing reveries. Noticing means being clever, which is hard work. All those years teaching the Romantics in my earlier go-round have caused me to repeat a lovely idea so often I suppose I believe it: that the external world is not just out there, but is created partly by our perception of it, that what we take to be alien objects are actually coordinate with our view of them. There's no world apart from our experience with and of it, and our own being does not rest inside us but in a series of fusions, symbiotic minglings.

Focusing so intently on the rocks and rills leaves me less room for keeping up with Carol's conversation. Noticing my absorption, or maybe just bored, Carol joins my silence. Rather than breaking it, I decide I'll switch my observing from the January landscape to my companion.

Carol, apart from being so zesty she could do as smelling salts, is magnetizing. Her facial bones are sharp, the chin narrow, and the forehead made sweet by bangs. She has gold-brown eyes and lion-pelt hair with streaks of brighter yellow. So soft I start stroking it.

That puts a temporary stop to the observing – and the walking. Carol kisses me, puts her own un-grabbed hand into my hair. It doesn't last but a jiffy, but still – still what? It's what it is, and what it is Carol could tell you better than I. I react to the kiss with stupor, Carol by smiling.

We begin walking again, and for the first time in this life or any other, I feel in complete accord with someone, can act and react without planning, wondering what the other might think. Fade and fall apart – ha! For all my anxiety in getting her to a date, these several months of half-baked plotting and impatient waiting, I have given little thought to her thought. That's strange, a state not fully explained by selfishness, though that's part of it. Have I found an accord with this girl or am I indifferent to her? I'm not trying to read her, recognizing that she isn't legible, and I don't want to oversimplify her. That's good, but have I simply found a drama I enjoy for all the pleasures it gives me, the meaty role just right for Tim? Could it be that the other roles doled out to those around me are nothing but supporting bits, the particular actresses irrelevant?

"You enjoying the walk, Carol?"

"It's fun, Tim, as it turns out."

"That means you didn't expect it to be."

"Right. I can't remember just walking, pointlessly, since I was six."

"Yeah."

My tone must have betrayed my chagrin. Carol laughs.

"No, really, it warms up the blood, walking here in the drizzle, wondering if we'll survive or slowly freeze to death like in the Jack London story."

"They'll find us tomorrow, permanently joined."

"Ice block Romeo and Juliet, sung about by bards, a legend for young lovers."

"Young lovers! That's a nice way to put it, Carol."

"Yeah, isn't it?"

What's going on? I wasn't much more clueless first time around, though I hadn't then been troubled with lines like this one.

We stroll, holding hands. It really isn't drizzling, though it's not gorgeous weather, more like terrible – dark, windy, thirty-four degrees. The trees are not the sort to sway in the breeze, so it's a bit like walking through an abandoned battlefield, stark and featureless. Still, it truly is blood-warming, the walk or Carol's mobile and affectionate presence. After the "young lovers" comment, she turns to unthreatening subjects, unquestionably out of pity for her shy, nervous, eager, scared, confused, know-nothing, happy friend.

But I decide to try.

"Carol I want to know you, not just to make assumptions."

She looks at me, saying nothing.

"I'm so self-absorbed."

"Tim, if you were self-absorbed, it'd never worry you that I'm a replaceable part."

"Thanks."

"It's not a compliment. We do know one another some. More will come."

"It will?"

"Oh, yes – and quickly, too."

"Why?"

"Because of our love – and the time. The time..."

I'm so moved by the love part, I let the rest pass.

"Carol, did you ever notice that, you know, we hardly ever notice things, mainly?"

"I don't mean to be rude, but what on earth did you just say?"

"I've been thinking that we go through life with blinders on, more like blindfolded. We don't really see the world around us at all."

I look at her, striding there with her muscular legs covered by a long skirt probably not warming her much in this Alaskan weather, wind blowing right up into her mid-region. She doesn't say anything but smiles, urging me to continue with this line, perhaps registering that I'm approaching comprehensibility. Maybe she isn't smiling, just clenching her teeth and shivering.

"Right now, for instance, I've been trying to make myself put into words what I'm seeing, exactly and in detail, so the words will bring into being that very world, as if the world were only there if I speak it. Browning said that, only about painting, 'We're made so that we first see what we've passed a thousand times, only after having it painted for us.' That's not right, but it's what he means: art makes the world for us and makes us in the world. The creative imagination doesn't represent what's already there; it creates what's outside us, what's inside us, and coordinates the two. It doesn't *show* us; it determines us. Carol, we aren't ever fully coordinated with ourselves or with the world. The dream of full presence can only be approached by an effort of art. What I mean is that trying to make prose poems in my head keeps me alive, guards me from going through these days, these precious days, without being in them at all. I want to live more completely. What it takes is noticing, pushing at the world so that it pushes back."

I'm sputtering in my eagerness, registering my preposterousness, counting on Carol to provide the brains missing from my babble.

"I think these trees look like stakes, crucifixion stakes."

"They do? Oh, I see. Yeah." With great effort, I choke off telling Carol what she means by that, explicating for her the connections between crucifixion and this dead park.

163

"As we move along through these trees, we're walking through a deep pattern of time, layers. And that's why crucifixion means what it does. Jesus's crucifixion took place at one time but is also there all the time, so it carries all that time with it, like the trees."

"Yeah."

"It's nice of you to let me try and say this, Tim. Let me go on, OK?"

"Yeah."

"I was so stirred by what you said. It made me want to cry, the golden days slipping by and we don't notice. We're corpses, dead and deader. So very very few days. And now thinking of these trees as crosses. But it's not sad, and it's not just in the past. I want to say more than I can. I guess it's all the life, the life that you are talking about. When you notice, even notice dead-looking trees, you're alive, even on this dumb walk, sorry, and that makes them live and us love. So, thinking of crucifixion makes me move more fully into time and hope, just like our walk, which shouldn't mean anything, but seems somehow pulsing with possibility and mystery, and makes me feel so close to it all. Even in this little blink, not even real. My older brother, I don't think you know him, he's at Ohio State, read me a passage from a book."

She pauses, but clearly means to continue.

"It's *A Portrait of the Artist as a Young Man*, by James Joyce, where the hero talks about being close to the wild heart of life. That's what I want to feel---dangerously close."

"To me?" I'm immediately sorry I said that, but she doesn't miss a beat.

"I need to think about that. I don't know if that's what I mean or not. It's more like, once you start, you live in everything, not just in a single person or tree or just one look or feeling. Let me keep trying. I don't mean to be rude when I say I don't think it's you. It's not that it's not you, but I was trying to talk about something bigger or different. That sounds rude."

"You're inside the feeling, and that's hard to express. But unless you try, then it doesn't exist. I can't say it, but it's important to try. If we take the risk to put ourselves in a way of thinking that we're both after, then the words and the world are one, an ecological system."

"A what? That's OK. I don't need to know. I'm trying to find out by talking. I'm trying to find out how all this is part of you, connected to you. Sure it is, somehow, but it's more like me opening something than you letting me do it."

"Yeah."

She's quiet, walking steadily, quickly, frowning too, but not in anger.

"Carol, you speak so lucidly. You never say 'uh' or 'you know' or 'like.' You have direct pipelines from your imagination and your heart to your tongue."

"Umm." She isn't listening.

"Listen, Ms. Rudeness, I was trying not to fixate on you, but that's all I did. I was thinking about how like cut grass you smell, how sharp your bone structure is, how your eyes dance, how uncomfortable your legs must be with a skirt, leaving your thighs and all open to the cold."

"My thighs and all. What are you bringing to life out here in this deserted park?"

I am, idiot that I be, offended. "Carol! I wasn't lusting after you or imagining looking up your skirt. It just was part of noticing you in detail, differently. Or trying. Trying to imagine so strongly there is no separation. You know, I wasn't just undressing you in my mind."

"Stop, Tim!"

"Sorry."

"I know, hun. I shouldn't have made the joke, but it was a joke. I know you were talking me into being, making me into art. I do understand. It just also seemed a little funny, that about my bare thighs."

"Yeah, it does."

"That's not flattering. Carol and her funny thighs, clown thighs, all blubbly and wiggly."

"Your thighs are solemn things. That's a guess, since you keep them hidden. Hint, hint."

Cold stare.

"I suppose you're right, though. My vision of the wind blowing up inside your pretty pleated skirt, raising it up among the trees, was not entirely artsy. It popped in, that pornographic picture, right into my exalted talk – and that's why I got jumpy. Mixed in with my observation of the twigs were some schoolboy fascinations. The more I talk about it, the more I really do seem like that fourth-grade schoolboy during recess."

"And you're not a schoolboy? I understand. Want to go find a playground so I can hang upside down on the monkey bars?"

"Oh yes! How did you know I had a panty fetish?"

"Everybody knows that about you."

"They do?"

"Tim! And what makes you think I wear panties? Who knows what I have up there? Khaki army shorts, burlap bloomers, nothing."

It seems a good time to stop and kiss.

·   ·   ·

We reach an agreement that walking and vivifying the world might now yield to something warm and tasty. Eating out was an uncommon practice my first time around, when my parents found occasion to visit a restaurant maybe bi-annually. I know three places in town, two diners and one that aspires to tearoom elegance. Carol, her opinion sought, leans gently but firmly toward the cheaper of the two diners. Even when I explain that I'm loaded even beyond the demands of the Helen Marshall Dean Dining Room, she still pushes gently away. My familiarity with that room, cloth napkins and all, derives from my annual birthday dinner first time through, when my mother took Harold to the swimming pool, to a movie, and then to the Helen Marshall Dean place to eat halibut. I remember those fish from the Harold good times, Mom at her kind-hearted best. But the diner will do: roast beef open-faced, mashed spuds, and gravy sounds terrific. Wonder how they make so much gravy, if "make it" describes its origins. The diner was close to the bus, so we can avoid extending our walk beyond our endurance. Likely, Carol has thought of that. She is unquestionably thoughtful, even if she hasn't thought specially of me, there in the park, amongst the crucifixion trees. I ought to forget that and think of Carol, what she was saying. Don't lose it. We seem to be losing so much.

On the bus (the fare covered by our school bus passes), headed for the Dan-Dee, we say little, because we feel so much.

. . .

I almost suggest salad, which would have given me away: no salads on the menu. Have I told her already of my sci-fi status (from which I am profiting so little)? No, though I was supposing there would come a time for it, maybe on the walk, and that hadn't happened, had it?

"What are you going to have, Carol? I'm from the future."

"Cheeseburger, Tim."

"I'm going for the gravy bowl, with the bread and last week's roast beef hidden beneath."

"My dad always gets that, 'always' being the once a year we celebrate by going out and wish we hadn't. Your family like that?"

"Exactly. Well, that's what I had remembered in 2016, but it's not quite true. My dad, you know him?"

"Not really. My dad likes him, says he's the most honest man he knows."

For some reason, I am so moved.

"I think he may set records there. You know what he makes, Carol? Fifty dollars a week, plus a tiny commission. He can't buy anything for himself. He got tickets for a Steelers game from one of the stores he calls on, a grocery store up in Midland, and took Joanie and me to Forbes Field. We went to this place close to the field. He urged us to get a second piece of pie. 'Have more pie. That peach pie is the best in the country.' I vow not to forget that again. I forgot it before. 'The best in the country.' And of course he didn't have any. Generally, you're right about eating out, but my dad, he's a celebrator. Even if he had money, he'd still never buy anything for himself. It'd be all holidays and special times."

I start to cry. It seems so already gone. Maybe it's that and maybe it's guilt, brought on by having forgotten, by suspecting I will forget again, by not caring enough. Maybe I can learn to care and to hold on. Peach pie.

Things are vanishing even now, slipping through our fingers. I keep stopping my crying, apologizing, and then starting back up. Carol is crying, too. Then she comes over and sits on my side of the booth, holding me.

"You kids OK? Oh, honeys, it'll be fine. Can I help? Things'll improve."

"We're OK, really," I say.

"Hi, Mrs. Poole," Carol says.

"You sure? You need something? Want me to call your parents?"

"Thanks, no."

"You know how it is."

"You bet I do. Hey, are you – don't tell me – Carol Blake! How are you anyhow?"

"Just great, Mrs. Poole. This is Tim Mills."

"Hi, Tim. My, how good-looking you are! Both of you! Are you OK, honey, you and your friend?" It wasn't clear which of us she is addressing. Her crossed eyes are shifting around enthusiastically, without any clear target. Carol accepts the challenge.

"Thanks, Mrs. Poole. We're fine. We're just feeling a little lost, as if what we want we'll never get, hard as we try – there'll be no time, isn't any time."

"Oh yes, I know. You poor dears. Just flash me a sign when you're ready. No hurry."

Soon I'm better, feel a strange mixture of sorrow and elation.

"So, you're from the future, Tim?" I hadn't realized Carol'd caught my sledgehammer announcement. She hasn't moved from beside me, nor lifted her hand from my shoulder.

"I guess so. Let me explain."

And I do. Right through the good food and maybe a half-hour beyond.

"So, my own memory of Harold has been replaced with you. That's interesting." Actually, Carol hasn't given much indication she finds my news all that interesting.

"That's one word for it."

"What does Joanie think?"

"She says it really doesn't matter. If this is a rerun or some half-assed experiment or just a delusion on my part, we have no choice but to take what we have as all we have and throw ourselves into it, moment by moment, doing our best. Mary says the same."

I suddenly wonder if I should've mentioned Mary. Carol shoots me a look I can't interpret, which doesn't distinguish it from most of the signals she emits: all are beyond me. Surely Harold hadn't been this inept.

Carol continues in a voice so soft, "That's wise, Tim. And true. Take what is as real, since there's no other choice. It doesn't completely satisfy me, though, does it you?"

"How?"

"How? You mean 'why?' I don't mean to criticize Mary and Joanie, but I think there's angles you haven't considered, Sam Spade. And I think you don't realize how troubled you are. Putting it the way Joanie and Mary do makes sense, but it's also a little like giving up, isn't it? They're right that that's how we live, not thinking much. But why not try to find out? There must be ways, not to be certain but to try. Not trying is what you were saying about not noticing, just zombie walking. Why be dead before you have to be? It won't last long."

She pauses, but I'm not tempted to interrupt. I can almost taste her earnestness.

"And you say you have most of your old memory, right? You say they messed up in filling you in on your Tim past. If that's so, and you know some of the future, it seems to me we have ways of finding out. For starters, if things turn out the way you think, then it looks like a run-through."

"Or I am gifted with the power to…"

"I'll take 'run-through.'"

"Then we know." I explain the baseball bet.

"I'm still not satisfied. There are other ways of looking at it, right? Fantasy, dream, memory-rewind? Can we keep at this, Buck Rogers?"

"You betcha."

"You were worried I'd be jealous of Mary, weren't you?"

"Yes." I never get used to Carol's delayed-action way of conducting the conversation.

"Well, I am, sort of. She's a friend of mine."

"Yeah."

"What do you think she feels about you?"

"I don't know. We've been buddies since we were two years old. I don't

169

recall that, but it's so. I think it was true of Tim and not exactly Harold, only Tim wasn't Tim when he was two, so it's very confusing."

"It counts for real, your counselors tell you. So, what do you think Mary feels for you?"

"Friendship, I guess, trust."

"Ummmm." Carol gives me another look I don't want to decipher.

. . .

The movie, walk to the bus, riding home, walk to the door: all the same. Glorious for me, so all-encompassing that it seems the very heart of being fourteen. I hope so. I hope everyone, at least once, has this experience. It all wouldn't seem so wasteful then, so empty. Carol and I exchange vows of love. I feel close to her – a little like everything we were talking about on our walk through the wet and cold, the way imagination can construct a sweet world and invite us into all that is unfolding right there before us. Carol seems passionate in goodnight kissing and not at all worried. Even then, I wonder if we are there in an absolute way, present to ourselves and the other, an experience that won't come ever again. But I have sense enough to toss that reflection away and enter into Carol's arms and heart, unable to distinguish either from my own. Still, something in me holds back. It is Carol who is moving, roving hands in decent zones, making buzzy noises. It isn't that I don't want to proceed – and proceed and proceed. But I don't, maybe so the evening will have no resolution. What is this beautiful girl doing rubbing against me, inviting me to hop into the sack? Certainly the last invitation is received and not sent, but all that trust she has for me, the fun she is having: I feel it so strongly I want not to advance, to stay inside what we have, to defeat time.

. . .

Oh, I believe in yesterday.

. . .

Everyone in Harold's later time knew that the fifties were sick, nowhere more positively than in its equation of sex with dirt: only crumbum girls had sex. Decisively freeing itself from that pathological nonsense, the sixties ushered in an era of easy sex, healthy views. Not for me. The more I come to feel a warm curiosity for someone, the more it seems wrong to roll around with them. True with Carol, truer with Mary, true with Donny, and yes, with rich shit Glenn. Even slutty Patty had fooled me into liking her and cancelling my sensible plans to teach her the joys of masochism. But it isn't my decency working but their own, and a lot beyond that – a sense that something beautiful is floating here in 1952, something that I not only should not defile but that might, if I'm worthy, enfold me.

CHAPTER 12

The next day I extend my curiosity by enduring a church trip with Mom and Joanie, Dad, as always, staying home. Predictably, I'm tempted by cynicism. After all, this is unreconstructed evangelical nonsense, a fifties version of know-nothing Christianity dirtying otherwise innocent East Liverpool. This particular merchant of salvation is housed in a split-level, often added-to, concrete-block cube, not high on the list of prestige assignments for ministers, even if there were discernible levels of quality among those choosing this line of work. All in all, though, this congregation probably gets the ministerial quality it wants: nincompoops reflecting Methodism's official aversion to thought. Getting together to pour contempt on the heathen, they batten on hell-fire talk that nobody in the house believes applies to her or, to be fair, anybody very particular, the conversation soon veering from hell to gossip, from serious sins to divorce, "running around," "carousing." These decent people get their mean fix here every week. Sounds bad, but maybe it isn't. Perhaps it drains what otherwise would fester, releasing some of the anger built up by fear, ignorance, and poverty, freeing them to deal fairly with life on the other six days.

The cost is high. "All my silver, all my gold – not a mite will I withhold!" This tuneful hymn is chosen as an apt accompaniment to the sermon, a vaguely accusatory discourse devoted to the slow pace at which the new rec center building fund is growing, threatening the souls of the community youth. And then there's the matter of the choir robes...

It really isn't so bad, and I have to work at the sneers. Why bother? I enjoy the show, certainly the music, and the many odd distractions. The choicest come in reading the windows put in as memorials to good servants of Christ now gone to their reward.

For Elmer Mauldin, Husband, Father, and Devoted Christian

He Died as He Lived, For His Lord

Wonder what that meant, dying for His Lord? Did he drop while resisting the pull of carousing?

None of the girls and boys I'm currently pursuing attend this church. I'd made a study of other teens likely to be here. Unhappily, the comely ones were younger than I, which wouldn't matter were they not quite so much younger, about three or four years. No pedophile I.

There's a tradition among the neighborhood church-going obliging each family to race home following the benediction and dig into a huge meal. I know this because the preacher regularly makes a joke about it, just to show what a plain-folks guy he is. "I don't want your roasts to burn and neither does God." Mom and Dad happily veer from this eating practice and maintain the same lunch-dinner weight ratio that obtains throughout the week. I have the feeling that this is Dad's decision. True, I attribute all happy practices to him, a verdict probably quite fair to my mother, so no need to feel guilty.

After two BLTs and some great baked beans (really were – navy beans with onions and, what the hell, ketchup) I try mid-afternoon to talk Joanie into joining me for a walk. She's willing to be with me but first suggests eighteen other activities.

"Lazy Daisy!"

"Timmy, it's four degrees out, slippery and dim. It'll be walking through an icy sewer."

"Just over to the playground."

"I'd do anything for you, but can't it be something else?"

"Bitch!"

Joanie is shocked, knows I'm kidding but still shocked. I cover it by attacking, wrestling her to the floor and tickling her in a playful as hell way. She twists around and my hand ends up on her breast. I hadn't been aware that she had breasts, but she does. This isn't my day. Joanie makes out not to notice, as do I. I play goofy big brother, tell her I'll take the walk on my own, expecting her to come along anyhow. She doesn't.

So I set off. It's miserably cold, but I move fast and am bundled up. I figure I'll make it to the park, retracing the steps Carol and I had taken (and wasting a good half-mile being angry with Joanie). True, it's a good twenty degrees colder than when Carol and I had traipsed here, but a loving sister would've come along. Yes! After ten minutes, I'd exorcised my horror at groping Joan and try to turn to other things. Only I can't find other things I want to think about. Its fun walking, in an animal kind of way, so I abandon myself to putting one foot before the other, noticing nothing.

Before I know it, I'm a couple of miles from home, in the park, making my way along a dirt road that hadn't been bad when Carol and I were upon it. Now it's a battlefield of frozen ruts threatening to lacerate the feet of the unwary. Staring intently at the ground and dancing an irregular jig on the small peaks, I fail to notice a car pulling up behind me, crawling on my tail.

When I do see, I'm hit by a wave of fear, Harold-like, forgetting my super powers. Jumping a good four feet – well, jumping pretty high – I spin round yelling, trying not to run away. Lo and behold!

"Betsy! Hi! This isn't even a road you're on."

"That's OK, I'm not supposed to be driving alone."

"What are you doing?"

"I stole a car and lit out for the forest."

"I'll come with you. We could go on a killing spree."

Her laugh is throaty and full – no tinkling bells for Betsy.

"So, Betsy, this parental vehicle you're in and ain't supposed to be, why are you driving it on this here rutted path rather than a proper road? You looking for trouble?"

"I saw you. I wanted to see you anyhow, so I put it in gear and followed. I thought we could go for a ride."

"You want an accomplice."

"I want you."

Who could resist? It's always a thrill to see Betsy, who makes me hot and uneasy in equal measure. It's also getting dark, and I figure she can get me home. I slide in next to her, very much next to her, and prepare to let her have her way with me.

"Call your parents. We'll be a while. I'll pull in at the Fleetwing. Got a nickel?"

I do. And I call, telling them I had run into Glenn.

I don't ask why we are going to be gone a while and Betsy doesn't tell me. She drives along, chugging a few miles over to the other side of the hill, through Calcutta. We chat away about indifferent things, Betsy as animated as she is mysterious.

"My treat. You get the popcorn. I mean, you run after it. I'll pay." This as she pulls into the Super 30 Drive-In (on Route 30, by gum), where in-car heaters promise a cozy time with a double feature starting at sunset, no matter how early that is.

Here's a rich fantasy bubbling up right before me. Betsy is outside my immediate circle, so there is, I tell myself, no way I can betray Mary, Carol, Donny, Glenn, Mother, or the Lord Jesus, even if anything develops. What might develop? Were Betsy a fast girl, word would have geysered up and spread. She's witty and adventurous, but why would she adventure into my territory? Who knows? She has the self-assurance that had cowed Harold and gives even Tim the fidgets. She's in charge in any case, but she's unconventional, and it might be she will decide convention can best be violated by – who knows? I'm ready.

She's wearing a tight white sweater and a distressingly long skirt, saddle shoes and bobby sox – has the prettiest hair and face, my God. And those curled-up lips, not as pronounced as Glenn's but still inviting lower class me to despoil them with wild kisses.

We bump over several little Super-30 hillocks to a far-left corner, hidden from the dozen or so cars spread throughout the field. Betsy settles the car, wrestles in speakers and heater, and smiles. "Well, sweetheart?"

"Well?"

"Popcorn?"

I get popcorn, Jujyfruits, and a pair of Cokes with her dollar, returning just as the screen lights up and thin sounds emerge from the speakers. The initial attraction is a plea for those in attendance to visit the very concession stand I've just left. "Let's all go to the Lobbb-beee, let's all go to the Lobbb-beee..."

"You warm enough, Tim?"

The in-car devices leak out irregular zephyrs of faintly warm (odd-smelling) air. I figure maybe Betsy means something else, so I move toward

175

her, heedless of the stick shift.

She cuddles up like a cat folding in for a nap. I hope she isn't bent on napping.

I'm for all-out unclean fun, but how might I bring that into being? Reviewing my repertoire, I find not one thing that might answer. She's a matter-of-fact girl who will perhaps enjoy some advanced something and think nothing of it. No, she isn't. She's direct in word and deed, but playing footsie at table, ear-tickling in church doesn't mean she's up for casual front-seat sex at the Super-30. It might mean that. I haven't the slightest idea what it meant or might not mean. Then there's that prosaic, decent note she'd sent. I have time to do this thinking, pointless as it is, because Betsy is watching the movie, sitting close enough but making no move to grovel.

I watch the movie, too, a Peter Cushing vehicle that doesn't seem to include vampires. The sound isn't clear, so I'm not sure what's going on. Mainly, I'm watching Betsy's legs. She's hiked her skirt up a bit, or it got caught on something. Anyhow, her legs are curled under her, as she leans into me, displaying skin above her knee. Not too much above the knee, but such heft is remarkable for the day and all the sweeter for being accidental.

Is Betsy enjoying this film?

"I think this movie is a sure bet for the Academy Award, Tim."

"Can't miss, unless there's dirty politics. Peter Cushing's been left out in the cold way too long."

"How about Claudette Colbert there on the bed. Is that a bed? Is that Claudette Colbert? She graces the role. Suppose this movie is meant to be out of focus?"

"Oh yes. Hand-held cameras – cinema-verite all the way."

"Uh-huh. Didn't realize you knew so much about movies, Tim. Impressive."

"I'm an impressive guy." I'm trying not to look at her thigh, at least not stare.

"Maybe. You're certainly as cute as any boy ever, I expect."

"Thanks."

"No need to thank me. It's not something to your credit. All you did was refrain from mutilating yourself. Cute is something foxes have too, or mice."

Betsy suddenly straightens up, turning to face me and, in the process, pulling back a little, elevating her leg, and, for a moment, exposing something white.

"You looking up my skirt, Tim? Never mind. I guess that's no surprise, since I had it hooked around my neck. Sorry I forgot to wear panties."

"You like to feel free. I understand. Me too. I switch to thongs when it's below zero." Something tells me I should give up trying to be witty. It's too much like a contest I'm not going to win. I've heard Betsy in action.

"Thongs? Never mind. I'm afraid you'll explain. Anyhow, I did want to talk with you a little. Do you mind?"

"Of course not. I think we can pick up the plot at any point."

"My guess is that Claudette Colbert is going to get buried alive and not like it, seek revenge in the third reel. But Tim, here it is. I have no reason to think you're not a good person. Of course I'm not certain, but I want you to know I'm not trying to insult you."

Somehow this doesn't seem a prelude to sex.

"What are you doing with my brother?"

"Geez, Betsy. I don't..."

"Sorry to interrupt. I don't mean whether you're touching one another or who's undressing whom. I figure that's going on. Glenn's good-looking and you're beyond that, so why not? I didn't mean that. Do you even like him, Tim?"

"You're worried that I'm exploiting him."

"Yes."

"It started out as cynical. I didn't know Glenn, didn't think highly of him for no reason at all, and had no interest in being his friend. I set out to seduce him and worse." Good place to stop. A little honesty is a dangerous thing, but I should have known this wouldn't do it.

"Worse how?"

"I hoped you'd let me off the hook. OK, here goes."

"Umm."

She's ootched closer and has, without my realizing it, taken my hand. "I originally figured I might seduce Glenn, use him sexually. He's very good looking, but it's more than that, something about his upper lip and the way it looks like a superior, rich-kid sneer. Where was I?"

"Your plan to trick Glenn so you could diddle him and go on your way."

"Worse."

"How?"

"I wanted class revenge, a way not simply to screw your brother but humiliate him."

"How?"

"I don't know. Make him crawl, make him do things he wouldn't like, make him into a masochist. A masochist is, you know..."

"As a matter of fact, I do. You wanted to chain him to the bed, dress him up in black leather, have down-and-dirty bondage fun, right, noisy lashing sessions?"

I thought she'd be furious, but her tone is light.

"Uhh," I explain.

"He really isn't a snob, Tim, but I figure you've seen that. My parents are, horrible snobs and, what's worse, dull. They deserve anything you can do to them. Want to humiliate my dad? You could chain him to the bed and go for him with a tire iron."

She leans over and kisses me, letting me know she's my friend, not on fire for my body.

"Tim, Glenn is impressed by you, so flattered you'd notice him, that he's without defenses. He talks of little else, asks me what I think of you, repeats what you say, makes plans for things you can do together, worries you'll lose interest in him or think of him as a pest. You knew all that?"

"I can see that, now that you say it. I won't lie, pretend I thought it out that well, but I'm not surprised, conceited as it is to say it. But Betsy..."

"Yes. Tim, Tim who looks up my skirt."

"Don't distract me, exhibitionist. I had realized that Glenn was not a generic rich kid but a generous person, is funny and warm – and courageous – being tender to another boy!"

"Look, Tim, I think it's great if you two are kissing and all that, and I'm not being coy: I don't care if you two have sex. That'll be great fun for both of you, if you care, even a little."

"I don't think it's likely we'll have real sex. It wouldn't be fair to him in this time."

"I know what you're saying."

"Do you? I mean – you gotta hear this – we probably won't have sex, not because it's bad or we are disgusted. I think we have just as much fun doing other things. But what you're saying isn't about that, I know."

"No, it isn't."

"I like Glenn a lot, a lot. I respect him. I won't lie to you: I think his feelings for me are more intense and focused than mine for him."

"That's it. You realize what's going on. I don't know if you care that much for Glenn, damn certain not in the way he cares for you, but I figure you won't deliberately hurt him."

"Oh no."

"Don't go so fast. I say I don't figure, but I also don't see too clearly how you can handle this and protect him so that he isn't hurt and real bad. But I don't blame you too much. You went into this recklessly, as you say, and you didn't have to say that. Now you're in it, you see what's going on. I don't think it's fair to expect you to engineer a painless exit."

"I don't want an exit."

"I was wrong to say that. There's no knowing how all this will end up, and I won't try to be a prophet – or interfere anymore."

"I understand."

"I know you do. If you weren't already spoken for, I'd move in on you myself."

Even I am alert enough to know she's being kind, letting me wriggle free. I pat her on the shoulder, a gesture that sounds ridiculous but is, for once, exactly right.

She gives me a peck on the cheek. And then she flips the ignition and we crawl toward the exit, lights off so as not to disturb the perverts parking there. Right as Claudette Colbert is emerging from the crypt to find Peter Cushing and rip out his liver, we pull onto Route 30, back into town. I don't think it was Claudette Colbert.

. . .

I get home, tuck myself in, and have a most unwelcome epiphany. Betsy doesn't mean what she had said about it being hunky-dory for me and her brother to have sex. And she's right. Glenn and I aren't in love, cannot honor the commitment implicit in sexual union.

And I begin to see it is the fifties which knows sex, not the sixties. Of course, equating sex with dirt is horrid, but the gratuitous shallowness of the next decades, where sex is no more than scratching an itch, is worse. Casual sex with strangers, sex to satisfy lust: we can sink no lower. If sex is disconnected from feeling, it loses touch with human value. Compared to sexual practices of the sixties, animals have elevated codes. And was I about to join their herd, selfish shit that I am, bent on contaminating this Edenic world? I hope not. One thing: my loves are so many and so various maybe I can find a way to be both non-celibate and non-brutish. I would pledge myself to it, were my pledges worth much.

• • •

I decide that the best allies in the do-gooder Rotary project are Mary and Jimmy, my most reliable and canny friends. As promised, Donny is added to the mix.

The fund-raising has proceeded so well we have more money than we need for this start. Our experts have been hauled in from down the river and get so interested they agree to waive much of their honoraria, don't "agree" but suggest it. I figure they see a scholarly book or two coming out of this, but they'd have that anyhow. Nice guys – actually, nice women.

We have meetings, discussions, problems. I sit back, let others dither, hiding my remarkable organizational talents. Which is bullshit. I try to keep myself out of the center because I see before long that I'm lousy as a boss. Harold had promoted leadership as his main talent and, being unchallenged, managed to elevate himself to the presidency of everything from the class to the Latin Club. What's happened? At least I recognize that I have trouble paying attention, forget what had already been agreed upon, fail to distinguish between good and lousy ideas. True, so why not admit it? I don't, though, not consistently, and the bumbling continues.

At one point, just for instance, Carol is agreeing with a fat girl that we need more group work, not just one-on-one. I think that's what they're saying. What's running through my mind – God help me – is a threesome with Carol and yon chubbo, who has a sweet face and the careful grace and delicacy acquired by a good many heavies.

"I hate losing the tutorials," I say, smiling broadly so as to maintain collegiality.

Everyone stares at me as if I have just announced that Mother will be happy to offer blow jobs to the first seventeen visitors arriving after four on Tuesdays.

"Er, Tim, I think we all agree with you." Jimmy jumps in to save me. "Carol and Mary Sue were just saying we needed group work on top of that. I think that's right, Tim. Maybe I misunderstood you."

Carol speaks slowly: "Misunderstood what, Jimmy? Tim's brilliant contribution?" She directs at me a glance something beyond withering, then melts into giggles. "Tim, if you'd try to focus your mind, Jimmy wouldn't have to keep covering for you."

Jimmy dives in: "On no, I..."

"Jimmy, even you can't make us believe Tim is in the swim of things."

"Yeah, what's your tale, nightingale?" chimes in an unidentified kid, wanting to distinguish himself by broadcasting a dislike for me. This isn't the first time he imagines he'll join a tide rising against me.

"Thanks, Jimmy. I see now. You want to *add* more group work. Absolutely. Listen, I know I'm not good at this. I can offer energy and money – I mean get money. But no brains, none. Just pretend I'm the janitor, which is unfair to janitors. Anyhow, pay me no never mind."

Humble pie right in the face of my squirty jealous rival.

Dean Nelson has made a pitch to the Rotary and got pledges lined up, but he suggests I attend a meeting with him and charm these old soft hearts into committing the bulk of the club's service budget to our Save the

Dropouts scheme.

"We are hoping to reverse the course of hundreds of individual lives and the city of East Liverpool itself. We will be the first town not only to honor its kids but to do something to keep hope alive. We won't give up on kids! East Liverpool will be called the Golden City, the City of Redemption; and this Rotary Club will not be simply the benefactor of that triumph. You will be, and are, the architect.

For the first time in American education we will be putting into full practice our wholehearted national belief in self-reliance, in never giving up. So what if kids have had a few problems? So what if others have lost faith in them? So what if they have lost faith in themselves? We will not lose faith. Keep the faith! We will draw in the best experts and the most tireless volunteers. No kid will lose here in East Liverpool! No kid will be left behind.

Because of this Rotary Club, we will reclaim the destiny of this great country and its youth. Out of failure we will craft success: out of shame and despondency, confidence and the will to be all that we can be. All that we can be: that is the promise we will make to our kids. We will make that promise! We will honor that promise! We will keep that promise!"

Right at that moment I could have been elected President by this group, porked their wives, sodomized their dogs. How I manage that vacuous blither without laughing I don't know. Yes I do. I manage it because my heart is in it. Nobody in the room is more moved than I. What a cornball. A plagiarist too, but that doesn't bother me a tittle.

I've found my niche: weaving enchantment out of mush, patriotism, and slogans later popularized by the military and the most contemptible U.S. President ever. I'm so good they vote to throw their entire service budget into this work. Too bad, old folks aid and Seeing-Eye dogs. Then a sentimental realtor moves to increase that service budget by fifty percent. He doesn't say how this is to be done, but the motion passes by acclamation.

Two days later another Board Meeting. Calling our collection a "Board" is my idea, nomenclature being my one strength. Dean Nelson reports on my Rotary coup, laying it on thick. Everybody, even my twerpy antagonist, loves me. I've taken pains to win him over – noticing him, smiling, calling him "buddy," pretend-punching his skinny shoulder.

I try to hook Carol and Mary after the meeting, but they're off to other activities, a choir rehearsal, home chores. Donny's there, however. I haven't ignored him lately – study sessions, sleepovers, even a hike. But our cuddling hasn't advanced. It's the old story: thinking of sex as conquest, I need to feel toward my object the pitiless glee with which a hawk views a crippled bunny. We're stuck. I can't claim much credit, so I'll say this: I never thought it was my moral will preventing me from sexual assault. I can fool myself often and a great deal, but I know I'm feeding on Donny's virtue, not mine. I'd make that clearer, were it clearer to me.

He's fumbling with his stuff, waiting for my approach. I half-hug him, trying to work my way toward some goal I don't recognize. Then it strikes me.

Before unfolding it, I need to find a way to acknowledge and avoid seeing that my bright idea seems to flat out contradict what I've decided. I will not lose sight of what I've learned or tarnish it. Still (you knew this was coming) there is such a thing as prudishness, a foolish consistency – and such a thing as running out of time.

Though I have three years and more, who's to say how that will play out? It's one thing to regard time as a fiction, but what is that to one locked in twilight? The days dwindle down. The possibilities here of a mistake, a lie from the heavenly sisters, surely grant me the right to explore some new territories, new bodies. No?

I'm trying to find a way to let horniness trump decency. Face it, pig!

Get drunk! Without the capacity to reason myself into ruthlessness, I figure nerve-numbing inebriation might do the trick. Getting smashed might get me laid. Donny'll do whatever I want, but... As soon as my thinking moves to Donny, the scheme dissolves. Resign yourself to living among humans, tiresome and restrictive as that it. Don't give up on depravity, but tonight just study with Donny, be friends. That's not bad, maybe as fine as it gets. And who knows what will come with the morrow – if there is one.

CHAPTER 13

The very next day, our shining basketball team has its first real test. We've played four games so far, against schools able, often barely, to scrape together a dozen guys for a squad. Our team is improving steadily and boasts three good players: Donny at one guard, Sammy at one forward, and Shaquille Mills at center. The other two starters, and at least two of the subs, are almost competent and understand how to play well enough to avoid crucial mistakes. I play center up in the key, clearing out the lay-up area for my teammates. Time and again, they dish me the ball so I can draw defenders, then feed cutters for easy baskets or sometimes signal Sammy or Donny to shoot from outside. Donny makes a surprisingly high percentage of these. Sammy makes almost none, though he loves trying. His form is terrific, but the fact that the ball so seldom goes through the net suggests that Sammy is cursed with a defective eye.

Coach Tarinello's equal-opportunity policy keeps every lurching kid attached to the squad and offers them playing time. I wonder if Coach is another victim of the celestials, a New Age, unisex soccer coach from the future looped back to this competitive age. I'm competitive myself. This very ferocity would have made the future tough for Tim, had he possessed one. Harold had learned to sublimate his own competitiveness into a foggy, multidirectional indifference. Unable actually to win at anything (apart from elections), Harold found competing a maladaptive trait and adjusted. Not so Tim, needing an all-out battle and now stuck with Nelson Mandela as freshman basketball coach.

Tarinello regards basketball as an enriching educational experience, open to all. I find myself longing for Sadon and his healthy intolerance for the ungifted. Sadon would see these try-hard incompetents for what they are: goddam chickenshits with marshmallows where their nuts should be.

So astonishing is our starting five, though, that we manage to build big leads and easily hang on against the pushovers making up our early schedule.

But now comes a different sort of opponent – a good team, or so says Tarinello. They're undefeated, and from a larger school, Canton McKinley, the basketball equivalent of Massillon in football. We are edgy and apprehensive, even me.

After four minutes, we readjust our emotions. I begin the game in a state of all-out hype, go way in the air for the opening tip and then call for the ball, spinning round my man and elevating so high that I come within an inch of dunking. That wouldn't have been the thing, not for my new unselfish ethos or for the rules of the game now in force. Still, so nervous am I that I take (and make) three of the first six shots.

Turns out we're so much better than this first-rate team I can sag back into my fake-and-feed mode, play defense, and get us up by a score of fourteen-to-three when Coach puts in the unables. Even they aren't so bad as to blow this lead, actually keeping us ahead by a fair margin, helped along by the Bulldogs' panic.

When it comes time to re-enter the first team, having scrubbed the bench clean, Tarinello inserts Donny and Jerry Kline (our other starting guard) but keeps me and Sammy, along with Wesley Putnam (our other starting forward) on the bench. Even Tarinello isn't loosey-goosey enough to welcome player involvement in such decisions, so I bite my tongue.

Once I relax, I enjoy watching Donny and Jerry play. They pass crisply, using the other three as decoys for a time and then, when Donny gets himself double-teamed and Jerry pulls another opponent out of position, feed the ball to an open klutz, who isn't a sure bet to make a shot, but makes some. When Canton Mac gets four or so unanswered points, Donny takes a shot. He's uncanny from outside, can drive, and plays smart and aggressive defense. Twice he steals the ball and scores. He's fast, seems always to be in the right place. He lacks my height and strength, unfair quickness, but he's playing in the same zones.

We win lop-sidedly. I get in briefly in the second half and employ the time setting up teammates. I do block three straight shots, which may be why Tarinello plops me. I come to appreciate what he's doing, can see that it's working. Against all reason, these unteachable kids are improving. In the process, they're having an extraordinary time. For one moment in their lives, they feel like winners, held up to something like admiration. Sure, their triumph, the cheering crowds are only a fantasy. But it's there and powerful.

I'm so moved, I don't mind playing only a little. What does it matter, really? Of course, if this doesn't matter, what does? I put that idea on hold, a good habit I haven't lost from Harold times: shelve worries that might be unsettling, promising to pull them off later, and then breaking that promise conscientiously.

I manage a potent imitation of kindly, figuring the thing to do with the drugged, tingly feeling I now have is to extend it. Therefore, I pick the least attractive, least talented kid on the team, and sidle up to him in the shower.

"Great game, Marshall!"

"Tim! Me? Gee thanks, Tim. Tim."

"Damn, Marshall, I didn't know you could play D like that – smart, quick. You know the court well, know where you are. Very smart, Marshall."

"God, Tim. You – I mean, Tim, you – Gee."

"Thanks, Marshall, but I'm just a freak – tall, which is a big advantage. I don't have to be quick and instinctive, which is lucky, because I'm not like you, Marshall."

"Nah – mumble, mumble."

"What?"

"I'm sorry, Tim. My name's Mickey, remember? Not that you should or anything. That's OK. Marshall's OK."

For the second time recently, I feel remorse. Mickey is one of those redheads bordering on albino: thin hair, transparent skin, blotching up at anything approaching embarrassment. Right now, he looks like a barber pole painted by a drunk.

"Mickey! Of course. Ah damn, forgive me. It's just that we've never had the chance to become friends. My fault."

"Muhhhhhhh."

"I won't get your name wrong again, I promise."

He looks at me, suddenly without embarrassment, probably wondering if I'm about to stick his head in the toilet, give him a swirly. Why would I talk to him at all, much less offer friendship? Good question. But I'm in deep and can hardly retreat from demonstrating the truth of what is certainly untrue.

"I mean it, Mickey. I get a lot of time to watch. Truth is, at first I was impatient being on the bench, but then I settled back. There's a way you can watch a game without really seeing it, and that's usually what I do. This time, though, it was more like I could see the way a coach might – not a good coach but a wannabe coach."

Mickey laughs, relaxing and casting off suspicion, his only defense. Other kids are showering around us, but for me the world contains only Mickey, crimsoned Mickey. Befriending this little ding-dong is tough going.

"So, anyhow, trust me. I sense that you don't."

"Yeah I do, Tim." He can't stop saying my name, for reasons I can guess.

"OK, Mickey. I'm sorry I haven't gotten to know you before now. But we'll remedy that, right?"

"If you want to." The words sound suspicious, but Mickey isn't.

"If I want to, massive cock, what about you?"

"Massi – that's good, Tim. My brother says I got no cock at all."

"It's fine, Mickey. Your brother's jealous, got a weeny barely bigger than yours despite being three years older."

"Four."

"Yeah, and a good brother, but not above envying how fast your dong is developing. He sees the handwriting on the wall, the shadows being cast by your growing whizzer."

"I'll tell him."

"Tell him if he wants to see a dick the size of Mt. Everest just check back in six months."

He laughs hard. Not a bad kid.

We've spent so much time in the showers, outlasting all others, that I'm wrinkling. By mutual consent, we make it to the tiny changing room, where Mickey tries to separate, probably not daring to press his luck. But I grab my pile of clothes and set up beside him. I'm being excessive, but the more I fake this friendship, the more I feel it.

Once dressed, I give him a light punch and a shove, then beat it off to catch Donny.

I'd made a friend, learned more about my coach, and watched Donny play so well.

"Wanta come over to my place, Tim?"

"Oh, yes."

"Great."

"You thinking what I'm thinking, Tim?"

"You bet."

I can tell he doesn't know what on earth he's thinking or what I'm thinking, but he's so inside my desires as to accede to them before they've announced themselves or are aroused. Right now, arousal is not an issue. But I do find myself pondering just what I *am* thinking, realizing without wanting to that I will never make the scenes in my head materialize.

Once in his bedroom, he excuses himself to go to the bathroom. As at my place, all bathroom activities are broadcast throughout the house. Donny is occupied washing something.

Soon, I found out what: his privates, moisture still on them when they're in my hand only minutes later. The thoughtfulness reactivates my sensitivity to Donny's fine spirit.

Still, here is a chance to find our way into the widely-known but always special pleasures of cocksucking, Donny offering to trade off, exciting in me a guilt zinger, then settling down to cuddle more mildly, as I pull him upright.

"Donny, do you like what we're doing? I don't want to hurt you. I've said that, but I don't think you hear me."

He's smiling, listening closely. I expect him to erupt with reassurances, attempts to stop all this talk, but he doesn't. He looks at me with eyes I cannot read, maybe pleading. If so, I cannot decipher the plea.

"Here's what it is, Donny. I think your participation in what we do is motivated by your desire to give me pleasure, even to anticipate it. I'm not saying you're disgusted. It's more like you are being driven by my desire, not yours, that you would never initiate these grab and rub episodes if I weren't so eager."

He still is quiet, seems to be studying me.

"I hope you understand. I want to know what you think. If you are different from me about the sex, please say so. Whatever you say won't change a thing. It'll make me feel good if you feel free. We have to be equal."

"I don't know, Tim. I understand what you're saying, but I don't know. It's all new to me. It doesn't make me feel bad to think about it – or to do it, as much as you'll let me do. I don't know how it makes me feel. I guess part of what you say is right. I like making you feel good, and it makes me feel surprised that you like my body."

"But –"

"Yeah. Would I want to do sex because I wanted to do stuff with you and not just..."

"Letting me do stuff to you."

"No! You make it sound like you'd be attacking me. I'm in this, too."

"Do you want to leave off for a while?"

"No."

"Do you want to soften it up, not go at it so hot and heavy?"

"No."

I'm stumped. Slowing down isn't what I wanted, and I can tell that Donny is telling the truth, letting me see what he recognizes about himself. And I know better than to launch again into lessons about cultural intolerance and future discomfort, being so certain what he'll say.

Before I can come up with different cautions, though, Donny takes over. "I want to be what you are, where you are. I mean, I want to be with you – just like now – only all the time. I want this never to end, you and me."

What have I done? I want to be with him. Let's never end this.

· · ·

If I had my way, dear,
We'd never grow old,
And sunshine I'd bring every day.

. . .

The one kid I seem able to keep from pawing is Margie, my wee research assistant. She appears to be having a great time hanging around me. Of course I'm in on the fun just as much.

I've concocted a true research project and have Margie doing oral histories for a book on the cultural past of East Liverpool. I invented the idea on the spot and then became infatuated with it. I've also suggested, in a tentative, half-assed way, that Margie go round asking kids about their views. Views on? Well, not exactly sex. I won't set out to get Margie in trouble, me either. But it strikes me that the girls in this town and this era are in a prelapsarian heaven, able to achieve true gender authority. Far more mature than boys, they exercise a range of flirting and suggestive talk without the risk of inviting what a decade later will be assault. For a short time, the culture veers off course, far enough to allow girls room to run and play. It's a dreamy hypothesis, but what I'm in seems more and more a dream. Of course it isn't that.

I set up a questionnaire for Margie, revise it after talking with her. This ragamuffin is smart, straightens out many of the twists I've inserted, those I admired most. She removes the padding, puts plain things in plain words.

"Do you talk dirty to boys?"

"On purpose?"

"What do you say?"

"Do boys ever say dirty stuff back?"

"Are you ever sorry you'd talked dirty to boys?"

My version had opened: "Do you find yourself ever taking liberties in conversations with boys, knowing you can do so without risk?"

The responses are so interesting I want to add more questions. Margie listens, says my additions are cool, and ignores them.

I do force her to accept bus fare and lunch money. Finally, I trick her into a shopping trip. She regards it as a pretend play-date, and I let her. She doesn't allow me to buy much, but I sneak in two pairs of marked-down shorts, a sweater, and an on-sale dress. I want to add coat and shoes, but I can see that Margie has stopped enjoying the buying part of this date, so we head over to the library to work.

"Margie, you're good at this."

"Ummm."

"No, really. You're great. You know that?"

"Ummm."

"You listening to me, squirt, mini-person?"

She looks up, smiling but hurt. What the hell is wrong with me?

• • •

"Mary, want to go for a walk?"

"Well, sure. A walk?"

"I thought it'd be nice. We haven't talked in almost eighteen hours."

"OK. Let's go down by the river."

"Want to go fishing?"

"Yes."

"Really? This is January."

"Best time for fishing. Uncrowded, no need for reservations."

"The reason nobody's fishing, dumbo, is there's nothing to catch."

"Fish hibernate?"

"I don't think so, unless there's ice. But they don't eat."

"Well, there's no ice."

"OK. I got two poles. Zebco reels even."

"Zebco reels? That's why nobody else bothers trying. They can't compete."

It occurs to me that I've ceded control of this conversation, but it's no strain letting her lead.

"Let's do it! It shouldn't be muddy."

"It'll be perfect, frozen into mounds we can sit on. Do you generally take a lawn chair?"

"No. For one thing, we don't have one. Oh, you were kidding. OK, Ms. Field and Stream, what'll we use for bait?"

"Worms? Insects? What do these fish eat? Old hamburger? Mizz?"

"Mizz is what you are. There ain't no worms nor insects nowhere; and hamburger won't stay on the hook, debutante ballroom girl. But we can make doughballs. We have to cook them. Can you cook?"

"No, but you can. Do it."

So we do it, adding stuff to the cornmeal base: ginger, powdered sugar, vanilla. End up tasting great. Were I a bottom-feeding fish, I'd go for it. Of course, the only fish we have in our polluted sewer, "Le Belle Ohio," are garbage hounds, and they'd probably prefer rotted flesh. But we make about four pounds of bait, fetch my gear, which does feature Zebco reels, eight spare hooks, and some sinkers Joanie and I had fashioned in a kit I got for Christmas.

This is exciting – a dumb idea, all the better for that. Harold had earlier (or later, depending on how you look at it) spent the equivalent of a full year of his youth fishing; but I can't remember him/me ever wetting a line in the winter.

"OK, Mary. We got what we need. Watch out fishies, here we come!"

"Let's go."

"You gonna change clothes, Mary?"

"Do I need those boots that come up to your waist? Waders? I don't have any. But you said it wouldn't be muddy. We're charging in where the big ones are, mid-river? Anyhow, these are old clothes, but thanks for your concern, *MOTHER*!"

"No, I didn't mean that."

"Is there a uniform? Will I embarrass you?"

"Ha! There won't be a soul there. No, it's ..."

"Lord Almighty, Timmy, out with it."

"You're wearing a dress."

"So? We gonna be tree-fishing? You think I'll get my fat butt bruised by climbing?"

"Your butt's not fat."

"How'd you know? Oh, yeah, nudey colony. But that was before I chunked up."

"Oh…"

"At a loss for words, class personality king? You know you won that vote, right?"

I hadn't known and am, again, uncomfortably conscious of the pettiness of my ambitions. Personality King! But being here with Mary, letting her talk quasi-dirty – that's real.

"Don't usually climb trees, but there's some down there, if we go to Bott's Landing."

"The very spot I had in mind, Bott's Land."

"Landing. Where boats come in, only they don't."

"Oh, that's why they let the trees grow, so I can climb and fish from them. See the fish, spot 'em where they lurk, which will even things up between me and an experienced angler like you. And you can see right up my dress, which is what you wanted all along."

"Mary! Not that you're wrong."

Mary jumps into my arms. We're in the middle of the street, and I'm carrying our poles, have lethal fish hooks stuck into my jeans. But I drop the poles, forget the hooks, grab Mary and kiss her. She responds, or maybe leads – and how light a load she is.

"Wait till we're down amongst the catfish, and only they can see us."

We don't end up at Bott's Landing, as I don't remember where it is, if indeed it exists. I expect the heavenly hussies haven't altered the river landscape, but who knows? What matters is that we can't find a path, have to scramble down the very steep bank, one used by the local pottery as a dump for spoiled goods and thus a little slippy-slidey. In summer, there are Amazonian weeds here that help prevent a tumble. In their absence, we're left to our own grace, considerable. Still, the bank, spotted with icy crockery, is more than even we can navigate easily. Make that *I* can navigate. About a third of the way down, I reach for a hunk of dead horseweed to control my descent, uproot it, and grab onto the closest thing at hand, which is Mary, more exactly Mary's foot. The result is an awkward downhill roll. To my credit, I manage to keep myself mostly beneath her, absorbing the sharp ruts, pointy rocks, and discarded pots.

It might have been worse. We finally get to the flat area preceding the river with only a few scratches. But in grabbing Mary's foot, hanging onto it for dear life, I've flipped her over multiple times, and, when we come to rest, her skirt isn't where it should be, is, in fact, clotted around her waist. Mary is atop me, her bottom in my face.

"Ah, Timmy?"

"Yeah, Mary?"

"You plan on maintaining this position for another hour or two?"

"Yeah."

"Can I pull down my dress?"

"No."

"Having me climb a tree would have been more suave. I could take a Kodak, you know."

"And I could paste it up in my locker at school."

"Timmy!"

"I'm sorry."

"Don't be. I don't mind panty talk, though it's embarrassing having you stare at them."

I don't know how to keep this going, whatever it is, so we walk to a clearing, drag over a log, bait our hooks, cast out, prop up our rods on v-shaped twigs, tighten the lines moderately, and settle back to see what we can attract, trying to ignore how bitterly cold it is.

"What's the world's record for fish – I mean how big?"

"From this river? Eight hundred and forty-seven pounds. A full twenty-four feet long."

"Sounds about right. Timmy, what do you think about sex?"

"With really big fish?"

She doesn't laugh. "With me."

What? In 1951, I figure, people might have sex, here and there, but they pretend it's just happening, rhapsodic energies taking over. Nobody says, "Hey, wanna fuck?" Respectable girls don't for sure. I know Mary didn't say, "Wanna fuck?" I might have handled that inquiry, since a part of me has been primed since the kiss. But "What do you think about sex with me?" is tougher, mysterious in its reach and scope. I don't want to "think" about it; I want it to happen. I'm much more a child of the 50s than Mary.

"Truth?"

"What?"

"I wonder if you wanted me to tell the truth, but of course you do. Really, Mary, I have no idea what to say."

"You don't have to answer if it makes you squirmy."

I roll over to kiss her – and who knows what else – tapping one of the poles with my foot as I do. I look and see what we're ignoring – fierce tugs on both lines.

"Mary! Grab your pole and jerk it straight to the sky when you feel him bite again."

She does. I do. We reel in respectable catfish, maybe a pound each.

"Are these record setters, Tim? They probably weigh, what was it you said, eight hundred pounds? I'd say we were close. Estimate. Yours is six ounces, which is low; mine is eight hundred and thirty-four pounds, which is high. It evens up."

We unhook and let the little slimers go – Mary needing no help – cast out, reset the rods, and settle back on our log.

"Mary, I'd love to have sex with you. But that's not quite what you asked, I know, and I don't want to duck. I'm just startled to be talking about it. Up there in 2016, people do talk about it, incessantly, but I didn't think people back here did."

"You probably thought only Mommies and Daddies had it, sex, blindfolded and silent, when they calculated it was time for the stork."

I'm say nothing, wondering what I ought to be thinking. Mary imagines I'm hurt.

"I wasn't mocking you, Tim. I'd rather die than hurt or lose you. We have so little..."

She begins to cry.

I wrap her in my arms. I hold her tight, rocking back and forth, wondering what it is we have so little of, trying to ignore that.

When we settle back into calm, I try reassurance. I'm not hurt, I tell her, smoothing her hair, kissing her wherever I can light. Her skirt is at full furl now, dragging the icy ground; and Mary has never been so appealing. Now is just the time to have sex. Only it isn't. Now is the time to tell Mary what having sex would signify to me.

"Mary, don't you think if we had sex that'd mean we're going to be married?"

"Married!" Her laugh is the most welcome song, and not just because it brings relief.

I let her exhaust her glee.

"Timmy, I was being unfair. I want to know what you think of me. Wait a minute." I had let out interrupting noises.

"That's not all. I really would like to have sex with you. I know it's peculiar to say it, but we're so close. Maybe too close. That seems like what you've said before. I don't want to have sex to trap you or make you feel something you don't feel."

I can wait no longer.

"Mary, I know you aren't scheming. You're perfect. I don't think of you as a part of the family. I think all the time about having sex with you, not just stealing peeks at your panties."

"Want another look?" She hikes her skirt up on the side, and then lowers it, not laughing, watching me closely.

"You know what I think? I may be crazy, but I'm here in a time warp."

"Go on."

"It's all so right, loving you, spending time with you, having sex sixteen times a day with you, in every position, some not known before. It's just so right. Yes?"

"I do think I see, honey. I know you don't think I'm trapping you, but something **is**. If you attach to me, it's like it's all over, all of it, worse even than if we were getting married, which, by the way, would be about as stupid as thinking we could set up a nudist colony here in East Liverpool and charge big membership fees."

She pauses, but I know she has more.

"I think there's more ways to think of it. I'm not saying having sex won't change things, but who knows? Why not think of it like this: we both want to. We neither one know what will happen if we do. Is that so bad, not knowing? Why can't we trust each other, do what we want, and see what happens? Consequences aren't the only thing to think about, and the future, for all we know, may be empty or dead. We love one another, so what are we waiting for – a time that may never come, may never be?"

I'm slack-jawed. I always thought that was just an expression, but I bring it to life, an ugly life probably.

"Yeah," I say.

"Yeah?"

"Everything you say makes so much sense. Why don't we trust each other, like always, and stop trying to predict what we can't predict anyhow? Why shouldn't we?"

"Timmy, do you...?"

But I'm on a roll: "Besides, this is so much better than fumbling around in the back seat of a car, hoping it will happen without you noticing."

She laughs again. "And in the dark you'd have trouble seeing panties."

"Or peeling them off."

"Right, peeling them off."

This is more than flesh can bear. I kick over the rods altogether as I roll onto the dearest kid on the Ohio River bank.

We have sex two or three times, depending on how you count. We remove only the necessary clothes, mindful of the cold, using discards to protect us from the scabby earth and rock. We have no condoms, so I employ the old and ineffective method of interruptus. In between copulations, we try other things. Neither of us knows a lot, but we fumble with lips and hands. So free are we, so at one, we can no longer distinguish between giving and taking pleasure.

CHAPTER 14

The next day is Sunday, church day. Joanie goes and I do too, as if it's the most natural thing in the world. Why not? It pleases Mom and amuses Dad. I mentioned before my father's regular absence. He drives us there and back, says nothing about church. Mom insists regularly that he is "a deeply religious man," but Dad never gives the slightest indication that any of this is true. Christianity, religion of any sort, seems no part of his life. As I've said, he's possessed of a generous, dear heart, but I never heard him invoke the Deity except in inventive swearing. I figure he is atheist through and through but encourages Mom to entertain any story that might comfort her. I don't know for sure. Joanie probably does.

"So, hun, what's the real reason Dad doesn't go to Church?"

"You know."

"No-wah! If I knew, I'd be the one telling *you*. Only desperation would make me humble myself to my little sister."

"So, why should I tell you? I keep it a secret and you're the inferior one. I tell and you gain on me. Why'd I do that?"

"If you don't tell me I'll throw you off the Chester Bridge."

"Ha!"

"We'd invite all your classmates to come and see – and cheer. You'd flutter down and they'd love you like never before."

She stares at me.

"OK, whiz-kid, so what's going on with Mom and Dad and Our Lord Jesus?"

"You know as much as I do, but I'm smarter than you, so I got it figured out and you don't, so how do you like them apples?"

What a pretty kid – such an open face, freckles even. She turns her bony shoulder to me, looks back over it, sticks out her tongue.

"OK. You're pathetic and I'm a fine Christian girl, so I'll throw out the lifeline, someone is drifting away – hey! She sings in such a pretty, low-toned voice that I'm arrested by the beauty of it and neglect to keep up the mocking game.

"Wanta sing together?"

Without answering, she starts in, me with her. We alternate the melody – pure happiness, even if the results are not lovely, which I scarcely think they are, though the hymns have a certain beauty, if you don't think too hard about the lyrics – which we don't:

A call for loyal soldiers comes to one and all,
Soldiers for the conflict! Will you heed the call?
Will you answer quickly, with a ready cheer?
Will you be enlisted as a volunteer?
A volunteer for Jesus, a soldier true!
Others have enlisted, why not you?
Jesus is the captain; he will never fear!
Will you be enlisted as a volunteer?

. . .

Love divine, all love excelling, Joy of heav'n to earth come down.
Fix in us thy humble dwelling; All thy faithful mercies crown.
Jesus, Thou art all compassion. Pure unbounded love Thou art.
Visit us with Thy salvation. Enter every trembling heart.

. . .

Sound the battle cry! See the foe is nigh! Raise the standard high!
For the lord!

Gird your armor on! Stand firm everyone! Rest your cause upon
His holy word!
Rouse them, soldiers, rally round the banner!
Ready, steady; pass the word along!
Onward, forward, shout aloud Hosanna!
Christ is Captain of the mighty throng!

. . .

"Wow. I could go on all day, Jesus Christ almighty. You have a glorious voice, hun."

"Like a diseased crow. I think Mom and Dad have made this agreement, a long time ago. She would go to Church and take us with her; Dad wouldn't go and not ever be asked about it. He wouldn't have to pray or sit through grace at meals. In return, he'd keep his ideas to himself, let Mom try to make us good Christians. Dad also would let Mom feed us a cover story about his own views. Of course none of this got spelled out. It just happened, like everything they do. Before they knew it, there they were, all worked out, settled."

"That makes sense. But Mom told me Dad was a true believer, just didn't like the organized church."

"Yeah, maybe. And maybe that's the sort of bushwah he lets go by."

"And that's what you think?"

"Yep, dumbo."

"You think he's an atheist."

"Yep, idiot."

"Thanks."

She seems chagrined that I don't respond in kind, abusively. Just the disappointment I was hoping for. "Hey Tales from the Crypt Girl, let's go over to the playground."

She looks at me suspiciously.

"Yeah, let's do. C'mon."

She's still mute.

"You can do your Gypsy Rose Lee act by the seesaw. I'll sell tickets."

She lunges at me, shrieking, moving quicker than I figured, toppling me. We sprawl, the two of us waggling, trying to remain unskinned and unpunctured amidst varieties of heavy, upturned furniture. I finally manage to extricate myself, use my little sister as a stepping-stone and head out the door, Joanie just behind.

We circle the block, Joanie still on my tail. I'm going almost full speed and not putting any distance between us. I cut into the thorn-bush-infested vacant lot, stop suddenly, crouch, and let the hurtling prettiness fly over my back. Luckily, her flight is mostly vertical, so I can catch and wrestle her to the ground. She screams in splutters and then knees me right in the nuts.

It's my idea to pretend that hasn't happened, but even the most rational plans will yield to excruciating pain. I writhe and moan, unable to exhale. Joanie starts to commiserate, changes her mind, rears back and laughs.

"Gotcha right in the warbles, huh, my brother with the sore dingleberries!"

"Call the ambulance – no, I don't want to live – call the mortician!"

Of course the agony abates. Joanie offers me a shoulder to lean on, allowing us to limp our way to the playground, right through the Canton's vacant lot and the Morrison's garage, which they keep open for just such traffic.

The playground is un-crowded, oddly, considering that it's a gray late afternoon, temperature all the way up to the twenties. There before us are three little turnips, maybe eight years old, so heavily clothed there's no guessing at gender.

"Push us on the swings, Joanie – please, please, please!"

"Who's that with you, Joanie?"

"Shhh. That's Joanie's boyfriend."

"Is not."

"Is."

"He's cute."

"Kinda."

"I'm Joanie's boyfriend. You're right. Name's Rudolph. And you know what?"

"What?" All three are grinning broadly.

"I'm also her cousin, brother, and teacher at school. Three-in-one."

"You are?"

"Yes. I'm also her dance coach and dentist. And I'm much better than she at swinging you on the swings."

"You aren't. What's your real name?"

"Helen," I said.

They don't blink. "OK, Helen, you push us, too."

I do. And play tag, hide and seek, and chase round the Maypole. We also race one another up and down the high slide (not to be confused with the low slide), until somebody, running too fast, catches a foot on the top step of the slide, and topples over and down, about ten feet, right onto the frozen ground.

"You OK, Helen?"

I am, no thanks to Joanie, who is doubled over laughing.

Soon the kids leave. "Bye Joanie! Bye Joanie's boyfriend!"

Joanie and I make our way to the seesaw, squatting at opposite ends. For a while we pop up and down, but even with Joanie perched at her farthest point and me up at the pivot point, we can't manage what you'd call balance. So we stop trying and sit suspended, enjoying the sweet weather.

"You have a boyfriend, Joanie?"

I expect a smartass retort, but none comes.

"You think I'm old enough? Anyhow, I don't think the boys are old enough."

"I see what you mean. Must be a problem. Girls seem about three times as mature as boys. Carol and Mary have that problem with me. Glenn's sister, Betsy, you know her?"

"I don't think so."

"She's a Junior. Scares me, she's so ahead of me."

Joanie doesn't seem to find that odd.

"Can I ask you something, Joanie?"

"Yes, of course."

"Do you have a boyfriend?"

"You already asked that."

"And you already didn't answer."

"Not really. There's some boys call me, you know."

"I guess."

"Well, they do. But that's it, really."

"Don't you want to have sex?" I hope I'm just kidding.

"Sure I do. Like anybody."

"You do? Nah."

"You asked. What'd you suppose?"

"I didn't."

"Well, do. Sure, I want to have sex. Like *you*!"

"Oh."

"You waiting for me to say something else?" This she puts in after a long pause.

"Yeah, I guess."

"Well, I'm not gonna."

"OK. Why don't you team up with Donny?"

"And you with Sally. Maybe the four of us could have sex all ways, huh?"

Doesn't sound bad, for a second, before conventional horror descends.

After this much time in the freezy drizzle, we're in need of warming, so we chase one another back home.

Just as we enter the kitchen, parents looking up expectantly, the phone rings – Mary.

"You want to talk to him? He's been terrible, Mary. I had to defend myself by kicking him in his bubbles. I don't think he's recovered. What? Yeah, he was beating me up – trying to. Yeah. Yeah. Over in the field. Yeah. You did? No! No, not me. When? Really. Yeah. Tom? He's nice. I suppose, Mary. Yeah..."

"Jesus, Joanie, I thought it was for me."

"You hear that, Mary? Yeah. That'd be soooooo mean!" She laughs hard.

"If you two are trying to annoy me, you aren't."

"Sorry, Mary. Some ugly injured boy here was talking and I couldn't hear you. Yeah. I know! Oh, I know."

"I'm out of here." I don't move, which probably dulls the threat.

Joanie hands me the phone, pinching my arm as she does and patting me on the cheek in a way she probably thinks I'll mind. I don't.

"Hi, Mary."

"Hi."

She's silent for ten minutes – ten seconds. Hell, she called me.

"I don't know how to tell you this, Timmy."

"What? What's wrong?"

"Something's wrong?" Joanie comes running over.

"Joanie, give me some privacy. Go in the kitchen with Mom." She does.

"OK, Mary. What's wrong?"

"I don't know how to tell you."

"Just go ahead."

Pause.

"Oh, Timmy..."

"Mary, just say. What's wrong?"

"I don't know how – "

" – to tell me. Christ, say it."

Silence.

"I'm sorry, Mary. I didn't mean to shout at you."

"We have to get married."

"Huh?"

"Do I have to spell it out? I'm pregnant. Don't tell me you're going to abandon me." She starts sobbing immoderately, very loudly.

"Shhh. What? You're pregnant? Holy shit." I hope I've kept my voice down and doubtless haven't.

She brings her sobbing under control: "You thought it couldn't happen first time, but we learned in Health with Miss Robinson that it can. You know Miss Robinson, with the real tight bun? She told us not to let boys talk us into having sex, saying it was safe first time and we wouldn't get pregnant because we would and oh Timmy what are we going to do?"

Finally, moronic me gets it.

"Well, Mary, how do I know it's mine? I think we should wait till the baby's born and see who in our town the little shitass looks like."

I have to hold the receiver away, so earsplitting is her response.

"Got ya!"

"You did. Hell, we only did the deed a few hours ago."

"That's why I called."

"You want to go back for an encore?"

"No."

"Didn't you like it?"

"Not as much as with Clifford." Clifford is a spectacularly homely dork.

"So, what was it?" I realize that's a little rude.

"I just knew you were pondering what all this meant and where we would go from here, and I wanted to tell you to stop it."

"Stop it?"

"Remember what we said. We both wanted to have sex so we did, and now that happened and now I am still me and you are still you and we don't worry. It was fun, right?"

"I'll say."

"Me too. So there we are."

"There we are."

"And Timmy?"

"Yeah?"

"Please don't marry me. Not this week. Bye."

"Mary, I think…" But she'd hung up.

. . .

Hang up the phone, turn around, and there's Dad, three ball gloves in hand.

"Not perfect weather, but how 'bout it?"

"Sure. Weather couldn't be better."

"That's what Joanie said. You two are so much alike."

I don't know when I've been so flattered, but saying so would be too personal for Dad.

Seconds later, we're outside playing variations on catch, Dad so happy, treating his kids as future major leaguers. Joanie is unusually athletic, and I realize quickly that *this* is my sport, my arm whipping around so naturally there's no knowing how fast I can throw if I try.

"Don't ease up, son! You got more on the ball than our whole starting rotation put together." "Our" is the Pittsburgh Pirates, whose pitching really does seem a match for their offense and defense, lousy, but surely several dozen levels above me.

We fight off the freeze by playing pickle, run-downs trapping the picked-off sucker. I know I've played it forever, Joanie too. Dad actually takes his turn as the runner, just the thing for his heart, but what the hell! It's the three of us, on a warm day at Forbes Field, against the Dodgers, winning this game and all games, playing pickle right into the World Series, the Yankees, bottom of the ninth... Dad lives his full imaginative life by way of me and Joanie and the Pirates, all of us triumphant.

• • •

I had forgotten what a bracing and, in its way, beautiful month February is here in golden East Liverpool in the fifties. Every day seems more promising and bright than the last, sweet days lengthening into sweeter.

Only a fool, double-drunk on nostalgia, would respond so positively. But the leaden weather does lend immoderate bliss to indoor activity. What could be finer than snacks, couches, a radio, and central heating – roaring gusts of comfort boiling up from bituminous coal? When Harold had reached the age of independence, he headed for sunny climes, where the outdoors beckoned one to vigor. He had never taken to vigor, so his indoor time was shared with a nagging feeling of being slothful and a sad son of a bitch, wasting his life in pursuit of nothing more worthy than the avoidance of activity. He seldom watched television, which he loved, hoping to dull the self-accusations, and he never investigated video games, knowing their pleasures would be too intense for him. But even grading papers with conscientiousness no students appreciated failed to justify him to himself.

Back here, however, nobody can be criticized for staying indoors weeks at a time.

•   •   •

Tuesday, I have a meeting, the Key Club, where we practice democracy under Roberts Rules. I preside and enforce the Rules as I understand them – perfectly. The issue before us: how to dispose of the money we've obtained from our sponsoring Kiwanis Club. The idea under consideration is to assume the heavy responsibility of planting a median island on the new highway. The highway isn't remotely "new," not even widened. We're to glamorize it by loading dirt into an island, then sticking in and watering plants. In return we'd get a sign:

WELCOME TO EAST LIVERPOOL
THE POTTERY CAPITAL OF THE WORLD
Island planted and maintained by The Key Club

The motion passes, after token discussion. To refuse would seem churlish, which is the last thing we teen enthusiasts are. The adult advisor said he'd have the beautifying greenery and implements waiting for us after our day of study and healthful play. When our never-more-than-tepid enthusiasm wanes, we begin to think that our agreement has been pro-forma, that the Kiwanis bosses have settled things and diddled us into spending *our* money on this purposeless project. There we are, though, we and the shovels and the bagged, spindly shrubs.

We gather at school after sixth period, eight of us, ready to get to planting, of which we know more than you would suppose, nothing. Mr. Schell, who runs the Heating and Plumbing Supply Company, loads us into the back of his pickup with the tools and vegetation, on our way to forced labor. We love it, we Key Clubbers, wobbling through the streets, seeing how long we can stay upright in the quivering truck without holding on. Very dangerous, but we feel anything worth doing is worth being stupid about. Mr. Schell cooperates by swerving and applying the brakes unexpectedly, throwing us into one another and the plants, allowing for a lot of grab and giggle, which is what we'd come for.

I wasn't kidding about the state of the greenery – scraggly, desiccated, brown round the edges. Probably they'd not been prizewinners in their best days, but in bad health and in late February they seem most suited for burial. Once we get to the island, cars rolling by coughing out the world's finest poisons, we stand on granite dirt, staring grimly at one another, now bereft of high spirits. This is a job for Superboy from the future.

"Hey, fellow keysters, I have an idea! By the way, you know what a keyster is?"

They looked less embalmed, my seven companions, and give me the opening I need.

"Here's a keyster and a goodun," I say, as, with some flair, I lower my jeans so that each gardening buddy and passing motorists will get a vocabulary lesson.

"So, that's a keyster," says Deanna VanClausen, a member of the Club only because I had put heavyweight pressure on her.

"It is indeed," I say. "But my idea goes beyond instructing you in parts of the body."

Our group is smaller than hoped for, some having chickened out. Glenn, for instance, is a member, but hasn't shown up, likely because he can't stand the proximity to Donny. Fine with me. I'm not anxious for a juggling act.

"So, what's your idea, Mr. 4-H?" This from one of the upper-class pretties.

"Well, as we dig, we play this round-robin game, with the loser having to remove an article of clothing, each time."

Nobody protests. Everybody looks surprised but not disgusted. That's a start. After I'd made the proposition, it dawned on me that the weather isn't perfect for strip games. But hell, we're all young, hearty, and horny.

"If we lose our shoes, how we supposed to dig?" asks a young dweeb. (This service club didn't attract all the hottest kids.)

No one bothers to answer.

"I know you're waiting for this, but who wins the game?"

"The winner is the last person with any clothes left, even if it's a sock."

"We'll be naked?" This from Dorko, who doesn't seem to mind much.

"No, Russell," says Donny; "you think Tim would embarrass us? That's not what he means. Right, Tim?"

Donny saves me. Nobody would strip completely, ever, in public. In the middle of a highway, no chance.

"How about we all play until one of us reaches near-naked?"

What do I mean by near-naked? Help, somebody!

Deanna: "Let's say bare belly, however that happens. That's not too thrilling, but it'll keep us out of jail. I mean, I'm not a prude, but I am not going to stand here on the Wellsville road in my bare keyster."

"Right. So, everybody knows, 'I'm going to Wheeling with my aunt who has syphilis and I'm taking along an apple, then the next person with a 'b.'"

We do movie stars, teachers, popular singers, eliminating Q and X. Meanwhile, we try to penetrate the boulder-infested earth, satisfying ourselves with smaller and smaller holes, finally stuffing the root bags into cavities barely matching the bag's diameter. We give up digging deep enough to cover and decide just to pile dirt and rocks up around the roots. Mr. Schell left us to our own devices to go get us pop. He must have gone to Oregon, so long is he away, allowing us to mess with one another.

The game proves un-titillating, as the too-easy demands of the alphabet quiz result in few and dull clothing losses after what seem like hours of play. To make up for this, we develop more ingenious means for touching one another, namely touching one another. The pretext is horsing around, throwing clods of dirt, wrestling, snapping bras (only once, as it isn't well received), and giving a wedgie to nerd boy. (Wedgies are a cruelty I import from the future. Don't say I'm wasting my resources.)

Right after we semi-plant the last dead stick, I feel a light warm weight attaching itself to my shoulders, Deanna having jumped on my back, laughing and kissing my ear. As if choreographed by the Celestials, the other kids occupy themselves at the far end of the island, removed from direct peeking by the forest we've just erected.

It seems so natural to continue. But somehow we don't advance, I don't

209

advance. Soon, Deanna slides down, pats my cheek, and goes to join the others.

Does this have a future? Probably not.

And why are we planting in February? Without protest? Without noticing?

. . .

The basketball team, still undefeated, has settled into a routine, me shooting only in a tight spot, of which there are none. Sounds boring, winning repeatedly, but it isn't. Our team spreads the ball around and plays tight defense. After a couple of blocked shots, opponents avoid the in close. We can then proceed to murder them on offense, where I feed and rebound.

It's such fun that we are, on occasion, guilty of over-passing. We so enjoy setting up shots that sometimes nobody takes one, dallying so long with set-ups that the odds catch up with us and the ball caroms off somebody and out of bounds. Still, it's what sports ought to be and never are, and we even extend the exhilaration into the scrubs.

After our sixth game, I decide to invite everybody out for pizza, financed by my ill-gotten gambling gains. I hatch the scheme as we're dressing, the locker-room having become an extension of our on-court fun, strangely synchronized. At any one point, all are at the same stage, one sock on, one coming on, belts a bucklin'. It's like the Ice Capades

"Hey, fat asses, how about we go for pizza, you too, coach, on me." Several start to make talky-noise, so I up my volume. "Really, on me. I won some money, happy to pay. It'd be great. We're a team, and why not? Hey, let's do it."

I can maybe explain my lame speech by admitting that my teammates look at me, not with faces alive with anticipation, but with puzzlement. At first I figure they're reluctant, but, if that *is* the case, it's not only that.

"Tim, what's peacha" asks Donny. He's one who looks more amused than mystified, maybe guessing something about my slip? Am I suggesting

210

pizza before there is pizza?

"Oh, sorry. I read about pizza. It's a great Italian dish, spaghetti sauce on piecrust. It's big in New York, I read, but I don't know what made me think of it."

They look at me with some alarm.

"Don't send me away to the asylum! Not another padded cell!"

Before this gets any worse, "I meant go up to Dairyland, have burgers and shakes – on me. You too, Coach."

Coach begs off. I figure some of the others might have pick-up arrangements that will shuffle them away. But no. Several make phone calls, but all end up coming, fifteen of us, two managers included.

We walk up to Dairyland, a freezing-wet experience. But nobody seems to mind. We've formed something like a colony, all coordinate. It probably won't happen again, I know that, know it because nothing like it had happened in Harold's lifetime. Nobody says anything very smart or amusing, but we feel the same currents running through us. We **do**. As a result, we spend well over an hour there at Dairyland, a stop that ordinarily maxed out at thirty minutes. I don't think I ever felt so easy and so unexceptional. I don't have anyone admiring me, nor do I feel pressed to get attention, give it, or reapportion it.

There are other people there, and we're not quiet, everybody talking at once. You'd think these others (adults in groups, families) would be annoyed. But they aren't. They smile, wave, stop by to say a word. It strikes me, all of a sudden, why I'm so surprised. Nobody dislikes us, sees us as a threat. How things are to change in the next decades, as kids, teens especially, become America's enemy, not because kids change but because the need for violent opposition, the irrational invention of menace, the demonizing of youth, grows exponentially. For now, there's enough good sense to allow kids to be human and for adults to summon the good-nature necessary to see it. This town is proud of its kids, loves seeing them happy.

Donny sits next to me, now and then presses his hand on mine or slugs me, and I do the same to the guy on my other side. We stay and eat little – nobody believes I have money, so people order sparsely and share even that. It's the finest time of my life, my lives. It sounds ungallant to say so, considering my encounters with Mary, Donny, Glenn. Turns out, for me anyhow, sex can't hold a candle to companionship. I'm tempted to call this discovery something basic about me or about the species. Better to call it something that happened. It happened and it couldn't last, yield any lessons, be transferred. Just luck.

. . .

Love doesn't make the world go round. Love is what makes the ride worthwhile.

CHAPTER 15

"Donny, how about I come over and study?" Donny lives a good three minutes from school.

"We can study each other's whing-whangs, you mean?"

"Donny! You're corrupting a minor. You'll go away for years."

"It'll be worth it."

We end up in Donny's room, working on World History, having covered American History thoroughly before Christmas. We're now studying (for one week) the classical world, having disposed of cave men in a three-day set of coordinated studies, lessons focusing on fire, saber-tooth tigers, cave paintings, and spears.

Just as we're finishing old Mesopotamia and Babylon – alphabets, hanging gardens, pagan Gods, you name it – there comes a knock at the door. As we're fully clothed, we have nothing to fear. We had nothing to fear even had we been naked and interlocked, as Donny's parents would have interpreted it as "boyish fun." They're not so much stupid as right, though they never do interrupt us, send messages by way of yelling, as do my parents. Rude though it sounds, it's easy to get used to, and it preserves privacy, which may have been the design. A knock, then, means Sally.

Sally greets us with some flaily contact, but less enthusiasm than usual. Her soberized version is worrisome, makes me appreciate how much her reliable energy means. You could trust Sally with a mission behind enemy lines, trust her courage and her competence. You're thinking Sally is extraordinary, and you're right, but what she has a lot of is there in lesser degrees in any number of kids, girls mostly but boys, too. How is it Harold had never seen all this firmly packed human value, or forgotten it so very quickly?

"Sally, what do you want?"

"Donny, what do you think I want? In!" The playfulness seems assumed, a bored actress playing 'Annie' for the six-hundredth time.

"You want to pester Timmy. He don't want pestered."

"Yes, he do!"

"Yes, I do."

Sally doesn't laugh, stands looking at me with a face so serious I feel as though it's a different child, one just told she wouldn't be having a birthday this year.

"Tim, can I talk to you about something? I'm sorry, I won't be long."

"Sure."

"I don't want to bug you, but I'm worried about Joanie, not that she can't take care of herself or anything, but you know how it is with girls."

I nod, instantly worried. Sally gets right to the point.

"This Carl Martin she's hanging out with, you know him?" With considerable difficulty, she pauses to let me answer.

"Yeah, he's older than me and Donny – and he's a butthole."

Sally nods agreement. "He's mean. I don't even think he's cute, but maybe he is.

Anyhow, I'm worried about Joanie."

"Excuse me, dearie, but how is she connecting with him? She's home every night. I'm with her a lot. I don't even see how she's talking to him on the phone."

"You know the Girl Scout meetings and the choir practices?"

"OK, I see."

"Don't tell your parents. I don't want to get her in trouble."

"I know, Sally. You got other sneak reports?"

I'm hoping for a giggle, but all I find is a glimpse of smile-lite.

After she leaves, I turn to Donny, only to find him turning to me. "Tim, I hate to do this to you, but I have a worry, too."

"Oh damn, Donny. And I was just – I am so sorry."

"Don't be sorry. Don't ever be."

He's looking at me so seriously I'm unable to understand – or to speak.

"We can do anything," he continues finally. "We'd better, you know. We'd better."

Now I really am speechless.

.   .   .

You cannot tell how soon it may be too late.

.   .   .

"Anyhow, Tim, you're gonna think our family is nothing but worries about yours."

"My mother's been diddling the milkman?"

Donny doesn't laugh. "I think Sally is going way overboard, not about Joanie – I don't know how to say this."

I see right away. "She has a crush on me."

"That'd be OK, but she hardly thinks of anything else. She worries about what you think. She doesn't see as much of Joanie, which worries her. She worries that telling you about Joanie and Carl will turn you against her. I'm afraid she'll make herself sick. I'm also afraid she'll do something to get your attention. And she doesn't seem happy. She's so quiet."

"This is my fault. Don't protest. Let me think. What I mean is, let me talk. Your sister has a crush on me. She's quite a kid, is Sally, and I think you're right, Donny, without me even hearing you say it. Sally shouldn't be underestimated. Words like 'crush' won't get us very far. It's worrisome that she's not as lively as usual, quiet like you say."

"You could talk to her, Tim."

"You think? What should I say?"

"You want *me* to tell *you*?"

"Yeah."

"Tell her not to – let's see – tell her you're both young and need time, both of you, to be friends, but with lots of different people, too."

"They tried to tell us we're too young. Donny, she's going to hear that as rejection. It'll hurt her. And with her not feeling at the top of things as it is... She's so vulnerable. Can you think of another way?"

"I think try getting her advice on Joanie. Talk to her about that. She'd be thinking of you as a friend who needs help, not as a hero."

"That's smart. I'll talk to her in front of you. Make it a council. Bring her in here!"

Before long, Sally has entered readily, soberly, into a discussion. She has ideas, though they all funnel into one: don't kick Carl's ass (yet) as it might drive Joanie closer to him; appeal to Joanie's good sense and boost her confidence. She probably sees pretty well for herself what is going on. Let that self-sufficient part of Joanie take over, give it a boost.

"Thanks, Sally." I try to pack all sorts of radiant good cheer into my voice. I'm not so stupid as to suppose the happies will immediately take up lodging, her deeper feeling moving out. It's a start. Or it would have been, had she not seemed – the word I've been trying to avoid – depressed.

•   •   •

Thirty minutes later, Mr. Fix-it has managed to get nowhere with the easier task of bringing Sis to her senses. Joanie stares at me as I wander in and out of the subject, trying to say nothing against Carl and failing, trying to protect Sally and succeeding. Instead of inviting Joanie's confidence, I've assumed it; instead of boosting her self-assurance, I've cracked it.

"Let's start over, Joanie. I love you."

She smiles, though I don't get the sense she's relenting, even as we hug.

"Please talk to me. I trust you. You know what you're doing. Despite what I said, I believe that. I want to give you a chance to talk this out with somebody who isn't judging you and doesn't assume he knows everything."

"That would be you."

"Fuck yes, me. Who the fuck else?"

All the fucks get Joanie to react.

"OK, Timmy. Yeah, about Carl. Everything you say. I don't know how you know, but I don't care. Probably Carl was bragging and you heard. If you shut up and stop advising, I can figure this out and maybe you can help."

"OK."

"Carl hasn't been nice to me, ever since he got me to start skipping things to see him. I know that."

"Want me to say something?"

"Yeah."

"It happens a lot to terrific girls. They get entangled with a guy who is cool, cool because he's meaner than shit. He's self-confident, that much is true, and it's attractive. But he's a sociopath; he doesn't have anybody in his world but himself. He doesn't set out to be mean, he just is. Don't think he's changeable. Once a girl gets entangled with his lethal coolness, she doesn't want to admit she was so wrong. Worse, she thinks she can fix the psycho. Worse, she starts thinking she deserves such treatment."

I notice that her bra strap has come unstrung, is dangling out the top of her blouse. It makes her look so unprotected, small.

Her poise holds for maybe ten seconds. Then she collapses into my unready arms.

"Oh Timmy, I feel so awful."

"You didn't do a thing. Want me to kick his ass?"

The joke is premature. "I did, too. I did, too."

"So, that's OK, honey."

"What I did was awful. I'm ashamed."

I'm embarrassed myself, don't want to hear, so I offer no help. Wonder if Carl is more selfish even than I? Joanie's sobbing increases. I have to say something.

"Look, dear sister, you mustn't feel bad. It doesn't matter. It happened. If it helps, you can regard it as a mistake, but I don't think it was even that."

"Oh, Timmy."

"Really, honey. In the big scheme of things, what makes the difference?"

For some reason, her crying gets worse.

"Joanie, Joanie, so you had sex. So what?"

"Had sex?" Her crying shuts off abruptly, turns to indignation, then to some kind of snot-producing laughter, all in six or seven blinks of an eye.

"Oh, I only mean..."

"I think it's clear what you mean. Had sex? Had sex? I'm twelve years old, evil boy. Had sex?"

"Yeah, well then, what are you so upset about?"

"He had me running after him, waiting for him when he didn't show up, even let him call me names."

"What names?"

"Stupid, fat, slut – stuff like that."

"I see. And you took it."

"Believed it, sort of, just like you say."

"Now big brother gets to plot fierce vengeance on this double-dyed bunghole."

"You and me together."

"Right. We should ask Mom for help, get her to apply some of those Biblical torments, adapt them to modern conditions. We can't slaughter Carl's first born or call down locust on his crops, but we can maybe paint his balls with Superheat."

"Make him cry in front of others."

"Yeah, we'll plot. And Joanie..."

"Uh-huh?"

"I'm glad you didn't have sex with Carl."

"God, Timmy. I was as likely to have sex with Mr. Backus the janitor."

"I can see why you'd think of him. Him and his mop machine. He's pretty hot, if you like hairy guys who are seventy, which of course you do, as who wouldn't? I do myself. But you really want to know why I'm glad you didn't have sex with Carl?"

"God, no! Stop talking about it."

"You gotta let me tell you why I'm glad you didn't have sex with Carl."

She tries to frown, but she's laughing by now. "OK, why are you glad I didn't have sex with Carl?"

"Because I've seen him in the shower. He has a wee-wee the size of..."
"Timmy!"

• • •

Two days later, after a happy quasi-date with Carol, more walking and even more kissing, I come home to a message from the Clinic. Dad's operation has been rescheduled for ten days from now, March 12. I have to talk about it with Mom. She is sensational in moments like these, cool and smart, without a thought for herself.

• • •

In between now and then, we have a talent assembly scheduled, the one featuring me and Judith Paderewski, with an encore, featuring me and Judith Paderewski. You'll recall that the first song, "If I Loved You," is a genuine duet – the encore, "You'll Never Walk Alone," isn't. However, we, make that she, turned it into one, knowing we may run out of time here and have to wait to the Spring Concert to release it. Anyhow, it takes me a good hour, spread over three practices, to convince Judith she wants to do it at either concert.

"But Tim, you do it really well; you do it beautifully. And that's the way it was written."

"Thanks, Judith, but it's a song written for a woman, a woman! Besides, who cares what its original purpose was, when you made it so much better."

"But it's so moving when you sing it. It's just right for you."

"You mean I sound like a woman. You saying something about my masculinity?"

"Yeah, Tim, you'd be better as a girl. You know what people say about you: 'There's a waste of a good girl.'"

219

I'm shocked. Even the mousy girls are self-possessed. No wonder poor Harold floundered, never had a chance.

Finally, she agrees to go with a duet that becomes complex, patiently waiting on the emotion to rise from the vasty deep, growing into a flood and blasting forth with sobby high stuff. I always liked the song, the opportunity it gives good contraltos to throb. Judith is no contralto, but her low register is so full and darkly toned nobody could tell that.

Neither Judith nor I is good at orchestration, which is to say we have no idea how to do it. Dr. Clendenning, however, gets interested and works up a boffo version.

A kid named John something is emceeing the show. John is a senior and the sort of people-pleasing fool for whom the 1951 term "dipshit" was invented. Such kids – numbering about one per class – often are thespians, announcers on the P.A. system, hall monitors, wearers of bow ties to dances, releasers of bad jokes, active in the wrong way in the wrong clubs, proposers of new ideas like a stiff honors system to halt the rising tide of cheating. They have depthless reservoirs of confidence and are so dull, so adamantine stupid, as never to register the responses of others. Nobody, not even lesser dipshits, likes them. No matter, these lulus imagine they are both popular and influential. The unshakable power of such baseless assumptions will carry them far in life, not only to top-of-the-lot car salesmen but to success in Hollywood, witness Mel Gibson; in crime-fighting, witness Hoover; in war, witness MacArthur; in jurisprudence, witness Clarence Thomas; in purveying C- wisdom to the national dipshit audience, witness Oprah; in sports, witness Pete Rose; in Presidenting, witness George W. Bush.

Even Harold, always short on people skills, knew how to handle this sort: listen to them, give them a perch from which to crow, flatter them. In return, one gets to register undisguised sneers. Dipshit Kings are incapable of detecting them. Just don't yell at them, strike them, or turn away as they are talking. Sounds easy, but it's dreadfully difficult. Try it.

I'm capable of doing anything for a good cause and am about peeing myself to advance this one, my own self-aggrandizement. I figure there are no encores in these shows and for good reason – time limits are set by school-bus schedules. But if it's the emcee's idea, if Oliver Out-Of-It is doing it for the good of the school and Virtue writ large, well then…

"Hi John. You don't know me. My name's Tim Mills. I'm only a freshman, but I'd consider it a great favor if you'd let me talk to you a minute, ask a couple of questions."

"Definitely, Mills. And I do know you, by the way, as it happens, and am happy to talk to you. How can I help you, Mills?"

My resolve not to punch this ass-face is being strained. Nobody says "Definitely." Nobody calls people by last names. Nobody says stuff drawn from antique plays like "as it happens." Nobody acts as if they're manning an information desk at a fucking library.

"You sure you have time, John?" He nods, with the graciousness of Queen Victoria. "Thanks a lot, John, I do appreciate it. I haven't been in a talent show before and know you've been in many and are running this one. I'm glad you are. We all are. Who else is qualified?"

I stop, worried that I'm drowning both of us in molasses. No need. John swells visibly, nods some more, even though there is no earthly way he could lay claim to "running" this show, or to having the qualifications for this or any other position.

"I wondered what it'd be like, John. Of course I've heard talent shows before, Horace Heidt. Here's what I'm asking – sorry to take so much of your time – those shows all are very mechanical, very predictable in their structure."

John (notice no nickname ever came his way) is trying to look bland, but he's puzzled. I have to remember that this guy could not outscore a crawdad in an I.Q. test.

"They are all alike. Each act gets the same amount of time, one after another, running like a model train, chugga-chugga-chugga. No imagination, no flair! If an act stinks, it goes once and that's it. If an act is spectacular, it goes once and that's it. Boring, boring, boring."

John is smirking still, but he seems to be quivering a little around the lips, maybe thinking I, though only a freshman without a first name, am mocking him. So I strike fast.

"But John – I know I'm bungling this, but I'm nervous. I've known who you are forever, but I never thought I'd work up nerve to talk to you. I know what you've done for this school and how original you are. I know you'd never be satisfied running a boring talent show, when it could be the best ever. So I imagined you'd be doing encores, time permitting, for the good acts, but I really wanted to know what you had planned for the lighting, whether you'd use those carbon-arc lights from the back. Reason I ask is, it'll change how Judith and I dress. I know all this is second nature to you, and I hope you'll forgive me asking, taking up your time."

"It's my pleasure, Mills. I'm glad to put my knowledge in your disposal. I have built up a lot of knowledge here and naturally I can understand – what I mean is, I'd like to know how you younger students, be you ever so resolute, can be expected to know what I know, you see, having not had the same ways of getting to that – ah – knowledge, unless there..."

His confidence doesn't seem shaken, but this poor demented groundhog has waddled too far from his hole, is dazzled by the brilliant sunshine of a sentence begun without an end in sight, and is now rolling down the hill, ass over tin cups.

"I see! I hadn't ever thought of that, John, but of course. Unless you tell us, teach us, we'll never know. We might try to trace your steps, but we'd have no chance."

"Right. Mills, I like you, so I'll tell you. Of course my duty is not simply to run this talent show but to plan it, not simply to plan it but to – what did you say? – create it, and create it as something new and not like any other – ah – talent show like they always have, boring-boring-boring. How did you put it? Chugga-chugga-chugga. Not bad. I like that, Mills. Yes! Chugga-chugga-chugga, indeed!"

I try to look as if I wished I had a pad and pencil.

"Yes, Mills, I intend to have fewer acts, of course, as you say and choose myself on the spot which acts should go twice – or three times." The last is true inspiration. "And which acts shouldn't go at all, time permitting, as you say." Even better, if nit-witty. "I can trust my instincts here, instincts and..."

"Experience?"

"Right. Instincts and experience. Right as rain, Mills."

"Thanks."

"Don't mention it, though I guess you already did, ha ha har! As for lights, Mills, this place is primitive, primitive! Those of us in theatre certainly expect more, demand more! And we get – well, see for yourself." As we're in the hallway of the central building and not the gym/auditorium/theater, there isn't anything to see for myself, which is OK, since he's interested only in the phrase, not its meaning.

After even more lavish ass smooching on my part, tip-giving on his, slack-jawed attentiveness on mine, condescension on his, I manage to escape. It would have been appropriate to the occasion for me to have backed away, bowing like Osric as I scuttle. But I have limits.

. . .

Only three days left now before Friday's bring-down-the-house, and I plan to rest up in the meantime, conserve my resources. Hey, this is a high school talent show, prelude to a CONCERT. We're talking stress most people will never have to bear.

Donny and I have a study session scheduled Wednesday, Glenn the next night late, Save the Children right before Glenn, and a surprise I'm planning on Friday with Carol. All one week before our Cleveland trip for Dad's surgery. Meanwhile, I need to figure out Sally's depression, in the absence of any available treatments for depression. The medical plan I'm cobbling together involves a two-stage campaign, as you'll soon see.

So, where to start? Chronology important to you, orderliness, or do you want the sex first? As it happens, you can have your clarity and eat it too, though what you and I regard as "sex" may not match up exactly. Anyhow, Donny and I are teaming up to learn the ins and outs of Roman civilization: its principle crops, rulers, accomplishments, and four reasons for collapse. And where do you suppose that little study-session will go? You and I are probably anticipating in harmony, but you and I may not be right.

"Where's Sally?"

"Huh? I really don't know, Tim, not really."

"Which means you do. I didn't think you'd do that, Donny, you sneak."

I'm immediately sorry. Donny's face incarnadines so quickly I want to call back everything.

"I'm sorry. I should have guessed you were keeping her out when I'm around, trying to help. I can be so thoughtless sometimes."

Still-flaming Donny looks me in the eye, but seems oddly distant.

"What is it?"

"I didn't tell Sally not to come in, not exactly. Actually, I told her you were coming, tried to make her excited about it, but she wasn't that I could tell. Sorry. I don't..." There's nowhere to go with that sentence.

At least, I'm not hurt. I'm thinking that, whatever this problem is, I can solve it. Eating into my confidence, though, is the certainty that I'm wrong.

"Tell me, Donny."

"She seems so unhappy. She's never been like this. Stays in her room."

"Will she tell you – what's wrong, I mean?"

"No. That's the thing. It's hard to get her to talk. She knows she's sad. She says she doesn't know why. I think maybe that's the truth. You think it might be?"

"I do. It might not be anything specific, like somebody did something to her. Sounds like she's depressed. I sort of thought that before."

"She's depressed, all right." Donny looks at me strangely, as if I'd done no more than offer a redundant description of the problem, not a diagnosis. Isn't depression reckoned as a condition back here in the 1952 now? Guess not.

Meanwhile, off in her room, this little girl is suffering. Right around the corner for her is an awful darkness, pain all the worse for having no source, everywhere and nowhere, more like an acid fog than a spear in the gut. I can't help thinking her condition has something to do with me. Trying to wean her of infatuation, I have been friendly but cool, just the wrong thing. Maybe what she felt for me was something more complicated than infatuation, assuming "infatuation" existed at all beyond the needs of those who applied the term in order to belittle and evade. So what? It's egotistical of me to imagine things are simple, that her depression is rooted in an obvious cause. On the other hand, it's one thing to say things are not as simple as unrequited love and another to dismiss the issue altogether. I don't know when I'd wanted anything so much as a release from the sense that I've done this, or that whatever "this" was, it wouldn't be "this" but for me. But for me, Sally would be happy still.

"What do you think about me talking to her, Donny?" I don't know why I'm losing confidence in my own scheme: talk to Sally, get her involved with – something.

"I don't know. She didn't say it, but she thinks of her room as – no, that's not it – she never cares who comes in. It might be good, you going in. But she'd worry about – you know."

I don't and say so.

"She might worry that she doesn't look pretty."

"She couldn't not look pretty. But maybe you're right. She might not want to be barged in on – and maybe she'd get it in her head that she was messed up or something. She ever wear makeup? I mean, does she usually?"

"I don't know. You thinking I could warn her and she could put some on?"

It isn't a common sensation for me this time around, but I feel lost, so Donny takes over:

"Sally might be better at working this out by herself. She knows we love her, and she'll let us know how we can help."

"That's wise."

"But... ? You're thinking something else."

"But maybe she won't work this out by herself. Maybe she can't."

That sounds so dire. It also suggests I know what I certainly don't.

"OK. Why don't you go in?"

And I do, first knocking. Her voice seems to emerge from a cave. Is she under the covers? Maybe I should go away.

Of course I don't. Sally is sitting on her bed, smiling without any spark. She shuffles herself upright and then sits again, retaining her automatic smile, directing her eyes right over my shoulder to the blank wall behind. She's beyond worrying about make-up.

"Hi. I've been missing you terrible."

"Me, too." Her smile is the deadest thing around still able to claim life, a phrase from Hardy, probably too overwhelming for what's before me. I hope.

"Look, old Sally, I need your help." Inspiration has come!

"You want my help?" She sounds almost imbecilic. This isn't even close to the right track. I try the jollies.

"You know why I really came in? I'm longing for a tickling session. OK?"

"If you want." She looks at me with an attempt at a smile.

I stand there helpless, unable to find a way to initiate horseplay.

While I debate what to do, Sally all of a sudden is in my arms, sobbing. She's also speaking, though I'm not able to make out much. I hold her, assuming it's best not to say anything. Besides, what can I say?

But I have to do something, am struck with this urgent need to act after a full minute of swaying there in the narrow trough between her bed and the wall.

I lift her chin and kiss her on the nose. "I'd do anything to help you, and I'll leave you alone, if you want. Donny feels the same, of course."

I brace for a new wave of sobs, but Sally moves back from me, wipes the snot off her lip, gives me a smile, wan but on the trail of the real thing.

"Thanks, Tim. I told Donny I don't know what's wrong. I shouldn't feel like this at all. I know I shouldn't."

"Has nothing to do with should. You do. We want to help. How about this, instead of me helping you, you help me? After all, who's important here?"

No laugh, but at least she doesn't try to produce one.

"What?"

"I thought I'd tap into your dark side, your criminal underbelly..."

"My insanity."

I try to keep from reacting: "Absolutely. And here's what we need: a scheme to enact vengeance on Carl for his shitting on Joanie."

"Tim!"

"Sorry I said shit."

"I don't mind. It's kinda funny. Not that what he did to Joanie is funny."

"She didn't tell me much, hardly any specifics. So, like you say, what we need is a way to cause Carl great pain, that lousy ass-faced moron, exquisite pain that lasts and lasts. Anything we can do, anything!"

"Anything!" She seems a little less encased in midnight.

"So long's we don't get ourselves caught and sent up the river."

"Yeah!"

"Can I come over Friday after school – we don't have a game, as it turns out – and scheme with you, just you and me?"

"OK." I'm hoping for more, a reaction pointing toward enthusiasm somewhere off in the distance. But I know depression isn't going to be touched by feel-good schemes. What we need is drugs.

What I say to her is pure dumb: "I'm going to make you better. Trust me. The reason you're feeling bad is just a matter of brain chemistry. I know this. Believe me. I understand it and can get some help, some medicine, some drugs. All legal. You're terrific."

She stares at me.

CHAPTER 16

A ship is safe in harbor, but that is not what a ship is for.

. . .

I'm still pondering Sally's problem as I crawl up the trellis outside Carol's bedroom. I think Harold had witnessed such a scene in a movie he'd loved a lot of years ago. My idea is to scale the trellis, hand over gloved hand (thorns). The plan has come to me as an image, and it's folded out into a scheme. This sort of thing might be defensible if it were spontaneous, which it isn't. I even write it down in my date book, so I won't forget or have it squeezed out by basketball practice, Save the Children, a choir rehearsal, a meeting of one of the twenty-seven clubs over which I preside, a SPEBSQSA affair, a Ping Pong tournament at the Cantons, a walk with Joanie, a diddle with Glenn, a study session with Donny, homework (honest and true, I do it).

Anyways, here I am scaling the trellis, initiating my plan to wedge some of the nakedly existential into my life, and hers. I half expect the trellis to collapse, her parents to burst out of the house and collar me, a neighbor to call the cops, a rabid watchdog to grab me, a lightning storm, a mistaken address, the right address but the wrong window. However, I make it to the top and slip my body into the room, one that holds Carol in her jammies.

The first thing I see is her eyes, which hold mine in a grip of embarrassment, as she crinkles her face in resignation before throwing her hands to her mouth in a good parody of theatrical melodrama: "the heroine is dumfounded!"

"How romantic, Tim!"

"You're being sarcastic."

"Well, 'romantic' isn't as fitting as 'stupid.'"

"Not very charitable."

"It's what it is. You trying to make sure we don't see each other? My mother finds you here, she'll lock me up – you, too. Breaking and entering, climbing and sliming, slipping and slithering, wailing and wedging... "

"OK."

"My mother will..."

"Why should she know?"

"That thing might of broke, you might of fell, you whisper like a foghorn."

"Let's be silent, then, communicate by touch only."

"Let's you go and we'll meet behind Clut's at lunch."

"Unfair."

"Not unfair. Not nice, though. Tim, I want to neck with you as much as you do with me. Hope you don't mind me saying that." Here she giggles and I, smooth operator, keep my mouth shut, wondering where she'll take us. "So, if we're headed in that direction, let's not mess it up by being – romantic and making things tougher on ourselves, Errol Flynn."

"One kiss."

"No."

"Oh, Carol, not one kiss?"

"Seventeen. Then you gotta go."

Seventeen kisses later, I leave. Carol would have thrown sense to the river breezes, so hungry was she for more. I know that because I was so hungry for her I would have braved a big crowd in Madison Square Garden, both sets of parents, and the Lord of Hosts. We're grinding into one another, but keep our hands away from just those sensitive areas we are dying to tweak. Guarded by clothes that remain unopened, we torment ourselves for a few minutes, then part.

"I think, Carol," I hiss back over my shoulder as I plant a toe on the trellis, realizing too late that down will be trickier than up, "we deserve a place in heaven for our virtue."

"Or stupid caution."

If she felt like that, why didn't she let on? But she shoves me down a ways into the thorns, shuts the window, closes the curtains – not so much as a blown kiss.

. . .

Of all the things happening, Save the Children occupies me most and interests me least. The traffic island with its fast-expiring trees is more engaging. I've been down to the beautified rock-pile twice since the planting, talking my dad into picking up a few of the others – Donny and Deanna and, once, Glenn – and hauling us there so we can loosen the soil and put on some fertilizer, which amounts to animal shit, undisguised. It does strike me that fertilizing in early March amounts to encouraging growth in plants determined to be dormant, but I enjoy the activity, and what's important here anyhow, my fun or the doomed plants? No chance to fool around more with Deanna. Dad is good at getting lost, doing God knows what for an hour, but the combination of competing lovers is daunting.

On one of the trips, a tallish, pretty, friendly Mary Lou – one of a dozen or so Mary-somethings in our class – comes along. She proves impressive at flirting, embarrassingly so, given Deanna's hovering. At one point, though, Deanna is drawn away to work with Glenn on one of the pointlessly pampered shrubs at the far end of the island. I manage to hide behind our bush and squat next to Mary Lou. Pretending to lose the spade I'm employing, I reach around her, lose my balance, and use her body as a fall-breaker, giving me a few seconds atop her, apologizing but not moving, while she tee-hees below. In extricating myself, I cup her right breast, squeeze it to signal that it's no accident, and giggle back. Trivial, except that Mary Lou leans over, not to protest the boob handling, but to whisper something in my ear, something I feel sure is a promise for future immoral activity. I do feel sure, but she's so close to my ear, nearly inside it, that it sounds like, "Spisss, spisss, spisss, spiss, spisss, Tsssimmy."

"Yeah. What did you just say?"

"I shay spisss, spiss, spiss, spisss, if you spiss, don't spiss spiss."

By then, Glenn and Deanna are approaching, probably drawn by the insect sounds coming from Mary Lou, and Donny is appearing round the fence with a small garbage can full of water. No chance to reach clarity right then, just stand, brush, and laugh it off.

Deanna and Mary Lou get along with the same easy understanding that appears to glue all the girls in this school together. They're in on something close to a shared ironic apprehension. Inside an absurd drama, they do what they can for as long as they can. In this play, those with all the power are so ill equipped to exercise or even recognize it that those dealt the poorest cards can easily win the early rounds. Boys have high-speed motor launches and girls rickety paddleboats, but it's the boys sputtering along. Girls know the rules, the course, the tricks of the game. Boys gun their engines.

But it won't last long, and the girls don't fool themselves about what looms ahead. All their élan seems shadowed by melancholy, some reserve or unwillingness to trust very far this temporary mobility. Before long, they'll be caged. No number of proms, phone calls to girlfriends making fun of boys, no quantity of superior insight and ability will alter the one future facing them. They can signal to one another, wave across the empty spaces to others walking parallel ditches. Awareness gains them nothing, and they waste no energy wishing it were otherwise. There are no prizes to be won, and though they feign interest in catching the best boys, it's a mock battle, much like a party game, where everyone ends up in the same closet, lights out, forced to plant the same dull kiss on the lips of males who vary as little as their haircuts or dreams. No point in competing, and they don't.

. . .

"All the privilege I claim for my own sex (it is not a very enviable one: you need not covet it), is that of loving longest, when existence or when hope is gone!"

. . .

Assuming Deanna likes me – she does – and assuming she saw Mary Lou's play for me – she did – one might have anticipated a little eye-scratching instead of the wry insouciance with which she reacts to Mary Lou's move to the front of the line. But me – I'm insulted.

With Donny and Glenn it's different. Near as I can tell, they'd had no past contact. Different interests (Glenn is no jock), different parts of town, different social classes. And now they're set at one another like two male wart hogs competing for – a third male wart hog.

"You wanta hold that a little steadier there, Danny?"

"Donny."

"Hold it steady, Dummy?"

"OK. You need help with the fertilizer bag, Glenn?"

"How you gonna help me with the bag AND hold the tree steady, how you gonna do that?" Glenn's doing a Bette Davis imitation, actually planting hands on hips.

Even Donny has his limits: "OK, Asshole," he says, stepping toward his tormentor.

It's amusing to watch. Donny sure doesn't look fierce. Still, small as he is, he's the one anybody'd back in a fight. Glenn is inflamed by jealousy, but not that inflamed.

"Don't flip, Donny. I was just fracturing you."

What a flood of look-at-what-a-regular-guy-I-am cowardice Glenn is flinging! I figure Donny will laugh and blow it off. He doesn't, so I do.

"You two guys oughta be friends."

Wrong line, could not have been worse.

"OK, so hate each other, but don't get into it here, please."

The "please" does it, as I knew it would. Both kids would slice off an eyelid for me. Backing off from a battle, losing face – nothing.

. . .

I wonder how aware either Donny or Glenn might be of the dangers right at the heart of the affection we're nurturing. Do they know how futureless all this is, what a mistake to move forward? Worse, do they imagine that we could sustain what we have, somehow ward off the terrors? How will they handle the agony when all the kissing has to stop, nothing to replace it but shame and denial? What are they, am I, thinking? What does thinking have to do with it?

A lot. This is planned, on my part, encouraged on theirs. Neither is unaware of what we're doing. Neither relishes talking about sex, but both make it clear they love it.

Here I am in 1952, a just-pretend. I hold only a short lease on the time and know it, though I let my four-year limit swim into view very seldom. My boy lovers aren't pretending, have no way of knowing that the future holds nothing, isn't there. Maybe they do know, consider the consequences, accept them. Maybe they're able to decide, which is more than I can do. I have been told by the celestials not to think of time – and I try, hoping to evade something. As if I don't guess, don't feel it all slipping away.

. . .

Bare ruined choirs

. . .

I said earlier I didn't find the Save-the-Children activity fulfilling. I lied. Within a few weeks this loosey-goosey scheme has grown legs or whatever sharp guys in 2016 will say about a booming enterprise. We have two hundred clients, more than fifty volunteers, a big hall at the Eagles Lodge, paper and pencils, good workbooks and plans, all courtesy of the Carnegie Tech pro, who knows her stuff.

We're told not to edit or correct the work of our mentees. Instead, we're to find out what interests the clients and discover ways to let them run with it – buy them books, take them to movies, supply them with materials. I don't know if it's that or simply the attention, but anybody wandering into our study hall would sense right away the good feeling, hear the hum of hard work as hard fun – whatever that might mean - whispered and earnest voices carrying on with urgency but no edge or anxiety. Sounds corny, but 'tis so.

It isn't that clients all start getting A's – too early to tell, though some of them by God will. It's more that they seem to care. We've been told by our expert to expect reluctance, some resistance to what might be felt as condescension, some anger rooted in shame. She makes it sound as if we need therapists as mentors, when what we have are steelworkers, gas-pumpers, meat-department managers, potters, and all the teachers in town. Turns out neither the kids being saved nor the saviors need cautioning. They like one another, once the shyness has drifted away. Often the talk wanders from the lessons to personal matters, to tips on dating (bad tips), on making money (bad tips), to general cheer-up (good talk), and, after a bit, mutual respect, reaching irregularly but often across lines of age, experience, and color. Most of the few black kids in town are in this class, sitting cross the desk from what are surely racist tutors. But the racism evaporates in the presence of an actual being – right there, breathing and talking.

How do I know all this? I don't know it; it's what happens. I take on the toughest case, a mean kid, mean-looking anyhow, hardened. Forced to attend by his anxious parents, he's determined to hate the whole experience, hate me, make me feel worthless. His name is Wallace.

"Should I call you Wallace?"

"Should I call you Timothy?"

"OK, how about I call you Wally?"

"How about I call you dispshit?"

"That'll be OK, fuckface."

What skill! From then on, Wally and I plow through the workbooks, along with reflections on the Pirates, girls, jobs, and school. Finally, race. Took us days to get here, but we do.

"The real worst part, I guess, is nobody talks about it. Just treat us as bad news, you know, or are real polite and beat it the hell out of there as fast as possible."

"Like you were a disease they might catch."

"Yeah, that's good."

"So, how do you get used to it?"

"Shit, Tim, you don't."

"Yeah, so what do you do with your anger?"

"What do you mean?"

"Why don't you just go round kicking the shit out of every white asshole you see?"

I realize I'm tempting him into an easy response, something like "Starting with you?" If so, he resists. "That'd be real smart. Just get me in jail."

"Which happens a lot?"

"My uncle."

"You know it's not always going to be like this. Things'll get better."

Again, there are so many responses available to him, easy ways to win the contest. But he doesn't regard it as a contest.

"I sure hope so. Thanks."

The thanking makes me ashamed, but I know from Harold days that "shame" is an unproductive feeling, so I accept his gratitude and squeeze his shoulder. Of course his culture, more macho even than mine, won't allow him to accept an encouraging squeeze. But he does.

• • •

The tutoring session runs late, or rather I do, but Glenn's parents hide any irritation they might feel at being kept waiting, motor running, heater purring. Actually, they seem to lust after me at least as much as their son does and their daughter doesn't – not lust, maybe, but something more deep-rooted. I make them feel smart and important. They feel I admire them, and they find so little admiration anywhere. But that isn't everything. They like me and know I like them – and I do. Their enthusiastic affection can hardly fail to find an echo. They're lonely, like all of us, and when an answer to that comes along, they're defenseless. Shallow and pretentious as they are, that isn't all they are. I slip them the key to something they thought they'd lost, or never had. Maybe it's the other way round. They make me see how loosely the privileges of class are tied to money, how deeply I feel exiled from the first, even when I have the second. In any case, I'm happy to see them, to see Glenn, and, wonder of wonders, scary Betsy.

I crawl into the back seat with the kids, do it with unaccustomed awkwardness, trying to be decorous, avoid body contact. The result: a hand is groping my ass so insistently I have trouble sitting, not wanting to cause injury or stop the fondling. By the time I'm settled, the hand is gone, with no clue as to which kid has welcomed me thus. Either is fine.

I feel a surge of pride in being there, a part of things. I badly want to become accustomed to what passes for privilege here in The Home of the Potters. I want to be part of their taken-for-granted. On top of that, the class thrills, I'm proud to offer my butt for other people's fun. Were I like most systematic mashers – a fitting word for my role – I'd protect my own flesh as ardently as I'd seek to expose that of others. But not me.

Maybe it's because Tim's body doesn't seem integral to whatever it is I am. More than not caring what others do to me, I welcome it. Want to see, feel, kiss, snuggle, insert? Why the hell not? Your pleasure is mine. The more you give, the more you have, as DHL was fond of saying, right as always.

I have a great plan, do-able now that Betsy is present and apparently free for the evening. First, I need to request what I know will be granted. "I hate to ask this, as you've been so kind to me so many times, but what I was thinking of will take us a while, keeping us up late, if that's OK. Do you think?"

They think.

"Do you suppose I could stay over? I know it's a school-night, and I normally wouldn't ask..."

Yes, yes, yes, our house is your house, we'll be so happy, don't get to see enough of you, one of our own.

We play "Risk," a game not yet invented, first constructing a game board: a map of the world, colored nicely, each continent divided up and named – Northern Europe, West Africa, East Asia. Then we make soldiers, gluing together cheerios into stacks and, Betsy's idea, dipping them in food coloring. I supervise this work, half-remembering and half-inventing rules. Daddy Downing makes the spinner and concocts out of wooden dowels the bigger pieces representing ten of the smaller cheerios armies, essential for serious imperialists.

It's nearly eleven by the time we finish preparing, but nobody wants to quit. I think the Downings have seldom had such fun, maybe never. The laughter is unforced, and even "Big Glenn," as he wants me to call him, drops his protective sarcasm. Betsy seems the only one outside the spell, but she's gracious enough not to break it.

People less mesmerized would have called it a night, but we start a game, adjusting the rules to make things fairer, prevent anyone from gaining a quick advantage. By 1 a.m., we have armies all over our game-board, each of us pursuing relentlessly the world conquest almost within our grasp. Had it not been for Betsy, we'd have kept at it until dawn. But she calls us to our senses, sends us off to bed, the parents as reluctant as four-year-olds leaving their toys.

Glenn and I waste no time. As soon as the door shuts, we clench – grinding, sucking, massaging with both hands. I lean back long enough to undo his pants, then rip off his shirt, actually tearing it.

"Sorry."

"Ummmph."

No jammies tonight. We hit the bed and we fuck, actually do.

"Did I hurt you, Glenn – hurt your feelings?"

"Hurt me? God, Tim. That was..."

"You don't regret it? You didn't mind?"

"Mind? God, Tim."

I want to know how he feels about sex. I've never done it, and certainly Harold hadn't. I've gathered enough from this initial try to be sure I'd like to do it often, but I also don't want to damage Glenn. Try as I might, I can't help but like him. Then there's the promise I made Betsy. I hadn't been thinking of that as her brother and I diddled, but now it comes on me with a rush. Have I forced him, coldly set about trapping his heart?

"Glenn, I loved that. I felt close to you and it was so exciting. But did you mind it, feel like I was doing something not quite right?"

"No."

"No what?"

"I loved it when we fucked, Tim."

We don't extend the conversation, just go to bed, cuddling close, hands folded together like old marrieds, confident and mutually protective.

. . .

Next evening, a bit before dark, I make it up to Margie's. I've never been where she lives, nor had Harold, though it's only a half-mile away. But it's a half-mile up the hill: across the railroad tracks, then the street, and then up into the thick trees, dirt roads, and dirt poor. Funny how these poor people, we poor people, maintain sharp and unmistakable distinctions. Margie and the hill folk are not in the town's worst area for human beings, the one most calculated to produce suffering. The very bottom was in a Bottom, Marshall's Bottom it's called, a pit that floods about every fourth spring, bringing mud where dust had reigned. But the hill neighborhoods are genuine third world: no windows fit their frames, no doors latch, no lawns are free of something rusting. A couple of the black families live up here, along with whites who have given up being racist and seem to get along well with neighbors.

Though I haven't till now visited, one and all seem to recognize me.

Probably they know Mom, who's acquainted with everyone and who, to give her her due, makes no distinctions. In my own marginally better neighborhood, tiny cheap houses but with doors attached and streets paved, you can be outside a long time in March and see nobody at all, so ubiquitous is the caving instinct. But here, adults and kids treat the smeary evening as if it were balmy beach weather. In the streets and yards, fixing things, messing around, visiting back and forth, they hail me with a pleasure and surprise that make me feel nearly as terrible as I should.

"Tim Mills! Good to see you! You must be hungry. Please come in!"

Every house I pass – I'm exaggerating but not much – offers itself as a restaurant, an oasis. Possessed by delight in finding me there and a conviction that I'm undernourished, men, women, and kids flock to me. I go in four or five houses – how can I not? – and manage to get away only after having milk or a Coke. Cookies, crackers with peanut butter. Few of the kids are my age; most are smaller, shy too. I play with them, and they enter in, as all kids will. Too bad I haven't returned to this time at age ten. I would have liked myself better.

Finally I arrive at Margie's house, nearly an hour after I'd planned. They drag me inside immediately, exposing in their one main room the signs of a meal just completed. Margie's parents ask after Mom, "a dear Christian woman," and then press me to eat.

"You know, Mrs. and Mr. Armstrong, I'm grateful, but I think I'd bust open if I did. It took me a good hour to make it down your street to see Margie. Everybody was feeding me."

They smile but aren't convinced I couldn't manage some cake. So, cake it is. Fine cake too, chocolate with a good two inches of frosting.

Margie held back when I entered, hiding behind three siblings. While the cake is being served, I make for the kids, roaring, pretending to be a bear. By this means, I manage to send them all, even the older boy, into hysterics, and cut out Margie from the herd.

"Mr. and Mrs. Armstrong, I wanted to thank you for allowing Margie to work as my research assistant. She's terrific. Actually, I wouldn't bother you, except for a small problem. I'm doing this project on the history of East Liverpool and have been relying on Margie's help. You see, she's been regularly going to the library for me, doing research. She does it very well."

I pause to see whether this is OK with all concerned. The Armstrongs are smiling cheerily. I guess that's good, so I press on. "Margie's also been doing oral histories, talking to kids her age but mostly elderly people about the old days, getting their memories down so we can collect them and write a personal account of the town, what it was like last century. Margie's been excellent at all this, and I wanted to thank you and also consult."

I should have quit sooner. By now, the parents' cheerful look is mixed with uncertainty, though they're still quite ready to trust me. But what exactly is it I'm doing with their daughter? A research assistant? Library? Talk to old-timers?

I need to slow down, and am about to when Margie saves me the trouble. "Tim asked me before Christmas about doing this research. I told you, remember? I've been working in the library and talking to old people like Mrs. Baker over behind Neville School about what it was like here back then. I can do it pretty well, Tim says."

"Oh yeah, Margie's smart and reliable," I add.

The parents beam. Margie tips the scale. They recognize her maturity and strength, are happy that I do, and know she'll not only do things well but will only do good things.

"My problem is pay. Please know I wouldn't bother you with this, if I could budge Margie. I got this grant from the Ohio Historical Society, that's the truth, so it's not my money at all. In this grant there's money for a research assistant. They're paying for it, not me. That's the money I can't get Margie to take. I've tried everything – from stuffing cash into her hat to hiding it in her schoolbooks. Nothing works. I even threatened her."

Looks of alarm.

"Just kidding. But can you help me? Margie has earned this money and should have it. It's only right."

Both parents look to Margie for cues. Disaster.

"If she won't take it, I'll get in trouble with the Society. It's against regulations."

Brilliant stroke. Margie slides into resignation with the speed available only to the pure of heart. Blessed are they indeed.

I extricate myself soon, make a clean get-away under cover of darkness. I feel better now and vow I'll come back up often, realizing I'll come back up never but pocketing that certainty for later remorse. That I'd managed OK with these poor, generous people is no credit to me, but I did give myself points for the hefty wage I will force on Margie.

. . .

Now for Sally. That's tough. Without the Internet, much less a developed drug culture, what can I do? How is depression treated in 2016? Uppers? I know weed is around now, given the plethora of warnings against it: pamphlets, movies like "Reefer Madness," and lectures from the YMCA director. But will marijuana help depression? I spend an afternoon in the library, fumbling about in the same outdated medical books that had given me nothing about Dad. They give me less here. The librarian tries to help, but she naturally regards depression as a bad mood. To her credit, she grasps the idea quickly and throws herself into the hunt. But there seems to be no quarry out there, not in books, probably not in the medical know-how I can tap into.

I think of the Cleveland Clinic, but don't want to arouse suspicion, in case I'm forced to descend into the criminal underworld, wherever that might be. My next thought, like yours, is Meilie. Terrible. Meilie is, apart from that betting ring, a deeply conventional guy with a moral code that's ferociously straight. Even a whiff of reefers or opium will send him right to Dad. The answer comes by accident, in a conversation with Betsy the morning after Glenn and I gave up our virginity to a good cause.

"Betsy, you going to an Ivy League school year after next?"

I'm joshing, witlessly and coldly, but Betsy, who misses nothing, lets it go.

"I'd like to, Tim, I really would. I've been talking a lot to Mr. Lee. I know he looks like a stuffed carp, but he knows what he's doing."

I find that hard to believe. Mr. Lee teaches Chemistry and coaches the golf team. He moves like a banana slug and looks like one, though Betsy's description works, too.

"He's been stuck here for eighty years, about, but he reads scientific journals, has written a few articles himself. He has a lab in his basement, does serious work. His wife works with him, and, maybe because of that, he doesn't think it's hellish for a woman to pursue science, organic chemistry in my case. Trouble is, some schools won't consider admitting women. It might work at Ohio State, but I checked and they weren't welcoming."

"So where, Princeton? Harvard?"

"I think Wellesley or Bryn Mawr."

"That's sensational, Betsy. You know, in my former life, I went to Case, became an engineer even, for a time."

What have I just said? Betsy looks at me with curiosity, high-voltage.

"Tell me what you mean."

I do.

"I'll be damned. And you're here with a new body and mind. So what's the connection to Harold? And why don't I remember Harold? Not that I doubt you."

"You don't? Harold has been expunged from your memory, replaced by Tim. That's what they told me."

"Are you happy with how you're spending your time, Tim?"

"No. I haven't had much of a plan, beyond narrow pleasures. And I think it's vile, hate myself for it, when I think along those lines, which I try not to do, which makes it worse."

"I didn't mean to criticize. Not at all. I like you, and I wouldn't think of judging you. I have no idea what I'd do."

"Thanks. You're one hell of a person. I know that's lame."

She smiles.

"You know, Betsy, what's happened without me knowing it is ... well, knowing you and Mary and Carol and Jimmy Canton and Donny and my own sister and (I manage not to forget) Glenn and even your parents – that's what's it's been about."

"How so?"

"I'm finding things out I didn't see first time. That's getting so interesting, it's doing weird things to me. Truth is, I don't know if I'm ashamed of what I've done. As things are turning out, maybe it isn't so bad, trivial as it sounds, as it is. But the good stuff wasn't planned, just happened. Can I help you with schools, applications? I do know a hell of a lot from first time around, about statements and that stuff. I was in that line. Could I help?"

She answers with a wink, an end in itself.

. . .

My talk with Mr. Lee, Dr. Lee, is immediately fruitful.

"Amphetamine sulphate."

"Huh?"

"For hay-fever, asthma, but in Europe it's sometimes injected. Makes you euphoric. Problems though. It was synthesized first in 1887, in Germany, I believe. Started using it as a psychostimulant in the twenties. The natural form is from the genus EPHEDRA; amphetamines are synthetic forms. Ephedra comes from China, a natural distillation from plants there. But nobody bothers with it now, since the synthetic form is easy to produce."

"I have a friend, Dr. Lee, who is seriously depressed, chemically depressed."

He nods, doesn't ask me how I know.

"I think amphetamines might help her."

"Yes, they would, without a doubt. But how you gonna get them?"

That's cutting to the chase. I take a deep breath, "I was hoping..."

"I'd make you some."

I wouldn't have considered that, but fine. Can he cook some up in his lab?

"If you let me supervise the patient, I'll do it. It's a powerful drug, Tom, and it could help many people. The government controls it, in the half-assed way we have of doing things. You can get Benzedrine inhalers easy, any drugstore, but not useful forms of the drug for what you're calling 'depression.' What was that drug? You tell me."

"Amphetamine sulfate."

"Good boy. Just wanted to see if you're an idiot."

"I see."

"I'll do it. Keep your goddam mouth shut."

"You can count on me. My name's Tim Mills."

"Sure it is."

CHAPTER 17

While Dr. Jekyll is concocting home-brew uppers, I hop a bus to the higher reaches of town, a park-like suburb, screened from the mill smoke by bumpy ridges. Odd how the old river towns manage small sections, all high up, as beautiful as anything in the nation. Wheeling has such sections, Steubenville, even Mingo Junction. The lawns are big and natural-looking, trees everywhere. There's a drawback, of course. Screen them how you will, they still belly up to heavy-industry cancer pits. All the same, I'm as impressed now by these uppity places as Harold had been. In a few decades such suburbs will lose their grace, as houses swell up like heated boils and the surrounding greenery shrinks.

It's Saturday, and there's little reason to suppose Glenn and family are home, country-clubbers that they are. Still, in March what must comprise main Club activities – swimming and golf – are impossible. Maybe the members gather for canasta or quilting. I haven't bothered to call ahead, as any idiot would, so anxious am I to get to Glenn. Why? You'll see.

Worst luck imaginable. Glenn III gone, Glenn II and Dorothy right there, unoccupied.

"*Tim*!! Wonderful to see you! Glenn, come here. It's Tim. What you doing standing out there in the cold? Come in!"

"I'm so sorry to bother you, Mrs. Downing. Very rude of me. I was just..."

"*Rude*? You could never be rude, honey." I think she's about to hug me, but it isn't a hugging era. So I hug her. She responds so eagerly I feel a nettling army of guilts, certain I've just pledged myself to something I have no intention of fulfilling.

When she backs off, I seize the moment. "You've been so good to me, Mrs. Downing."

Tearfully and with a courage appropriate for some occasion actually calling for courage, she gulps, "Oh Tim, honey, couldn't you call me Dotty? Or Mom?"

The last comes out so wistfully, hopelessly, that only someone even more lickspittle mean than I would have backed off.

"I am proud – honored – Mom."

Perched on the edge of a quaking emotional precipice, I am – never doubt the power of prayer – rescued by Glenn II, who has no paternal designs on me. He gets me off the porch into the warm, gives me news on Glenn's whereabouts, gets us Cokes, and sets off with me in his Cadillac to pick up Glenn from his scout meeting.

"That's nice of you, but I should have called ahead. Don't mess up his meeting."

"You kidding? He'd poison my oatmeal if I let him stay there while you were here."

"Well..."

"You know how much he likes you, right?" He examines me closely. I feel accused, though I doubt that he is accusing.

"Does he?"

He *is* accusing, doesn't speak but narrows his eyes significantly.

"I admire Glenn, Mr. Downing. He's a good friend."

Not enough.

"He's a smart kid, generous and funny. He's also kind."

"Yeah?"

"Can I say something?"

He winks.

"Mr. Downing, I don't know if you realize that Glenn's not at all a snob."

"And you figured he would be. Still, why are you friends?"

This is getting prickly. "I can't explain our friendship very well, to be honest. We get along, have a lot in common – you know, talking about school and girls and sports. I guess you're right. At first I was a little wary, imagining that all rich kids were shits."

This is the right note, though I hit it by chance and pretty late in the conversation. Mr. Downing laughs:. "Yeah, well, most rich kids *are* shits. You know some of the little assholes living up here, right? I always worry Glenn is one of them."

I nod.

"Tim, you're good for him. I've never seen him so happy. Maybe what I took as his rich asshole quality was, all along, just him being miserable. He seems like a real kid now – for the first time since he was about ten. Thanks!"

Wanta make me feel worse?

Fifteen minutes later, Glenn, rescued from his scouting fun, is with me in his bedroom. I notice for the first time a bookshelf, recessed and partly hidden by some curtains. This seems so unlike Glenn, I wander over for a look. In with a depressing amount of Lloyd C. Douglass is a sizeable collection of 20s writers (Fitzgerald, Anderson, Hemingway), along with Twain, Poe, and Dickens. What in hell? These must be Betsy's.

"Glenn, what a great library!" I'm only a leaky bladder away from asking whose it is.

"Thanks. I got them all with money my rich grandma sent me – still sends me. She makes me buy books with it."

I'm examining some Fitzgerald, looking for signs of use, finding them. "Makes you?"

"Nah. She doesn't care. Betsy got me started. There's this book guy in Pittsburgh, and also Ogilvies gets them for me." I recognize in Glenn the same restraint I'd exercised a second ago. He's keeping himself from adding, "I hope you don't think I'm a dick for reading. I also masturbate and beat up little kids and normal things, too."

I'm still holding the book, trying to adjust to this unexpected information. Is everybody here secretly ripened and complex, demanding of me more than I'm prepared to give? Puppies from the past is what I expected, and now get full-fledged wonders. Hell!

I take a deep breath, ready myself for a different kind of conversation with a different kid. What can I say about *This Side of Paradise*, which Harold hadn't read? Try *The Great Gatsby*.

Try Glenn across the room, dressed only in jeans, smirking at me and standing before his big bed, beckoning.

He had turned on old ELO station WOHI, playing a Frankie Lane hit, "Ghost Riders in the Sky," surely one of the oddest songs ever to make it big: "If you want to save your soul from hell a ridin' on this range, then cowboy change your ways today, or with us you will ride; a tryin' to catch the devil's herd, across the cloudy skies." Not sexy music, but it's loud and covers our upcoming noise. But my lust alarms me. I haven't come here *for* sex but to talk about sex, apologize, get straight with this interesting boy. Does he think I want only his body?

Something about that thought, the conversation with his dad, the books, Glenn's belly – suddenly I see myself too clearly and want a way to escape, not from the room so much, though certainly that, but from what I've become.

"Did you think I came here only for sex, Glenn? Never mind. Let's not, though."

"You want to stop. You don't want..."

"No, that's not what I'm saying. I'm not trying to end our relationship and find a way to make it look good. No, I don't want to stop. But I do worry about you, the future, what I'm doing to you, what kind of person I am."

"You're not doing anything **to** me, Tim. Don't leave."

"You don't know, Glenn."

He suddenly seems angry. That doesn't fit with what I know of Glenn, but what do I know of Glenn? Little enough that I shut up and let him go on.

"I know you don't mean it this way, but it's not very flattering. It's OK for you, but you worry that it's not for me. Like I'm a baby and you need to take care of me. I don't know how I might feel about it later. How could I? I might call myself a fairy. I might tomorrow, only I won't. Even if I did, so what? Why should I stop doing something, if I don't want to and don't have any reason to and hope you don't either? We're here now. I don't want to lose this because of what might be a month from now, when there won't be a month from now."

He pauses but isn't finished. He's excited and incoherent, but I catch the drift, realize I'm being taught something – and becoming scared.

"Tim, I do see what you're saying. If we heard that a couple of guys were doing what we do, we might call them names. I don't think we would, me and you. Here's what it is for me, though. I don't care. It's more. I care about you and what's going on. It's the best thing I've ever done, and not just the sex. I never thought I'd know somebody like you. I think this is the best thing that'll happen to me in my life. I'd sooner die than stop this."

. . .

Not knowing when the dawn will come, I open every door.

. . .

He isn't being dramatic, delivering a speech. He's making himself clear, laying bare his young heart. At least I keep from echoing his declaration. There is much to admire in Glenn, more than I'm capable of recognizing. He is funny, smart, and dear. He has few or none of the class blemishes I'd attached to him. But I would not choose death over losing him. Without deserving any of it, Glenn still pulls out of me a condescension that allows me to keep my distance. Even I cannot be so craven as to make declarations, add more lies to what my presence and rutting activities have proclaimed so loudly.

Poor Glenn. Someday, when he's working dutifully at his law firm, this reckless, boyish romping will come flooding back, and it will hurt. His feeling for me now constitutes his being. He's remade himself to fit what I want, all in the name of extending that affection. Glenn has in him a radiant selflessness that gives him range for invention, and he would not stop inventing new ways to be, faithful to a dream that is like a flowing cloud. He is devoted, ready to find new parts to play, but he will run out of costumes and we will run out of thrills. Clear as day. But I wonder if I'm settling for clarity, stabilizing myself and forcing Glenn to do all the shape shifting, refusing to take risks for no better reason than wanting to avoid confusion. I find it easy to say I don't feel all that much for Glenn, as if such feelings descended on us, just happens, and were not a willed activity. Only people selfishly guarding themselves against others take on such ignorance. Ignorance isn't the right word; cruelty is. Were I a better person, a halfway good person, I would not hesitate to answer Glenn's call.

• • •

With only a week remaining before the big talent assembly, not to mention Dad's operation, I decide I should spend a Sunday at home, finding out more about Joanie and tolerating my parents. Such a nice thing to do! Joanie has recovered from her non-sexual escapades with the as-yet-unpunished Carl and is not above registering, but just to me, her sarcastic disbelief in my enthusiasm for a Sunday drive. What could be finer, I suggest, than going out into the countryside, exploring some obscure byways?

My Dad reacts with enthusiasm, as if taking off on roads is one of the few heady pleasures he allows himself. Behind the wheel, he can relax and fool around. He's as close both to taking control and to losing himself as he ever is. I haven't made myself aware of it before, but on these drives he is garrulous, exercising a self unlike any of his others. My mother says only pleasant things, suppressing her repetitive anecdotes and predictable opinions. Our car is old, the bottom of the line when new, but it's clean and friendly, so even Joanie and I, cramped in the tiny back seat, enjoy ourselves.

The county is webbed with thousands of tiny roads, many unsigned or with absurd markers like "10." Most are paved, but you never can predict how long the pavement might hold out. It's hilly country, heavily wooded, presenting always, even in its present unleafed state, the illusion of limitless uncharted territories. Around every corner there are more trees, often a woods, sometimes a creek or a bog, some meadows – now and then a trailer, abandoned mattress, or a house. We ignore the latter and fall into the dream of being outside of familiarity altogether. Locked in a mystery, the car weaves round, never allowing anything steady. Landscapes are on the move, melting one into another. Just as we draw close to failure, to a destination, Dad veers off, past new woods, fields, worlds.

"I see something you don't see, and it's in the shape of a big blubbery butt."

"Joanie!" Mom says, laughing.

"Like Mrs. Nickle's butt," Dad says.

"It *is* Mrs. Nickels' butt, right Joanie? I saw her back there leaning over a fence, butt unfurled. That it?"

"Too late. We passed it."

Someone in a helicopter would have seen us meandering through just a few square miles. Someone with a watch would have clocked us at maybe two hours. But there was no helicopter and no watch. We sing, play games, are silent, and loll. I don't think first time around I took note of such times, probably resented them, imagining they were keeping me from who-knows-what fun with friends I didn't have.

I'm very glad I've been given the chance to find this pleasure. It's something only a family as uneasy as mine could manage. I find myself thinking that it's the best I've found back here, lost as it was on old Harold. They hadn't told me I'd have the capacity not just to screw hapless teenagers but to swim in quiet waters. During this ride, I become fully present, losing that cursed double consciousness, the sense that I am watching myself, scoring my every move, much like a judge at a diving competition. Now, it's as if I have no self. Happiness is all around me, in and through me. It is part of me; I am part of it.

Emerging from the maze and chugging into our garage, parents and kids divide, Joanie jumping on my back and riding me onto the porch, through the door and into the kitchen.

"Can you help me with my homework, Timmy?"

"No, I'm busy!" I'm so pleased she asks and she knows it.

"Oh-----you are not! You never do homework."

"And you never need help. I do homework. I'll put it off, though, just to feed you the answers, keep you from flunking out and taking to the streets, earning a small seedy living with your small seedy body. You still having trouble with long division?"

"It's a relief map I'm making – you know, mountains and valleys."

"And lakes and rivers. Why don't we create one in that metal thing in the garage, that oil pan? We could use the motor we were playing with, line the pan with something thick and have water flowing. Whatdya say?"

Most kids would have retreated to the original idea, a commonplace relief map, crusty lump-slops spread around in globs that even the most charitable vision would never mistake for mountains. Not Joanie.

"Yes!! We could color the plastery stuff. And use some of those river pebbles we collected, you'n me, make it a prize-winner. Whatdya mean, something thick?"

"Maybe ask Dad what would work."

We do. He knows. Shows us quietly and as quietly retreats.

Joanie and I construct right through supper. As we're occupying the kitchen, and as our activities are by parental decree more important than eating, Mom sidles in, edges snake-like toward the refrigerator, and slaps together sandwiches for us. Her sandwiches lean toward the rudimentary, in this case, a full two-inch thick hunk of processed cheese slammed between Wonder Bread slices, flavored with Miracle Whip, with a side of nothing at all. And milk.

"Thanks, Mom." She's already sliding round the corner.

"Oh, you're welcome, kids."

"That's really nice of you. Thanks. Isn't that nice, Joanie?"

"What?"

"The sandwich Mom made us so we could keep going. And the milk."

"Uh huh."

"Joanie!"

"What, Timmy?"

"Tell Mom 'thanks.'"

"Thanks, Mom. I love these cheese sandwiches. Thanks."

Then hissing to me: "Tell Mom 'thanks'? What's wrong with you?

These taste like thick dust, yellow ball gloves. She likes doing it. Can you eat this? What's wrong with you?"

Hissing back: "The thought's sweet."

"I guess. It's what she does." Then, back to normal. "Is that where the Rocky Mountains are? Right next to the Mississippi River? Is that the Mississippi River?"

"Yeah. The mountains are OK. Maybe a little close to the water flowin' there along the path of the yeller Mississippi, but the glop ran. They're on the right side of the continent, more or less. This supposed to be to scale? We got Iceland bigger than Africa. Let's put more colored rocks at the poles, blue like the Aurora Borealis."

"They have those at both poles? The Northern Lights at the South Pole?"

"They shine at *our* poles, also there where Hawaii runs into Japan."

. . .

Feeling all cozied, I decide it's time to add another virtuous girl to my list of conquests, a short list now, but with many elbowing one another to get on it. I think of Patty and recoil in horror. It hasn't been easy mashing her back into acquaintancehood. She still acts as if we are lovers, separated by an unfriendly fate. A phone call to her, much less a date, would land me back up to my nose in Okefenokee.

Mary Lou? That brief encounter with her left breast had been nice, and she had whispered into my ear inviting things. Or had she? Maybe she was telling me to move my hand. But she's worth a try. I mean, how can she resist? Easily, I expect. But here goes, "So, Mary Lou, would you like to go to a movie Saturday night?"

"A date, Tim?"

"Absolutely."

"Tim, why would you ask me?"

"What do you mean?"

"I'm surprised at you."

"What do you mean?"

"What do *you* mean, Tim?"

"I'm confused, Mary Lou. I just want to know if you'd like to go to a movie, on a date, Saturday night."

"Of course I would, Tim, and you know that."

"Great."

"But I don't think that's very nice of you."

"Huh? I thought you said you wanted to."

"Of course I do."

"I thought we were friends. I really like you. I thought you liked me."

"I thought so, too, but this isn't nice. What about Carol? What about Mary?"

My face lights up like a smoggy sunset. She might as well ask me about Glenn, about Donny. Does she know about Patty?

"Gee, Mary Lou, I only meant a date."

"I know, but think about Carol and Mary. Are you trying to hurt them?"

"My goodness."

"Are you trying to hurt me?"

I shut up, having nothing to say. Then I do. "I don't think that's what I'm trying for, Mary Lou. I can see why you'd think that. I feel so lost. Do you think there's something wrong with me? I guess I don't have any right to ask that. Mary Lou, really, I don't know what I'm doing. Yes, I do. I'm being selfish."

"You are."

"Yeah."

"I wish you hadn't called."

"Can we pretend I didn't, go back to where we were?"

"I don't think so."

I go no further down the list.

• • •

Wednesday, Assembly Day, finds Judith and me dressed to the nines, throats sprayed. Dr. Clendenning has worked out a new version of the climax to our first number:

Longin' to tell you [slow way down, soften] but afraid and shy,
I'd let my [very slow] gol – den chan – ces [slower still] pass me by.
[speed up to a snail's crawl] Soon you'd leave me,
Off you would go in the mist of day,
[slowest yet] Nev – er, nev – er to know [hold note forever]
How I loved you [long pause]
If [pause] I [pause] loved you.

Since the section is repeated, given both to Julie and Billy, we aren't a quick act. To make matters worse on the timing front, Dr. Clendenning calls us out of class second period to load on us yet another way to prolong things. "Got this idea, kids."

Judith and I bob our heads,

"The Never-Walking encore is great, but don't rush into it. You're going to get applause like thunder. After a minute of it, I key the orchestra at measure eighty-four there – see?"

We see.

"I'll cut right into the applause with the orchestra, forte. Then you both start in at 'Longin to tell you'---alternating phrases until 'Never, never to know,' where you both sing, a duet, louder than hell, dramatic, ear-splitting sweet. Tim, you go high and Judith, you pick up the harmony, and then whisper the last phrase, 'if I loved you,' in unison, and dead soft, I mean really soft, slow too, of course."

"OK."

"You better go back to cutting up frogs. I'm not supposed to interrupt your work."

On our return---"Judith, what do you think of this?"

"I think it's a little show-offy, even without the encore."

"Me too. Should we say we don't want to do it?"

"Huh? I want to do it."

"OK. A little show-offy is good. But this'll extend our time, a lot. Let's save the other number for the Spring Concert."

"You think we shouldn't just take over the talent show entirely, Tim? John would approve, of course, if you convinced him it was his idea."

"You're right about John, evil one, but do you agree to limit ourselves to merely half the whole program this time out?

"OK. That's good."

It is good. Sure enough, we finish the duet, embrace, bow – holding hands. The cheering comes crashing down like an explosion, on and on. Judith and I stand there, smiling like goofs, forgetting (at least I am) that we'll be doing the last part over again. After a minute that seems like ten, here comes the orchestra behind us. Luckily, the lead-in isn't short, which gives us time to regroup and the audience a chance to sense that something is happening.

"Longin' to tell you..."

Immediate hush.

Finish, further atomic blasts, retreat.

Then, faithful to his imbecility, John grabs the mike, shouts down the shouting and gives forth the news, we had, true, planted but hoped he'd forget, "How about an encore? Yes! We haven't done encores in the past, but I've never been in charge in the past, and I say encores are the thing – so we'll do that thing and have an encore."

You lackwit! Busses leave on schedule, other acts are waiting, we've taken too much time as it is.

I look at Judith, who's thinking the same thing, nudges me, so I go out, grab the mike, and attempt some damage control. "Thanks, John, but there are other acts we want to hear and not much time, so thanks to all you friends from Judith and from me. We'll howl at you another time – and that's a threat!"

John looks none too pleased, seems disposed to force an encore. But when the audience laughs, he adopts my words as his, accepts the good will, and proceeds. Drawing back into the side hall, Judith and I are slow beating a retreat, still lost in our mutual daze. It occurs to me that John might possess further, more crapulent ideas, and that Judith and I should duck out of his sweaty-palmed reach. But it's high emotion, romantic and dangerous, and it holds us in its spell, right here in this huge cementy hallway leading nowhere in particular.

Plain Judith is pretty enough now, bright and alive, but she seems ready to leave. I've come to recognize that, celestial promises notwithstanding, my peers seem to find it easy enough to keep their hands off me. They do not pant as I pass; they do not roll over on their backs with feet pawing the air; they do not rip bodices or heave. Certainly, Harold had achieved nothing like Tim's success, but Tim has failed to line 'em up and knock 'em down. In seven months, I've had what sticklers for the truth would count as three sexual encounters, with Donny, Glenn and Mary. Groping Patty (Mary Lou, Deanna), kissing Carol: those pleasures might be preludes to more – and might not. Most likely not. If any are to develop, so will the friendships, the sense of ease and trust.

I had supposed sex would be isolated, uncomplicated. Wasn't that the big advantage given me, a chance to maximize pleasure, minimize involvement? Instead, I have found it as complicated having sex this time through as not having it was before. I had supposed I'd find mere friendship laughably naïve. It isn't. I have really screwed nobody. I've slowly advanced toward the intricate state of loving some. The sex that has occurred has been produced by circumstances both broader and more inclusive than I ever expected. I'd planned almost nothing that has come about, written no scripts that have been followed.

Judith hangs out with me a minute – out of kindness, the unintended consequence of which is that we're sitting ducks for John, who plows straight at us after introducing in his inimitable way the next act, dance stylings by Debby Ann Naylor, who (Harold knew) seizes every opportunity to don spangles and tap her way into our hearts. But she never makes it past the vestibule, the left ventricle, sad Debby Ann. Debby Ann is loyal to her dream, and it repays her with mockery she finally is unable to ignore.

"Hello there, kids! I like the way we turned your encore into the next act. Classy, class---eeeeee!"

"Liked your introduction, John."

"Yes you did. I mean, you and I know these things, Tim. Excellent singing, Janice."

"Judith."

"Oh yeah, that's what I meant to say. Judith, of course. Easy mistake there, but..." John ran out of steam, tried to fire up again. "Liked your act there, Juiced-Up Judith. Good lungs you got, and I'm not being foul-minded either, ha ha."

Judith and I edge back, keeping our eyes on John, just in case he decides to come at us.

"I want you – don't go away."

"Well, we have to..."

"Wait. Don't think of going. I have an idea or two up my sleeve, once this oddball girl gets through with her dance. I guess you could call it a dance, ha ha."

I look at my watch. Hallelujah! "I'll bet those are some ideas. But John, there's only about a minute until the bell. Looks to me like Debby Ann is going to tap right into the night."

"Like fun she is!" said John, who begins a rapid twirl that will launch him back into his emceeing action. But he slips, does John, halfway round, his shoulders and upper body having moved too fast for his fat butt and heavy feet. The result is an undignified sprawl, accompanied by a yip that turns into low-pitched but loud baying.

"Oh my God! I'm hurt. I broke my leg. Help me!"

Judith and I somehow keep from laughing, but neither of us squats to help. John makes a few scrambles, trying to get upright with such haste that he once again fails to get his lower body beneath his upper and takes another sliding spill. By this point he's sniveling, not softly.

"Are you hurt, John?" This, naturally, from Judith. I'm hoping that John has fractured at least one leg, his skull, all ten fingers, and his ass bone. I hope he has lost the use of his eyes and nostrils and sustained internal injuries, mortal.

Just as a weeping John makes it to his feet, pants torn right down the ass-crack, and starts plunging toward the auditorium, the bell rings. Debby

Ann, ever the pro, transitions into two fast trip-and-grab moves, bows, and exits with dignity, as the one-thousand-odd kids empty out faster than the calendars flicking by in old movies, years moving before you can count or even see them, the auditorium steadily darkening.

CHAPTER 18

Next on the schedule, drawn up with the needs of others in mind, more study with Donny that isn't exactly study. This time, Donny's parents sit me down for their family five-o'clock dinner. They'd fed me before, but usually sandwiches-on-napkins or, touchingly, trays brought up to Donny's room. Now, the five of us jam into the antiseptic kitchen, mooshing ourselves around an oil-cloth-draped table. The food is right out of Mom's mental cookbook but much better, probably because the cooking grease, lard in short, is differently aged.

"Tim, do you like school?"

Donny's dad, equipped with a face too small for his body but otherwise unremarkable, is at least as shy as mine, shares also his distant devotion to his kids, determined to help without making them ashamed. I like him right off. He doesn't want me to like him. He wants me to be at home and be friends with his son.

"I do, sir. It's fun, most of it, and it gives Donny and me a chance to study together."

"That's good."

"You know, lots of times we find ways – mostly Donny does – to make what seems pretty boring in school quite interesting." I have no idea what I mean, though I'm confident I can expand, even produce instances of whatever it is, if challenged.

Donny looks at me as if I were impersonating a comedian. I take it as a challenge. "We were studying Mesopotamia. In school, it was awful. But Donny had the idea to make it a game, where the winner gets to slug the loser in the shoulder---and mine's still sore."

Donny's mom and dad both register alarm, so I hastily add, "That's the rules. Anybody fooling the other is required to give him a knuckle-punch in the shoulder. Like this..." I pretend to punch Donny's mother. She squeals, flinches, laughs, and then gives me a shove, almost toppling me off the narrow kitchenette chair.

"Donny won so often I had to see a doctor, deep bone bruises, fear of fracture. That's why I am eating so fast, so the pain isn't drawn out. Nah, it's because the food is so good."

Blah, blah, blah. But it does relax Donny's dad, who tells two jokes and several tales from his youth, tales calculated to make him appear bumpkinish. The mom tells a few stories, also, confining herself otherwise to pushing food at us, replenishing already-full bowls.

"So, Sally, do you want to see my bruised, battered arm, what's left of it?"

Sally has been quiet but not dramatically gloomy. She seems no part of things, and my plan to include her, draw her out, is flopping.

"What?"

"Wanta see what your brute brother did to me?"

Sally doesn't smile, but tries to. "I don't know." I'm glad I have the amphetamine in my pocket. Dr. Lee seems confident that we have what we need and that it isn't lethal, probably. He made it into sort-of pills, mashed-together granular products, loosely cemented with some kind of gelatin. I have a big supply, about half of which I've crammed into a paper bag. And no, I haven't tried any on myself.

We get through dinner well enough, all of us, conspiring to ignore Sally, not knowing what else to do. As we're shoving back, pretending to help clean up, only to have dishes ripped from our grasp, I sidle over to Sally. "Can I talk with you?"

"Yeah. Only I need to do some things in my room. You going to be here a while, I guess, but don't stay, you know, if you got other stuff to do. I don't..." She trails off dismally, seeming to slump against a wall, without having a wall to slump against.

"Nah, Donny and I will study for a while. How long?"

"I don't know."

"Forty minutes?"

"OK."

261

. . .

"We got any homework to occupy us, Donny?"

"Sexual education."

"Can I tie you up, force you to wear a dress, suck on your toes? You can take notes to use in our report for Miss Blaine's creative project."

"We can do a demo – everybody join in."

"You're a pervert, Donny. I'm warning you now, don't you put your hands on me or I'll scream. I know where those hands have been."

Donny responds by shoving me back on the bed and jumping on top, worming his body in squirmy waves over my middle. Then he rolls away and has me unzipped and exposed in something less than half a second.

Within half a shake, Donny and I, though neither one naked, have lowered, opened, bunched up enough cloth so we can reach everything we want. It'd been a few days since we'd had access to one another's bodies, not long, but we're ravenous. Trying to avoid ejaculating, I don't. Nor does Donny. Exciting mutual orgasm, though it'd been more sublime had it not occurred three minutes into our groveling.

"Oh Jesus, Tim. I got you all sticky."

"What do you suppose that is all over your stomach?"

"I guess it is. What's that you said last time – reload?"

So we move to more of the same, with fewer obstacles (clothes) and then no obstacles and then, what do you know folks, to the thing itself, extended as far as we are able.

Exactly what I had vowed not to do, not to plant this experience, this image in his head and leave him – who knows? – marked, debased? Just how did it happen, this all-out sex, sex it will be hard to think of years hence – or tomorrow – as normal fun?

I did it, that's how it happened. There is no "it," just deliberate action, my action, my selfishness. I have trouble being honest, but no trouble at all being dog-dirty mean.

Donny – I'll spare me the details – tells me how terrific this all is, how he wants to go on, right now and into the future, how he never imagined life could be so fine. The last declaration gives me no hiding place. So I take refuge, as well as I can, in vows for the future, in forgetting what's happened, in turning the talk to Sally.

Donny says it will be better to go into her room by myself, so I do. Sally's room is as small as his but in another part of the second floor of this poor house in this poor neighborhood. Harold had never noted the fact, but I do now: of the twenty-five thousand citizens, twenty-four thousand are poor, the one thousand who are not, mostly barely-not. The houses where I live are only twenty-thirty years old, are wee, constructed of the cheapest materials. Donny's part of town, older and grimier, has probably once regarded itself as on its way to something better and built homes on a classic urban model, crowded together and tall. His area had held its own for nearly half a century but had then started to crumble. The houses, like Ozymandias' tomb, do not hold up against the ravages of time. East Liverpool is now riding the back skirts of a one-time prosperity, rooted in iron, steel, and pots. The small wave has crested. There's just enough money around now to fool most into thinking the town can be a settling place. They're putting down roots in an ash pit.

I know better than to burst in on Sally: I knock, she answers in a voice below dismal, made more alarming when I see that she is trying hard to be cheery. She seems so forlorn, sitting on the edge of the bed, as if comfort had never come close to her and never would.

I go straight to what I have to offer. "Sally, I know you're feeling terrible. It's called depression, and I can help."

She stares at me, her face registering nothing I can decipher.

"Here's what I think. You feel low and awful, don't want to be with anybody and don't want to be by yourself. Things that used to make you happy, don't, and you have no idea what's wrong. You think it's something in your head, since you can't see any other reason why you're feeling so bad. You stay away from people. It isn't getting any better. It's getting worse."

Sally is paying attention, whether because I'm making sense or because she doesn't have the energy to kick me out, I can't guess. She says nothing, doesn't change expression, so I forge ahead, caught up in my pedagogical fervor.

"The problem is chemical, the chemistry of your brain. I won't lie to you about other things that may have – gone wrong. I don't want to dodge my own responsibility. I might have been more sensitive. I should have been."

She's looking both confused and distressed, and I realize I'm speaking for my benefit. It had seemed generous at first, but it's the opposite. Too late to explain, so I hustle on.

"Your depression is caused by a deficiency of dopamine and adrenaline in the brain. It's something like that. Dr. Lee, the chemistry teacher, told me all this. In the future, Sally – listen to me now – " (I say that as a spill-over of my own eagerness, not because she's ignoring me) "there will be ways to treat depression by chemicals. It'll be common, and people won't have to suffer as you are and think they're going crazy."

"That's what I think."

Her first words, and I have wit enough to shut up and let others follow. Slowly, between long pauses, they do. "I feel like you said. All the time. Not like anybody did anything to me, or good or bad stuff happens. It's always the same, though sometimes worse. Nothing helps – or makes things a whole lot worse. I still like things, but it doesn't change anything. Not even Mom and Dad, not even you, not even Donny, not even Joanie."

For the first time, she registers some unmistakable feeling, even if it's grief. Her face contorts, and I'm sure she's going to break into tears, fall into my arms. She doesn't. "I feel like this all the time. I can't remember feeling any different. If I did, it doesn't matter. I try to feel different, but it's better to stay away from people. I'm going crazy."

After the first spasms of pain, wrinkling across her face, Sally has fallen back behind the blank features that seem to fit her not at all, to fit no one who is alive. Her voice seems to come from an unwelcome imposter. Worse than colorless, it's inflected in arbitrary and unsettling ways that make her sentences seem inhuman, produced by a machine programmed by another and defective machine. I think a part of Sally recognizes her depression, and, wanting to protect others, tries to inject spirit here and there into her voice. The result is a mad set of emphases and tonal variations, more horrorshow frightening than a monotone would have been. The last sentence came out as "OK? Thass nice OF you?, TIMmy?" Would healthy doses of speed re-splice the circuitry inside this little girl?

"I don't know when it started. One day I just didn't care what I was wearing. Then maybe the same day and maybe later I realized that I didn't care about something my mom said about why wasn't I studying and I had better adopt better habits or I'd never get anywhere. She wants me to go to college because she never went. And I usually would have gotten all mad about her saying that, but I didn't. I didn't think she was right. I didn't care at all. I didn't care about much. I didn't care about anything."

She stops. Letting her talk may have been a great idea, but what's emerging wouldn't have struck the untrained ear as therapeutic work. It scares hell out of me, but I don't know how to stop or redirect it. I would introduce a new topic if I knew how to do so. I'm willing again to suggest that I had failed her, but I'm helpless in the face of her icy disease. Who is being drugged here – and for what? My eagerness to erase begins to seem, like so much of my life here, all of it, self-serving and small.

"It's like always being sick but not having a lot of pain, any."

The room is collapsing around us both.

"Here, take one of these. I'll get a glass of water."

"OK."

The dosage is guesswork. Dr. Lee told me to use half a pill and watch to see that "the patient" doesn't "respond badly." There's no point seeking clarification: he'd never done it before and isn't a pharmaceutical expert. He's an eccentric high-school chemistry teacher, willing to give it a go. What sense does it make? He'd never even seen "the patient" and was taking the half-assed description of a fourteen-year old as a diagnosis. The old fool plunges into the work, producing dangerous drugs, as if it were one more science fair project. What experience does he bring to bear, what authority? Half a pill? What could that mean? These pills are all different sizes and crumble like doughballs made with insufficient stickum.

Oh well.

I excuse myself, run down the hall to Donny's room, update him on things, and return to observe. The idea of going back to her pain makes me clammy. What do I look for as a reaction to the drug, and what to do if I find it? What if Sally's eyes roll back in her head? Maybe she'll froth, swallow her tongue, scream, lose consciousness. Jesus.

I do nothing to reassure Sally when I get back, spilling the beans about how little I know, and that little not much less than Dr. Lee. Again, I start a stumble toward the personal, gulp and stutter and retreat.

"But amphetamines do really work to make you feel better. 'Uppers,' they come to be called, because they make you feel up, positive, peppy. They also get called 'speed,' since they give you, you know, speedy feelings, like energy."

Sally stares at me. Think of how a lizard might regard you were you to give it a freeway traffic report. Sally's eyes are not uncomprehending, just cold and unchanging. No matter how closely one examines those eyes, how exacting the measurements, there'll be no changes, no reaction to what I'm saying, to variations in lighting, to dust or cinders, to explosions.

Just to avoid her zombie blankness, I suggest we play a game, tic-tac-toe and then "squares," to pass the time while the uppers bring her up, worse luck to us all if they don't. I want Sally's return to good times as badly as I'd wanted anything. I would gladly trade a lot for this little friend's happiness, including fame, sex, and winning local elections. Sally herself is worth it, and I keep myself from considering how selfish my anxiety might be.

Forty minutes later, I complete the last square on the sheet, count up to see I've lost, and look up to tell Sally. I'm met with eyes that seem to me different, I can't think how exactly, but then – they are sparkling. They move, catch the light. She isn't smiling, but she is, for the first time in weeks, alive and with us.

"Sally!"

"I know, Tim. Don't say it."

I don't. I hang around a bit just to bask in our success. For old time's sake, I wrestle a bit with Sally, let her jump on me, knees in my chest. What the hell. She's there again. I break free from our romp to run after Donny, to show him his rejuvenated little sister.

Of course it's temporary, but so what? I call Sally that night and she's back where she had been – but not quite. She's had a glimpse of her old chemical world. It isn't enough to do anything about the depression, but it does plant a hope that makes the depression easier to bear. Dr. Lee has told me it'll take several weeks before Sally can start easing off the drugs and let the "natural feeding system of adrenaline and dopamine" take over. How he knew that, I had no idea. It's counter-intuitive, isn't it? Wouldn't she get so used to the amphetamines that her feeding system would shut down? But I guess it's shut down as it is, and what the hell do I know?

I pass on to Sally the increased dosage OKed by Dr. Lee. I tell her he says she should take the tablets whenever she needs to, but no more than one every three hours. What he'd actually said was a little different. I'd talked with him right before I called Sally.

"How about the dosage, Dr. Lee?"

"Did you give her half a pill?"

"Yeah – well, no; I gave her a whole one."

"She still alive?"

"Yeah."

"That's OK, then. Made her feel better, right?"

"I'll say. In about forty minutes. That sound right?"

"Yes, it does. As I don't know a thing about it, anything between thirty seconds and a week would sound right."

"She reacted well. She seemed to be in the world for the first time in weeks."

"Good."

"So keep at it?"

"Of course, nitwit."

"How much?"

"Huh?"

"What dosage?"

"Oh yeah. Tell her to take them as often as she needs. She's the best judge."

"No limit?"

"Of course a limit, nincompoop! This is potent stuff. She could overdose and die. No limit? What a stupid kid!"

I don't think he was joking.

"What limit, then?"

"Well, what I said is true about the patient knowing best. Since they make her feel better, why should she suffer? You don't want her to suffer, do you?"

"No, but..."

"I know. Just fracturing you, oddball. Isn't that the way you talk?"

"Sure is." Sure isn't, at least I don't think it is. Is he ever going to impart information I can use?

"OK. If she doesn't react – get sick, get hives, get dizzy, or die – and since she tolerated the one-pill, well then – how long ago did she take that pill?"

"Five hours, I'd say."

"Too long. No wonder she's drifted back to where she was."

"If five hours is too long, what wouldn't be?"

"Four. Sound good to you?"

"How in hell would I know?"

"Just kidding, Billy. Let's say four hours, if that keeps her up."

"Thanks so much, Dr. Lee. I don't know what..."

"OK, kid. Just don't let on. I don't want to go into business in this line, and I don't want to go to the clink. But you seem like a good kid. You doing this for a friend, right?"

"My friend's little sister. She's only twelve."

"Well, that's good. Hope you don't manage to cook her brains. Just kidding, jackass. Gotta go."

• • •

Thursday after school I make another trip to Donny's, mostly to see Sally, though it's also nice to have time with Donny. Not to get stale, we back off and do nothing but what we can manage with our hands – including holding onto palms and fingers. Why is this so fine? I can produce things that sound like answers, but I don't have anything but a set of possibilities that could be convincing. And it's important to find the answer, the one that doesn't exist. Maybe I feel so close to Donny I can give him happiness without extracting even more for myself. Maybe I derive all my joy from self-congratulatory estimates of my altruism. Maybe I find this a cheap way to purchase a delicious self-approval, equip myself with a self-serving story for my grandchildren. "Gather round and let boompa tell you how to treat a sexual partner, how it's all about warmth, making sure your partner has a chance to think and breathe."

After a while, we lean over toward the other.

"I don't want to scare you, Tim."

"You won't."

"I want to be with you always, married. Nothing will ever be as nice."

"No it won't."

"So?"

"Soon as it's legal, we'll do it."

. . .

All those who try to go it sole alone,
Too proud to be beholden for relief,
Are absolutely sure to come to grief.

. . .

"So, Sally. Did you take another pill?" I can see she has. I explain again Dr. Lee's regimen: take the pills for three months, more or less, then try cutting back a little to see if the natural chemical feeds have started working. If they have, keep slowly, very slowly, reducing the dosage. If not, go back until the reducing doesn't bother you.

She looks at me with an impish smile: "Carl?"

"Should we get him?"

"Yes, Tim. Get him!"

"You have any ideas how?"

I'm convinced she doesn't, but her eyes take on more light. "Goddam right I do!"

"Sally!"

"Shit yeah, damn it and hell, I do."

"Spill it."

"What is it Carl's most proud of?"

"Being mean?"

"Yeah, Tim, is he mean to you? Just for instance."

"Me? Of course not. He's mean to... I see."

"You got a pretty face, Tim, which is lucky, cause you don't have a packed attic."

Who is this kid? Bubbling up from the lower depths, she now is queen of the waters.

"So, we got this guy who loves being mean to girls, making them worship him so he can humiliate them, right?"

"So we humiliate him."

"Absolutely!"

"Yeah."

"But how, Sally?"

"We bring your girlfriend in, use her as, what do they say on that show, bait?"

"What show?"

"Oh, you know."

I don't, but I'm starting to get the idea. What girlfriend does she have in mind? It wouldn't be very gracious to ask. Carol? That's my guess.

"Oh yeah, I know. So what does she do?"

"Well, we get her to pretend to like Carl, go out with him. I mean *really* like him."

"Uh huh." C'mon, Sally, give me particulars, names, one name anyhow.

"We fill Carol in on everything, get her to plan with us."

270

"Like what would she do, Sally?"

"Like get Carl to think she's hot on him, you know, pretend to be hot for him a lot, agree to go out with him, then really give it to him."

This is starting to make some kind of vile sense.

"Disgrace him, make him look ridiculous."

"Make him never want to be mean to a girl. Never want to go out with a girl again. Never want to be in the same room with a girl again. Never want to..."

"OK, Cricket, I get the point. You're giddy. As for Carl, I'll take degradation. Make him a laughing stock. You got an idea, I mean a specific idea?"

"Tim!"

"What? I just asked if you had an idea."

"I get embarrassed talking about sex."

"No, you don't. Besides, how's this about sex?"

"Carol tells him her parents are going to be away. This is after she sets him up, gets him to think she wants to, you know, have it with him. You know what I mean?"

"I'm shocked, but yeah. So, Carol pretends to have feelings for Carl, then tells him her parents are away – away?"

"For the evening. Playing canasta. Your parents can invite them."

"Ha! But OK. Say that works."

"Well, then, she gets Carl over. This is after she has him all set up before, you know, all hotty. Then she tells him – this is embarrassing."

"Spit it out, Sally, or I'll give you something to be embarrassed about!"

"OK – don't look at me – Carol tells Carl to go into the dark living room and GET READY, GET READY, you know, as she wants to slip into something comfortable. She tells him not to leave or anything, just GET READY. You know what I mean? GET READY? While she slips into SOMETHING COMFORTABLE."

"You hear that in a movie?"

"Yeah."

God! "OK."

"So she tells Carl to get naked, like you say, because she wants to get sexy

– don't look – and when Carl gets all naked and very hotty in the dark room she turns on the lights and says "SURPRISE" and the whole school's there. And everybody laughs at Carl and points at his, you know, dingy, and laughs."

"That's a vile scheme, Sally."

"What's that mean?"

"It's sensational."

She beams.

• • •

The night before our Cleveland trip for Dad's operation, he calls me out of the dining room, asks if I wouldn't like to drive with him for ice cream. Dad has few quirks, but one of them is that ready-packed ice cream isn't fit for consumption. Lover of cow-fat that he is, cream on cereal, butter on everything, Dad drives us down twice a week to Wilda and Bert's Store, where they mash several pounds of ice cream into a quart container. More expensive, but good value, doubtless, in terms of pennies per ounce. But it isn't value that interests Dad, it's quality. He hates the thin fluff put out for the undiscriminating. It occurs to me as we get in the car, and he mentions again his views on ready-packed, that this is about his only deeply-lodged point of intolerance. Discriminating ice-cream eaters unite!

"Joanie and Mom coming?"

"I told em we needed some man-to-man." He laughs in embarrassment and as an apology. He hates to impose, take up my time.

Then it hits me. He wants to set things straight in case it's a long recovery. I'm fourteen, but the MAN around. I don't know if Dad notices Mom's competence. Maybe he does. Anyhow, here we are in the car, me in the front seat, where I've been about three times before.

"Tim, I'm counting on you to help your mother, if things go wrong. I mean with the operation. I know you don't want to talk about it, but it's important. There are two house payments left, that's all, and there's money in the bank for that and the other bills. I'm afraid the insurance won't cover a lot more than the funeral. I'd be happy to do without that myself, just put me out with the trash. But it'd break your mother's heart not to do it right, what she thinks is right, so follow what she says. The insurance man's number is in the desk. There'll be a little money left over but not much for your college, and Joanie too of course. I figure you knew that or could guess, but you two will be able to go to college, I know, one way or another, on your own. If it all goes OK tomorrow, your mother and I will be able to help."

I can think of nothing to say.

"That about does that. There's another thing I want you to do, but I'll bring that up on the way home."

Two quarts of ice cream and two comic books for Joanie (and two for me) later, we're in the car again, for Dad's second proclamation.

"Now, listen to me, Tim. You know the Romanelli family, up in Midland, have the store there – yeah, I know you know. Anyhow, they're friends from way back with several people in the Pirates organization. Chief scout, first-base coach. You know that?"

I don't and say so.

"Well – hear me out – you know how you had those scouts watching you last year?"

No, but I don't let on.

"They want to look at you, the Pirates. Not in Fort Meyers, but end of the month, when they come back North. They won't call it a try-out, but that's what it is. Between you and me, our pitching is pretty thin." (Between Dad and me and every other baseball-literate citizen.) "So, Vito will get in touch with you when it's set up and you have to promise me you'll go."

I'm quiet, trying to absorb this, not even knowing what position I play. Pitcher, apparently. That seems to fit our pickle-playing fun and my own fantasies. Why not? Harold hadn't really played baseball, beyond elementary-school sandlot, but that was Harold and this is me. Dad takes my quiet as hesitation.

"You don't have to, son. You don't want to?"

"Even if I didn't, I'd do anything for you, Dad. But I do want to and I will – and you'll be there, too."

Dad is driving, as he always does, as if he's making love to the wheel, all scrunched over, protecting it with both hands. I've never seen him lift a hand except to signal a turn. Now, looking straight ahead, he does, but slowly, almost furtively, reach his right hand over and take mine, squeezing it so gently I think it might be my imagination.

Much as I want to, I can't keep myself goddamn it from crying. I keep it quiet, so Dad can pretend not to notice.

. . .

That was the last. Before the operation, Dad is too busy trying to keep everyone upbeat to get personal. Even after they have given him his pre-op relaxing shot, he is anxiously looking around, trying to spot any sign of fearfulness and counteract it.

"You know, we need to replace that dice football game. We've played it so much it's looking like real chewed-up turf, the board is. And Risk that Tim invented needs to have a better.... I had this idea myself..."

That was it.

Right up to the end, he occupies the central role only to keep himself out of the center. The jolly innkeeper part is the last one for which he was suited, and he wasn't much of an actor to begin with.

. . .

In his epic *Young Men and Fire*, a book Harold had taken into his heart and then transferred to Tim, Norman Maclean discusses the last minutes of the life of Harry Gisborne, in his day the leading expert on fire blowups, a blowup being one of those nightmares nature uses to kill the young and gallant. Blowups occur when conditions are freakishly, fiendishly perfect. A fire, even a small fire, can explode into something more than a fire, a storm of flame, eating up oxygen so fast there is none left for anyone in the area trying to breathe, even if the heat from this inferno were bearable. And it wouldn't be.

With a bad heart much like my own father's, Gisborne had climbed the steep hills of Montana's Mann Gulch to test his fire blowup theory. He was there on November 9, 1949, only three months after the Mann Gulch fire had burned to death thirteen young smokejumpers, young boys, really, who thought they were being dropped out of the sky onto a routine mop-up and found themselves finally where Harry Gisborne came to be and my dad, too.

At last making it to the top of the scorched gulch, within feet of the wooden crosses marking where each of the dead young men had lost his race with the fire, Gisborne took out his one pair of good binoculars and warded off the attempts of his companion to make him rest. Studying the lay of the land, the pattern of the fallen trees, and the location of the corpses, Gisborne saw that the fire had made its own tragic weather system, the walls of the gulch forming banks to reflect back into the hills both heat and air currents, creating a self-sustaining whirlwind. Such a system, feeding on itself, cannot last long, but in this case its short life didn't help the boys who were losing theirs.

Gisborne, recognizing at a flash what had happened two nights earlier, saw just as quickly that his theory was wrong, wrong from beginning to end. "Well, damn!" he said to his companion, "would ya look at that!" He explained what he saw and started laughing, then sat down at last to take a breather. Within a minute, his companion knew the old mistaken man was dead. He propped his body up with rocks, just so it wouldn't roll down the steep hill into the Missouri River, and went to get carriers.

Maclean muses on Gisborne's death, as he muses on the deaths of the boys, his own wife's, and the one shortly awaiting him. Not a bad way to die, he says, "excitedly finding we were wrong and excitedly waiting for tomorrow to come so we can start over, get our new dope together."

Also not a bad way to die occupied with the lives and needs of kids, kids and the games they play, repairing old ones and thinking up new ones for tomorrow.

CHAPTER 19

The next two weeks are crammed enough with ritual and fuss to keep us from thinking much of what has happened. Mom, it seems, spends half the time crying and the other half learning things she'll have to know. Joanie seems defeated at first, but then takes to helping Mom and straightening crooked things. Reluctantly, she slowly allows a part of herself to be dragged back into the life of a vital and connected kid.

I'm no use myself, not that there is any need for me. I do discover close up what Harold had avoided, grief. Nothing this time through surprises me more. When the same dad had died on Harold, nothing inside had been troubled, nothing that Harold could locate anyhow. He had accepted the role of the sad kid, the pitied kid, though, to his credit, he hadn't exploited it often. He didn't seek out situations where his presumptive grief would stand him in good stead. Inside those situations unavoidably, though, he sometimes milked them. In succeeding months, Harold had thrown himself into helping his mother, arranging driving lessons and getting her enrolled in a small college up the river in Beaver, so she could change her substitute teaching status to full-time and support the family. Harold had tutored her, resenting fiercely the time wasted and the mother who was asking nothing from him.

This time, I don't try to help much, do almost nothing. The step-by-step grief manuals that are later to appear probably would have consoled me, given me thoughts to think and ways to formalize feelings I could neither understand nor narrate, probably given me more manageable feelings to feel. Now, "How you doing?" makes no contact, often as I hear it. "Better" "Fine" "It'll take some time" "It's Mom and Joanie I'm worried about" "I've been better."

I've murdered my father this time around, one might say. To my credit, I reject that sensational formulation after entertaining it for a few minutes, reject it as being far too satisfying. It isn't wrong, but it's not profound. The desire to do-in the dad, after all, is banal. I have larger crimes for which to bring myself into the dock.

Twice now, I have spent time with this gentle-hearted man and managed to avoid him. First time around, in the previous 1958, Harold had been at home when news came of his father's death. Dad had been sick for years, seriously sick for months, and had, three days earlier, been taken to the hospital. Harold and Joanie returned from college, he from Case Institute and Joanie from Pitt, to form a unit for the deathwatch. After two days, Joanie had driven from the hospital to the house to get some sleep. Mom wouldn't dream of leaving, but it seemed to please her to have us do so. Joanie came back half-a-day later and I took my turn.

The hospital was on the other side of town, down close to the football field, so it took me a good fifteen minutes to drive home. Harold had been awake, off and on, for a long two days, napping in chairs, and I spent the driving time thinking only of how tired I was and deserved to be and how fine it would be to sleep in a saggy old bed that had always seemed to me the very acme of comfort.

So when the phone call came, there I was, comfortable and warm, unlike Joanie and Mom, unlike my dad: "Harry, this is Joanie. You should come on down now. We need to — Dad just died."

In the fortnight following the death, I (Tim now) do almost nothing for anybody else, devote my time to grief. The days bleed into one another as if the sun were not moving across the sky and sinking into the black earth, over and over. I allow myself to burrow into my monochromatic world, feeling nothing more than a dull ache in my tendons. Keeps me from sleeping, as if I were a minor league pain-pill addict trying to go cold turkey. Even less dramatic than that. Pain so commonplace it probably afflicts dogs and barnyard fowl.

Joanie tries to tend to Mom and to me, Mom herself spending energy offering me consolations I try to find irritating. The only thing that stands out is an incident at Gilbert's Funeral Home. What had been Dad is pumped full of something, rouged and skin-glowed, looking like a mannequin made of impermanent clay. According to the tribal practices of our Appalachian town, friends are required to come to Gilbert's during "viewing hours" in order to file past the casket, look at the mortician's taxidermy work, and offer words of kindness to the family, lined up beside the casket like a receiving line at a debutante's ball.

Mom, then me, then Joanie, arranged by age in a gender sandwich. The spectators try hard not to say something insensitive, forcing them into repetitions, intimate friends and bare acquaintances expressing their condolences, respects, and assurances of Christian salvation in phrases that vary not a tittle. Under other circumstances, it would have been funny. Under these circumstances, it's funny, though only a brute would register that fact, sink to that level, allow entrance to the risible. I forgot to say that part of the formula required of each person running the gauntlet of our receiving line is, "He looks go good."

"I'm so sorry, he was so young, at least he's not suffering, he looks so good, he's with God now, anything you need, my condolences, so sorry, I'll be glad to – dear Joanie, I'm so sorry, he was so young, at least..."

Absorbing dozens of these ritual recitals, anyone – well, maybe not anyone, maybe hardly anyone, maybe only Joanie and I – would get restless. It's not a question of doubting the sincerity of our friends, our parents' friends, but of being faced with the equivalent of a comic jack-in-the-box, popping up predictably at the same turn-of-the-crank.

After a while, I try timing each encounter, thinking I can distract myself by making a chart, predicting the fastest, figuring averages and means. But the close attention to wristwatch required by such a scheme demands more self-possession and downright rudeness than I can muster. Then I try counting the people in line, hoping to draw comfort by noting the steadily decreasing number of tormentors still to come. But the line winds round a big potted plant (made of shiny cloth of some sort) and into a hallway, so that particular recreation is a flop.

So preoccupied am I with my failure to find distractions, so busy casting about for more, that I don't see Mrs. Wooburn approach. Mrs. Wooburn is an amazing woman, a fat and quaking soul who never seems to be the same size, have her flesh arranged in the same way: now her legs are club-like, now sharp like needles; now her breasts sag and now point toward the sky. The only thing reliable about her body is its mobility. It never is still, seems always to be slipping downhill or flying cross the room. She teaches third grade, does Mrs. Wooburn, making a startling intervention into the psyches of each of the young lives she finds occasion to interfere with in the course of her duties. Mrs. Wooburn saw Jesus, spoke with him and once told us the Son of God had felt her leg while she was on a ladder cleaning the windows, which she did every spring and we should too if we wanted to maintain a reputation in the neighborhood for cleanliness which was a very important reputation to have and would stand us in good stead when it came to bad times which would descend on us all and don't forget good hygiene habits, especially when it came to the next world where cleanliness counted. Students of Mrs. Wooburn all got 100% on their tests, because Mrs. Wooburn would accompany all the questions with the answers. When the results were in, she'd parade us around into all the other classrooms, perfect papers unfurled. The other students snickered; we had no idea why. In her zeal to treat soul and body and to inspire orderly habits inside and out, Mrs. Wooburn made each student, every day, record the details of his (and, more degradingly, her) health regimen, including tooth-brushing, hand-washing, hair-combing, and bowel-moving. There is no truth to the rumor, spread by liars or the forgetful, that Mrs. Wooburn required further details. Oral report, yes, but it was sufficient to give a snappy yes or no. Mrs. Wooburn had no wish to intrude.

Anyhow, here she comes, overwhelmed with feelings too stormy to be contained. Mrs. Wooburn was often overwhelmed with feelings, one of the most unforgettable features of her pedagogical plan and presence, but this is extraordinary, even for her, this assault on my poor mother, first in line. So tidal-wavish is Mrs. Wooburn's sympathy that she's weeping copiously, not only from the eyes but from the mouth. The result is that she sputters, sloushing her words as her flapping lips try and fail to hold back the moisture arising from her true sympathy. "Show shvery shorry, oh shamay shjesus our shlord shelter shush all, poor shlamb, show shvery shevery..." She has no more finished showering me, moving on to the funeral director, who has come up at an unlucky time to whisper something and has been mistaken for one of the family, than Joanie hooks her mouth in my direction and stage-whispers, "Show shvery shvery sorry, oh jesusush shour shlord..." We start giggling, strangle the giggles, break out again, and keep up that excruciating alternation until finally the last well-wisher has told us Dad is now with Jesus. The fuck he is!

. . .

The anguish hits me once we get home, socking me in like a thick and featureless fog. Then it's gone. Two weeks later, I wake up in my old state. I suppose I'm altered somehow, but I'm aware only of one thing, a small thing. Having murdered my father, like old Oedipus, I might have been able to muster grand narratives with which to torment and exalt myself. But, as I say, I can't. I try, but I know I never hated my father, wanted to rival him, wanted to take from him what he had. This time around, I have felt warmer toward him, more respectful, but I know him only a little better. The tragic energies that might have been vibrating through me simply are not. The part of my dad lodging with me has been present during the grief, but has not caused it. It is present now, in my rejuvenated state, and does not poison it. For some time I cannot place what it was that I had retained, the remembrancer. Then I know. I miss him.

. . .

He was my North, my South, my East and West,
My working week and my Sunday rest.
My noon, my midnight, my talk, my song;
I thought that love would last forever:
I was wrong.
The stars are not wanted now; put out every one,

Pack up the moon and dismantle the sun,
Pour away the ocean and sweep up the wood;
For nothing now can ever come to any good.

. . .

I now have my own life to think of, at least that's what I do. Both Mary and Carol have been attentive, dear – Betsy too. Also Glenn and Donny, more awkwardly. The single unformulaic friend is my oldest, Jimmy Canton, who simply makes himself available for any emotional engagement I might require. The selflessness in his always-round-the-corner availability was there the first go-round, but I hadn't noticed it really. This time I do.

But it is to Carol I turn my immediate attention. To Mary too, but more to Carol. I try to think it's not because she is one of those on my list, the very top of the list, who remains unfamiliar with the fruits of true intimacy. So I call on her, finding her unexpectedly alone.

"Hi Carol."

"How you doing?"

"I'm OK. I really appreciate all your kindness."

"Not kindness, Tim. I love you."

That catches me off guard, the easy way she moves into and out of concern, asking if I'm grieving, hearing I'm not, refocusing our talk into the present, away from death. In a couple of seconds, she has us back where we had been, reforming the environment and rescuing me.

I can't get my voice under control immediately, but don't want her declaration to hang in the air, so, what the hell, I quiver and quake. "Carol, I can't tell you how much I love you."

"You do it without words, mountain man, scaling trellises, seeking the most remote peaks."

Carol reddens suddenly, then tries a laugh, giving me the chance to match her large kindness with a tiny one. Her sophistication has its boundaries, and body talk marks one of them. Or so I imagine.

"I'd pursue you anywhere – into the foulest sewers, the top of the highest skyscraper in town where the chiropractors are, the bell tower at school, the boys' toilets."

"Let's get out of here, Tim."

"Yes, I'd love to---take a walk, talk."

"Neck."

"Carol!"

"You know what, Tim, for a visitor from the future, which you tell me is free and loose, you don't seem to me either. It's not like I got naked and jumped you. I just said 'neck.'"

I see her point. "You said that you wanted to neck, Carol. You're not supposed to want to neck, here in 1952. You're certainly not supposed to say you want to neck."

"You an expert on how girls are supposed to act in 1952?"

"Got me there. I'm not an expert on how girls in any country, at any time, under any circumstances, act, want to act, are expected to act."

"Nor am I, Tim. Didn't mean to make you feel bad. If you want to talk, that's fine."

"Both. Both talk and neck."

"If both it is, we'd better go someplace."

"We could go to Jimmy Canton's house. He'd hide us."

"He'd do anything for us. But what if we got caught. He'd be the one getting into trouble. That'd be mean."

"Yeah. You got any friends where we could... ?"

"Mary."

I'm now the embarrassed one, can't even produce a laugh.

"Tim, do you suppose Mary and I don't know?"

"No."

"You must think we're stupid."

"No."

"You probably think that if we both knew, we'd mind."

"No?"

"Yes."

"You mind."

"Yes."

"Mary minds."

"Yes."

"I would, too. If you were in love with me and, say, Carl, then I'd mind. A lot."

"Carl? That cool dude? Maybe I will love him. I hadn't thought of it, but that's an idea. I'll call Mary."

"He was mean to Joanie."

"Actually, I knew that. Sally called me. We got this revenge plan afoot. But you're changing the subject."

"Wasn't me changed the subject."

"Was."

"Yeah, well, Carol, I think it's kind of..."

"What?"

"I don't know. How can you be so cool about Mary? That's not what I mean. I mean, I don't know how I can love you and Mary and why you don't..."

"Get annoyed?"

"Yeah."

"You think I don't care."

"I don't know."

"You think Mary doesn't care."

"I don't know."

"We care. You aren't listening. So do Donny and Patty, I expect, and all the other people you've made love you – what's his name, Glenn, and probably several dozen others."

"Oh damn."

"But it's not your fault, Timmy."

"Thanks."

"You couldn't help it."

"Thanks."

"Sure you could. It is your fault."

"It is, Carol."

"Please don't confess something."

"I set out, when I came back here, just set out to have sex with as many people as possible, screw them, fuck them, and hell with them. That's what I set out to do. It was deliberate. I set out to do just that, and no more."

"That first day in class. You set out to fuck me?"

"Carol! No."

"And when you first saw Mary this time around, you started right off making plans to fuck her?"

"No."

"Patty?"

"Well, that's true, but I haven't."

"Yet."

"Yeah, yet, but I won't."

"I know. Sorry. So who else did you plan to fuck?"

"Carol, do you really mind not saying that? It's..."

"It's mean, is what it is. I'm a little hurt, I guess, though I'll get over that and don't you start apologizing. It is what it is, and I like you a whole lot more than I'm hurt and I understand better than you think. OK, I'll stop."

"I set out to get at rich kids — that was the plan, but..."

"It didn't get beyond poor dimwit Patty, who enjoyed it anyhow. Look, dearie, I don't want to hurt you. Let's stop this."

"I want to say, but I don't know what I'll say till I say it. Can I?"

"I know what you mean."

"I didn't set out to have sex with you. I never imagined that. This Timmy character that I am isn't in any better touch with himself than old Harold. But that doesn't mean anything to you, or to me either. When I first sat behind you and we started playing around, you being so witty and open and flirting, I just wanted to keep that going. I didn't think of it advancing. I just wanted you to be kidding around about my belt and wearing my underwear, just trusting me. More than trusting me, though, playing with me, letting me play with you – play and invent and love – and never, ever stop. We'd outwit time."

"Uh-huh."

"I didn't have a plan. Still don't. I thought I had a plan with Patty, though, and then with Glenn. You know Glenn?"

"Of course. I mentioned his name not two minutes ago. You have the bad memory problems of a seventy-year-old man, or whatever you are."

"I do. I've had sex with Glenn. That was part of a plan, vicious, like with Patty, only worse, because it might do a lot of damage to him. The odd thing is I've come to admire Glenn, like him. I do, Carol. He reads, has depth. Anyhow, we're close friends, which wasn't part of the plan. I think Glenn doesn't think the sex is that big a deal. Anyhow..."

"You want to keep going, honey?"

"Yeah. Well, I've had sex with Donny, too."

"I figured."

"So sex with him wasn't planned."

"Uh-huh."

"Yes it was. I saw him the first day back and got all, you know."

"All erected."

"That's exactly right."

"But when I started hanging out, trying to seduce him, and then... Is that awful?"

"I think you know."

"It is, right?"

"It isn't."

"Oh."

"Anybody else you set out to dick and then decided you'd love instead?"

"Miss Hawke, lovely Adelaine Hawke."

"Goes without saying. So, where can we neck?"

"I say we take our chances on right here where we are. Does the door lock?"

"It does, but what if they come to the door?"

"Better they get mad about a locked door than about your bra hanging around my ears."

"And me in your underwear."

This is more than I can stand. More than Carol can stand too, I guess. I know. I get the door locked, barely, before Carol has pulled me onto the bed, rolled over on top of me, and used one hand to pull at my ears, while the other unbuttons my shirt.

We're not quiet. All these weeks, months, Carol never far from my heart, or my arousals, come on me like a flood, as if there were no intervening time. We're back in Latin class, trading clothes. I'm moving slow now, Carol too. It's as if we want to prolong it all, the touching and the looking. We take forever undressing one another, fondling as we go. At one point, Carol pulls my half-way down underpants back up. Taking the clue, I do the same with hers.

Then we both snake our hands inside – so much for delaying things. Knowing so little about the procedures we're enacting, we do whatever comes to mind. Our underwear suddenly is off and our hands get replaced by direct contact. My passion, shooting through me, still cannot keep pace with the feeling of tenderness I have for this lovely, oohing girl. With Mary, with Donny, with Glenn, the sexual eagerness has become more complex as things proceed. The simple desire to accomplish, to possess, becomes mixed with concern, a slight distance. As my mind and feelings expand, nothing happens to my zing, even my focus. It's more as if I'm aware of two bodies at once, two packs of feelings. With Carol, this doubling is much stronger, and I think I take into my own mind her vagina, her threatened hymen, as much as my own member. Saying this, I know how vile it sounds, how ferociously sexist to take possession of her feelings and her body. Too bad. I'm as worried about causing her pain as if it were happening to me. So I don't hurt, at least I hope. I keep sinking my body lower on the bed, as her grinding quickens. I want her to have this sex without rupture and pain. And she does.

We cuddle after, saying little, realizing we're now again fully aroused. But we re-dress one another, stealthily unlock the door, and make our way down the stairs and into the kitchen, planting ourselves at the kitchen table, books out, pencils at ready, so the returning parents will find only good friends, good students. They come in not two minutes after we have the stage set.

It's only after the parents have served us cookies and fussed a bit that we realize we have, surely with some degree of awareness, done what we had threatened at our first meeting. Carol stands up fast to get a dishrag to wipe up my milk slop and almost immediately sits down again, clutching at something behind her.

"What's wrong?" I hiss.

"Shhh." Carol is brick red. Thinking she's in pain, I start to stand in order to help, then feel a sharp pain in my ass, my nuts. How have I not noticed before? How have we made it downstairs? Carried along by ecstatic wooziness, we've been unaware of our ill-fitting undies. Carol's narrow hips have somehow held up my biggies, and I have fit my bulk into her tinies. And now we have to put up with it. Suffer.

"What'll we do?" I ask. Carol breaks into giggles, igniting the same in me.

"Whooie!," she says, leaving me bound within an ever-tightening girdle of agony.

Carol stands, carefully, keeping her legs at a spread-eagle. To the bathroom she goes, returns, and slips me a handful of cotton under the table. I follow suit and come back hunched over, aroused by the thought of Carol with nothing but open air under her.

So, after an indecently short interval wherein we pretend to complete our homework, I invite Carol to walk me to the mailbox. The mailbox! Again, my double-barreled intelligence fails me, and I can think of no better excuse for pulling her outside on this miserable March day than a letter to mail.

"Tim, just leave it and we'll mail it in the morning."

Does Mama want me to possess her daughter there on the fake Persian rug?

"Oh, thank you, but I want to get it into the hands of the mail department, you know, the Postal Service, right away. You understand, Mrs. Blake?"

She doesn't, looks at me as if I'm a lunatic, but lets me go. I'm sure she would have held her daughter back had she been quick enough to think of a reason, but she's even more lummoxy than I. In ten seconds we're out the door.

"You still have my panties, Tim! You going to take them home, wear them to bed?" She laughs loudly.

"Your mother will hear, you jackass you! And yeah, I want *all* your panties. I'll wear them and you go bare-assed."

"OK."

"Carol, as long as you aren't guarded by panties, you know what I think?"

She puts her hand right on my ass and starts rubbing, "I have no idea."

"I think it would be a shame not to save all that effort and time."

"I'm not as lazy as you. Let's proceed."

In the oozing sodden weeds and brambles, a field handily set two lots down from Carol's house and offering, even in this winter bareness, plenty of cover, if practically no comfort. Who notices?

Carol is on top again and attacks so vigorously she is not for long intact. Our sex is so prolonged, it occurs to me that we must adjust our story to accommodate visiting a mailbox in another town, Chester perhaps, when finally she shudders and recklessly yells – as do I.

We use my panties to clean up the blood, not much. Her panties, I keep.

My jacket is mucked up with thistles, late-March muck, insect spittle, and Carol juice. I see that as I take it off later in my bedroom. It would be so corny to keep it as is, so I do.

CHAPTER 20

The very next afternoon, right after school, I find myself walking over to Mary's, basketball practice having been cancelled. "I have nothing more to teach you guys." "Sure, you do." "Well, yes I do, but you need some rest." "No, we don't." "No, you don't, but I do." "No, you don't." "No, I don't, but if we practice every weeknight except Friday, you know what'll happen?" "What?" "You'll get used to it." "So what?" "You don't wanna." "How come?" "Look, am I just a coach or am I a teacher of life lessons?" "You're just a coach." "Ha, ha, so listen to me, green twigs, don't ever get used to anything." "Why?" "Just don't. Whenever you get used to something, stop it. Whenever you get comfortable, make yourself itch. Whenever you get good at something, quit."

So I'm free to walk right up and ring the bell and find Mary and her big unaccusing smile on the other side of the open door.

"You've been ignoring me, Timmy."

"No!"

"Use me and dump me. Yesterday's rutabaga, chewed on and discarded. No taste left. No more mystery. Better to have sex with yourself than old Mary. Mary's just a..."

She's laughing, but I am suddenly so sad, it's all I can do not to burst out crying. Mary senses this and folds me into her.

After a bit, I regain my composure but don't leave her arms.

"Timmy, Timmy. I'm sorry. You feel better?"

She's rocking me. Finally, I move my hands from her back up to her neck, then hair, pressing against her, straightening slowly so as to get more of my torso in contact with hers. Still crouching to adjust for height, my sensitive parts find hers and push. Just pushing, not grinding. What am I, an animal? Yes.

Mary responds by licking my ear, not delicately.

"What about your parents?"

"They'll enjoy watching."

OK! Within minutes, seconds, there we are, where we both want to be. Well, maybe we hadn't planned being on her front-room floor, scratchy rug rubbing raw our exposed flesh, but otherwise it's so fine. I want it never to end, for time to freeze or explode.

"Will we ever stop doing this, dear Mary?

"Not so's you'd notice."

"That's good, no that's wonderful. We'll do it all over town, in the boys' and girls' bathrooms at school, on the floor of the State Theater balcony, at church---everywhere."

"Sure," she says.

"And never stop, never. We'll be doing this in 2052. Why not?"

She smiles at me, doesn't say anything.

. . .

At home, things slog along, one misery after another. Joanie develops some kind of infection, she is told, but I know it's not an infection at all – another in the long line of benefits I haul back from the future. Thus far, I have imported illegal drugs to Sally, some basketball moves I'd seen on televised NBA games, death to my father, the happy diversions of *Risk* and *Twister*, and not one damn thing else. But my time here is just starting, sort of, and surely I will soon find ways to transform me, my friends, and the entire East Liverpool metropolitan area.

As I was saying, Joanie is told by the local quacks that she has a skin infection, when it's simply a rash, caused by an allergic reaction, an allergy as hidden in the mist of the future as the double helix, Minecraft, electronic nose-hair trimmers, and Attention Deficit Disorder.

"Joanie, honey, just try a different soap. That perfumed stuff is bad."

"Really? Timmy, you a doctor up there in the future?"

"I am."

"You are not."

"Might as well be, dummy."

"So, don't use the soap?"

"Use soap. You wash, don't you, every month or so? Well, use Fels Naptha or Lava or something, not Lifebuoy."

"Uh huh. Fels Naptha and Lava will take my skin off. How about Ivory."

"Perfect. Any other problems, just come to Doctor Tim, Dermatologist. That's what I am, dermatologist, meaning skin doctor. The skin problems haven't been invented yet, but they will be and then we'll have the specialist doctor. Maybe the doctor comes first, in the usual way of progress. Use the term, sis, and impress all your ignorant but well-meaning friends. Der-ma-tall-a-jist. Hey, Joanie, are you surprised at Mom?"

"You know she registered for class this summer? I guess you know that."

"Yeah, but half the time she's moving forward and the other half she's weeping."

"Tim!"

"I'm sorry. I think you see the good stuff and I see the annoying."

"OK, let's not talk about it. You gonna get Carl?"

"You heard Sally's plan, right? You women know everything. You rule."

"Tim, you think that?"

"Well, no. It's all sort of private, isn't it? I mean, it's not that you control the game."

"I'll say."

"But you're so much more easy about stuff, know more. I think the word is 'wiser.'"

"Girls are not just one thing, Tim. We're not all the same. And why you calling us 'women'? That sounds goofy. They do that in 2016?"

"Not really, not twelve-year-olds – nobody calls them 'women.' You're right. I don't mean all females. I mean you and Sally and Mary and Carol. Look, I've been given all these things, as I told you, by the celestials or whatever they are. But, even with those boosters, I'm not close to being as cool as you four. Take sex. I still think of it as dark and sly, coercive, like military tactics, taking the enemy by storm. And you, you see it as funny.

Jesus wept!"

"Tim."

"Yeah?"

"Listen to what you're saying. Sounds like you're worshipping God or something, not talking about ordinary girls. Just because we aren't morons. We're not exalted. We don't make fun of boys, only some of them. Don't think we live in some other world. That's kind of nice, but it's kind of stupid too."

"That's harsh."

"No, it isn't. We have fun because we're friends. I like Sally, and Carol and Mary are great. We trust each other the way friends do. Like you and Donny, Glenn too – Jimmy Canton for sure. It's not so different, I'll bet. I don't think you should make so much difference between girls and boys, Timmy. Didn't they give you equipment for that?"

"For what?"

"For not being dumb about girls. Women! Mom, for instance."

"We back to Mom?"

"You should be, and be more patient. She isn't asking for much."

"Wants me to talk, say Dad was a Christian saint. It's like she never knew him."

"She knew him. It's her way, that's all."

"It blows."

"Huh? Why does it bother you so much?"

"I see. It's me, not her. It's women, I guess. I never thought of Mom that way, as a woman."

"I'm not asking you to."

"Oh."

"Just be nice."

"OK."

"Just be nice."

"I said OK."

"Just be nice, you fucking boy."

"Joanie!"

· · ·

I figure I'd better get to it, before my guilt subsides.

"You doing OK, Mom?" The two of us, freezing on the back porch. She makes room for me on the swing she'd had me put up a month before it's fit to sit outside.

She bursts into tears and lets fly her well-practiced declarations. "How hard, the most wonderful man, he's with God now, we had such a fine time." Unfeeling of me to be annoyed. A good son, a moderately decent person, would have comforted her, hugged. I'm able to avoid outward show of irritation. I don't argue with her about Dad's place with Jesus. I don't get up and leave.

"Uh-huh," I agree, then I wait. She takes my hand and starts in on me: man of the house now, take care of Joanie, protect her. Then she surprises me, smiles too. "We'll all be just fine, Tim. You'll see."

"Mom, you know there's money Dad didn't tell you about. He and I had this scheme, me and Dad did, and made lots of money. Part of it went for his operation – " moving quickly – "but there's a lot left. Dad wanted you to have it to tide you over. Right now it's in the bank under my name, just to keep it as a surprise for you. Dad figured…"

I'm making this up as I go along. Inspired. Dad's scheme. She'd buy that, never question its legitimacy. No need for details – the NL Playoffs, Meilie, Satanic gambling.

"He asked me to tell you to pay off the house right away, the two payments remaining. Also buy a new car. A good one. He said. And pay for your school. That's why you need a good reliable car, a Buick."

Dumb idea. She flinches.

"Dad said."

"A Buick?"

"It was what he wanted. And there'll still be a great deal of money, Mom. About one hundred thirty thousand. Really."

"Heavens!"

293

"Dad figured you wouldn't want to move, but he asked me to help you find contractors to fix up the house and get you first-rate appliances. And he wanted you not to have to worry about college costs for me and Joanie. He said to invest what's left after these other things – about $100,000 – which will give you a safety cushion, and also a little extra money, just on the interest – about $400 a month, I think, free and clear."

"Timmy! You're a good boy."

For the first time, maybe the first time ever, I look at her. She really doesn't care about the money. She cares that I'm talking about Dad.

"I miss him so, Mom."

I let her hug me. I had ended up in her arms. It was me that made the first move.

. . .

A few days later, just as a variation on grief, and fornication, I stop by to see Margie. She opens the door before I knock, seems not at all surprised to see me. I peek inside, find nobody else. She shuts the door behind her, moves out with me into the dirt road – must be a mush-pit when it rains. How does her family maintain such good nature, such dignity? I feel sure I would sink into the surroundings, all tar-paper and wood too old to do its job framing windows, crumbling and barely holding in the glass, second-hand Formica kitchen tables steadied with match books under the legs, clothes which balance repeated washings with increased patching. Still, they prevail – Margie, her parents, the neighbors.

She jabs my arm, driving us away from the house, taking tiny steps just short of a run. She has on a thin sweater, no sort of protection, but I suppose it's all she has, and I'm not about to embarrass her again about clothes. I've accomplished so little with her wages, so little even toward keeping her warm.

"You knew I was coming, Margie? You got magic powers?"

"When you showed up, just then, I was just going out on a research trip."

"Damn, Margie, I wasn't checking up. You sure you know what you're doing?"

She looks hurt. For once, I notice. "Not that you're not a lot more capable than me. It's true of all you women, but you're the worst. You make me feel like I'm four years old and you're my baby-sitter. Hell, you could run the school you're going to. Why, you could do anything. You could... Youch!"

She stops me by slugging me again much harder in the bicep with her fist, middle knuckle extended.

That hurts, but not as much as I have hurt her. Actually, I don't think I have hurt anybody. Maybe Patty. Maybe Glenn too, Donny. Maybe Mary, since I'm not tied to her as I should be. Carol too. But even I can't make myself an all-out villain by such mental twistings, which are, among other things, insulting to the others. Is it so bad being pawed by me? They get to paw in return, and do so eagerly – not such a bad trade.

"So, where we going, assistant? I'm here to escort you."

"Like a date."

"Not 'like.'"

"OK."

Margie walks so fast, skipping, that I have to hustle to keep up. She cuts through some rocks and dirt, what was once maybe a lane up the hill to a tiny house rapidly being overtaken by the jungle vegetation around it. For all that, this cabin seems sturdier than most of the slightly bigger homes below. Also, there are curtains in the window and a welcome mat in front of the heavy door.

"OK, Margie, where are we now?"

"Old Mrs. Billingham. Her place. This is my third time. She's really nice."

"You interviewing her, right, for the project?"

"Uh-huh."

"You keeping track of your hours?"

"It's not work. And she gives me cookies. She'll give you some, too."

"And I'm paying you for your time. Listen, Margie, since you're such a liar, *I'm* going to tell *you* how many hours you've worked. That's fifty hours, unreported, and I'm paying you five bucks an hour and not a penny more. So how much is that, brick-head?"

"Tim! I couldn't. Let's go in."

We do. Mrs. Billingham, to all appearances living alone at age one-hundred-plus, is so happy to see Margie she doesn't mind me tagging along. I sprawl on the floor, loudly claiming my right to be comfortable, not wanting to call attention to the fact that the number of people in the room outnumber the chairs by one.

Cookies come, glasses of water, cloth napkins. Margie takes out her pencil and pad, and the old lady starts in where she had, I guess, left off. "We tried hard in those days to pretend we never had the miseries, pretended even to ourselves. But I can tell you, honey, we had 'em. Just like you, if you're old enough, and don't you dare tell me – I ain't here to embarrass you. You was askin last time about that and about birth control. We had a lot of stories and that's all. My mother told me to wash out with hot salt water right after. Some tried laxatives, some tried sauerkraut, I won't tell you how. Nothing worked. We was just one step away from chants and spells. Lots of girls, kids not much older n you, got pregnant trustin these things, honey, and there wasn't much you could do about it, though not a few tried, and that's another story."

This continues for a good hour, wandering from one distressing topic to another and, often, back again. It's as if I'm not there, as if these two women, despite the ninety years separating them, are locked into perfect understanding, moving together in coordinated strokes, like a ballet. Margie is nodding, laughing in time. How can she keep up, understand all this? Lots of it baffles me. I'm back to where I was before Joanie corrected me: girls inhabit a higher sphere.

By the time we leave, I am lost in admiration for these two, for the melancholy understanding these women share. Ten more minutes and I would have fallen head over heels for Mrs. Billingham. That's already where I am with Margie.

. . .

"I thought the Rotary wanted me to talk about Save the Children."

"I thought so too, Tim. I don't know how one thing turned into the other. I don't think I forgot, but maybe I did. Getting old."

"Oh screw it, Dean Nelson, you'll never get old."

"OK. Did you say, 'Screw it,' young Tim?"

"Sorry."

"Don't be. You can get away with anything, being as kind as you are to so many kids, Donny and Sally among them, especially them, I expect."

He grins. Dean Nelson always says the right thing, puts everybody at ease, every scared and ignorant kid, which is all of us. He's responsive, reads every student so well because he wants to help, not impress, them. He seems to have no ego and pulls things out of us, out of me, we didn't want to release, had little idea were there.

"You know my dad died."

"I do know. I've been talking to your mom. She's one strong woman, and you've been very good to her."

"I mention it because I don't have him here to talk to. This might go past what even you can be OK with, but I feel bad you thinking I'm some kind of saint. If only you knew, and I want you to know. I'm not a good person at all."

"Tell me anything, Tim." He gets up from his desk, moves round on my side, and grabs my shoulder, ooching me over beside him on the couch.

"Dean Nelson, if you were my dad, you couldn't make me feel worse right now, thinking I'm what I'm not. Kind to Donny and Sally, to other kids? One of the reasons Sally got so depressed was that she had a crush on me that I didn't do much to stop. Tried, but I could have done better. So, helping her was (a) easy and (b) mostly to get rid of guilt. That's too simple, but it isn't wrong."

He nods.

"Well, here's what's worse. I plotted to have sex with Donny. And we have – had sex. I came to admire and respect him along the way, but that doesn't change what happened. I worry that now I've made him do something that'll screw him up."

"You didn't make him do anything, Tim. I know that. Hell, you suppose he didn't want to have sex with you?"

"Huh?"

"He didn't tell me that. I have eyes. You know what I mean."

I don't.

"Tim, Donny is like my own son. I don't feel like protecting him or anyone else. Protecting gets a good name and doesn't deserve one. With Donny, it's pretty simple. I trust him."

"But don't you think he might be vulnerable to someone like me?"

"I hope so. I know more than you suppose, Tim, and your worries are piffle. Blow them away. He's no more vulnerable to you than you are to him, so, as you say, screw it."

"What if later on he thinks he's a queer, or whatever other cruel term is around?"

"Not a worry. Trust me. Nothing to worry about."

"How do you know all that? I mean, how can you... ?"

"We have a way. And Tim, Donny won't be damaged by what you two are doing. Neither will all the others."

"The others? You know about them?"

He winks. I hurriedly change the subject, fearing he might start naming names.

"So anyhow, Dean, it's a panel discussion on Communism."

"Right. They expect you to echo back to them their views and show how resolute you are, steeled against the wily lures of the Commies lurking about town."

"I saw one outside Meilie's yesterday, guy in a raincoat. How long do I have to talk?"

"Somewhere between ten minutes and six hours."

"They have strong views on the subject, I'm sure. You know, I feel very positively about communism. I feel even more strongly about anti-communism."

"I know. That's why I picked you. You just go up there and tell them your ideas on Joe Stalin and Joe McCarthy and how not one of the local Rotarians knows a damned thing. Tell them they're a bunch of insecure men, strutting around in defiance of a phantom enemy. Just you tell 'em."

"I'll do no such thing."

"Oh, you will."

"You scare me. Telling me what I'm going to say and encouraging me to go about buggering the student body."

"Exactly. Not all the student body will take to buggering, but you'll not be bothering those not ready for it. You have advanced instincts that guide you. Trust me, Tim, you are not capable of hurting anybody. At least, capable or not, you won't be doing it."

"Advanced instincts for well-formed booties. There's a gift. I'm going to go now and bone up on Karl Marx. Don't want to be stumped by those scholars up at Rotary."

"You're just saying that, trying to be snide. It's not in you."

"Are you a member of some heavenly female chorus in your spare time?"

"Young man, are you getting fresh?"

. . .

The panel is nowhere near as incendiary as Dean Nelson seems to be anticipating – or having me anticipate. The members are so dead set on regarding me as a trophy they can display with great pride, that they turn my most obnoxious assertions into occasions for enthusiastic nodding. Even the other panelists disarm me by agreeing. Who can sustain arrogance in the midst of such harmony? Not even me.

For example----

Me: "Communism is Utopian. It forms a world where all truly are equal, where greed and acquisitiveness no longer rule. It's a place where the needs of all supersede the needs of the few. No oppression, no hogged-up property, and nobody lives off the sweat of the poor."

Mr. Ennis: "I agree with Timmy. That's a true Christian world."

Mr. Moots: "I hadn't heard it put that way before. Thank you, Timmy."

Mr. Probst: "If you want to run for Governor, Timmy. I'll vote for you!"

Laughing and clapping.

Who can stand against that? It isn't a panel on Communism. It's a meeting called to exchange glad-handing. These men like me and they like one another, listening intently to petty problems, ignorant views, stale jokes. Marx would have been moved. I think Jesus wouldn't have liked it much. Nobody is suffering.

. . .

The meeting to firm up plans to humiliate Carl is preceded by some hot sex with----guess? Actually, it's two of my lovers, one Friday night and one Saturday morning. And it isn't so much sex as cuddlies. Donny and Mary. Both involve bedrooms, and both feature a good hour of nuzzling and slowly undressing, long pauses between bits of soft cotton and starched shirts. Both crawl along with no particular end in view, but are so fine my eyes lose focus, little sparkly things appearing at their corners. Makes me worry that it's blood pressure, a problem Harold had experienced, along with the sparkles, not brought on by good sex for Harold, that's for sure.

The cuddling and slow fiddling: why not keep that up forever? Why have "sex" at all, why end it? Delaying, ooching, talking, giggling, putting odder and odder things into odder and odder places to see what happens: all that occupies our best attention. It seems much more like making love, creating what we already had over and over again, expressing our affection and playing with it, bringing it into new forms, risking embarrassment, keeping one another amused, keeping warm. Am I making it sound too much like building sand castles, mutual crayoning? We're playing a game with uncertain rules, trying to make dead sure it never ends.

. . .

At the vengeance meeting itself –

"So, we all know Sally's great plan. I know Carol's already at work being nice to Carl. Right? How's that going?"

Carol answers me with a long stare.

"Well?"

"Well, like I was telling Betsy [Betsy has joined the cabal, along with her brother, Donny, Carol, Mary, Sally, and Joanie, Jimmy Canton being way too kind to be involved in any meanness, no matter how richly deserved], things have been going not really great for our plan. I have been with Carl, but..." She trails off in a muddled muck of self-consciousness so unlike Carol I think she's joking.

"What? He's not going along? Don't say he isn't interested in you, Carol, cause that can't be, and I'll know you're fibbing because besides you being hot, nobody named Carl could resist hooking up with a dame named Carol, just cause Carl and Carol looks so good carved on trees and scrawled on toilet walls."

She doesn't laugh. Nor does anyone else.

"What's going on? We're going to humiliate this asshole, right?"

"You really want to, Tim?" This from Joanie.

"Sure. We all do, right? Right?"

Looking around, I see a half-dozen unenthusiastic faces. What the hell?

"Somebody tell me. Couple of weeks ago you were all wildly vindictive, ready to draw his toenails out with tweezers, put his balls in a vise. Now – what's happened?"

Silence.

"Carol?"

"Huh?"

"Huh? What happened in the last ten days?"

"Ask yourself. You as anxious to hurt Carl as you were then?"

"Of course. What's changed?"

Nobody speaks, which forces me to think, the last thing I want to do. Maybe it isn't quite as important to me, not quite, but still...

"So, did Carl be all mean and bad to Joanie or what? Ten days makes no difference, does it?"

"Did he be bad?" Betsy smiles at me, also digging her elbow into my ribs, easy to do as her armchair is next to mine. "Are you, Tarzan, as anxious now as you were then? So what happened? Ten days happened."

"That make it different?"

Betsy looks at me seriously, but it's Joanie who answers, "More different than you could know right now, Timmy. I'm sorry."

Sorry? Everybody looks sorry. Sorry about what?

"Sorry about what? Donny?"

His answer is to look away. I leave off asking. What's going on? Carl is Carl, no different. What's this about ten days? It's only time, a short time. I don't understand, not that I want to.

. . .

At least Jimmy Canton isn't mysterious, is his usual calm, friendly, inventive self. Now that spring is here, it's time, he says, for our annual carnival. It's one thing I remember vividly from Harold times, and apparently the readjusted Tim has taken part in them, too.

These annual carnivals are more important to the neighborhood as a rite of spring than are the Jesus-Is-Risen services, egg hunts, or new pastel coats. They attract the attention of everyone the age of Jimmy and me and younger, especially younger. Perhaps we're carrying on too long, the two of us, with an activity that speaks loudest to the nine-year-olds. But it is roaring fun, and Jimmy's unchecked enthusiasm allows me to pitch in unembarrassed. I'd never met anyone so devoted to good times and to easy friendship. Who else could give me permission to do what I so wanted to do?

Now, the carnival is a trifle amateurish, a severe critic might say. Luckily, we have no severe critics around and wouldn't have noticed if we had. We've developed a tradition, a set of tried and true acts, attractions, food booths, games, and surprises. One surprise we always have is "MOVIE TIME," which features some of the Canton's home movies and three store-bought comedies (Three Stooges, a cartoon gala, and a loser called "Fisherman's Luck"). Our family has a projector, Jimmy's a screen, and we set it up in his garage. Most of our featured live acts also take place in his garage, behind a curtain (sheet), in front of some benches Jimmy and I had made years before from scrap lumber, covered with old roofing shingles (brown). They have stood up well, if unevenly, over the years, these benches, rarely collapsing.

Reenlisting our old acts turns out to be tougher than I'd imagined. Billy Thompson, for instance, gives me a cold "no," despite my chumming him up. For years, Billy had displayed his somewhat disgustingly double-jointed elbows to the crowd (maybe eight kids) who had paid a penny each for the spectacle. "No," he tells me, despite my joking so well. But then he says yes to Jimmy, naturally, as Jimmy doesn't pull out all the homosocial stops or suggest that Billy is his dearest friend. He just asks him to do it as a favor. Nobody can refuse Jimmy.

Well, yes they can. My own sister, my own Joanie, says she absolutely won't humiliate herself another year with her poetry reading, even if we keep the sheet drawn and her identity a mystery. And Mildred Todd from up the street says she isn't taking baton anymore and really doesn't think she can twirl. We still have the tapping Bailey twins, magnificent even on the dirt floor, and Glenn Hall's magic act, the one talent that really is a talent, not to overlook Cub Scout Troop #Seven's gymnastics show, climaxing in a pyramid made a little risky by the advancing bulk of some of those accustomed to take top positions. We also have returning the song stylings of Glenda Diggs, shadow pictures by Jimmy's sister, and the trained cats of Nadine Simms, a show worth seeing some years, though the cats have not always cooperated fully or at all.

And there's more. We have outside in the field next to the Canton's a fishing pond with prizes, a basketball hoop for those wanting to win a stuffed animal (one is all we have), a hop-scotch competition, face-painting (my idea, imported from the future, and now using house paint, which is what's on hand), and food stands, dependent on the local mothers, who always come through. In a good year, we cleared almost four dollars. Not a bad day's work.

Afterwards, Jimmy and I have to concede that our take is lower than usual. We allow many free admissions, even free cookies, but we always do that, so that doesn't explain our slumping income. I suggest that we are saturating the market. Jimmy thinks we are depending too much on attractions, that the future is in games, and that we should invest our profit from this year in prizes. He has a point. Once our stuffed animal had been won, we could offer little incentive for shooting the basketball or hopping scotch. I suggest we build a dunking pool next time. Jimmy, who seems to like every idea, agrees. I should add that the reason he likes every idea has a lot to do with his ability to make ideas work, to build things, think things through, endure setbacks, and get help. In a sane world, he would be President.

Yes, the carnival has been a financial disappointment, were one set up to be disappointed, which left us out. We agree, Jimmy and I, that the enthusiasm level has never been higher and that the quality of the acts has been astounding, as good, nearly, as any traveling show that comes to the open fields housing pro carnivals or even the high-class performers at the Ceramic Theater. Blackstone the Magician has been there, along with The Mills Brothers and Fred Warring. Fred Warring had brought a stripped-down version of his "Pennsylvanians," but still...

CHAPTER 21

Seems as if every day gets longer, at least in terms of the number of non-school activities I can fit in. How could that be? Turn the corner and there is Donny or Glenn with pants on the way down, Mary or Carol with skirts coming up. I'm speaking in artful poetic figures here. Nothing gross. And not just sex, but good times. I can't remember ever having such open conversations, everyone so friendly and eager. Maybe the celestials are slipping me drugs.

It's as if boring things, classes and routine matters like dressing and peeing, are so compressed they almost don't exist. What happens at school amounts to sweet encounters, plans concocted, promises extended, discoveries made. No tests? No lectures? No attendance taking?

I find myself one day at East Junior High, in the eighth-grade class containing so many pretty kids, Joanie and Sally prominently. (Why Sally, who lives on the opposite end of town, is enrolled there troubles me, but not for long.) These two have arranged for me to come in and talk about structuralism. You heard right. I have been telling them about it, without, for once, commandeering the ideas as my own. And they thought it'd be just the thing for Social Studies.

"It's a way of seeing the world as a set of systems that operate on their own. The economy is one such system, but that's not a good example. The clearest is nature, what comes to be called ecology, the way everything feeds off everything else, adjusting in complex ways to imbalances. It's the **system** that works, not God or man or consciousness. Another good example is language, which is entirely independent of human beings. We enter into it and try to employ it, but we don't invent it. It'd be more accurate to say it invents us. And blah, blah, blah."

Amazingly, they had been rapt, these two kids, sitting at our kitchen table, and book me that very week. The speech in the massive junior-high auditorium goes wonderfully. How? I worry and fuss about it, but can't have pitched it to their level. Worse, I tell them all I'm from the future and somehow feel called upon to let them in on the fact that the hour of structuralism is short indeed: no sooner are people declaring themselves structuralists than it is being repudiated, as the flood of post-structuralism, of deconstruction sweeps in. On and on I go. And they cheer, stand and cheer.

"I shouldn't tell you this, but all this won't happen until the 1970s and 80s."

Wild cheers.

"The problem with structuralism turns out to be that it IS structured, assumes the existence of stable and permanent centers, when in fact one can always dissolve those centers, more exactly, show how they are merely constructed. Thus, the most powerful tool we develop gets itself called 'deconstruction,' opening up the world for endless play, dynamic movement from one conditional, contingent center to another."

Nodding, humming in concert, and then more cheers.

"One of the most interesting post-structuralists turns out to be Michel Foucault, the source of what becomes known as cultural studies, the analysis of cultures as complex systems of power, generating truth, or what is taken for truth. By this standard, power does not work by censoring uncomfortable views but by generating those views in the first place. Truth, then, is not found, not out there somewhere in an innocent state waiting for us. Truth is manufactured, constructed by power."

"Anyhow, thank you very much for your polite attention. You'll be glad to hear that I called Isaly's and arranged for them to deliver Eskimo Pies, three for each of you. Also, they're packed in dry ice, which you're welcome to play with."

They're glad to hear that. But the applause, which rolls through the auditorium and out into the streets, exceeds by the size of the sky even the joy of ice cream.

. . .

I grab Joanie that evening for a walk, around a neighborhood that seems oddly deserted. The houses are there and some dogs, but not the usual scurry of kids and adults. Probably something going on at the Church. Aside from the Cantons and a couple of Italian families, everyone goes to the same Methodist Church. Maybe that's it.

"Honey, what was I doing at your school?"

"We invited you, Timmy."

"I gathered, but I don't seem to recall that. What I meant, though, was that I was giving a talk on some stuff forty years in the future, boring stuff, too, and everybody seemed interested. Couldn't have been, but pretended to be."

"They were. We were."

"This is me, Joanie. Don't shit me. And why was I there talking on structuralism of all things? I should have been saying that later on they discover that cigarette smoking causes cancer, so better smoke while you can. What's going on, honey?"

She looks at me with such sad eyes, doesn't say anything.

"Where is everybody?"

"I don't know, big brother."

"I think you do."

"Timmy, please don't go on like this."

"I'm mystified."

"No, you're not. Not really. I love you."

Even the Cantons aren't home. Is there an atomic alert or something? It's getting dark, but I can see no lights anywhere.

. . .

"Mary, dearie. I'm so glad you're home."

"You wanta go fishing?"

"For what? Ha ha!"

"For that, of course. But for our old friend, the catfish, right? Speaking of which I have a poem for you, dearest Tim. And here it is:

> *If I were to live my life in catfish forms,*
> *In scaffolds of skin and whiskers at the bottom of a pond,*
> *And you were to come by one evening*
> *When the moon was shining down into my dark home,*
> *And stand there at the edge of my affection,*
> *And think, "It's beautiful here by this pond.*
> *I wish somebody loved me,"*
> *I'd love you and be your catfish friend,*
> *And drive such lonely thoughts from your mind,*
> *And suddenly you would be at peace,*
> *And ask yourself, "I wonder if there are any catfish in this pond?*
> *It seems like a perfect place for them.*

"Mary, that's so moving. I'm your catfish friend."

"I'm yours."

"Oh God. I know that poem. Richard Brautigan, 1970s, 80s?"

"That's right. Very popular around 2016, Tim. You knew that."

"But Mary?"

"Don't ask, Tim; it just is. You know."

"I don't, but you do. That's enough for me, old lover, new lover. Forever lover."

"Let's keep it on tune."

"I knew it. You're gonna dump me for Carl."

"Among others."

"Mary, that's not funny."

"Sorry. You're not possessive, Tim, just think you are. It's all one, you know."

"We're all one?"

"Yep, you and me and Carol."

"And others too, right?"

"I'm glad you see that."

"Who are you?"

"Just who you think, dear, who I've always been."

"Can I come over?"

"What was it Gertrude Stein said of Oakland?"

"There's no there there."

"There's no here here."

"Oh, Mary!"

"Don't be scared, Tim."

Scared? Me? Ha. Yes, I am.

"I'll always love you."

"Oh, Mary. That makes it all-----." She didn't seem to be there.

. . .

Next day after school, school seeming to last only fifteen minutes, I get into Betsy's car to go see Glenn.

"Betsy, have they cut the school day?"

"I don't think that's it, Tim."

"What is it?"

"You've been asking around, right?"

"I have. Seems like time's screwed up, and I end up places I hadn't planned on being. And last night, there didn't seem to be anybody in our neighborhood. And where are all the kids at school?" It now struck me that hardly anybody was there. And where are all the other cars?

"How come there's no traffic, Betsy?"

"You'd know better than anyone, old dear."

"Old dear! You know how much I pine for you, Betsy?"

"As much as you do for my brother?"

"I am sorry about that. I know you asked me not to get too involved, not to hurt Glenn. I guess..."

"You guess having sex with him five or six times a week might not have been the best way not to get involved."

"You know."

"Who wouldn't?"

"I have no defense."

"You need none. Glenn's been so happy. You've authorized him."

"You talk the way people do in 2016."

"I know."

"How?"

She looks at me. "You've made Glenn think about his being in a new way. You remade his life. That was something."

"So, now we can go on without guilt. Glenn and I can try new things."

Betsy smiles.

"So, we keep going, keep romping."

She looks at me.

"Betsy, what's happening?"

"Oh, Tim!"

"OK, how about you and me having sex. I'm not bad."

"You're a whole lot more than 'not bad.'"

"So?"

"It's all up to you, of course, but you won't."

"I won't?"

"That's all there is to it. That's all there is."

"All?"

. . .

The next day there doesn't seem to be school, but there's a phone call from Pittsburgh. "Tim, this is Branch Rickey."

"Lord God."

"No, just Mr. Rickey."

"Yes, sir, how can I help you?"

"Well, I'm hoping you can indeed help me. Our season hasn't started, and it already looks gloomy. I'm not a gloomy man, Tim, but I've been around this game long enough not to fool myself. I'm an excellent judge of talent."

"You are legendary."

"Be that as it may, I can look about me and see talent, if it's there. I see precious little here, Tim, precious little. I hope you aren't distressed by my candor."

"Not at all, sir." Wonder if he knows how bad the fifty-two Bucs will actually be, not just bad but the worst team in modern times. Out of one-hundred-fifty-four games, this team will win forty-two. It's almost difficult to win so few games, a fact driven home by the inability of any other team ever to do it.

"I've been talking with Mr. Galbreath, and he agrees we need to take some chances. Between you and me, Tim, a team somewhat less wretched would not dip this deep into the chance bag, if you follow me."

I do.

"I'm putting our manager, the long-suffering Billy Meyer, on the line. He has a proposition for you, one I hope you will entertain favorably. Any questions or doubts, Tim, you come straight to me. Hear?"

Before I can reply, another voice comes on the line, gravelly and mean-toned, a caricature of old baseball dogs. Even his voice has tobacco spittle on it.

"Mills? Billy Meyer. Heard about you from Ray Manizotti and Lou Romanelli down in Midland, old friends of mine. Say you have a fastball better than Feller's. I'd like to see, kid. I don't care if you're four years old. You able to throw like Manizotti and Romanelli say, we can use you. We got two, maybe three pitchers that I can think are not plain awful when I'm drunk. You got me?"

"Yes, sir."

"Don't call me 'sir,' little boy. You anyways near as good as Ray says, you'll be making way more than me. Come up today, OK? I got your address. East Liverpool, right? Be down to get you."

"You will?"

"Not me, simpleton. I'm not so low in the toilet they make me drive cars. I've got a coach coming. East Liverpool, right? Don't say. I know it's right. Bring your glove. Be there is ten minutes, car will."

It's a good hour to Pittsburgh. More. How can a car be here in ten minutes?

It's here when I look out the window, and before I know it we're at Forbes Field. I'm in a uniform, on the mound. Here I am, Clyde McCullough catching, replaced in a bit by Joe Garagiola. I look around at the other pitchers warming up: Murry Dickson, who one year won twenty and lost twenty, too, a young Bob Friend, at the beginning of a good career, Ron Kline, in the middle of pitching lots of innings, seldom well. Mel Queen, Bill Werle, others. The infield is not the strongest part of the team, though, like Friend, Dick Groat is there with wonderful things before him. However, so is a guy called Clem Koshorek, 5'4" and not even fast. The outfield is better – Gus Bell, Frank Thomas, Bobby DelGreco, and, sweet Mary, Ralph Kiner.

"Sure hope you can help us, kid."

"Thank you, Mr. Kiner."

"Anything you need, let us know. We'll make it easy for you. No rookie hazing. Only don't be too sure." He winks. Ralph Kiner! Fifty-four home runs in 1949. He will win the home-run title every year he is with us.

I stretch and throw. And again. And again. My arm seems to become stronger as I pitch, holding back impossibly long and then whipping forward way too fast, as I shift my weight. One-hundred-four mph they say. Without speed guns, how do they know? I discover I have a curve ball, even a screwball.

"Need to work on your change, kid. You learn to change speeds, you'll be OK."

"So, can I work in the minors or something? I'll work really hard."

"Minors? You're my starting pitcher, opening day. Two weeks. You're a thirty-game winner if I ever saw one, even with this team, which'll give you almost no runs. But you won't need 'em."

. . .

There's a note on the kitchen table, refrigerator notes having to wait on refrigerator magnets, still off into the future.

Timmy dear,
The school called about the election. You won.
I'm so proud of you. You're a good son.
There's meat loaf in the refrigerator.
Goodbye and love,
Mom

. . .

I hadn't known there was an election. That seemed par for the course, considering the last few days, or weeks, or whatever. Election for what? Why? When had I run? And who voted? There didn't seem to be any electors around anywhere.

I touch the kitchen table just to assure myself that solid is solid, that it's there and I am, too. I try to see my reflection in its surface, a dumb idea, as it has no reflective properties. I kick myself in the shin. Hurts, which is reassuring. There *is* an explanation for all this.

I go out on the back porch to smell the spring air. There are birds around, proof that no atomic attack has occurred. The birds are there and the sweet air. No trains are going by, but often there are gaps of an hour or so between the restful, happy clickety-clickety.

For some reason, I start to feel uneasy. I think about drifting over to the Cantons or calling Carol. Carol seems the best plan.

"Carol! Is that you?"

"How could you not know? Am I your bed partner, or am I not?"

"Carol, I'm scared."

"I know you are, Tim."

"Is it OK?"

"I love you."

"I love you so – but is it OK?"

"It's more OK than you can know."

"Will I see you again?"

"Not so's you'd notice."

"What does that mean? Are you leaving me?"

"You know it's not that. Tim, remember that joke from your time, the one where two friends, let's say you and me, meet outside the psychiatrist's office, and one says, 'Are you coming or going?'"

She's quiet, so I have to say, "I don't remember."

"Well," she says, "the other guy says, 'If I knew that I wouldn't be here.'"

"Oh, Carol. That mean coming and going are the same thing, neither matters, both matter, it's all..."

"Well, Tim, here's more, from your favorite artist, Andy Warhol. I was thinking of it on our walk, remember, when we were noticing things and you were looking up my dress."

She's quiet. "Don't go, Carol."

"Warhol says, 'The more you look at the exact same thing the more the meaning goes away, and the better and emptier you feel.'"

"Emptier?"

"Better, Tim, better."

Then silence.

• • •

I go back into the kitchen, sit at the table. Somehow it makes my panic subside a little to stroke that table, old cheap Formica, solid, even pretty. I go to the frig, still there, and get out the meatloaf. Delicious.

"Joanie?"

I thought I heard somebody behind me. It's become very dark, so I can't see too well.

I feel good, though, so light and soft, drifting again. The table is still there, and the meatloaf and the note. "Goodbye"?

It's so dark, and someone is behind me. I should be frightened, but I'm not. I knew all along, knew about the future and the past, about the sex and the fun, about all these dear kids and the games and singing and the carnival. It's not like I knew what it meant, this time around or before. This time around I was here. So was the table.

I have the feeling I always will be here, but that is nonsense. Somewhere out in the bird-filled, sweet air is something not me, and somewhere I can never land. But that seems OK. Here today...

"Joanie?"

I'm surprised it is so dark.

Now is a good time to think. Funny how, when you decide you are going to think, you don't. At least I don't. There doesn't seem anything in my head.

"Tim?"

I figure now is the time. As they said during the last war, "This is it." Why not? I'm ready for anything they can throw at me, even more women at kitchen tables like the one that has been there only a minute before.

The darkness has lifted.

"Dad?"

"Hi, Harry."

"Where are we?"

"We're right here, son, right here."

"OK. And Dad, where will...?"

"Just remember, son, what Yogi will say: 'The future's not what it used to be.'"

I'll remember.

UNATTRIBUTED QUOTATIONS

Scattered through the novel are phrases, snippets, poems, stolen as follows:

B1203

Purchase other Black Rose Writing titles at www.blackrosewriting.com/books
and use promo code PRINT to receive a 20% discount.

BLACK ROSE
writing™

CPSIA information can be obtained at www.ICGtesting.com
Printed in the USA
BVOW02s1625300116

434810BV00001B/1/P